BLACKOUT

A CROSSBREED NOVEL

USA TODAY BESTSELLING AUTHOR

DANNIKA DARK

Also By Dannika Dark:

THE MAGERI SERIES
Sterling
Twist
Impulse
Gravity
Shine
The Gift (Novella)

MAGERI WORLD
Risk

NOVELLAS
Closer

THE SEVEN SERIES
Seven Years
Six Months
Five Weeks
Four Days
Three Hours
Two Minutes
One Second
Winter Moon (Novella)

SEVEN WORLD
Charming

THE CROSSBREED SERIES
Keystone
Ravenheart
Deathtrap
Gaslight
Blackout

These violent delights have violent ends.

- William Shakespeare

Chapter 1

I DUG MY KNEE INTO THE Sensor's neck, pinning his unshaven face even harder against the concrete. "I thought February was supposed to be the coldest month."

From his seat on the man's back, Christian twisted the wrapper off a peppermint. "I can't say I've noticed a difference."

"Well, I'm getting hot."

"Take off your fecking coat."

"Get off me," the man growled.

I had his arms pinned, and every so often, he'd test me.

"People pee in alleyways," I pointed out. "There's no way I'm setting my leather jacket on the ground."

Christian crunched on his candy. "Then perhaps next time you should capture your victim in front of a café where there are chairs to drape your garments over."

"You're the one who dragged him into the alley."

"It's a dead end."

"Like all your past relationships?"

"Nobody died at the end of mine. Can't say the same about the men in your past."

I glanced up at an Italian-looking man on a balcony three stories up. After lighting up his slim cigar, he flicked the extinguished match into the dumpster below. The longer we sat there, the more onlookers we were going to attract.

Christian eyed the man with measured interest before tucking his wrapper into his coat pocket.

I shook my hair out of my eyes, my back muscles beginning

to ache as I kept the man's wrists pinned to the concrete. The hole in my jeans ripped wider, exposing my knee. What I really wanted was to stand up and stretch, but we had to restrain this idiot until the Regulators arrived. I'd already blasted him once, but I didn't want to use up all my energy. "Got another one of those mints?"

"Sorry, lass. My last one."

"Liar."

The radiant sunshine took the chill out of the air. No wind, no snow, and to top it off, the temperature was hovering somewhere in the fifties. You could never predict what the weather might do in Cognito.

"How long does it take for Regulators to actually show up?" I complained, my face flushed and sweat tickling the back of my neck.

Christian glanced at his imaginary watch. "Dead or alive is a flexible option. Care to switch plans and call the cleaners instead?"

"That works for me."

Our prisoner grunted defiantly, so I put more pressure on his wrists. While Christian was only jesting, sinking my teeth into this animal and sucking the life out of him tempted me in ways I couldn't articulate. We'd spent the past week tracking this scumbag after receiving an anonymous tip that he was selling sensory child porn on the streets. Traders lifting experiences from certified pedophiles and offering them for sale was the lowest form of sensory exchange.

Some shady sellers argued that buying an experience wasn't the same as committing a crime. They called it Sensorship—a play on words using the Sensor name to describe prohibiting the sale of emotional experiences derived from criminal acts. It was a bullshit excuse. Deviants fed on those insidious desires, and eventually a sensory exchange wouldn't be enough. Had I caught this asshole before Keystone came along, I would have tortured him for a long time before killing him. He wasn't a big guy, but you had to be careful when fighting a Sensor. They used their gifts as a weapon, filling their attacker with paralyzing feelings of pain, sometimes even death.

"I hope they cut off your hands," I muttered.

Christian scratched his beard. "That's not all I hope they cut off." He turned a sharp eye toward the man. "I think we should switch places. I feel a little gassy this morning. Let's turn him faceup so I can rest my arse on his—"

"Good afternoon," a voice boomed from behind me.

Chills ran down my spine. They always did when either Regulators of the Security Force or Mageri Enforcers were around. That rogue side of me wanted to bolt. They rarely introduced themselves or cared about anything other than conducting interviews and serving warrants.

"I'm Merry, and this is Weather."

I furrowed my brow and peered over my shoulder. Two blond Chitahs approached, katanas fastened to their hips. The one in the red coat had wispy hair down to his shoulders. His mean-looking friend had a wide Mohawk trimmed short, which would have been the most distinguishable feature about him had it not been for his unibrow. Unlike his partner, he wore the standard Regulator attire of all black, his long coat open so he had access to his sword.

"Have a gander at the two pussies," Christian murmured. "Aren't they a fetching pair?"

Christian didn't hold Chitahs in high regard. Hell, he didn't hold *anyone* in high regard.

Merry, the long-haired one, looked unfazed by Christian's irreverent remarks. With one hand on the pommel of his sword, he tilted his head and regarded the Sensor beneath us. "I prefer to get the jokes out of the way so we can get down to business."

Christian turned the ring on his finger. "Have it your way. You can tell me all about how your garden grows later, Mary."

"It's Merry with an *m-e*. Is this him?"

I quickly replaced my knee with my foot and stood up. "Yep."

Merry strode around to the other side and squatted in front of our prisoner. He removed a folded-up document from his inside coat pocket and held it in front of the man's face. "Jefferson Randall, by order of the higher authority, the Regulators of the Security Force hereby place you under arrest. You're a declared outlaw, and as such, we have a signed warrant for your arrest. You will be placed in the Breed jail and remain there until the hearing when the court determines your fate."

"For what?" the man growled.

"On the charge of illegal sensory exchange."

Merry leaned in tight, and his upper and lower fangs slid into view. "For crimes against children."

"I'm not doing anything every other Sensor isn't."

"You can plead your case to the court, but we've already detained five of your customers, and each has confirmed that the sensory exchanges are illegal in nature and, if I might add, dastardly. If you choose to run, I'll slice off your testicles. The warrant requires that we hand you over alive, but it doesn't specify in one piece."

"I would have pegged your buddy as the menacing one," I said to Merry.

Most people were easy to read, so it made me wonder how a seemingly affable guy like Merry could be so blasé about mutilating his prisoners.

Merry's golden eyes swung up to mine, and he rose to his feet. "A kind face reveals nothing about the man beneath. We all wear masks."

I bit my lip and stared down at Jefferson. "Mind if I test that theory? He's not technically in your custody just yet, is he?"

Merry stepped back and inclined his head. A gust of wind blew a broad swath of hair across his face, but the shine in his eyes pierced through and kept watch on my every move.

Christian grinned wolfishly. "If you're planning to blast him with energy, might I suggest you go for the manly bits?"

"It hurts worse in the head," I informed him, my foot still on Jefferson's neck.

With lightning speed, Christian flipped the Sensor onto his back. "Do you have any personal experience to back that up?"

Jefferson tried to spit on me, but it landed back in his face.

I scrunched my nose at Christian's suggestion. "Maybe you should check him for genital lice before I put my hands down there."

"Fecking not."

I snorted and took my foot off the man's neck. The moment I let my guard down, assuming he'd behave around Regulators, he seized my ankle, fingers searching for bare skin.

Before so much as a flutter of sensory magic entered my body, Merry's sword sliced through Jefferson's wrist. Blood sprayed against the concrete as the fat-nosed deviant clutched the bleeding stump and bellowed in agony.

Merry positioned his blade against the man's throat. "Do that again, Sensor."

The dare went unchallenged.

Regulators carried out beheadings, and while not all of them participated in the executions, the job required a merciless outlook to hold that position. A man who didn't bargain. A man whose every action was supported by the law.

I clutched Jefferson by the balls. "Lights out."

The Sensor convulsed, eyes bulging and mouth open in a silent scream. He was still reeling from the loss of his hand, so I gave him extra—enough to knock him unconscious but not kill the bastard. Two Regulators with sharp swords were standing too close for me to do anything brazen.

"Your name?" Merry asked.

I stood up to address the svelte man with the small mouth and narrow nose. "Raven."

"Fitting."

Christian stepped into view. "We're done here. Say your goodbyes to the dry shite, and let's go."

As he stalked off, Weather rubbed his nose.

I rocked on my heels and gave Merry a detailed appraisal, from his shiny black boots to his black gloves. "What's up with the red coat? I usually see you guys in black."

"I recently transferred from Alberta, Canada. Up there, our coats are red. My new boss hasn't pressed the issue on my attire."

"Maybe he'd rather pocket that money since you already have a uniform."

Weather folded his thick arms and huffed like a bull about to charge a matador. "Are you accusing our superior of stealing?" *Slander laws, Raven. Shut up and get your ass out of here.*

"Just kidding," I sang, remembering they could smell fear. Ignoring Weather's question, I kept my attention on Merry. "Don't file that little fireworks show I did in your report. Not unless you also include the part where you let it happen."

"Let me allay your fears by giving you my word as a Chitah." Merry bowed, his eyes never shifting away from mine.

Unnerved by the intensity of his gaze, I clumsily turned away. Once I caught up with my partner, I glanced over my shoulder to spy Merry kicking Jefferson in the ribs.

"That was unrewarding," I said. "It's like those fishermen who do a catch and release. I don't know if I'll ever get used to this."

Christian squinted, his sunglasses still in my truck. "What are you prattling on about? He's going to jail and missing his good hand, if you get my meaning."

"What if he has friends in high places who owe him a favor?" I kicked a pebble, and it skidded into the street. "Sometimes it feels like we're wasting our time if they're just going to be free to walk the streets again."

"Do you want their head mounted on your wall? Or perhaps you just want to eat them." Christian gave an older lady passing us a toothy smile. "This is what we do with our prey. If you kill every one of them, you'll steal all the joy away from those Regulator shitebags who dress up and play God."

I unzipped my leather coat. "Jefferson's a declared outlaw. That means dead or alive."

"Viktor's orders. Unless we have to defend ourselves, he wants the plonker alive. That way they can squeeze him for information on all the men who sold him those vile memories."

"You and all your squeezing."

Christian rocked with laughter. "You can't just kill a man in the light of day while people are shopping for bagels and walking their poodles. Besides, Viktor takes a cut out of our checks each time he has to call in the cleaners."

My brows popped up in surprise. "I didn't know that."

"Jaysus. Do you think people clean up bodies and blood out of the goodness of their heart?"

"No. I just thought the higher authority paid for it."

He chortled. "They won't even buy Mary Contrary a black coat."

A teenager squabbling on her phone passed by us, taking up most of the sidewalk and forcing me closer to Christian.

"Why didn't you give Weather the same shit you were dishing to Merry?"

He gave me a pointed look. "Never trust the quiet ones."

We reached my blue truck, the doors still ajar from us having jumped out to chase our target on foot. Luckily, most criminals didn't see anything worth stealing in an old pickup. The radio was the original, and I didn't keep any fancy electronics in there. The only loot a thief would find was two dollars in change from the coins in the ashtray.

Now that I had my own vehicle, spontaneity was my new best friend. My truck symbolized freedom, and besides, driving it made me feel closer to my father. It didn't erase the emptiness of life without him, but having it in my possession made it easier to let go.

"I need a big assignment," I said decidedly, resting my arm on the hood. "I mean... I'm glad we busted that guy, but last week Viktor had us scouring pawnshops for illegal weapons. Meanwhile, Shepherd was given a case tracking down a Mage killer."

"Aye, using one of the weapons that *we* found."

I circled to the driver's side. "It should have been *our* case."

We both got in and slammed the doors.

Christian dusted off his dirty pants. "You don't see Blue and Niko whining about searching for a lost dog."

I took my keys out of my coat pocket. "That was a bullshit assignment. Viktor should never have accepted it. He probably owed someone a favor. Why else would he have Blue and Niko tracking down a fucking wolf? If some high-and-mighty Shifter official decides to run away and live his life in the woods, that's his business. What's the point of rounding him up and bringing him home if he hasn't broken any laws? We're not animal control."

Christian belted out a laugh, and it was as dark as a sinner's heart.

"What's so funny?"

"Nothing, Precious. Just drive."

Small victories were best celebrated with an Angus burger, and I knew just the place.

"Nice wheels," Betty gushed, gesturing out the window at my truck. "I saw you drive up in it, honey. I'm so glad things are looking up for you."

Betty always had a way of making me feel good about myself, even when things were bleak. It was nice to be able to share glimpses of my life with her that weren't a train wreck.

I smiled up at her. "I haven't seen you in a while. Where have you been?"

"I'm not dead yet." She put one hand on her plump hip. "I went on a cruise!"

That explained her light tan and redder-than-normal dyed hair. For a woman of almost eighty, she was as vivacious as anyone my age. But I'd never seen her in anything but a dress and apron, so I had a difficult time imagining her on a lounge chair with a fruity umbrella drink in her hand.

"My kids all chipped in for my ticket," she bragged. "Everyone came along. The grandkids were a handful, but we had a marvelous time."

"Which islands did you see?"

"The boat docked in a few places, but I didn't get off. I once read a story about a woman who missed her boat in Mexico, and they found her five years later, living as someone's love slave."

Christian choked on his ice water.

"Don't believe everything you read in those tabloids," I cautioned her, holding in my laugh.

"You're probably right, honey. Just last week they had an article about a vampire baby."

"Now *that's* fecking impossible," Christian retorted.

I kicked him beneath the table.

Betty didn't bother taking out her pen and pad. "Same as usual?"

"Yes, ma'am."

"One Angus burger with extra cheese and a side of onion rings coming right up." She turned on her heel and headed to the kitchen.

Christian stretched his arms across the back of his booth. "That's a wee bit presumptuous of her. What if *I* was hungry?"

"You haven't been hungry since 1948."

He turned his head to look outside. "Perhaps you should wash your hands before you wrap those dirty little fingers around your hamburger. You've been scuttling around in the alley."

I glanced at my palms and shuddered when I thought about all the things they'd touched in the past half hour. That launched me out of my seat and into the restroom. As I lathered my hands with pink soap, I stared at my reflection in the mirror. I'd never age another day. No wrinkles, no grey hairs, no sagging skin or age spots. The only hint of my age would be a glimmer of light in my eyes, something that inevitably happened with the ancients as their Mage power increased. As I looked into my own mismatched eyes, I almost didn't recognize the person staring back. Pieces of my past were missing, and without those memories, the fabric of my identity would always be frayed.

Know thyself.

Christian's words resonated with me. Funny how right he was.

I washed a smudge of dirt off my chin and, for just a split second, thought of Fletcher. He crossed my mind at random moments when I was least expecting it, and I didn't like the invasive nature of those thoughts. Forgetting him wasn't as easy as it used to be. He didn't creep into my nightmares anymore, but I'd spent far too many waking hours pondering his whereabouts. We hadn't uncovered any clues since his escape, and Viktor said that would take time and I needed to be patient. If patience was a virtue, I planned to be the most virtuous woman in Cognito.

Once I collected my thoughts and dried my hands on a paper towel, I emerged from the bathroom and noticed the additional head count at our table. "Where did you two come from?"

Gem peered over her shoulder at me, the sun glinting off the rhinestones framing her sunglasses. "The dungeon of gloom."

Claude scooted against the window to let me sit across from Gem. "What's shakin'?"

"What brings you guys into the city?"

"I can't stay at home with all this sunshine," Gem explained. "Claude let me tag along so I could do some shopping."

Claude rested his elbows on the table and flashed a smile. "Gem's like a rechargeable battery, and she's running out of juice. I told her I'd drop her off in the city on my way to work. We were stopped at the intersection when I spotted your truck."

"We're celebrating," I informed him. "Another case closed."

"Congrats."

A woman outside passed by our window and stared at Claude. When he held her gaze, a rosy blush tinted her cheeks, and she beamed. He had that effect on women and made no apologies. Men with golden locks and sensual lips like his rarely did.

Gem glanced down at her laminated menu. "Darn. I should have ordered the strawberry shake instead. It says here it's made from fresh fruit."

"Then change your order." When I raised my hand to flag a waitress, Gem seized my wrist.

"No! I don't want to be a bother."

I put down my arm. "They don't care."

She sighed and pushed the menu toward the edge of the table. "But I do."

Claude suddenly reached across the table and gripped her hand. "What's wrong, female? I can scent you're upset about something more than a milkshake."

She put her hands in her lap and frowned. "I electrocuted Hooper."

Hooper was the Sensor that Gem was seeing.

I blinked in surprise. "As in… dead?"

"No! He's not dead."

Christian concealed a smile by turning his head toward the window.

"It's the downside of being a Mage," she said, alluding to the obvious.

Sexual energy in a Mage needs a place to go, but when you're not dating another Mage or a Vampire who can handle it, that meant an energy blast.

Christian put his arm around her. "Boy meets girl. Boy seduces girl, and girl electrocutes boy while giving him a hand job. It's a tale as old as time."

She elbowed him in the ribs. "We didn't go that far. If I can't control myself with a little heavy petting, what happens if we make fireworks?"

I snorted. "That's one way to put it."

Betty returned with my food and set a vanilla milkshake in front of Gem. "Sure you don't want anything?" she asked Claude.

He smiled handsomely at her, enough to substitute for a tip. Betty hurried off with a jaunty smile on her face.

"So what do you plan on doing today?" I asked Gem.

She straightened a lock of her lavender hair in front of her face, and it sprang back in a natural wave when she let it go. "Walk around, shop, and maybe go relic hunting. Sometimes I find rare books in the pawnshops."

"That's our book nerd," Claude said affectionately.

She pushed her shades up her nose with one finger. "I prefer the term bibliophile."

I gobbled up two onion rings, suddenly reminded of how Christian and I had met. He eyed them briefly, and I wondered if he was thinking the same thing.

Emotions in check, Raven. Claude the Sniffer is sitting beside you.

Gem sipped her milkshake and moaned with delight. We'd all been suffering through sugar deprivation, thanks to Kira's organic approach to cooking. Ever since Viktor had taken her in as our domestic help, our diets had dramatically changed due to her lack of knowledge when it came to processed food and sugar. Gem slid the tall glass over to Claude, who removed the straw and drank straight from the glass.

I watched him set the glass down. "Are you originally from around here?" I asked, suddenly realizing the question might be too invasive. Because we all presumably had a dark past, we never asked each other probing questions. Not unless someone volunteered that information. But idle chitchat in a diner was hard to avoid, so I let the question linger to see if he would answer.

He licked the ice cream mustache from his upper lip. "No. Pennsylvania originally."

"Did you fight in the Battle of Gettysburg?" I quipped, remembering how he once mentioned he was centuries old.

"That would have meant joining the army and my name going into the record books. Most of us protect our names from legal documents." He slid the glass back to Gem. "It was difficult to leave the state or country in those days when the draft was going on. The world was smaller back then, and everyone knew everyone. During the war, we either paid substitutes to take our place or faked health problems."

Christian tilted his head to the side. "I once met a man who cut off his own foot to dodge a draft."

Claude's leather jacket creaked as he sat back. "Sounds delightful."

I took a huge bite of my burger, listening to the conversation as they reminisced over evading the military in times of war.

Christian's phone vibrated. "Jaysus wept. All this fecking technology. Can't even have two seconds to enjoy a meal."

"What meal?" Gem asked, gesturing at the empty table in front of him. "I don't see how you can just sit there and smell all this divine food." She pulled the straw out of her glass and licked the bottom. "I could just eat all day long."

Christian put his phone away after quickly checking it. "Aye, and you can start with Raven's bovine sandwich."

A pickle slapped onto my plate, and I looked up. "What do you mean?"

"Now that we're available, Viktor has another assignment that begins now."

"Can't it wait?"

Christian laced his fingers together. "By all means, take your time. We're on our way to look at a corpse, so be sure to finish every last juicy bite."

I set down my burger after Christian managed to kill my appetite. "Just when I thought I was going to end my day on a normal note."

Claude chuckled. "What gave you the idea that our lives were normal?"

"Want to hitch a ride with us?" I asked Gem while grabbing my jacket.

Her sparkly shades slid down to the tip of her nose. "Alas, my schedule today is full, and I don't have room anywhere to squeeze in dead bodies."

Just as well. Gem didn't like seeing that stuff anyhow.

After I got up and waited for Christian to scoot out of his seat, I stared at all the uneaten food on my plate.

"Do me a favor and don't let my lunch go to waste," I said to Claude. "Betty doesn't like it when people leave a full plate behind."

His handsome features twisted with horror. "But I just ate three helpings of meatballs before we left."

Poor guy. I almost felt sorry for him, knowing he would do it.

I patted his shoulder. "Take one for the team."

Chapter 2

I SWALLOWED HARD, STANDING AT THE feet of a dead man. "That's really disgusting."

Christian knelt in front of the headless body. "I couldn't agree more. Corduroy trousers are the uniform they issue in hell."

He poked at the pool of blood on the linoleum floor but didn't taste it. It looked fresh, and there were spatters of it on the walls and countertops where it must have sprayed.

I swung open the fridge. "What do you think happened to it?"

"Perhaps it grew legs and walked away." Christian rose to his feet and jerked open the oven door. "I can't say I've ever seen anything like this before."

"Talk about losing your head."

He wiped his bloody finger on a clean rag. "Perhaps someone wanted a trophy above the fireplace."

"Viktor said it just happened within the hour. Why didn't the higher authority send in the Regulators or cleaners?" I nudged the body with my foot. "What's so special about this guy?"

The doorbell rang.

"That's him," Christian said, bustling to the door.

I waited in the kitchen of the upscale apartment and looked at the stainless-steel appliances, which were spattered with blood. A pool had soaked right through the accent rug and spread across the black tile. This guy was loaded, but an accent rug? I opened the fridge and looked inside. Yogurt, chocolate-covered strawberries, a vegetable platter, wine—there was no way this portly man lived here alone. Maybe his wife got tired of his complaining.

Wyatt appeared in the doorway, and when he got a gander at the body on the floor, he pulled his knit hat over his face. "Son of a ghost! I'm *not* doing this." When he tried to turn around, Christian blocked the doorway, gripping the doorjamb on either side. Wyatt shoved at him to no avail, the hat still covering his face. "Viktor said you needed me to help with something on your assignment. I thought he meant hacking into a computer or cracking an electronic safe. Nobody mentioned the Headless Horseman."

"It just happened," I pointed out. "Maybe you should have a look around before he floats away into the oblivion."

Christian snatched Wyatt's hat. "See anything, Spooky? Because we can't make a positive identification until we've located his head."

Wyatt scowled. "Do you know how creepy a floating head is? That's what happens when it separates from their body. And you can't have a conversation with it. They don't have any lungs."

"They're dead. They don't have any lungs to begin with."

"Don't be such a fanghole. You're not the one who has to see it. Besides, you don't understand how it works." Wyatt stepped over the corpse to stand beside me. "It only matters what *they* think. If they can't see their body, they don't think they can speak. No lungs, no throat—it's all psychological." He unzipped his army-green jacket and tucked his thumbs behind his skull belt buckle. "What happened?"

Christian gripped the doorframe above his head and leaned forward. "The higher authority believes this might be one of their own, but they want a positive ID."

"Did you search his wallet for his assigned alias? It's all in the system."

Christian gave him a lethal stare. "You wouldn't be here if we had a wallet, now would you? And even if we had one, we don't have a face to match his license."

"Why is this our concern?"

Christian let go of the frame. "Because it's what we get paid for, you dolt."

I rubbed the goose bumps on my bare arms.

Wyatt noticed my black tank top and jeans. "Where's your jacket?"

"In the truck."

"Where's your bra?"

"Are you going to help us or not?" When I took a step forward to walk around the body, my heel slipped in blood, and I hit the tile.

Wyatt howled with laughter as I lay there in a puddle of blood, which had splashed everywhere.

"This wasn't in the brochure," I muttered, cringing at the severed neck.

Christian grabbed my hand and hauled me up. "Best we leave Spooky alone to summon the spirits while we check out the place for clues."

I shook blood off my arm and used a dishrag to wipe off my hands. "This apartment belongs to a woman. They might live together, but if so, she wears the pants in this relationship."

"And how did you come to that conclusion?"

I pitched the bloody rag into the sink. "Because men don't buy flowery accent rugs. There's no beer, no leftover pizza, and no manly furniture. Besides, I looked at the contents of the fridge, and there's no way I'm gonna believe that he's a salad-eating man."

We roamed into the living room and looked around. The closed drapes blocked out most of the light, but one of them was fluttering.

I pulled it back and revealed an open window. "What do you make of this?"

"We're not here to investigate a murder, only to identify a corpse."

"Indulge me."

"Route of escape?" he offered, approaching the glass.

We eyed the three-story drop. It wasn't that far, and a Mage could have healed. A Chitah might have scaled the walls, or maybe a Shifter flew out the window.

But something about it didn't sit well with me. "This *just* happened. Seems like crawling out a window in broad daylight would attract attention."

"Aye," he agreed, circling the grey sofa. "Perhaps it was a jilted lover."

I scanned the room. Not a petal fallen from the fresh flowers on the glass coffee table. No overturned chairs, no blood, no ripped cushions, and not a single fringe on the area rug was out of line. "Who reported this? It doesn't look like the guy had time to scream, let alone dial for help."

Christian sent a message to Viktor and waited before reading the reply. "Window washers. The window was open, and one of them sensed a murder had happened. According to Viktor, they didn't enter the apartment."

"So the window was already open," I said, stating the obvious as I rounded a swivel chair. "Maybe the killer changed his escape plan when he saw the workers outside on the scaffold."

"Then *they* would have seen the killer poking his head out, and we'd have witnesses. He never intended to bail through the window. It was already open."

I rubbed my nose, the air heavy with the scent of red roses. They were the kind of flowers you gave to a lover on a special occasion. I walked around in search of photographs, but it was futile considering Breed weren't supposed to keep pictures of themselves outside of their fake licenses, which were all issued with alias information. Not everyone followed the rules, perhaps out of vanity or a secret desire to remember their lives, so I kept looking.

Wyatt circled around me in a flash and searched the bedrooms down the hall. I rummaged through the drawers of a console table but only found pens, notepads, candles, and several lighters.

"Whose name is on the lease?" I asked.

Christian peered behind paintings on the wall. "Viktor didn't say, and we're not to ask. He doesn't want us questioning anyone in the building. No neighbors, no witnesses, no leasing office."

"I found the freshy," Wyatt said grimly. He strode into the living room, shoulders stiff and lips pressed tight. "Well, half of him."

"Ask him who the murderer is," I said, hoping we could wrap this up so I could go back to my Angus burger.

Wyatt snatched his beanie from Christian's hand and tugged it onto his head. "That's not the half I found. Now he's stuck to me. Thanks a lot."

Christian wasn't about to tolerate any complaints. "Then ask the body to write down what he knows."

"It doesn't work that way unless he took a pen and paper with him in the afterlife."

"For feck's sake."

"Does he know where his severed head is?" I anchored my hands on my hips, watching Wyatt stare at a void space beside him. "Maybe he can point the way."

"Well?" Wyatt asked. "Where's your head?" After a moment, Wyatt turned as if watching someone walk into the kitchen.

We all followed, and Wyatt stopped short of the body. "It's in the freezer."

When he made no move to go after it, Christian stepped around him and opened the freezer door. He pulled out a severed head, holding it by the frosty hair. "Now that's a morbid sight if I ever did see one."

Wyatt spun on his heel. "I'm gonna have nightmares."

I jerked my head back. "Why? You've seen dead bodies before. Besides, the eyes are closed. It's not like he's looking at you."

"Yeah, but his ghost head's not in here, and I've searched the place. That means his head moved on to the next life but his body didn't." Wyatt reached for his collar and pulled it away from his neck as if he might vomit.

"Go search the house again—you probably missed it. Try looking out the open window in the living room. Maybe he wanted some fresh air and couldn't get back inside."

Wyatt gave me an indignant look and stormed out of the room.

I leaned against the counter, the body to my left. "Why do you think they put it in the freezer?"

Christian stepped over the corpse and lowered his arm. "It was facing out, so he wanted the authorities to admire his work."

"How do you know?"

He stepped close, his gaze hot. "Don't ask a killer that question."

My pulse ticked faster.

"Has anyone ever told you how fetching you are?"

I glanced down. "I'm covered in blood."

Christian looked at me the same way I'd looked at those chocolate-covered strawberries. "And do you think that turns me off?"

"I bet you're easy to please on a date. Not that I would know."

He gave me a hot look that could have incinerated my panties. "Don't make plans on Valentine's."

"Are you asking me out on a date with a head in your hand?"

His fangs slid out, and he leaned in tight. "I'm not asking, Precious."

Moments after he stepped back, Wyatt appeared in the open doorway.

"The spirit head's gone. My work is done."

As he spun on his heel, I chased after him. "Wait a second! You can't just leave."

After he flung the door open, he stopped in his tracks and turned. "Hold your ponies. I can't have a conversation with a headless body, but you want me to stick around here long enough for it to bond with me? You guys are a couple of fruit loops. See ya."

Christian stood a few paces behind me, the head still in his hand. "What's gotten into him?"

"Your cologne?"

"Whoever did this had a sharp blade," he remarked, showing me the severed neck.

I averted my eyes. "The victim also trusted him enough to let him inside and offer him a drink."

"A drink? And how did you come to that conclusion?"

"You should know better than anyone, my Irish friend. When someone invites you into their house, why else would they go to the kitchen?"

"Maybe it was the maintenance man coming to repair a drippy faucet."

"Does the maintenance man wear a sword?"

Christian's face went stony, and he tipped his head to the side. Then he looked around and noticed what I'd already observed: there was no sign of a struggle. It wasn't uncommon for Breed to carry weapons. After all, I wore daggers in plain sight. But a maintenance worker or deliveryman wouldn't arm themselves. That meant the victim either knew the murderer or had reason to trust an armed man.

The unmistakable click of sharp heels on a hard surface made me turn. A brunette with bright-red lips, black gloves, and a pearl necklace froze in the open doorway. I was sure she also had on clothes, but she flashed out of sight before I could look at the rest of her.

"Oh, no, you don't," I growled, racing out the door after her. She had already reached the end of the hall and was pushing through a door.

I skidded into a stairwell, but she was already on the next landing down. I had on my red sneakers, and that meant no woman in high heels was going to win this chase. Halfway down, I jumped over the rail to the landing below. Before she could descend the next flight of stairs, I snatched the back of her black dress, and she whirled around, throwing a blast of energy into me.

I smiled. "Thanks for the energy drink."

She wrenched away and managed three more steps before I jumped on her back and we went sailing to the landing below. We hit the concrete with a thud, and the bone that snapped wasn't mine.

I sat up and rotated my shoulders, making sure I hadn't dislocated anything.

"I'll kill you!" she screeched unconvincingly, her jaw clenched as she rolled over and hugged her arm against her body.

Winded and sore, I scooted back against the wall to catch my breath. "Not if I kill you first."

Christian and I watched the haughty woman rip back her silk drapes to heal her broken arm in the sunshine. Christian had already set the bone so it would fuse together seamlessly. There was a moment when I almost pitied her, but that thought perished when she took an imperious tone with me and demanded I get my cheap shoes off her precious oriental rug.

"Don't you think breaking her arm was a bit extreme?" he asked me quietly. "She doesn't look like a killer to me."

"Guilty people don't run."

"Aye, but you're also drenched in blood. Perhaps you gave her a wee bit of a fright."

He had a point. "What did you do with the head?"

"I put him back in the freezer to chill out for a while." Christian waltzed over to the woman and gestured for her to take a seat.

She gave me a venomous look before kicking off her broken heel and sitting down on the couch. "Those Manolo Blahnik heels were one of a kind, made especially for me."

I jutted my hip and folded my arms. "You shouldn't have run."

"Excuse me if I had a knee-jerk reaction to a vagrant, covered in blood, standing inside my apartment while her Vampire companion is flourishing my lover's head in his hand."

I met Christian's gaze. *Lover.* This was getting interesting.

Christian circled behind the sofa and leaned over the back, his fingers laced. "You say this is your home?"

She touched her flushed cheeks, her gaze settling on the red roses on the table. "Yes, I rent this property. How do I know the higher authority hired you?"

I strutted toward the swivel chair and plopped down. "Because you'd be dead otherwise, don't you think?"

"Was that your friend I saw loping down the hall?" Her lip quivered when she looked at the flowers again. "What happened?"

"That's what we're here to find out," Christian said coolly. "Who's the numpty we found in the kitchen?"

When she removed one of her black gloves, she smacked him in the face with it. With a cross look, Christian straightened up and circled to the front of the couch. He shoved the flowers aside and took a seat on the glass coffee table. I waited anxiously to see if it would hold his weight or crack.

After popping a peppermint into his mouth, he continued. "Can you tell me the name of the dearly departed?"

"Walter. Do I have to give his last name?"

"If we're to identify him for a proper burial. Let's start with your name."

She reclined her head, eyes closing. "Elaine Sanders."

Christian crunched on his candy. "Why do I know that name?"

Her brown eyes popped open, and she gave him a peevish glance. "I'm an official representative of the higher authority. The man you found is Walter Hughes."

"Does he live here?" I asked, wondering if maybe she was his sugar mama.

"No."

"But he has a key."

She shifted, looking away and fidgeting with a gold bracelet on her wrist. "Look, if you must know, I'm bonded with another Mage."

Bonded being the Mage equivalent of marriage.

I leaned back and crossed my legs. This lady's story wasn't anything I hadn't heard before. "So... you own this little apartment and share it as a rendezvous point with your lover? That explains why it doesn't look that lived-in. Why did you kill him?"

"Do you really think I'd murder my lover in my own apartment and come back?"

"Maybe you got spooked and ran. But you had a little time to think about it and decided to come back and clean up your mess. You're not off my suspect list until you can provide an alibi."

She gave a dramatic sigh while tucking her skirt beneath her legs. "I just came from work. There are at least ten people who can testify to my whereabouts all day."

"Does your husband know about this little arrangement?" Christian asked.

Her expression remained as rigid as her posture. "He doesn't know about this place, and I'd like to keep it that way."

Elaine was avoiding eye contact with Christian the way most people did around Vampires. She didn't know we were only here to identify the body, but anything additional we learned would go straight to Viktor.

Christian kept his voice steady. "Do you think your husband might have found out?"

Her eyes rounded, and she shot to her feet. "Absolutely not! Henry would never do anything so obscene. You better think twice about implicating an official of the court. I've taken every measure to keep this affair private."

"Can *he* provide an alibi?" Christian asked.

She shook her head. "Your clumsy efforts to solve a crime will tarnish his reputation unnecessarily. The scandal could jeopardize our positions. Merely questioning him without sufficient evidence is slanderous, and I won't stand for it." Elaine wrinkled her nose at me. "I'm going to have to replace that chair."

I glanced at the bloodstains on the upholstery where my arms had rubbed against it. "You're going to have to replace a lot more than that, starting with your refrigerator."

Her dark eyebrows pressed together. "I don't know what you mean."

Christian cleared his throat in what was an obvious attempt to shut me up. "Is there anyone else who knows about this place?"

Elaine shook her head.

"Are you sure?" he pressed. "A best friend, a delivery service..."

"No one." Her lip quivered, and she steered her gaze away. "This was the only place we could have uninterrupted privacy. Walter didn't have a mate, so he didn't have to make any sacrifices. But he felt it was imperative to protect my reputation, and going to hotels or on trips would create too many opportunities for mistakes. My face is recognizable among the elite, so having a place of our own was his idea. My husband and I don't work the same hours, and he's not the doting kind who calls when I'm away. Walter and I planned for this weekend. I came up with a ruse by convincing my husband that I had a meeting with a designer. Walter was so excited."

That explained the roses. He must have shown up early with flowers and the chocolate-covered strawberries I'd seen in the fridge.

Christian leaned forward. "You said Walter didn't have a mate. That's not a Mage term."

She rubbed her forehead. "Walter was a Chitah."

Ahhh. His dark hair had thrown me off, and since his eyelids were frozen shut, I hadn't seen his eye color. That explained why she didn't want anyone finding out about the affair. Her husband would probably see it as a slap in the face that she'd chosen to have an affair with a Chitah—and a defect at that.

"Would you have knocked or just walked in?" I asked.

She jerked her head back. "Why should that matter?"

"Because he let someone inside the apartment. You have a peephole, and I'm guessing if this place is a secret, he would have looked out first. But if you had a habit of knocking, he wouldn't have thought twice about opening the door."

"I have a key," she said. "We both do. I've never knocked."

Christian rose to his feet and put his hands in his coat pockets. "Would he have ordered delivery?"

She huffed out a laugh. "We never order that garbage."

I wiped my arm on the sofa as I sat forward. People like her probably thought they were too cultured to eat a little chow mein or pepperoni pizza. "Well, you two obviously can't go out to eat at a restaurant."

"We've also never had an entire weekend together," she said with derision. "Walter stocks the kitchen in case I get hungry, but I don't come here to eat."

Christian jerked his head toward the kitchen, calling me away. I followed him through the archway.

"What do you make of it?" I asked.

"I think her husband found out and took matters into his own hands. That would explain the head in the freezer—something for her to find."

"Yep. That seems like the obvious choice. But if their relationship was a secret, then why did Viktor's contact send us in first? How would they know who was staying here and what was going on?"

Christian scratched his beard. "I wouldn't be surprised if they kept files on all their people. It wouldn't be hard to make the connection if she signed the lease in her name. Now that we've identified the body as her lover, it's business as usual. They send in a qualified Regulator, and after the inquisition, the cleaners take care of the mess. I'm assuming if Elaine had been the victim, there would be special protocol to follow. They're trying to be discreet, especially if they think she's dead at the hands of her lover. The higher authority doesn't like scandal. Can't let that information get around before they tell her husband, the poor bastard."

I leaned my back against the doorjamb. "We better give Viktor the scoop."

"Aye. We've got everything we need."

"What about her husband? I think we need to call him over."

Christian chortled. "Only if you want to see a real bloodbath. Viktor gave us orders not to question anyone, and we've already broken his rule. I think he'll give us a pass on this one, but don't push your luck."

I opened the fridge and grabbed one of the chocolate-covered strawberries. "Want one?"

"Over my rotting corpse."

"Or his," I said, stepping over the body. After finishing the last bite, I tossed the stem in the sink. "What's the male equivalent of a mistress? A mister?"

Christian sighed, his gaze distant. "Second fiddle."

Chapter 3

BEFORE WE LEFT ELAINE'S DEN of iniquity, we reported to Viktor to make sure he didn't need us to pursue the investigation any further. Satisfied with our findings, he let us off the hook, and we instructed Elaine to sit tight until the Regulators arrived. Heading back to Ruby's Diner while covered in blood was out of the question, so Christian and I went home.

After a quick shower, I headed down to the dining room, drying off the ends of my damp hair with a towel. When I walked in, I took a moment to admire the unpolished beauty. Candlelight from the chandelier suffused the room, soaking into the rustic wood table and illuminating the stone floors. Aside from a few upgraded rooms, our modest furnishings removed us from modern civilization. I would never have thought I could get used to the quiet, but Keystone wasn't without its charms.

Christian and Viktor were having a quiet conversation in one of the booths against the wall that separated the dining and gathering rooms. They were cozy, like what you might see in a restaurant or bar—vinyl benches and wood tables that comfortably seated four per table. Each of the booths was placed next to one of the open archways that overlooked the gathering room. No one was in there, but the firelight in the hearth burned bright.

I fell back a step when Viktor looked up. "Blue said you wanted to see me, but I didn't know you were in the middle of something. Do you guys need another minute?"

Christian scooted against the wall, inviting me to sit beside him.

When I sat down, the fat candle against the wall flickered and almost went out. I draped my towel over the back of my seat and shivered.

Viktor's grey eyes glittered from too many spirits. "Can I pour you a glass?"

Before I could answer, he filled an empty goblet he'd set aside and slid it in front of me. After he topped everyone off, Viktor swirled his glass and held it beneath his nose. "This was a very good year. My village in Russia had a record heat wave. Nothing makes you feel more alive than the sun beating down on your shoulders. Our winters were bleak and long, and summers were like your spring. So to have that year of blessed heat—I can still remember running through the high grass and how cold the water felt when jumping in. That was the year I became a man."

Viktor didn't have to elaborate on what he meant by that.

After savoring another mouthful of wine, he swirled his glass, lost in the memories. "To you... this just smells like another red wine. But someday when you're older, you'll recognize the scent of yesterday. It's jasmine on the breeze, old leather, a fragrant wine... or maybe for you it will just be hamburgers grilling in a diner."

Alcohol acts as a time machine. I knew all about how it lifted a person out of the present and into the past. And right now, Viktor was on a one-way trip to another century.

"Do you miss your home?" I asked.

"You never miss a where. You only miss a when. If I returned, it would not be the same. Home is not a place—it's the people you love and the time that you inhabit."

My glass clinked against his. "I'll drink to that."

Viktor became nostalgic when he drank aged wine. Mostly, we were subjected to humorous stories of his past—many of which might have been tall tales—but after a few more glasses, his mood would shift to a sullen one. Usually by then, he'd revert to his native tongue, and the rest of us would retire to our rooms.

Christian ran his finger around the rim of his glass. "Is there a reason you summoned us here?"

Viktor swept back his silver hair and grumbled. "I received a call shortly after dinner, and I spoke with my contact for a long time to assure him that you were not involved."

"In what?" I asked. "The murder? What the hell gave them that crazy idea? They're the ones who called us to check out the body."

"Not that one. The woman."

My breath caught.

Christian leaned forward. "You mean to say that Elaine Sanders is dead?"

"I didn't do it," I cut in, fearing our tumble down the stairs might implicate me. Not to mention the blood on her clothes from when I'd wrestled her to the ground. "Her arm broke during a fall, but that was the only damage done. We told you everything, Viktor. I swear it."

"I believe you. But you must appreciate how it appears. The Regulators arrived to find her deceased, and you were the last people who saw her alive."

"Suicide?" Christian offered. "Her murdered lover had banjaxed her career. The poor woman was an incapacitated, blubbering mess."

"Let's not exaggerate," I said. "But Christian has a point. Her marriage was probably over—maybe her career. I can see how sending in Regulators would spark rumors. You can't trust those guys with secrets. Maybe we shouldn't have left her alone."

Viktor held his glass. "Unless she cut off her own head, suicide is unlikely."

I stared at my sweatpants, wondering where it all went wrong. "We told her to lock the door. How long did it take the Regulators to get there after we left?"

Viktor swayed his head from side to side, and his mouth turned down as he struggled to remember. "I'd say... maybe twenty minutes?"

"For feck's sake." Christian rubbed his face. "The killer was watching us the whole time."

I put my elbows on the table and cupped one hand over the other. "So Elaine was their target to begin with. They probably saw her go up and realized she had company."

"Why would you assume they weren't *both* targets?" Viktor asked.

"Because Walter was a nobody. Elaine's an official for the higher authority and had her reputation to protect. Walter probably got there early, put the strawberries and wine in the fridge, set the flowers on the table, and then answered a knock at the door."

"And the window?" Christian asked.

"Maybe he opened it when setting out the flowers. Chitahs have a strong sense of smell, so he probably aired out the apartment because of the roses. Claude's always mentioning how odors bother him after a long period of time."

"Aye. That might explain why poor Walter didn't flee or fight. Either his sense of smell was also defective, or the roses masked the intentions of his murderer."

"Do you think the killer was hiding in the apartment while we were there?"

"No. I would have heard him." Christian drank his wine and then set his empty glass on the end of the table. "Does her husband have an alibi?"

Viktor rubbed his cheek. "Da. My contact discreetly confirmed that he's been at work all day, oblivious to the fate of his woman."

"The more I think about it, the more I'm convinced it wasn't the husband," I said. "Would Walter have really opened the door for her husband? Someone would have thrown a punch and knocked shit over."

Christian steered his gaze over to me in a deliberate way. "Maybe Walter wanted to play hero and tell Mr. Sanders once and for all how it's going to be. Do you realize that the majority of victims know their killers? You have to rule out family and friends before you can conduct an investigation."

"Even if Walter had opened the door by mistake, there would have been a struggle the moment he caught sight of the sword. Chitahs have the advantage over a Mage, remember? Walter could have taken him out with a single bite."

"Perhaps he was afraid of nibbling on a member of the higher authority."

"He could have claimed self-defense."

Candlelight sparkled in Christian's eyes, and he gave me a fiendish grin. Sometimes he gave me that look when we had quarrels.

Viktor cleared his throat. "My contact documents the private residences of his colleagues. The victim did nothing to conceal her name on the lease, and property purchased by officials is reported to specific channels. This is not common knowledge, but it helps their investigator track criminal activities. They assumed she was the one reported deceased, so we were called to confirm her identity and search for clues."

"I still don't understand why it's not a job for the Regulators or even Mageri Enforcers. Why have a third party involved before anyone else conducts their investigation? We basically contaminated the crime scene."

Viktor lowered his voice. "They believe someone is targeting the higher authority, but they are keeping it quiet. She is the fifth victim on the panel."

My pulse jumped. "How many members are there?"

"I do not know the exact number as there are more members than the seats filled at their trials. They rotate."

"Why not warn them?"

"It would instigate panic. Not just among officials but also everyone in the city. Just imagine."

"*Jaysus,*" Christian breathed.

Though I knew the seriousness of the crime, I wasn't certain I comprehended the full impact. "But the Regulators can protect them. They'd be on high alert."

"It's bigger than that," Christian said. "Some of the panel members might flee, and factions living within the city would see that as a sign the law is crumbling. The higher authority is the only thing keeping order in the major cities. The murders expose their vulnerabilities and could incite an uprising. Sometimes, all people need is a push."

I gulped down my wine. "I think my head is about to explode."

Viktor tugged at the collar of his pullover. "Because this is not our case, we must keep quiet about the assassinations."

I shook my head. "It won't stay a secret for long. Elaine was bonded to another official."

"The Regulators will talk," Christian added.

Viktor filled his glass. "Not if they're using the same men to investigate each crime."

Christian leaned back. "I wager they have a trusted team for just such occasions. How considerate."

"The higher authority plans for every occasion, including their own demise." Viktor's expression grew dim, and he drank more wine. After a few moments, he began singing a Russian song—something old and melancholy.

Kira appeared in the doorway, as quiet as a ghost. Her long nightgown swished above her bare feet as she crossed the room and helped Viktor to stand. I didn't interact with Kira beyond passing her in the hall and nodding. She made no effort to communicate with us and preferred keeping her distance. But despite her quiet demeanor and invisibility, she looked after Viktor whenever he got this way. Blue had always been the one to take the drink from Viktor's hand when he'd fallen asleep in his chair, but she'd usually cover him with a blanket and let him sleep. Kira would walk him to bed—perhaps something she'd done a million times with her own father.

Once they left, I emptied the bottle into my glass and enjoyed the full-bodied flavor dancing on my taste buds.

Christian brushed his hand against mine. "Have I ever mentioned that I love it when you're feisty?"

"So *that's* what that look was about. Sometimes I can't tell if you want to kiss me or kill me."

"Me neither."

I leaned back. "Why would the killer go to Elaine's secret-rendezvous apartment instead of her house? Her husband's also a target, so he could have killed two birds with one stone."

"Officials have personal bodyguards, men who protect them night and day. You can bet your sweet arse she left behind her guard when she met up with Walter. I don't know the facts of the other cases, but I'd wager they were all slain when unguarded. The apartment made her vulnerable."

"We should have stayed."

"If there's one thing I've learned, it's that you can't turn back time."

I reached up and touched my chest where my ruby necklace used to be. No, we couldn't turn back time. But what if we knew what was coming? My mind drifted to something else that had been plaguing my thoughts for the past few weeks. "I can't stop thinking about Crush. Fletcher's out there somewhere, and it won't take long before he goes after him. If he can't get to me, he'll go for the one thing I care about."

"Your da can take care of himself."

"Yeah, if he knows what's coming. Maybe I can't protect him, but the least I can do is warn him."

"That a Mage is after him? That his daughter is still alive? Which part would you start with first?"

I gazed at the white candle, the wax melting down the sides and piling onto the silver holder. Not much time had passed since Fletcher's escape. He was probably settling in to a new place and getting his bearings before plotting revenge. Fletcher knew who I worked for, and if that intimidated him, he might go after my father instead. I knew how his mind worked, and that knowledge kept me awake at night.

Christian put his arm around me. He had an uncanny knack for calming my nerves in the most unexpected ways. Sometimes it was a brush of his hand against mine, and other times it was a tender look. But he hadn't made any moves since our assignment in Canada. My intimate memories of Christian before my abduction were gone, but not the ones that followed. I thought about that night often. Not just his passionate kisses and sexual moves that left me boneless, but other memories resided in my thoughts. Like the tender way he held me in his arms as we watched the fire, how he tucked my hair behind my ear when he thought I'd fallen asleep.

As much as he professed to being incapable of love, I'd discovered his secret.

Christian had a tender heart.

But something held me back, kept me from reciprocating the desire to build a foundation together. My stolen memories left a lasting impact on my ability to develop our relationship any further. I didn't deny him affection, but how was I supposed to get serious with a man after one night of passion? There were too many past conversations, too many shared moments that were now absent, thanks to my maker. What if I had asked Houdini to take away my feelings for Christian? Would I be going against my own wishes by pursuing this?

Without answers, I was left in the dark.

Regardless, I felt good in his arms. Safe. Listening to the steady beat of his heart. His body heat warming me. His strong arms holding me as gently as a dandelion in the wind.

Until he pushed me away.

Shepherd swaggered into the room and gave us a cursory glance before lighting up a cigarette. The black T-shirt and jeans weren't his usual attire for working out, so I gathered he was seeking companionship. Shepherd and Christian clicked, and it wasn't unusual to find them having a drink.

Sensing I was about to become a third wheel in the bromance, I stood up and grabbed my towel. "Well, time for me to wander the halls for a few hours and discover a new room. Sleep tight. Don't let the Vampires bite."

As I passed by Shepherd, I looked over my shoulder at Christian. Yeah, this situation created all kinds of complications. He couldn't even respond since Shepherd might pick up on a rogue emotion. Instead of giving me a smile or a wink, Christian patted the table, inviting his friend to sit and talk.

Shepherd waited patiently for Raven to leave before strolling over to Viktor's alcohol cabinet. "How does whiskey sound?"

"Don't mind if I do," Christian said.

Shepherd held the cigarette between his lips as he returned to the table with glasses in one hand and the bottle in the other. After filling each one halfway, he took a seat. His eyes skated over to the dining table and the candles burning in the chandelier. Kira usually put them out in case wax dripped onto the table, but sometimes, she forgot.

"Something on your mind?" Christian asked.

Shepherd reached for the square ashtray by the wall and flicked his ashes. "I'm thinking about leaving Keystone."

"We've all had those days, you morose bastard." Christian sipped his whiskey. He always told it like it was. "But we don't exactly have anything waiting for us on the outside."

"I'm dead serious."

Shepherd thought back to a few weeks before when he'd gone out walking in the snow. Blue found him sitting on top of a frozen pond, in a stupor. She brought him back inside by the fire and said, "Don't let your love for her be the thing that destroys you."

Maggie had once been the center of his universe. He still remembered her infectious laugh and the way she'd make fish lips in a futile attempt to kiss her own pregnant belly. Blue didn't know that as torturous as it was to lose Maggie, Shepherd had put away that pain the day he buried her killer. It was his baby who haunted his dreams and consumed his thoughts. With each passing day, his boy would grow, and Shepherd would never get to see it. The idea of kidnapping him was starting to nestle in his thoughts like a thorn. It would be the worst possible scenario. They would live as rogues, and Shepherd would have no source of income. Both his scars and the boy's would make it easy for bounty hunters to track them down. It wouldn't be long before the boy grew to resent him. The fact that Shepherd would never have shared memories with his own son stole what little contentment he'd found with Keystone.

"Don't be daft," Christian said, drink in hand. "Viktor threw us each a lifeline, and that's what's keeping us from turning into one of the shitebags we're hunting. Get langered and get it out of your system, but keep away those thoughts before they fester."

"If it's all the same to you, I'll make my own decisions." Shepherd knocked back his drink and set the empty glass on the table.

"And have you informed your partner?"

Shepherd ran a hand over his buzz cut and felt a spot on his nape that needed trimming. "All Wyatt needs is that damn vending machine and a computer."

"I beg to differ. Who's the one who saved his life that time when those street thugs came at us with guns? And what about the time someone followed Wyatt home from one of his surveillance jobs? The rest of us told him to drive in circles and lose the guy, but you're the one who ran out of the pub after him."

Shepherd remembered that night. Wyatt had been in panic mode, so Shepherd jogged what must have been twelve blocks before they met up at an intersection. He jumped in the driver's seat, took over that little car, and drove like Jason Bourne to lose the fucker who'd been tailing Wyatt after he'd been caught setting up hidden cameras outside a gangster's meeting spot. Shepherd remembered how shaken Wyatt was by the whole thing, being unarmed, as usual. It wasn't the first time Shepherd had saved his ass. That was one reason Viktor had paired them up. Wyatt was the brains and Shepherd the brawn.

Shepherd took a long drag from his cigarette. "Viktor can find a replacement. A guy like me ain't hard to replace."

Christian stroked his beard, his black eyes trying hard to read Shepherd. "If it were that easy to find replacements, don't you think we'd have a bigger team? It takes the man a long time to find whatever it is he's looking for—a person he can trust who'll be loyal to the organization. You should thank the heavenly angels he took you in."

"You've never thought of leaving? I mean for real."

"Aye, but I came to my senses." Christian swirled his drink. "We've all got a million reasons to leave, but maybe all we really need is one to stay."

Shepherd was a man of routine and order, and lately, those two things had parted ways. The stable ground he'd once walked on was shaking again, and if he wasn't careful, he might slip through one of the cracks.

"If you leave, there won't be any coming back," Christian reminded him. "Take a vacation for a fortnight. Viktor has no qualms with any of us taking a break to get our head together. But if you commit to leaving Keystone, you won't get a second chance."

Shepherd refilled their glasses. The slow burn of whiskey steadied his nerves.

"Maybe you should talk to someone about what troubles you," Christian suggested. "Get it off your chest. If you don't think Wyatt'll take you seriously, I'm always here. Just don't think you can cry on my shoulder and hug it out. I'll not be your gal. It's probably not as big of a deal as you're making it out to be."

Shepherd cut him a sharp glare. "It's a big fucking deal. I just don't know if talking about it will dig my own grave."

Christian's eyes slanted away as if he understood. He lifted his glass in a toast. "*Sláinte.*"

"Cheers."

They each took a drink. Alcohol gave Shepherd permission to forget his problems. It blurred his thoughts between past and present. It made sleeping at night a hell of a lot easier.

"I can't make your decisions for you," Christian finally said, resting his arms on the table. "But ask yourself if leaving will fix your problem. Will it truly? Because if the answer is no, you'll be in the exact same position with nothing to give you purpose in life. What'll stop you from crossing the line? Each one of us is a weapon of some sort, and Viktor knows how dangerous we are in the wrong hands."

Shepherd tucked his chin in the palm of his hand. He glanced down at the scars on his right arm, which weren't as bad as the left. The cigarette smoke between his fingers created a haze, but through the haze, he remembered receiving each and every cut. Fifty-three in total on his entire body. Sometimes he counted a few more or less, but that was the number that came up the most.

"What if I can't find a reason to stay?" Shepherd asked in all honesty.

Christian knocked back the rest of his drink and slid toward the end of the bench. "Then at least tell us your troubles before walking out the door. By then it won't matter, and you owe us that much. I'll be the one scrubbing your memories of your time with Keystone, but I can't touch the rest. That's yours. If you become a menace to society, then at least we'll understand your motives. But whatever you do, don't run." Christian leaned in tight and locked eyes with Shepherd. "If you run, we'll have no choice but to hunt you down. And you know what that means. I'll have to do a full memory wipe. Not just Keystone, but everything before and after."

After Christian got up and left the room, Shepherd stared vacantly at the empty seat in front of him. A cold dread washed over him. He knew damn well about the agreement they'd each made when joining Keystone, and that was a crucial part of why he was thinking about running away.

Forgetting Keystone would mean forgetting his son.

Chapter 4

PATRICK BANE SURE DID LOVE his balls. It was the night before Valentine's Day, and though Patrick hadn't announced a theme for his party, the obvious red décor and flower arrangements said it all. Keystone was invited and present, but most of us had split up to do our own thing.

As a member of the higher authority, Patrick had all the luxuries a Mage could afford. His mansion had a grand front room and two curved staircases joined by a balcony on the second floor. The marble floors gleamed beneath an opulent chandelier dripping with crystals. Cocktail tables were spaced apart and covered in white linen. Each table had a cluster of red candles surrounded by lush red rose petals. As usual, Mr. Bane's staff had their hands full with passing out champagne and desserts. Each woman who drifted by left behind a cloud of perfume, and most of the men were dressed up in their finest attire. It became a game to guess which century each person had been born in based on their outfit.

Instead of standing, Gem and I had chosen a table with tall chairs. Most of the men were underwhelmed with my leather pants, but Gem stole the show. She'd decided a red dress would clash with her hair, a pale-violet ombré that faded to silver-tinted ends. Instead, she'd purchased a black cocktail dress with a giant heart cut out of the back. Beneath it, she wore a red lacy top to make the heart design stand out. Her platform heels were also black, but they each had small roses stitched into the fabric along the bottom. Few women held a candle to Gem's unique sense of style. Her outfits were whimsical and thought out for each occasion.

"Patrick always has the best nonalcoholic drinks," she gushed. "And you can tell the difference."

I munched on another chocolate-covered strawberry, pieces of the chocolate shell cracking and falling onto the white tablecloth. "Why didn't he have this party tomorrow?"

Gem set down her glass of sparkling cider and gave an elfin smile. "Most people have plans on Valentine's Day. Wink, wink."

That reminded me of my date with Christian. I tossed the strawberry stem on a small plate and licked the chocolate off my fingers. "Is that what you and Hooper are doing?"

Her eyes sparkled, as did all the glitter painted around them. "Alas, Hooper's not into commercial holidays. But tonight is the first real date we've had in a long time."

I glanced around the room. Women in red gowns and expensive baubles were stealing the attention of every available man. "Are you sure he knows you're on a date?"

"Bartenders make a lot of friends. Someone he knows recognized him and asked if he could make them a drink that they aren't serving here. People say he's the best mixologist in town."

I folded a rose petal in half. "Is it because he spikes the drinks?"

Her eyebrows gathered. "I never asked. Bartenders aren't supposed to do that unless it's one of the specialty drinks in the bar. He could get fired."

"People love their Sensor magic. Maybe he makes a little cash on the side at public events like these."

Confusion swam across her face. People frowned upon misused magic, especially at elite parties such as this one. What Sensors did was seen as a novelty, but their powers could also be dangerous if used irresponsibly. In my failed attempt to carry on a normal conversation, I'd inadvertently planted seeds of doubt in Gem's head that would likely lead to a blowout later between her and Hooper.

Well done, Raven.

Wyatt cut through the crowd and swaggered in our direction. To say that Wyatt had charisma would be an understatement. What he lacked in style, he more than made up for in personality.

He'd shined his black cowboy boots, and his dark jeans had a nice press. But Viktor had taken the jacket off his own back so Wyatt could conceal his T-shirt, which said: I HAVE A HEART-ON. Blue had remarked on the homonym, and that opened up a heated discussion on the ride over.

Luckily, Viktor hadn't mentioned my leather pants and red sweater. I was woefully underdressed, but nothing else went with my apathy.

"This party is out of sight," Wyatt said, his olive-green eyes sparkling with merriment. "Plenty of desperate women who don't want to be alone tomorrow. They say it's a trivial holiday, but I call bullshit."

I leaned back in my chair. "Ah. *Now* I get why they hold these parties the day before. Looking for an easy lay?"

Wyatt collected the pieces of chocolate I'd spilled on the table and ate them. "I'm not complaining. My loins need to be ungirded once in a while."

When Gem's nose wrinkled, he winked at her.

Violins and cellos played from a nearby room where people were dancing. I glimpsed their happy faces through the open doorway over my right shoulder. Christian was somewhere in there, but I suddenly found myself wondering how long I could look at him without drawing attention. This wouldn't be such a difficult position had Viktor never established the rule regarding sexual relations between partners.

Then again, I could totally see his point. Christian's whereabouts had become a distraction for me throughout the evening.

I slid off my stool. "I'm going to mingle."

Wyatt waggled his eyebrows. "Happy hunting."

Viktor was in a tight circle with Patrick and a few other men dressed like penguins. They stood beside one of the grand staircases, champagne in hand. Patrick's little boy was sitting on the floor, a dull look in his eyes. He had on his black cape and mask, something he must have enjoyed as a means to escape the drudgery of staying out of trouble and making a good impression on behalf of the host.

Poor kid. Nobody brought children to these parties, and he'd probably rather be upstairs, playing with his toys.

I dragged my gaze up and saw Shepherd sitting directly above him, his face visible through the gaps in the staircase. He didn't like social gatherings, and to be honest, neither did I. Dressing up had its moments, but I couldn't relate to these people. They were snooty, self-centered, aristocratic assholes.

"You look like you could use a drink," a tall gentleman said. He handed me a champagne flute and lifted his own to his lips. "The representation of other Chitahs here is abysmal."

His bright-yellow eyes looked at the pockets of partygoers with derision. I sipped my champagne and noticed his soot-colored hair. Most Chitahs had blond or reddish hair, but the lighter shades were always preferable. This guy was incredibly tall, so I felt it necessary to say something incredibly inane.

"How's the weather up there?"

He lowered his glass and studied me for a beat. "I should ask you the same."

I could smell him, and it wasn't cologne but a heady scent that made me take a step back.

"What is your Breed?" he inquired, tilting his head to the side.

Panic rippled through me when I noticed his nostrils twitching. "I'm a Mage."

Not entirely a lie.

He reached up and slowly traced his bottom lip with his finger. "Is that so? Come forward and let me look at you."

I jutted my hip to the side. "I never show my assets on the first date."

His face softened, but not the three creases in his brow. "Do you fear me? Or do you see me as more than just a mortal enemy?"

"I've got nothing against your kind as long as you keep your fangs to yourself."

A smile touched his lips, and his eyes sparkled like yellow citrine in morning light. "You have nothing to fear from me, female. If your kind weren't so intimidated by my people, we might actually find common ground and quit warring with one another."

I gulped down my champagne. "I once knew a Chitah detective who seduced Mage women before killing them. He used his venom to overpower his prey. So it's not like the distrust of your kind is unwarranted."

He drew a deep breath and set his half-empty glass on a tray moving by. "It's unfortunate that one foolish man can alter perceptions because of his misdeeds. As long as men shape their beliefs by the actions of the past, the chasm between our Breeds will always exist."

I couldn't help but notice that during our conversation, we were garnering stares from people around us who were pretending not to look.

"So… what do you do for a living?"

He stirred with laughter and put his hands in the pockets of his long black coat. "A little of this. A little of that. And you?"

I rocked on my heels. "A little of this. A little of that."

"I'm Quaid," he said, bowing. "And you are?"

"Raven. What's a nice guy like you doing talking to a girl like me? Don't you have important colleagues around here to schmooze up to?"

"I don't like seeing a female alone. Especially one with ruby lips turned in a frown."

I felt my cheeks flush.

"It's refreshing to speak candidly with another person."

Christian eased up next to Quaid. "Did you know the real reason women paint their lips pink and red is to resemble their fanny? Shagging is all men think about, so it's the only way that women can hold our attention."

I gave him a mirthless smile. "I'm sorry, do I know you?"

A man suddenly appeared at Quaid's left. "Sire, the host wishes to speak with you before you leave."

Quaid bowed and dutifully stepped away to do what everyone at these functions did—make connections.

"You make interesting friends," Christian remarked, walking me to a private corner away from the crowd.

"Jealous?"

"Of the Overlord? Hardly."

"Overlord?"

"Are you familiar with the Chitah hierarchy? Everyone belongs to a Pride, and every Pride is ruled by a Lord." He peered over his shoulder and discreetly pointed at Quaid. "And *that* one rules them all. He's their version of a king."

I suddenly felt dizzy when I remembered the asinine things I'd asked him. *How's the weather up there?* Good job, Raven.

I smacked Christian's chest. "And you walked right up, talking about vaginas! What is wrong with us?"

He chortled, and I didn't know whether to laugh or cry. "Come now. What happened to the old Raven who didn't give a shite what people thought?"

"That was before I had a boss. Had it been anyone else, no big deal. But the Lord of all Lords? I'm so fucking dead."

The power suddenly shut off, and the music died. People looked around the room, which was now insufficiently lit with candles.

"Looks like someone forgot to pay the light bill," I quipped.

Christian leaned in sexily, and for a moment, I thought he might kiss me. "You know what those leathers do to me."

I blinked in surprise. "Someone might hear you."

"No Vampires on the premises. Besides, parties like these are too loud, and another Vampire would hardly take notice. Hundreds of different conversations going at once, women cackling, glasses clinking, not to mention all those hooves stomping about in the ballroom."

"So noise doesn't bother you?"

"Aye, it bothers me. But I mute out the world until the only sound I can hear is the gentle ticking of your heart."

"That's a little creepy."

Despite his admission, a flurry of tingles raced through me as he stepped closer, his finger tracing down the curve of my breast. No one could see us in the shadowy corner. I wanted to kiss his Adam's apple and fall into his embrace. I also wanted to pull him into an empty room and do bad things.

Time stopped when an explosion rocked the mansion, sucking the air right out of my lungs. The sound was so earsplitting that I temporarily went deaf, all the cacophonous noise around me muffled. Christian pinned me to the wall, his body shielding mine. Once I counted all my limbs, we looked around to make sense of what just happened.

Some guests were on the floor. Others hunched over with their hands covering their ears. Black smoke billowed in from the back, but I didn't see any dead bodies or damage.

A bevy of men moved like hockey players on ice, circling the Overlord. Facing outward, they drew their swords and formed a ring of steel before ushering him out the front door. Several people followed suit, searching for their party and rushing out. Moments later, pandemonium ensued. Cocktail tables were now obstacles as people flooded out of the adjoining rooms.

Christian and I sprang into action, searching the crowd for our team. Though my ears were still ringing, a crying child caught my attention. I swung my gaze to where Patrick and Viktor had been moments earlier and saw they were okay. But the little boy was in a fetal position on the floor, hands over his head. Shepherd jogged toward them just as Patrick scooped up his little boy and hurried off. Viktor appeared unhurt and caught up with Shepherd.

I headed to the back, where I'd last seen Gem and Wyatt. Christian disappeared toward the other side of the house. Broken glass from the champagne flutes crunched beneath my boots. No one in my line of vision had purple hair, and there were so many people pouring out of the ballroom that I found myself swimming against the stream.

"Gem!" I shouted.

I turned left and skidded on the marble floor where drinks had been spilled. Inside an empty dining room, candles flickered beneath a painting of a foxhunt, and trays of uneaten food covered the table.

Arguments erupted in the hall, one Mage blasting an agitated cougar who had shifted during the melee. I scuttled around them and smacked into someone while turning a corner.

"Niko," I breathed, gripping his shoulders. "Are you okay?"

His black hood fell away. "Where's Viktor?"

"He's fine. Christian and Shepherd are out there, but I can't find anyone else. Gem and Wyatt were sitting at a table around the corner just a few minutes ago. What happened?" Smoke funneling in from an open doorway in the back grew thicker and burned my eyes. "Is the house on fire?"

"Someone set off a bomb," he said. "Be careful. Some use them as tactical diversions to get people to run in the opposite direction. Stay inside until we know what we're dealing with. Ready yourself and watch for anyone who looks unusually calm."

"Take my arm," I said, leading him through the smoky hallway. Niko wouldn't be able to navigate with all these people running about, not to mention the fallen objects on the ground. "Don't these rich people know how to fight?"

"Their first instinct is self-preservation."

I pulled my collar over my mouth and coughed. The acrid smell of something burning filled the air. Charred flesh? Gunpowder? Chemicals? I couldn't really describe it. At the end of the hall, we were suddenly immersed in darkness. When the air thinned, I looked around and saw we were in a kitchen. Flames ate up the curtains, and pieces of wood littered the floor from what looked to be ground zero. Shards of glass were everywhere, even embedded in the wall next to me. Drywall burned around the edges of a hole that was once a window, by the looks of the damage. I could actually see outside.

Niko stumbled over a chunk of the wall, so I let him lean on me for support. Aside from a small push dagger on my belt loop, the only weapons I had were my own two hands.

A crumpled body in the corner had charred flesh, and another was missing a leg. They must have been Patrick's staff.

"Two casualties," I noted, heading for the back door. It was still intact, and when we stepped outside, I noticed a charred spot on the patio where the concrete had broken apart. My eyes finally stopped burning, and I coughed a few times to clear my lungs.

"How many bodies?" he asked.

"None that I can see," I said, bewildered as I searched the darkness.

Car alarms wailed from nearby, but the panicked shouts faded as more people left the premises.

I branched away from Niko and approached a fountain. My Vampire eyes were adjusting when I suddenly tripped and hit the ground, my face buried in the grass. When I lifted my head and rolled over, I scuttled backward from a decapitated body.

"What is it with me tripping over corpses lately?" I grumbled.

Inside, fire extinguishers hissed as white smoke poured out from the gaping hole in the wall. Several guards rushed onto the scene. Two approached me, and the husky guy with the flashlight knelt down and shined his light on the body.

The other guy reached in the fountain and lifted something out. "I found the head."

Nauseated from the smell of burning flesh, I struggled to a standing position. "I need a vacation."

Patrick's guard rested his sword on my shoulder, just inches from my neck. "Throw down your weapons."

I looked into his brute face, wondering how many cannoli he'd eaten before he decided to get off his ass and check out the crime scene. "I didn't do this."

"She's right," Niko affirmed, his voice commanding. "We're Keystone."

"I don't care who you belong to," the guard replied in a higher-pitched voice than before. "It looks like we got a dead body, and your friend was hovering over it. So you're gonna shut your mouth and let me do my job. *Capisce?*"

"Let her go," Christian boomed. "She was inside with me, and we have witnesses."

"What witnesses?" the guard asked, refusing to buy any of this.

Christian folded his arms. "The Overlord. Now saunter on."

Flashlight beams streaked around the property like club lights as guards searched for clues.

The Don Corleone wannabe lowered his sword when he saw the malice in Christian's eyes. "Stay here. All of you."

I moseyed over to my crew, eager to get away from the body.

"Feck me. They're contaminating the entire crime scene."

"Do you think the blast killed that guy?" I asked.

"It's too clean," Christian pointed out. "Someone set off the bomb as a diversion. Bombs cloak any lingering scents left at a crime scene. *Jaysus*, will you just look at them? It's like watching the Three Stooges."

"The bomb was a good idea," I said. "If we'd just stumbled upon the bodies, they would have held everyone for questioning. The blast created a panic, and everyone's long gone by now—especially the killer. Who had swords on them?"

Niko opened his coat, revealing his own. "It's not mandatory to leave them behind—just a courtesy to the host. Most comply, but we're not everyone."

We turned our attention to where guards were dragging a second body from behind the shrubs. My stomach knotted when I noticed the decapitation.

A few people trickled out the back door to see what was happening. Gem and Wyatt appeared, and when Wyatt got a gander at the bodies, he made a fast exit.

Gem passed in front of us to get a closer look and whirled around, covering her mouth.

"I take it you two didn't see the bodies in the kitchen?" I asked.

"We couldn't see anything because of the fire extinguishers."

"Where's Viktor?"

A cold breeze ruffled her hair, and she clutched her arms, shivering. "Shepherd drove him back home."

Relief. Our number-one priority was Viktor's safety.

"Has anyone seen Blue or Claude?" I asked.

"Claude's inside, talking to one of the guards," she said, gesturing toward the window. "I think Blue's falcon is scouting the property for runners. Has anyone seen Hooper?"

"If he didn't leave, he's probably looking for you," I suggested. "People were trampling each other in there like the Running of the Bulls."

"Why don't you call him?" Niko suggested.

Gem's eyes brightened. "Good idea! Since we came here together, I don't think he'd ditch me. Can I borrow someone's phone? I didn't bring mine. No pockets on the dress."

Christian handed his over. "Ask him if he has room for more. Shepherd has the Jeep, and some of us need a ride home."

"You can always squeeze into Claude's Porsche."

"I'd have more legroom tethered to the hood. We're not all gonna fit, so we need an extra car."

Patrick emerged from the back door and made his way over to the fountain. He bent down, presumably looking at the head, and righted himself. "That's Representative Alexander Warren."

Christian and I shared a look at the startling revelation that it was a member of the higher authority. We knew they were being targeted. But here, at a high-profile event?

"What about him?" a guard asked, lingering near the second body.

A ring chimed from the dead man's pocket.

Christian and I steered our gaze to Gem, whose phone was ringing in synchronicity with the dead man's. When she realized the same thing, she turned as white as a ghost. Her eyes rounded in horror, and she stared for a frozen moment at the body in the shadows.

A breath later, she surged forward, and the scream she unleashed made everyone's hair stand on end.

I flashed toward her and seized her wrist, but she wrenched away and gave me the most heartbroken look, tears welling in her eyes. Her brows slanted in disbelief as the phone continued ringing. Christian removed it from her hand, and when he ended the call, the ringing stopped.

I squinted as light accumulated within her palm. Gem threw her arms forward, and an energy ball the size of a grapefruit shot forward. Two guards ducked as the crackling blue ball went sailing by and exploded into a line of trees. Not nearly the same intensity as I'd seen her use once before, but anything larger might have killed someone.

Gem fell to her knees, exposing that perfect red heart on her back. The wail that poured out of her was devastating.

Christian walked off to make a positive ID, and I felt utterly sick to my stomach.

Niko knelt on the ground and pulled Gem into his arms. "We need to go," he said to me. He tried to help her stand, but her legs were like jelly. Niko knew he couldn't carry her away from the scene, so they stayed as they were.

Claude burst through the back door, nostrils flaring and a wild look in his eyes. When he spotted his partner in a heap on the ground, the smell of her anguish must have burned his nose. His lips peeled back, revealing all four canines. I looked warily at him, wondering if he'd flip his switch in front of all the armed guards.

"Give her to me," he snarled.

When Niko coaxed her to her feet, she saw Hooper's body again and screamed. I felt a catch in my throat when I saw the depth of sadness in her expression. All the mascara and eyeliner had smeared down her face, glittery makeup gathering around her chin as the tears kept streaming down.

Gem had great empathy for others, and because of that, she had always found it difficult to be around murder victims. While she wanted to have more involvement in dangerous missions, it would ultimately destroy the Gem we all knew and loved. Not everyone was cut out for a job in which investigating dead bodies or killing someone was part of the job description. Gem was incapable of shutting off emotions like the rest of us. She wore her heart on her sleeve, and right now it was shattered.

Claude lifted her into his arms, holding her tight against him. Niko followed behind as they left the scene.

I heaved a sigh, still in disbelief. "What do we do?"

Christian pursed his lips and looked thoughtfully at me. "I'll talk to Patrick and give him Hooper's identity so he gets a proper burial and any family is notified. Stay here." Christian branched away toward Mr. Bane while I lingered on the patio.

"We need everyone to clear the area," a voice boomed.

I turned left and spotted two Regulators on the scene—Merry

and Weather. It wasn't uncommon for Regulators to be present during social gatherings held by a member of the higher authority. It gave people what was clearly a false sense of security.

"No one leaves the premises until we've completed our investigation," Merry announced, his blond hair pulled back in a tight knot. "Stay within fifty feet of the house—if not inside—and secure the area. Do not allow anyone else to leave the party."

"Too late for that," I muttered.

He turned a sharp eye toward me and closed the distance between us. "So we meet again, Raven. Were you first on the scene?"

I gave him a brisk nod. "Yes."

"Interesting. Remain here."

"What about all the people who bailed?"

"Believe it or not, in cases like this, assailants like to remain behind to revel in the damage done."

"You should search everyone's weapons," I suggested. "The murderer will have blood on his sword."

Merry gestured to the fountain. "Not if he rinsed it."

After a pause, Merry delivered a look that sent a chill down my spine, and I realized that every single person standing outside was a suspect, including me. "Rest assured, Raven, we're very thorough."

Chapter 5

MERRY WASN'T KIDDING ABOUT HOW thorough they were. Christian and I waited for two hours while they conducted a detailed investigation, documenting everything in their report. They examined the bomb fragments and confirmed that explosives had been set outside the house. From that, they concluded that the intent wasn't to cause mass casualties but to cover up any trace evidence. After investigating the crime scene, they questioned us separately. While we all knew one of the victims, they didn't feel that Hooper was the primary target.

I stoked the fire in my bedroom, grateful to finally be home. Still shaken by the events of the evening, I hadn't changed out of my leather pants and sweater. I set the fire poker down and rubbed my eyes. It was past midnight. We'd waited at Patrick's until Shepherd returned for us. He hugged the turns as he sped back home, and we were all anxious. Not only because of Hooper, but because a public attack against the higher authority seemed like an impossible feat. How could someone have slipped through the party with explosives and not a single Chitah have picked up the scent? Had Patrick's guards been asleep? Why target someone in the most public of places, risking capture?

When the door opened, I stood up.

Christian entered the room, his gaze drifting to the fire.

"How's Gem?"

"I don't hear her anymore," he said, closing the door behind him. "I think she's done weeping for the night."

I strode to the left side of the bed and sat down in the wooden chair by my desk. "Is Claude still draped over her like a tablecloth?"

"Aye. Things didn't go well when Blue tried to pry him off the poor lass."

"I couldn't even get in the room. His switch was flipped, so it wasn't worth the trouble."

"Even Niko's struck by her loss." Christian rounded the bed and sat across from me. "He's standing vigil outside her door."

"Tomorrow when she's more lucid, she'll kick everyone out. That's what a woman does when her heart is broken. She grieves privately."

"I thought she shared her pain over a pint of ice cream with a sassy best friend."

I crossed my legs. "When Gem's ready to talk, I won't be the first person she runs to, anyway."

"And why's that? You're of the female persuasion, and you two get on fine."

"Gem needs someone who's good with words. I'm not exactly a pillar of strength when it comes to comforting people in their darkest hour. I'm too impervious to death."

Christian's laughter was as dark as a bottomless pit. "Aye, perhaps she needs to lean on someone with a heart."

"Hey, I have a heart. It's just a little dusty."

"I wouldn't say that," he said so quietly that I wasn't sure I heard him correctly.

"I'm here if she wants to talk, but I respect her right to privacy. When I went through that rough patch, she did the same for me. It meant a lot that everyone gave me the space I needed." I shook my head. "Why Hooper?"

Christian flicked a glance at the desk beside me. "Wrong place, wrong time? Perhaps that's why they dragged the body into the bushes. They didn't want anyone mistaking him for the primary target. Or maybe he witnessed something going down and hid."

"I didn't really know him, but he seemed like a decent guy. Gem liked him."

"Infatuation, to be sure. But not love."

I snorted. "How would you know the difference?" I gave him a dubious look before switching to a more benign topic. "I hope we're off the suspect list," I said, steering my eyes to the fire. "There was a moment where I thought Niko and I were done for since our scent and emotional imprints were all over the place."

Christian gently rubbed his hand across the scarlet bedspread. "You haven't changed your mind about our date, have you?"

"Given the circumstances, do you think it's appropriate?"

He rose to his feet and stood in front of the latticed windows. "Since when have we ever done anything appropriate?"

I smiled ruefully, admiring his tall stature. It might be interesting to see what kind of evening a man like Christian Poe would plan for a woman. "We'll see."

"You're a terrible tease, Miss Black."

When I stood up and stretched, a few joints cracked. "Has anyone seen Wyatt?"

"I heard him in the kitchen earlier but not since."

I was curious what had happened to him at the party. He chatted with Hooper on a few occasions, and I wanted to get his take on things. When Christian followed me out of the bedroom, we parted ways, and I headed down to the second floor and peered into Wyatt's computer room. All the lights were off except for the one inside the vending machine. I'd never actually been in Wyatt's bedroom. When we used to rotate laundry days, he would always leave his clothes in a basket outside his door. Wyatt slept on the same level as Christian and me, only on the opposite side of the mansion. I ascended a winding staircase, the cold of the stone floor penetrating through my socks. When I passed windows overlooking the courtyard below, I glanced down. The heated pool was lit up with blue and green lights, but I didn't see Gem floating on the water as she often did in the evening.

Wyatt's door was closed, but I could see light seeping into the hall from the cracks. I rapped my knuckles against the wood, certain he wouldn't hear me over the Pink Floyd song blaring from his room. After another knock, I cracked the door, recognizing the song as "Brain Damage."

"Wyatt?"

I stood in the doorway and took it all in. Surprisingly, Wyatt didn't have electricity. As far as I knew, no one's bedroom was wired up. Gem compensated with candles and battery-operated lights. Claude had lanterns affixed to the walls.

In the center of the room was a massive black sectional that looked more like a giant square bed than a sofa. The arms nearly reached the end, and it faced left toward the fireplace.

Instead of greeting Wyatt, I had to soak it all in. The entire left wall had black shelving, cabinets along the bottom that flanked the fireplace, and blue cylindrical lanterns on the dividers. The colored glass gave it a futuristic and masculine vibe. I neared the shelves, my eyes wide.

Upon every shelf was a bizarre mixture of gargoyle and cat figurines. Mostly gargoyles. Some were reading, some were guarding, and others were leaning on shields or holding swords. One had a serpent tongue sticking out, and they were so morbid that I couldn't stop gaping at them.

"Trippy, huh?" Wyatt asked. "I use them to ward off spirits, keep them out of my domain."

"And the cats?"

"Same. There's old folklore about cats seeing spirits, and specters usually do their best to avoid them."

"Does it work?" I asked, shuffling sideways to look at them all.

"I'm pretty sure it does, because the spooks have always kept out of my abode. Back in the day, Gravewalkers used to keep a lot of cats. Viktor doesn't even like the one we have lurking around outside, so that's all I've got to secure my ass and give me privacy."

I glanced back at the door and blinked. The entire wall around the door was black with a Pac-Man mural. The lines were bright blue, the dots and Pac-Man neon yellow. Several ghosts were chasing him, a red one right on his tail. "Since when do you like Pac-Man? I only ever see you playing that new stuff with all the rapid gunfire."

"It's apropos, don't you think?"

"In what way?"

Wyatt kept speaking in that lazy stoner voice. "It's symbolic of a Gravewalker's constant plight. Just trying to get through life, but all the ghosts are chasing him."

I studied the dots on the board. "You trying to eat all the food. That's about right."

"I'm pretty sure the guy who conceived this game was either a Gravewalker or knew one. He understands."

"Your man card is revoked. Where's your bed?"

Leaning on the opposite arm of the sofa, a lazy smile stretched across his face. "You're looking at it, buttercup."

Well, it was certainly big enough.

"I used to have a round bed, but it was a pain in the ass," he said, staring at his toes as he wiggled them. "My feet were always hanging off the edge. I roll around a lot."

I reached the edge of the sofa. "Well, now you have nowhere to roll except into the fire."

When the Pink Floyd song blaring from his wireless speaker ended, Wyatt lifted his phone and started swiping. "I need a mood lifter."

"Are you stoned?"

"This isn't a good time of year for mushrooms, so I had to break out a doobie."

"Don't tell me you grow those."

"I don't grow anything. They're wild and free."

I made a mental note to avoid any mushrooms at mealtime. If Kira was collecting herbs or anything else from the wooded part of our property, she might not know one mushroom from the next.

"Ah, found one," he said. "You like Electric Light Orchestra?"

"Who?"

"Sacrilege. Here. Listen to 'Mr. Blue Sky.' Everybody knows that one."

"Can you turn that down?"

When the volume lowered, Wyatt tossed his phone aside and reclined his head. He was lying with his arms and legs spread as if someone had shot him down.

"What happened to you earlier at the party?"

"I split from Rollergirl. After she finished her drink, all she wanted to do was find Hooper. Nobody needs a third wheel, so I took off. Headed to a room on the other side of the mansion where they were hoarding all the good food. You know, like those ham rolls and fancy crackers. Then all of a sudden…" Wyatt made a sound like an explosion, his arms reaching up. "Not a comforting sound for a Gravewalker. That means freshies, and freshies love nothing more than finding the nearest Gravewalker." Wyatt raised his head, his eyes glazed like two donuts. "Did Hooper suffer?"

I sat on the arm of his sofa. "I don't think so. He wasn't into anything illegal that you know about, was he?"

Wyatt shrugged. "Who isn't these days? Everything's illegal. Even my 'shrooms."

Whether Wyatt wanted to admit it or not, Hooper's death had affected him. Enough that drugs were his coping mechanism for the moment.

"I have a bad feeling about all this. The higher authority asked Christian and me to check out a murder scene. It wasn't a job, just a favor. I can't talk about it, but something colossal is brewing, and I feel like I'm sitting on the sidelines."

"Can't stop inevitability," he said, rumpling his hair. Then he crawled toward the middle of the bed and sprawled out, facing the ceiling. "What if none of this is real? What if when we dream, *that's* the real world, and this is really the dream?"

"So when you die in the dream, you die in real life?"

His eyes widened. "What a conundrum."

That must have been his word for the day.

Wyatt's gaze grew distant. "What if all the spirits are going back to the real world so the real version of them can die, and those who stay behind are saving their own lives? Does that mean their real bodies are without a soul?"

I sighed. Another few minutes of this conversation, and he'd probably be pontificating over the nature of man, ghost, and a higher power.

No, thanks.

As I left Wyatt to discover the secrets of the universe, I realized he was right. You couldn't stop inevitability. Like the way all the events had fallen into place in order for my Creator to find me. Houdini might have sold me back to Keystone, but Fletcher—who hadn't even been looking for me—had seen the ad. And *known*. If there was an order to things, why the hell would the universe let Fletcher get away instead of giving me my revenge? Houdini said it was to give me another chance, to go through the ordeal a second time with new eyes. I felt stronger the second time around, and I finally realized that Fletcher was neither god nor devil. Oddly enough, my time in captivity had been a healing process. After living in the Breed world, I finally saw him as a man and not a monster. I hated that I had to go through it a second time just to come to that realization, but suffering often leads to empowerment.

I pressed my back against Wyatt's door, the song changing to one by Toto. It reminded me of when Crush would invite his biker friends over for barbecue and they'd sit outside and talk about road trips.

At least it wasn't Air Supply.

My thoughts drifted to Gem.

Poor Gem.

Hooper didn't deserve an ending like that. At least their relationship had never graduated to anything beyond casual. We all knew better than to get involved in something serious—that kind of relationship wouldn't last with a job like ours. Would Viktor allow mates and spouses to live in the mansion? Even if he did, their lives would always be in danger because of our jobs.

Then my thoughts drifted to Christian and the mysterious feelings I had for him. Mysterious because of the memory wipe. Should I allow them to flourish? Thinking about Gem's current situation made me hesitate. Our jobs were dangerous, and I might be setting myself up for heartbreak.

It also reminded me of the danger I'd inadvertently put my father in now that Fletcher was on the run. How deep of a loss could I sustain before it broke me? My fear was that one day, I would find out.

Gem slowly opened her eyes. Tears had dried on her lashes, and she wiped away clumps of mascara that had settled at the corners. She stared at a string of tiny battery-operated lights just beyond a sheer blue fabric panel hanging from her canopy bed.

For the first time in many years, she felt hollow, and that feeling frightened her. She didn't want to lose herself again.

Gem grew up wondering what it felt like to be loved. The idea of love had become a curiosity, one that often steered her toward the wrong people. She connected with men but never loved them. Losing Hooper gutted her. Not because she saw a future with him, but because he was a light in this world and deserved a happy ending of his own. Had they never met, he wouldn't have gone to the party, and he'd still be alive. He'd still be at work and planning a trip to South America.

It felt as if years had passed since they'd left Patrick's house, and most of the events following were a blur. She remembered Claude carrying her to the car and then passing her over to Niko, who somehow squeezed into the Porsche with her in his lap. Maybe they were afraid that if they let go, she might run. And that was probably true. All Gem wanted to do was run from the pain and guilt, because sitting still hurt too much. She never even had the chance to say goodbye.

She steered her thoughts away from the actual murder, not wanting to burst into tears again. Part of her wanted to believe this was nothing but a nightmare and Hooper was still alive.

Now she was in her bed, keenly aware, thanks to Claude snoring at her feet, that none of it had been a dream.

Gem had never experienced love, so she wasn't sure how to label the emotions she felt for Hooper. Adoration? He told the best stories and was a doting companion who always made her feel special.

Still staring at the twinkling light in her dark room, Gem swallowed a lump in her throat. A few small candles in colorful jars were flickering, and she soaked in the colors as if they might wash away the memories. She had a sudden urge to go downstairs and float in the pool for a while. Gem soaked in life and enjoyed it, but when negative energy seeped into her thoughts, floating canceled out all the noise.

Crestfallen, she forced herself to think of happy things so she wouldn't wake up Claude with heavy emotions. Right now she just wanted to be alone more than anything. It took some effort, but she managed to free her legs from his warm and rumbling chest. He continued snoring like a sleeping lion. When she swung her feet over the edge of the bed and looked down, she realized she was still in her party dress.

Why did I wear this? she thought, tears welling in her eyes.

Had she jinxed the whole evening by dressing for a funeral? Gem couldn't get it off fast enough. After the fabric fell to the floor and she stripped out of the red lace top beneath it, she put on a knee-length nightgown and fastened her kimono robe around her waist. Her quartz pendant felt hot to the touch, so she took it off and placed it on the bedside table. It had absorbed too much of her grief, and she wouldn't be able to wear it until the sun removed all that negative energy.

She stopped at the foot of the bed and looked at her shelf by the window. Rocks and gemstones were inanimate things she could love, and she'd spent years adding to her collection. She suddenly had an urge to knock the shelves down and throw the crystals everywhere until they shattered.

Misery wasn't supposed to touch her anymore—it wasn't allowed.

She quashed the urge to destroy everything she loved and instead hurried to the door. Claude didn't wake as she snuck out of the room and closed the door behind her.

"You're up," a voice said, making her jump.

Gem clutched her racing heart as she looked down. Niko was propped against the wall, his knees drawn up as if he'd been sitting there for a long time, a katana still affixed to his side.

"What are you doing out here?" she asked, but the inane

question barely made it out before she wanted to swallow it back down.

"Forgive me for not making you aware of my presence," he said in earnest. "Would you like to sit?"

"I was just going—"

"To swim," he finished.

She blinked. "How did you know?"

"Because it's what you do."

It was foolish to think that any of them could hide their idiosyncrasies. Each of them managed their pain differently. Viktor drank his away, Shepherd would exercise or meditate, Raven took those precarious walks on the roof, Wyatt disappeared into his room and played music, and Gem floated.

She took a seat to his right and shivered when her back touched the stone wall.

Niko shifted around as he removed his long black coat. He handed it to her, and she draped it over her bent knees, pulling it to her chin to bask in the heat.

"Did you warm this?"

"Being a Thermal comes in handy."

"Thanks."

"If you don't mind my saying, your light looks better. Did you get some rest?"

"Some," she admitted, wiping the smudged mascara below her eyes. "I must look like a raccoon."

Niko held a smile in his voice. "I didn't notice."

"Consider yourself lucky."

"I wouldn't say that."

Her stomach dipped when she realized her faux pas. "I'm sorry, that was rude. I don't always think before I speak."

"Needn't apologize. Being authentic is an honest way to live, and I wouldn't change it."

She stared at the wall in front of them. A candle burned in a lantern several feet to the left, bright enough to wash the floors with soft light. "Occasionally, I regret choosing to be a Mage."

"We all go through those regrets in our early years. Somewhere in your five hundreds, you learn to accept that life is painful."

"If I'd stayed a Relic, I'd be an old woman by now. My life would be almost over."

"And you would have missed all these opportunities you have now to understand the depth of pain and accept it as part of the natural cycle. Mortals are always in a hurry to do things, but they never understand that the most important thing they can do in life is change. Change themselves, change the world—that's *our* burden to carry as immortals. It's what we do here at Keystone. We make sacrifices to make this world a better place. Sometimes people have to die for that change to begin. These are things you'll learn when you get as old as me."

"Old as dirt?" she quipped, her joke falling flat. Gem wondered about Niko's previous remark. "What do you mean by my light looking better? What does it usually look like?" She tried to broach the topic of his blindness with sensitivity. "What do I look like to you?"

Niko turned, his almond-shaped eyes seeming to look her all over even though he couldn't see her physical form. Despite the low light, his pale eyes sparkled. "I have nothing to compare you to, but you are... lustrous. Your light is unique—a deep amethyst and silver that sometimes floats like a ribbon when you walk by."

She caught that image and held it in her mind for a moment. A tear escaped and slipped down her cheek. "What did Hooper look like?"

Niko put his arm around her. Gem didn't really want to know the answer, because it didn't matter anymore. Hooper's light was forever extinguished.

"There's something I want to tell you, but I don't know if I should."

She sniffled. "What?"

"You might despise me for my timing. I don't wish to say anything cruel just to dim your pain."

"Well, now you *have* to tell me." She leaned away to get a look at his face but couldn't decipher his expression.

His brow furrowed, and when he tipped his head forward, his straight black hair created a curtain. She wanted to reach out and tuck it behind his ear.

But Niko must have understood how important it was for the sighted world to see facial expressions, because he brushed his hair back with his fingers. She briefly wondered about his age when he was turned, but it was difficult to tell with immortals. She guessed maybe thirty. In his time, that was probably middle age for most men.

His lips thinned as if an internal battle was waging. "How do you feel now compared to earlier this evening?"

"I don't understand."

He stroked his bottom lip.

"Just say it, Niko."

"Hooper wasn't allowing your relationship to develop... genuinely."

Gem noticed his word choice. Language was her trade, so she knew the importance of phrasing. "Do you mean something to do with his Sensor gifts?"

Niko bowed his head.

Gem sighed, embarrassed that someone had noticed. "I think I knew that already."

He blinked, astonishment flashing in his eyes.

"I'm not as naive as I look. I had a feeling something was going on after the fourth time we went out. He always fixed my drinks or handled them. But you know what? I didn't care. Even if he was spiking my drinks with Sensor magic, he made me feel happy. I liked being around him, and maybe it was all just an illusion, but it was a nice one."

"Do you feel differently about Sensor magic than you do drugs or alcohol? I just assumed..."

"I know what you mean." Gem drew her legs closer, her bare feet chilled. "I think Sensor magic can be a beautiful thing, and even though it has addictive qualities, I struggle with believing that what he did was wrong. How can joy be an addiction?"

Niko's voice softened around the edges. "It can be the worst kind. Deception plays with your heart, not your mind or your desires. And your heart is a very precious thing."

Gem choked out a sob that came out of nowhere. "It's all my fault. I shouldn't have invited him. I shouldn't have let him go off and leave me alone. They kept asking to speak to him privately, and I told him to go. All I wanted to do was make him happy."

Niko put his hand on top of her head. The gesture was so odd that she wanted to laugh. When the pad of his thumb found her cheek, he wiped away the tears.

"Do you want to touch my face?" she asked, knowing he sometimes did that to get a sense of someone's features.

"No." He withdrew his hand. "I wouldn't want to learn what your sorrow looks like."

She essayed a smile. "I guess you're right. Nothing worse than a wrinkly, wet face with swollen eyes. Can you really tell what a person looks like that way?"

"Not the way you think. But I'm curious like everyone else. Some people have a strong nose. Others have a stubborn chin. Dimples and lines are curiosities, and the differences intrigue me. But sometimes, for just a moment, the light shapes itself, and I think I can almost see a person the way they really look."

She wiped her nose and realized she was doing it all over his coat. "I'll give your coat to Kira to wash. I've cried all over it."

"Let your heart mourn for as long as you need. Hooper's deeds were misguided, but if it's any consolation, I think he did it because he cared about you. Enough that he thought it might give him a better chance. People cheat in life because they're afraid of failure." He leaned forward to get up. "Would you like someone to keep you company? Blue? Maybe Raven?"

Gem didn't want to see anyone. She had no plans to go down for breakfast in the morning or match the doleful smiles that passed her in the hall. She didn't think she could bear anyone saying how sorry they were or talking about Hooper in the past tense. She needed to get through this night and then figure out how damaged she really was from the loss. Even if she didn't love Hooper, he was still a charismatic and thoughtful guy who had deserved a long life.

Gem wanted to remember him in a good light, because she feared she might one day grow to resent him for making her an addict to his affection.

"Gem?"

She snapped out of her thoughts. "What?"

"Maybe you need someone to talk to."

"I don't want to see anyone, not even Claude. He means well, but could you peel him off my bed and tell everyone I need privacy? I just… I need…"

Without waiting for her to finish, Niko bowed. "As you wish, braveheart."

Chapter 6

M Y KNEE BOUNCED UP AND down while I waited impatiently on the bench near the front door of the restaurant. Every time someone strolled in, a blast of cold air chilled me all over again.

"I thought you had reservations," I said, shivering from the gust of wind.

Christian leaned forward and twiddled his thumbs. When he looked over his shoulder at me, his fangs were out in a vicious display. "That fecking arseface knows I called a week ago. It's in his bloody book. If they can't find a table, they need to throw out one of these shitebags and make room. And if that eejit walks over one more time and offers a glass of water while we wait, I'm going to rip his heart out through his belly button and serve it on a platter to the next customer who steals a table that should've been ours a half hour ago."

I crossed my legs. "Stop. You're making my nipples hard."

"I approve of that dress, by the way."

He meant my ankle-length cotton skirt that any decent Puritan holding on to her virginity would approve of. Because Christian wouldn't tell me where we were going, I didn't want to dress like a slob. I also didn't want to be underdressed in winter, so I'd put on knee-length boots, a long skirt, and a sleeveless turtleneck. I wore my trench coat this time, and though I'd initially taken it off while we waited, the parade of customers going in and out had forced me to put it back on.

I felt a sharp stab of guilt when I thought about Gem. "Maybe we shouldn't have gone out. It's a little insensitive."

"You heard what Niko said this morning. The poor lass wants her privacy."

"Yep, and now we look like assholes. We could have at least made her something to eat."

"I'm sorry your beau is dead, but here's a salad to brighten your dreary day." Christian gave me a pointed look. "I'm sure that's precisely what she wants."

"You know what I mean. I know she doesn't want to see anyone, but it feels dismissive that we're out on a date. That was pretty traumatic, having to see Hooper with his head lopped off."

"Now you're making *my* nipples hard. Can we not talk about expired corpses on a holiday?"

"You mean the day a naked baby in a loincloth shoots unwitting victims with an arrow?"

"Aye. The very one."

I glared at the man who stood at the lectern as if he were guarding the pearly gates. Past him, customers were drinking cocktails at a horseshoe-shaped bar. The host had suggested we sit at the bar if we wanted to eat, to which Christian had replied, "Over my rotting corpse."

This place was a little ambitious of him. Fancy dresses, expensive jewelry, jazzy music, women who didn't have weapons strapped to their thighs.

"Looks like you weren't the only one who made reservations on Valentine's. But why would you pick a place called Denial?"

Christian sat back and crossed his legs. "It had a nice ring to it."

My lip twitched.

"Go on and say it, lass. I can see the joke festering in your eyes."

"Are you going to order the empty plate, or is hunger still your denial?" I chortled and admired the Rolex on his fine, strong wrist. Then I skimmed over the rest of his attire, a crisp white button-up beneath a charcoal vest and matching trousers. He'd taken off his leather gloves and put them in the pockets of his trench coat, and though he wore a tie, it was slim and tucked beneath his vest. All he needed was a newsboy hat and a pocket watch to complete the period-piece ensemble that stepped out of last century. "When is the last time you went out on a date? And that Chitah you asked out while you were spying on me doesn't count. I mean a *real* date."

"1935."

"Your clothes look older."

"A man never throws out a good suit."

"I hope he throws out his good underwear."

When the host immediately seated a couple who'd just walked in, Christian launched to his feet.

I stood up and grabbed his arm. "It's not worth it."

He turned so slowly that my belly did a little dip. "I want more with you than a few dalliances. I can't pretend to know what it is you require in a man, but I'll not let you starve to death on my watch."

I stifled a laugh as he turned to the host.

Christian's patience was wearing thin, and I watched curiously to see how it would play out. "We've been sitting here sucking air while you've seated others. Is there something I'm not aware of in the reservation process, aside from you checking off my fecking name and giving us a table?"

The older man with the caterpillar mustache sighed before leaning in and lowering his voice. "Sir, we're a respectable establishment. Interbreeding makes people… uncomfortable." He made an insincere effort to appear apologetic.

Christian looked over his shoulder at me, obviously seeking my opinion on the matter.

"I've changed my mind. It's worth it," I said, giving him the all clear to make a scene.

Some of the elite didn't like mixed couples of different Breeds. Christian was clearly a Vampire, and as far as this guy was concerned, I wasn't.

Christian reached across the podium and snatched the man's tie, jerking him forward. "I'll thank you kindly to seat my companion and me at the finest table in your establishment. If I so much as see the bathroom or kitchen door, I'll throw you in a pool filled with eels."

The man instantly snapped his eyes shut, avoiding Christian's Vampire charm. "Sir, it's manager's orders. My hands... they're tied." Sweat beaded on his pasty brow. "It's a pleasant evening, and we want to keep it that way. Most of our customers, as you can plainly see, are the same Breed."

Christian slammed the man's head against the clipboard. "You spineless little gobshite. I should drain you."

The man clapped a hand on his neck and reared back. "How dare you threaten me!" He searched his immediate surroundings, hoping someone had overheard.

I found this all too amusing and simply admired Christian's bravado.

Christian straightened his vest, a baleful look on his face. "I just cleaned this jacket, so you're lucky this time."

The man smiled willfully.

Christian eased up to him, his tone thick with malice. "But one random night, when you're walking to your car after a long day seating customers, you keep an eye on those shadows. I don't forget anyone who does me a bad turn. And on that note, we bid you a good evening."

The man stood slack-jawed, and Christian's dark laugh as he turned away made the man clutch his throat again.

"Well played," I murmured, passing a couple of Chitahs. "I thought for a minute you were going to start a war for me."

Christian held the door open. "You'll know when that day comes."

I tucked my hands in my pockets and turned away from the street. "Maybe the universe is telling us to go home," I said, trying to thaw out his mood.

"The universe can shove it up its arse. Now we go to plan B."

"Explain."

"I drop you off in an abandoned building and run an errand."

"Errand?" *I just bet.* "If this is some kind of joke where you go home and I'm left sitting in a warehouse, think again, Vamp."

Christian rolled with laughter. "Jaysus wept. Have you no faith in me?"

"Sure. I trust Vampires all the time."

He put his arm around me and led us to his car. "I promise I'll have you home in one piece."

"Are you sure about that?"

He gave me a guarded look. "A promise is a promise."

When Christian Poe said he was going to drop me off in front of an abandoned building on Valentine's Day, he was not kidding around. Shortly after leaving the restaurant, we drove to the other side of the Breed district, and Christian let me out of the car in front of a tall building.

"Wait here, and don't go inside," he instructed me.

Really?

Waiting out in the cold lasted five minutes before I tested the unlocked door and entered the ten-story building. The main lobby had trash on the floor and nary a place to sit my cold ass. I tried all the doors, but they were locked.

Except one—the staircase. Curious and bored, I let my adventuresome spirit take hold and went up. The stairwell was a lot warmer than the lobby, and the exercise would not only get my blood pumping but also kill some time. The doors on each floor were locked, so I kept going up until I reached a narrow staircase that didn't have a landing at the top, just a heavy door with a broken lock.

I stepped outside and looked around, my breath heavy and feet sore. The stars shimmered above me like tiny diamonds pressed against black velvet. And oh man, what a view. It was a tremendous vantage point for admiring the cityscape. Some parts of Cognito were artsy and others a slum, but all districts were equal in beauty from the rooftops.

While turning in a circle, I couldn't help but notice a large mattress. I scouted the roof, wondering if I'd barged in on someone's makeshift home. What threw me were the black satin sheets tucked around the edges and a deep-red blanket folded on top. And then as I stepped closer, I noticed an ice bucket with a bottle of vino inside and two wineglasses sitting on cloth napkins.

Ah. So *this* was his master plan. Impress me with fancy dining and then… well, what exactly? Get me drunk on an abandoned rooftop? Unbridled sex? Holding me beneath the stars and declaring his everlasting love and affection?

It had to be the sex. Christian wasn't the cuddling type.

While I debated on whether to be insulted or flattered, I sat on the mattress and waited as the minutes ticked by. At least my boots were warm. I folded my legs beneath me and wondered what Christian was doing. Was he in a club somewhere, hitting on a busty blonde and having a private laugh about leaving me out in the cold? He had a dark sense of humor, and I wouldn't put it past him.

My heart ratcheted when the hinges on the door squeaked. Christian's dark shape took form as he kicked the door shut behind him.

"Did you really have a reservation at the restaurant?" I asked.

He gave me a cross look, a white cloud of smoke escaping his lips as he strode toward me with a black bag.

"What's that?"

Christian set the large thermal bag in front of me, and a savory smell hovered in the air while I unzipped the top.

I drew in a deep breath, my mouth watering.

"Angus burgers, onion rings, and hot coffee," he said in that lovely Irish brogue. "I decided against milkshakes since I wasn't sure if I'd find you frozen to death."

I pulled out a thermos and then another. "Where did you get these?"

"Your friend Betty sold them to me from her personal stash."

Good old Betty.

The first thing I did was shove an onion ring into my mouth

before they got cold. "I like this plan better than fine dining. The less silverware the better."

He removed his coat and draped it across the ledge. "Burgers on a rooftop," he muttered. "You should strive for better things in life."

"Should I remark about the mattress, or do you want to sit down and join me?"

His lip twitched as he sat down, one leg folded underneath him and the other foot propped on the ground. To my surprise, he didn't balk about eating. Vampires don't require food to survive and often decline it entirely. Maybe he joined me so I wouldn't be eating alone, but I watched him unwrap his burger and take a monstrous bite. After a few quiet moments, it felt like a real date. His eyes sparkled a little, and I was certain he made a grunting sound as he ate more. Christian reminded me of a well-mannered man who was starving to death and yet trying to retain his social graces.

"You can lick your fingers," I said. "I won't tell anyone."

He flashed me a hot look and wiped his mouth and beard with a paper napkin.

I couldn't help it. Maybe it was him pulling out all the stops, or maybe it was that damn suit, but I got all tingly looking at Christian. The way he hungrily chewed on that burger reminded me of his voracious appetite in bed. And yet there was also an indescribable feeling coming over me... like déjà vu. My thoughts drifted back to the night when Christian and I had sought shelter in an abandoned building in the Bricks, but when I tried to remember our conversation, a shooting pain burrowed in my head.

I winced and set my burger down.

"Something wrong?" he asked.

"No. I was just trying to remember something."

His jaw tensed. Christian slowly opened a thermos and sipped the steaming coffee.

"Why did you think a fancy restaurant would impress me?"

"In my experience, you don't impress anyone by pinching pennies."

"We met in a dive where I was scavenging for food. I'm obviously not a cocktail-and-lobster kind of girl. This is all you had to do. Burgers, a rooftop, and… okay, we have to discuss the elephant in the room."

When I patted the bed, he looked genuinely disappointed with himself.

"I overshot with the mattress."

I snorted. "I bet hauling it up those stairs was a logistical nightmare."

"Praying to the heavenly angels that it wouldn't rain was another. Then I would have had to go to plan C."

My brows popped up.

"And you're not finding that one out," he said.

"Viktor's van?"

Christian would never take me to a hotel and make me feel like a prostitute. No, he would seduce me with wine and a Tempur-Pedic on a rooftop. It was almost funny. Almost. But his unconventional courtship also appealed to the romantic side of me, because Christian knew what I liked.

After I finished my onion rings, I wrapped up my half-eaten burger and stuffed it in the sack. "That's all I can manage."

"You're shivering," he murmured, moving the paper bag aside and scooting closer. When he wrapped his arms around my shoulders, I warmed from the inside out. Meanwhile, my mind warred with what I knew about Christian before Houdini versus what I knew about him after. He seemed like two different men.

"I understand," he said, his soft voice wrapping around me like a blanket.

"What do you mean?"

"The headaches. I have a keen awareness of what you're doing when we're together. You're trying to remember all those missing pieces. That's why I'm doing all this, Raven. I'm trying to fill those holes with new memories."

"I always wanted a guy who would fill my holes."

Christian threw back his head and laughed. I loved the sound of it up close, and my toes actually curled.

"*Jaysus*, woman. You're a handful."

I tilted my head back, my breath skating across his neck. "I'm also a mouthful."

His breath hitched, and his Adam's apple bobbed as he swallowed down his reaction. I was so close to his neck that the heat coming off his skin warmed my cheek. Viktor had mentioned how certain things in my life would trigger memories of the past, and for me, that trigger would always be Christian's blood. I remembered the tantalizing flavor and his sweet blood coursing through my veins like fire.

When Christian dipped his chin and looked down at me, he gave me a hot look.

Without any preamble, his mouth brushed against mine, searching for permission. His tongue swept across the seam of my lips, and my hand slid around him, discovering the hard planes and ridges of his body beneath his vest.

My lips parted, and Christian delivered a smoldering kiss. His rough hand held the nape of my neck as he caged me with his heat. I suddenly felt feverish, every stroke of his tongue inserting fantasies into my head about him lifting my skirt. The kiss was hot and sensual, and I moaned as my heavy boots shifted in my attempt to straddle him.

But Christian wouldn't allow it. He held me still, not allowing me to take it to the next level. When I nibbled on his lower lip in protest, his hand slipped inside my coat.

"Your breath is atrocious," he growled, delivering another crushing kiss.

Served him right for buying me onion rings.

His tongue pressed against mine, the rhythm unraveling me at the seams. Damn him and that sexy beard. I couldn't get enough of his whiskers, his hands, his mouth. The kiss lengthened, burning like a timeless fireplace. Memories of sex with Christian flooded my mind, and yet there was an undercurrent in the way he kissed me that wasn't sexual at all. I felt an intimate connection threading between us that overpowered my senses. It was the strongest thing I'd ever felt, and it consumed me.

Suddenly, I got scared. "Wait," I said, breaking the kiss. I reared back, panting and out of breath. My heart was racing a mile a minute, and I still couldn't shake that intense feeling.

His hand fell to my thigh, and he squeezed it. "What has you spooked like a horse? Is it because of Gem?"

My eyes flicked up. Could he see right through me?

I'd lost my mother at an early age, one of many reasons I'd pushed my father away as I got older. Deep down, I was afraid of losing him too. Now that I finally wanted a relationship with him, my life as an immortal had forced me to let go. Christian was addressing another elephant in the room—my fear of intimacy. Part of it was due to my stolen memories, but I was also afraid of love. What if he didn't love me back? What if he died? My job wasn't the only thing at stake; there was also my heart to consider. I still felt as if I didn't know Christian well enough to give him more.

Not yet.

"Is that how you're going to live your life?" he went on. "Sabotaging relationships because you're afraid?"

"Don't flip this around on me when you're the one who's always scoffed at the idea of love."

"That's because it's a canker sore in life, and I know the damage it can do."

"But you're still pursuing me."

"Aye."

"Even though it could end in ruin."

"Aye. But I'm not running from it because I'm afraid of death. There are things far worse in this world than death."

I wiped my mouth. "Like keeping our relationship a secret?"

His black eyes narrowed.

I stood up, cold from losing the heat of him. "You dodge me whenever someone walks into a room. We're constantly looking over our shoulders, worried someone might pick up on an emotional imprint, a smell, or even a look. How long can we keep doing this?" I turned away to face the city. "Is it worth our jobs?"

Hearts was what I meant to say.

I was torn between keeping it casual or getting serious. How long could I live a lie? Eventually the lies would catch up with us.

"I've always lived my life in the open," I said, gathering steam again. "All this cloak-and-dagger shit is wearing thin, and if I'm going to take a man in my life, then maybe I want someone who isn't afraid to fight for it. If something isn't worth fighting over, maybe it's not worth having."

Christian rose, and I felt the heat of him behind me. "Are you asking for me to fight Viktor on something you're not even sure you want? You asked me to go slow, and we're coasting along in the slow lane. I don't know how much you've changed since…"

I walked to the ledge and sat down, unable to straddle it with my long skirt on. "You intentionally picked a restaurant that no one on our team goes to, didn't you? It wasn't to impress me—it was to hide."

Christian approached the ledge and warily glanced at the street below. "What would you have me do?"

I raised the collar of my trench coat up to shield my neck from the wind. "I don't know. I'm not trying to lay any blame on you, but I wish… I just wish I had my memories back. Maybe then it would be an easier decision."

He rocked on his heels, his hands in his pockets. When he spoke, his words were quiet and to himself. "So that's what it's going to take."

"Why do you even like me to begin with? Infatuation with a crossbreed? My sparkling personality? My kill ratio?"

Without warning, he grabbed my hand and pulled me to him. I teetered on my tiptoes as his arm snaked around my waist and he cupped my neck. "You're timeless." He looked at my blue eye and then my brown. "Your eyes are like heaven and earth, and I'm trapped somewhere in between."

I found myself unable to breathe. Since when was Christian so tenderhearted? I enjoyed his dark sarcasm, his sexy swagger, the way he could take down any man with his bare hands, and most especially the way he smelled when I was right up close. But all these soft words had me dumbfounded. Part of me wanted to stab him in the throat with my dagger, fearing this was a joke. The other part wanted him to lift me in his arms and carry me away.

Then a thought pirouetted in my mind. Where would we go to be intimate if we couldn't go home? A park bench?

"So... do you want some wine?" I asked, stumbling over my words.

"No. It was a foolish thought to begin with." He flicked a glance over to the blanket, which the wind flipped over and was dragging across the dirty asphalt.

"I like it up here," I confessed, not wanting him to think the entire evening was a failure. "Just look at the view. This is what I live for."

We simultaneously turned our heads to look at the city lights, which spread out like a carpet of color. Intersection lights changing, the mellow gold from the street lamps, sporadic windows lit up with no apparent pattern, green trim around the tallest building, blinking neon from a movie theater and pizza place next door, white car lights rolling down the streets and turning corners like in a video game. The city breathed life, and it was pure magic.

"Thanks," I whispered.

"For what?" A soft chuckle rolled in his throat. "I've ruined a perfectly respectable holiday."

"For driving in the slow lane. For not demanding more or less. I don't know what I'm doing, but I feel like you're the only one who gets me. I'm not sure why I feel that way."

"I do, Precious," he whispered. "I do."

"I trust my instincts, and that's why I believe that everything you've told me is true. Honesty matters to me more than anything else. And family."

"You're telling me that you never fib?"

"Not about the things that matter."

"Then you have my word that I'll never deceive you."

With my hands flat on his chest, I sank into his embrace. The icy wind wasn't so bothersome anymore. In that second, as he shifted his stance and held me tighter, I blinked at an unexpected occurrence happening in my line of vision.

I intentionally widened my eyes, uncertain if maybe I'd blinked or had something in my eye. The city lights were flashing. "Did you just see that?"

I pushed away and faced the horizon.

Just then, giant sections of the city went dark, cascading like dominoes falling in random directions until the only visible lights left were the cars.

"What's happening?" I wondered.

Christian approached the ledge, his hair whipping in the wind. "Blackout."

Chapter 7

CHRISTIAN AND I SAT ON the rooftop for an hour, waiting for the power to come back on. No sense in driving when the intersection lights weren't operational. We drank hot coffee, talked about our past cases, and tried to one-up each other on who had the craziest stories. Christian told me about a Vampire who used to pose as a mannequin in one of those window displays. Some immortals had simply gone crazy. Others had strange fetishes. Since it was in the human district, most immortals who took notice said nothing. He had alabaster skin so pale that anyone could have mistaken him for plastic. Christian had worked as a bodyguard, and his boss used to get coffee at the café across the street. One day, a saleslady appeared in the display and began to undress the Vampire. When his trousers dropped and she pulled down his shorts, a scream pealed out, and she shrank back in terror. The Vamp was so startled by her reaction that he ran into the street naked, only to get run over by an ice cream truck.

I'd never laughed so hard. Christian had a deadpan way of telling stories that painted a vivid picture in my head. And it wasn't the wine, because we hadn't uncorked the bottle. And it wasn't blood sharing, because I hadn't uncorked *him*.

It was the first time I really saw a glimmer of the man I must have fallen for. We probably had moments just like this, only different stories—different conversations. Christian and I had great banter and never took each other's sarcasm personally. I was a button pusher, and that didn't bother him.

Time skipped by like a stone, and before I knew it, my Mage clock alerted me it was close to midnight.

I shoved the blanket off my lap. "We better get back before people start to talk."

When we rose to our feet, he cupped my neck and brushed his lips against mine. "Shall we give them something to talk about?"

My jagged breath escaped, and he inhaled it as he moved his mouth over mine in a kiss that consumed me.

Christian suddenly jerked his head back and looked around. "The power's still out."

"That's weird. I don't think we've ever had one that went on for this long. I mean, the power to Crush's trailer went out a lot, but that had to do with the ice pulling down the lines."

He grabbed my hand and tugged me along.

"What about all that litter?" I asked, laughing as we left behind the evidence of our date.

"We haven't got time. I didn't realize how late it was. We need to get out of the city."

Christian wound up ahead of me as I hurried down the stairs, trying to keep up in a tight skirt that hindered me from moving freely. The caged air inside the stairwell combined with chasing after Christian warmed my blood. My extremities started burning from the heat, and I rubbed my ears. It reminded me of the times I'd slept in buildings like this to stay out of the wind and snow. Not only did stairwells offer privacy and protection from watchful eyes, but if the roof door was open, you could build a fire in there and not die from smoke inhalation.

We strolled through the lobby, and I put my hands in my pockets to warm them.

As soon as Christian reached the curb, he pivoted on his heel. "What's wrong?"

His jaw set as he looked around. "The car's gone."

I chuckled at that. "Your precious Honda? I told you I should have driven. Nobody would have tried to steal an old truck."

Dogs barked in the distance. It didn't seem like a typical night, and the noise pressed all around us. Sirens, shouting, glass breaking, and other sounds that I hadn't been able to hear at the top of a ten-story building.

I stuffed my hands in my pockets. "I don't know how we're going to explain what we're doing here, but call Viktor. He'll send someone out to get us."

Christian annihilated the distance between us. "My phone was in the car. I wanted to give us privacy."

And both of us knew I'd left my purse at home since Christian had offered to pay for everything.

"I don't suppose you have a spare phone hidden in one of those boots?" he asked, his stark features no longer carrying the same warmth and humor as moments earlier.

"No, but I have a dagger. Will that help?"

"We can't even call a cab."

"We can hail one."

He folded his arms. "And what'll you pay him with? Your good humor?"

My gaze dragged down. "You don't have a wallet in those fancy trousers? Let me guess, you left it in the car."

"After I bought your burgers, I tossed it on the seat."

I smiled. "This is a fine mess you've gotten us in, Mr. Poe."

"Your unflappable charm won't get us out of this one." Christian glanced at his watch. "Cab drivers won't be working in these conditions anyhow. Wyatt will notice."

"Notice what?"

"Our absence. Keystone is powered by candlelight, but Wyatt spends most of his time in the office. He'll be going through withdrawals by now and checking into the problem. He'll alert the team, and they'll realize we're not home."

"Why does that matter?"

He took my arm, and we headed down the dark street. "Looters don't waste time when the lights go out for more than an hour. They can steal merchandise without worrying about security cameras, alarms, or the police."

"Since when are you scared of a few looters?"

"That's just the beginning. There's a darker side to blackouts—something you're not seasoned enough to have witnessed."

My heart picked up speed. "What's that?"

"Have you ever stopped to ask yourself what *immortals* like to do when the power goes out? Anarchists crave a lawless world. Electricity creates an illusion of order, and without it, people become savages. I've seen it happen before. Let's hope the lights return soon."

When we turned right to what was usually a busy street, darkness enveloped us. The streets were eerily empty, and the moon had crested the tallest building. In the distance, flames poured out of a shop. Men were running to and fro, but they weren't carrying buckets of water. They were dancing and throwing objects at the windows to shatter the glass.

"*Jaysus,*" Christian breathed, swinging his arm out in front of me so fast that the next thing I knew, I was pinned to a brick wall. He flattened his back against the wall beside me. "Don't move."

A shape lumbered into view.

A lion.

I'd never seen one up close, only on TV. His heavy paws came to a full stop in front of us, and he turned his massive head to look at me. The wind ruffled the fur on the regal mane crowning his face, and he stood as tall as my shoulders when he raised his head high. He was magnificent, but anyone that close to a predator has only one instinct, and that's to run.

"Shifter," Christian said, gripping my arm. "Don't run. He's harmless if you leave him be."

"What if it escaped from the zoo?" I asked quietly.

"Then try not to look like a gazelle."

After a few deep breaths, the lion lost interest and trundled up the sidewalk in the direction we'd come from.

I blew out a breath. "What if he had eaten me and left my remains all over the street?"

Christian held my hand as we continued our journey. "Nobody likes a litterbug. I'd have gathered your bones and taken them home."

"Kindling for the fire?"

"Worry not, lass. I would have had Shepherd reassemble you with a little glue and twine. Prop you in the corner of my bedchamber with a burger sack in your hand."

"I'd blend right in with your décor."

When we reached the fire, there was no point crossing the street to avoid the men. We continued our quickened pace, not showing any interest.

"Burn!" one of them cheered. "Burn, baby!"

"Fucking Shifters and all their property," his buddy yelled. "They don't rule this city. We do!"

I briefly wondered if the lion we'd passed was the shopkeeper, and I felt immediate sympathy. A lot of immortals didn't like the way Councils carved aside land and property for Shifters. Some Shifter businesses catered mainly to their own kind because they didn't want to deal with the animosity from other Breeds.

The heat from the flames warmed me, but not in a good way. I let go of Christian's hand, thinking how inappropriate our public display of affection was when someone's dream was going up in flames.

Without a sense of law and order, ancients apparently indulged in fantasies of taking matters into their own hands. Revenge on a neighbor, stealing Sensor-spiked bottles from a seller, or burning establishments that didn't fit in their perfect world.

And worse, a Mage who normally abstained from juicing might suddenly get the urge to drink someone's light. Who would find out? Especially with everyone running amok.

"I'm sure the lights will come on soon," I said. "People need to chill out."

"Are you telling that to me or yourself?"

"Outages happen in the summertime, don't they? When the power grids are overloaded. The only time we get them in winter is when there's an ice storm. It's probably just a blip." I came to a grinding halt and pulled a dagger from inside my boot.

Christian scanned the streets before looking down at me. "What are you doing?"

I used the sharp edge to cut through my skirt and rip it all the way around above my knee. "Ever tried running in a long skirt? If something happens, I'm not about to be that girl in a horror movie who trips and falls." I cut a slit down one side just to make sure I had enough room to move my legs freely.

"You don't think your legs will call attention?"

"I really don't give a shit. I just had a lion look me over as if I were fast food. What would have happened if he tried chasing me? I can't flash in a long skirt," I informed him, kicking the fallen fabric into the gutter. "I'm used to men ogling my legs. And they can ogle them all they like when they're wrapped around their neck and cutting off the circulation."

"I made a promise to protect you."

I tucked my knife back in the sheath. "You also gave me a funny look while doing it. What was that about?"

"I promised to get you home in one piece. Maybe I wasn't entirely sure if you'd survive a second round with me in bed."

I cackled. "Ah, so the mattress wasn't just for show."

"Can we not quarrel? I need my hearing to make sure a rhinoceros isn't charging after you. And you should lay off the profanities. A lady doesn't swear."

When he turned, I wanted to kick him for that remark. But instead, I began admiring the muscular globes of his ass through the fabric of his trousers. He'd left his jacket on the roof, so I had a full and glorious view since his snug vest stopped at the waist.

Christian looked over his shoulder at me, and the bemused look in his eyes briefly flickered to something hot when he caught me eye-licking him. "You keep giving me that look, and we'll never make it home."

I snapped out of my fantasies and caught up with him. "Where are we going?"

"The human district is safest for now."

"Ruby's."

"Come again?"

"It's the one place that everyone knows I like to go. If Viktor gets worried enough to send someone looking for us, they'll go to all our usual hangouts. Probably the bars first, but eventually, someone's going to remember the diner. If no one comes, we wait it out until morning. They're open twenty-four hours."

"They'll close if their stoves aren't working."

"Are you kidding?" I snorted at the idea. "As long as they've got pie, cake, and coffee, they'll stay open."

"Can't sell coffee without a working pot."

"I happen to know that they keep kettles and propane burners in the back for emergencies. We once had a blackout during a storm, and while the food stopped, the coffee kept coming."

He raked his fingers through his hair. "It's probably a two-hour walk from where we are."

We both stopped and looked at each other.

"Are you thinking what I'm thinking?" I asked.

He surveyed the street. "Aye, but we have to stay close. I can only shadow walk where there's absence of light, so that means avoiding the main streets. Too many car headlights. I also don't want you wearing down your battery."

I adjusted a loose button on his vest. "Don't worry about my battery, Mr. Poe. I'm sure if I run low on energy, you'll find some way to… recharge me."

He growled sexily and tugged a lock of my hair. "*Now* you're feeling amorous?"

"Danger turns me on." While it was just a joke, I wondered if there might be some truth to that.

Christian's head turned sharply, and that was when I caught sight of what was fast approaching.

Four men headed toward us with a purposeful stride. Mage power dripped from one of them, his fingertips a dim blue as he clenched his fists to control what was clearly sexual energy. It buzzed through the air in fervent waves that crackled against my skin. This added a whole new level of fuckery to our situation.

I reached down and pulled the stunner from inside my boot. "Let's do this."

Chapter 8

SHEPHERD EXECUTED HIS LAST PULL-UP and dropped to the floor. After an intense workout, his body felt tight and hard, like a lockbox protecting all his valuables. He guzzled down a bottle of water then poured the rest over his sweaty head before tossing the plastic into a small wastebasket near the exercise equipment. The power had been out a while now. Since the gym was one of the few rooms with electricity, he'd brought a couple of lanterns down so he could let off some steam. Shepherd glanced up at the lofty ceilings, the absence of artificial light unnerving. Bad shit went down during an extended outage. He hadn't noticed it until Wyatt's curses filled the quiet hallways. Poor bastard was helpless without all his computers.

Shepherd snuffed out one lantern and carried the other up to the dining room. As soon as he opened the door, Viktor and Claude broke their conversation.

"What's up?" Shepherd asked, setting the lantern on the floor.

Viktor stroked his beard. Usually, the whiskers on the sides were short with the goatee around the mouth longer, but it looked as though he'd skipped his daily trim. "Christian and Raven haven't returned. I want you and Claude to look for them."

Shepherd furrowed his brow. "What gives?"

Claude still had on his black tank top with the RAZOR SHARP logo on the front. He was also sucking on a red licorice stick. "I drove through the Breed district on my way home, and people are out in spades."

"Looting?"

"Burning businesses, from what I saw."

"Shit. Already?"

"You bet." Claude wiggled his candy around. "I went inside a convenience store to grab some licorice and lotion. People were acting like it was the apocalypse."

"Do I want to know why you were buying lotion at this time of night?"

Claude tapped the licorice stick against his nose and winked. "I have dry elbows."

Short-term blackouts were never a cause for concern, but as the hours ticked by—especially at night—people would walk on the dark side.

Still sweating, Shepherd pulled up his white T-shirt and wiped off his face. "Anyone try calling them?"

"No answer," Viktor replied. "Christian would never stay out in this unless something was wrong."

"Fine. I'll go."

"We both go," Claude interjected. "And I drive. My car's faster."

Shepherd didn't like riding shotgun, especially in small cars. So he raised his arm, showing off the sweat stains, and took a whiff.

Claude wrinkled his nose. When the prospect of Shepherd's sweaty body rubbing all over his seats registered, he chewed the end off his licorice. "Never mind. You can drive."

Shepherd chuckled. "What's the matter, pretty boy? You don't like the way I smell?"

"You slay me."

"Keep your phones on," Viktor said, ignoring their nonsense. "If we hear from them or they show up, I'll send a message."

Shepherd gave a casual salute when Viktor rose from the table to leave the room. He couldn't help but notice their fearless leader had buttoned his cardigan incorrectly, because there was an extra button hanging at the bottom.

The man had a lot on his mind.

"Meet me in the car," Shepherd said. "I need to go upstairs."

"To shower?"

"Nobody's got time for that. I need to grab a few weapons. Do you want me to bring you anything? A dagger? A gun? Maybe a crossbow?"

Claude rose from the table, showing off his extra four inches of height. "Bring me a package of those little white powdered donuts out of Wyatt's machine."

"Power's out, remember?"

"He's got a key."

"Which is probably glued to his private parts. If you think you can pry that from his cold dead hands, by all means."

Claude lifted his chin and swaggered toward the door. "Challenge accepted."

Shortly after Shepherd gathered a few weapons, they hopped in the Jeep Wrangler—which looked more like a war machine, thanks to some of his modifications—and headed out in search of Christian and Raven. Guns weren't effective with all Breed, but he still brought his Glock just in case he needed to slow someone down. Hopefully, things hadn't gone to hell. As they drove through the human districts, looters were attempting to rip open the security gates outside liquor stores and electronic stores. They'd smashed out the windows of one place and were hauling ass with armloads of stolen goods, including giant television sets.

One lady was pushing a grocery cart filled with meat. Shepherd didn't know where the hell she thought she was going to keep all that stuff with the power out. Some people just didn't think.

Claude licked his fingers, his lips dusted in powdered sugar.

Shepherd gave him a sly look. "How did you get the key?"

Claude finished chewing his last donut. "Wyatt was reluctant at first. I told him I could always go to the nearest funeral home and make an open plea that if any spooks want Gravewalker services, all they have to do is come home with me and search for a key. You never saw him leap out of a chair so fast."

Shepherd belted out a laugh. "I'll have to remember that next time."

Claude wadded up his wrapper and tossed it out the window. "I think he taught me a few new curse words. What's a fuck nugget?"

Shepherd pulled the Jeep up in front of Flavors, a club they frequented.

"Someone took precautions," Claude said, pointing out the open window at the main doors, which someone had boarded up.

"Can you pick up Raven's scent?"

Claude gave him a cross look. "The only scent I'm picking up in this sweatbox of yours is body odor. Raven has on a certain perfume tonight, so I might be able to pick up the trail. Keep driving. Maybe I'll get lucky."

Shepherd put the car in drive. "What are the odds that your dumb ass is going to sniff them out in a city of four million? I ain't got enough gas for this shit."

Claude rubbed his nose. "With your pits reeking, you make a good a point." He zipped up his leather jacket. "Does Wyatt keep a spare hat in here?"

"Glove compartment."

Claude rummaged around until he found the folded-up knit hat. He had a mess of blond hair to stuff beneath it, but once it was on, he gave Shepherd a wild look. Claude was as Chitah as they came, golden eyes so bone-chilling that most people couldn't hold his gaze for more than a few seconds. It was like staring into the eyes of a savage animal.

"I don't know if sticking your head out the window is such a good idea," Shepherd finally said, giving him the side-eye. "You know how excited you get."

Claude rubbed his smooth chin. "Afraid I'll flip my switch and damage your precious car?"

"Maybe."

Claude had flipped his switch around Shepherd but luckily never attacked. He described it as being able to see and hear what was happening but having no control. That didn't exactly sit well with Shepherd. If Claude wasn't in control, then that meant his primal side was. Chitahs had animal instincts like Shifters, but they didn't shift. Some speculated that Chitahs might be mutated from Shifters, becoming a species in which man and animal had merged into one.

Shepherd tightened his grip on the wheel. "If you get a whiff of one female in trouble and smash through my windshield to get to her, I'm making you pay for damages."

"Stop the car."

Shepherd slammed on the brakes.

When Claude got out, Shepherd thought he was going to storm off. Instead, the man climbed onto the hood and mounted the roof.

"Jesus fuck," Shepherd muttered, throwing open his door. "What the hell do you think you're doing?"

Claude looked like a runner at the starting line. His nostrils flared as he raised his head. "They probably went to one of our hangouts. Just circle the area, go to the next, and let me do my thing."

"I don't have a roof rack for you to hold on to," Shepherd pointed out.

A look of irritation flashed in Claude's eyes. "Then drive slowly. I've got long arms, so keep the front windows open, and I'll be fine."

Shaking his head, Shepherd hopped in the Jeep and coasted down the road. Claude had a point. If Christian and Raven were still in the city, they might have walked to a regular hangout. Scents faded by the minute. Since Claude had a keen sense of smell, it was worth a shot.

Shepherd hadn't seen a cab driver since entering the city. If something had happened to Christian's car, they were probably stranded. Nobody wanted to be out in this mess, especially when traffic lights weren't working and people were driving like assholes.

After a short drive, they reached Nine Circles of Hell. It hadn't been a hangout until Hooper and Gem started seeing one another.

Damn. What a fucking shame about Hooper. Shepherd hadn't known the guy very well, but he'd seemed all right. Had a job, kept his nose clean. Yet none of that mattered in the grand scheme of things. Innocent people were cut down every day for no good reason. It made you question the point of life.

His thoughts steered briefly to Maggie, but instead of lingering on her as they usually did, he thought of the boy.

His boy.

Shepherd's chance at being a dad was over. That ship had sailed. But buried beneath all that common sense was another voice, one that whispered dark ideas in his ear late at night.

Kill Patrick.

Steal the boy.

Leave Keystone.

Every day he stayed with Keystone presented another opportunity of running into Patrick. Going to that Valentine's party had done a number on him, especially after the explosion. He didn't need a constant reminder of what he'd never have. How was he supposed to move on and forget?

When the crowd thickened, he slowed his Jeep. Unable to see what was going on, Shepherd turned left to avoid trouble.

"I need to leave," he mumbled to himself.

Thoughts of his son were consuming him to the point that he couldn't focus on his job. Did Patrick scold the child? Punish him? Force him to read emotions he didn't want to? It sure as hell wouldn't be long before he started telling the kid lies about Shepherd. This was one big clusterfuck. Kidnapping an official's child would automatically brand him an outlaw, wanted dead or alive. The boy would grow to resent him, and they'd always be in danger from either Patrick's men or bounty hunters. Damned if he did and damned if he didn't do anything about it.

He clenched his jaw, realizing he was returning to the same conclusion—he had to leave Keystone. If he stayed, it wouldn't be long before he did something stupid. Either that, or his own personal shit would become such a distraction that he'd put his team in danger.

Something thumped against the car, and he blinked, snapping out of his daze in time to see a body go spiraling toward the curb.

He'd accidentally clipped a pedestrian. Shepherd slowed to a stop and looked back to see if he was okay. The man sat up, rubbing his noggin. Unless he was a Relic, he'd be fine.

As soon as Shepherd took off, he heard shouts overlapping from behind. When he stopped, the brake lights lit up a group of angry men who were swarming together and heading for his Jeep.

Claude knocked on the hood. "Better get a move on. They're pissed."

"No shit, Sherlock."

When a baseball bat slammed against the back end of his Jeep, he almost got out to kick some ass. But his team was more important than his ego, so instead he got the hell out of there.

Until he looked in the rearview and saw them flashing after them.

"*Ffuck.*"

Millions of people in the city, and he hit a Mage.

Shepherd made a sharp right turn, careening through the streets like a juggernaut. One of the men reached his door and tried to open it, so Shepherd took out his gun and fired a warning shot right in the man's arm.

Up ahead, a roadblock. Cars were stopped at an intersection, drivers yelling at each other. Shepherd had no choice but to stop. Claude suddenly ran down the hood and jumped, clutching a light pole and scaling it to the top. Watching the pretty boy in action was a fucking sight to behold. He was swinging from poles like Tarzan. Shepherd didn't need to see Claude's face to know that his eyes were black and his canines out. Claude moved like a jungle animal when he was in primal mode. Another Chitah chased after him, and when Claude reached the opposite intersection light, he turned around, and they collided midair. The two men fell to the concrete below, but Shepherd didn't have time to watch. The man he'd struck with his Jeep had yanked the door open.

"Got a problem, Mage?" Shepherd aimed his gun and fired. The bullet struck the man in the shoulder, knocking him back.

Shepherd jumped from the cab, his black boots hitting the concrete with a commanding thud. "This isn't gonna end pretty."

Claude rose to his feet, blood staining his face. His eyes locked on a man rounding the front end of Shepherd's Jeep. Claude's mouth widened, revealing all four canines. With alarming speed, he torpedoed after the man, who flashed out of sight.

Shepherd drew back when the Mage he'd shot grabbed his arm holding the gun. A blast of energy jolted through Shepherd, causing him to drop the gun. The energy wasn't strong enough to knock him out, but it still hurt like hell. Maybe it had to do with the guy's injuries, or maybe he was just a weak-ass Mage. Regardless, it pissed Shepherd off.

With his good hand, Shepherd casually reached behind his belt and pulled out a serrated stunner from the leather sheath. "Shouldn't have done that, compadre."

He wielded the blade just as the Mage blasted him in the chest.

Chapter 9

I WASN'T SURE IF IT WAS adrenaline fueling my veins or Mage light, but the four men approaching us from across the street were about to require a pain prescription. They were eyeballing me as if I were some kind of Mage juice box.

Most men crashed into each other like a couple of apes, but I'd learned through Niko that doing the opposite was sometimes more effective in combat. Make them think you're going in for a collision and then execute another maneuver. With a firm grip on the handle of my stunner, I streaked toward one and ducked. When I circled behind him, I plunged my knife into his kidney. The Mage fell like a stone, and I regretted not having armed myself with more weapons on my first real date with Christian.

"One down, three to go," I announced.

Christian threw a deadly punch at one of the men, who spun around like a top. The Mage clutched his shattered jaw before pulling healing light from one of his buddies.

Bastards. I hated cheaters.

Two men flanked Christian. One of them put on a show, flashing around until Christian gave him his undivided attention. The one behind him reached in his coat pocket and pulled out what appeared to be impalement wood.

The moon and stars supplied enough light for me to see that the man coming at me appeared no older than twenty, but this wasn't his first rodeo. He looked confident and experienced, and the worst thing I could do was underestimate my opponent. He didn't look like a Learner, especially the skilled way he gripped the blade in his hand. Probably a stunner.

And I could use that stunner.

This guy wasn't too big, but he looked to be five feet eight inches of pure dumb. Tough guys could kick ass, but a jughead with no common sense could still lose a fight no matter how big and bad he was.

My brain switched gears, and I settled on a new tactic. I flashed toward him like an inexperienced Mage, sharpening my light and filling my hands with energy. Only a novice would knowingly juice up another Mage with his light. As soon as I blasted him, he reached around and drove that stunner into my back. It would have been pointless to fight him for the weapon. This way he was practically giving it to me.

I let my knees turn to spaghetti noodles, and I fell to the ground, faking paralysis.

"Got her!" he boasted.

No matter how many times it happened, I never got used to a knife in my back. Being immortal didn't remove pain, but when you no longer feared death, it was amazing the things you could do.

I grimaced against the concrete, my hair obscuring my view of the action. I needed to stay absolutely still for him to buy my act. Otherwise, I'd lose my only chance to take him out.

Where the hell is he? Has he turned away yet?

Christian must have caught on to my plan. After I heard a body hit the ground, he said, "Only two of you left? Have you ever fought against a Vampire and won? Do you know how easily I can compress your skull? That's right, boys. Keep coming." And right then, I knew he'd diverted all attention away from me.

I reached over my shoulder, but my fingers barely touched the handle. Then I tried grabbing the dagger from underneath, but it was impossible to reach.

"*Ohhh*, you've got to be kidding me!" I growled.

Of all the places he could have stabbed me, he chose the one spot on my back least likely to get scratched when I had an itch.

I tried propping my elbow against the concrete to force my arm higher, but it wasn't enough. I sat up, blinking at the two men surrounding Christian.

One flashed at him and brought down the stake. Christian parried the attack, the wood splintering against his shoulder but not sinking in. When he raked his hair back, his lips were curled in a snarl, fangs gleaming in the moonlight. I wasn't sure if it had to do with someone almost nailing him with impalement wood or tearing his favorite suit.

Christian locked eyes with me as I stood up. Something inexplicable transpired between us, as if we were connected in a way that transcended thought. Succumbing to that instinct, I flashed into his arms.

Without missing a beat, Christian reached behind my back and yanked out the dagger. I nearly collapsed from the pain, but knowing what had to be done, we simultaneously turned, our backs united.

Christian went for the big guy wielding the impalement stick. Eager to have my revenge, I lunged at the jerk who'd stabbed me in the back.

I leapt into his arms like a child, wrapping my legs around his waist and locking my ankles. He didn't have time to react before I sank my fangs into his neck. The Mage bellowed, yanking my hair in a desperate grapple to pry me off.

Resisting the force of my head being pulled back, I drank hard and fast until his knees buckled. When he fell onto his back, I quickly let go so my arms wouldn't get pinned beneath him. His blood wasn't vile with dark deeds like other criminals I'd taken out, but it was no cabernet sauvignon, either.

I slammed the man's palms against the concrete, locking my fingers with his and squeezing them tight. "Lights out."

My palms heated when his Mage light pulled to the surface and entered my body. I understood why juicing could be an addictive pastime. Dark light from evil men made me sick, but this guy was probably going along with the herd. His light wasn't pure, but as it poured into me like a river of raw power, I got a buzz that made me tingly all over. When I felt his core light just within reach, I pulled hard until a loud crack sounded, light snapping against my palms like a whip.

I sat back, blood still wet on my tongue. Foreign energy tangled with my own, its presence as pervasive as poison ivy.

The man's eyes widened when he felt his immortality slip through his fingers. No pity lived in my heart for any man who would stab me in the back.

I wondered if he was a Healer, because I felt the wound in my back seal together from the introduction of his core light. Now fueled with energy, I stood up and watched him scuttle backward before running down a dark alley.

When I looked back at Christian, he was hunched over a body. With a slow and deliberate turn, he stood up and held out his hand. In his palm, a heart.

He tossed it at my feet. "Happy Valentine's Day."

My Vampire sexuality mystified me. Christian offering me the heart of an enemy sent a thrill between my legs like nothing else. The gruesome visual would have sent a normal person running, but moonlight painted everything a different color. Christian inhabited my heart. I'd never had anyone willing to kill for me—no one except for my father. And yet time and time again, Christian was by my side.

I put away lost memories and reveled in the creation of a new one. This intimate moment we shared of fighting to keep each other alive was everything. The romance, the laughter, the rooftop dinner, the kiss, and even the danger. All the dots connected. No holes, no missing pieces—just one fantastic evening that was intact and all mine.

We moved toward each other as if magnets were drawing us together. The intensity of his gaze was hard to decipher. His looks of anger and lust were often one and the same. When I reached him, my panties practically disintegrated. Christian pulled me to him by the back of my neck and kissed me hard. I moaned into his mouth, and he lifted me straight up and kept walking.

We were shadows dancing in the dark.

My back struck a solid surface, and Christian pressed against me as my feet touched the ground. He gripped my bare thighs beneath my modified skirt, and I melted against his touch.

I tunneled my fingers through his hair, his mouth still on mine. Christian was a phenomenal kisser. His tongue did things to me that fantasies were made of. He knew when to go hard and deep and when to draw back and leave me wanting more. Maybe it was centuries of practice, but I wasn't complaining. I could kiss those talented lips of his forever.

And I was also certain that if he kept touching my legs and sweeping his tongue against mine, I might actually climax.

Christian ripped my panties on either side and let the material fall to the ground. When he wedged his hand between my legs, parting them, my breath hitched.

"Someone might see us," I said through shallow breaths.

He pressed against me even harder, his fingers stroking me. "I need to be inside you, Precious. Let them watch."

The hot look he gave sent a tremor of anticipation through me. Christian *liked* the idea of people seeing us. I craved his warmth, so I grabbed his firm ass and pulled him even closer.

"You like that?" I asked, noticing his fangs sliding into view.

"Aye," he breathed, anchoring his hands on my thighs.

I squeezed again, and this time he groaned.

Christian nestled his mouth against my neck as I reached for the front of his trousers. The top button was easy enough to unlatch, but my brow furrowed when I didn't feel a zipper.

"Buttons," he rasped.

His breath heated my neck, my vein pulsing for him. I felt a gentle scrape against my skin as he restrained himself from taking what he wanted.

"Trousers like these were normally held up with suspenders," he said matter-of-factly, stroking my vein with his tongue.

"Shut up, Poe. I don't want a history lesson in men's trousers."

I worked on the buttons, but there wasn't enough give in the material and no way to do it without a few popping off. "I'm ripping your pants."

His head fell back, eyes closed and breath heavy.

Car horns blared in the distance, and the sounds of the city overlapped until they became white noise.

We were in a scramble, buttons falling to the ground in a desperate struggle to get him inside me. When I freed his shaft, gripping the hot length of him and rolling my thumb across the blunt tip, he lifted my thigh and buried himself to the hilt.

Christian cursed under his breath.

I gripped his shoulders, taking every inch of him. He cupped my ass, our lips close but not kissing. Feeling his erratic breath against mine fueled the fire raging between us. Christian suddenly rammed hard and deep. When I cried out, his hands moved away and flattened against the wall.

"No," I whispered, clinging to his neck. "Keep them on me."

"I can't," he bit out.

"You will."

"I'll hurt you."

I killed the debate when I sank my fangs into his neck. Christian bucked, and I held on as I sipped his dark, lustful lifeblood. It flowed down my throat like sweet desire, awakening an ancient heat inside my veins. I wanted him to unleash, and he'd never do that as long as he had to handle me like a porcelain doll. I only needed enough to match his strength.

I retracted my fangs and ran my tongue over the mark.

"You're killing me," he ground out.

"*Now* touch me. Don't hold back—I want it all."

Christian's hands slid beneath my skirt, his fingers scoring my hips. I vaguely heard someone walking down the street, briefly stopping at the entrance to the alley. Maybe they couldn't see us in the shadows.

Maybe they could.

The first time we'd had sex, it was passionate. This time we were fucking. And I didn't care. I wanted unsentimental, lascivious pleasure. I wanted friction. I wanted that feverish heat and renegade pleasure.

Christian hoisted me off the ground and pinned me against the wall. "*Jaysus,*" he whispered. "You're so fecking wet."

I rode him. My boot heels anchored against the brick wall behind me, and my bent knees clamped against his hips like a nutcracker. I was chasing my release while riding the length of him. Christian's blood lingered on my tongue, but he made no attempt to drink mine in return.

He looked up at me with ravenous hunger. It made my belly clench, and as I stared deeper into those obsidian eyes, my oncoming orgasm shimmered around me like tiny pulses of light.

"You're gorgeous," he whispered.

I threw my head back. Every muscle seized as pleasure ripped through my body like white lightning. I moaned, not caring who might hear. Christian buried himself inside me, drawing out my release as he kissed and sucked on my neck.

Breathless, I lifted his chin and planted my lips on his. The kiss went deep, our tongues intimately twining until he pinned me hard against the wall and slammed his hips into me, his tempo frenetic.

When I cried out, he covered my mouth with his hand. So I pricked his finger with my fang and tasted his oncoming orgasm.

Christian growled fiercely and suddenly pulled out. His head dropped on my shoulder as he came, his body trembling. There was a moment when my cheeks heated, and I wondered if I'd done something wrong that he would rather have finished on a brick wall than in me.

"Why did you do that?" I whispered.

When he stepped back, my feet touched the ground.

Christian tucked himself away and fumbled with the remaining buttons on his trousers, his cheeks flushed and lips swollen from my kisses. "You're like a package of dynamite," he said, still out of breath.

And Christian didn't lose his breath. I'd seen him shadow walk miles and not so much as sweat. Maybe he had a way of controlling his body, but with me, he couldn't.

Now there was an interesting thought.

I pulled down my skirt and buttoned my coat up, the loss of heat making the breeze unbearable. "It's not like I can get pregnant," I muttered.

"Aye. But you're wearing that short little number, and your knickers are lying in a heap on the ground."

Ah. In the heat of the moment, it hadn't occurred to me how I didn't have a way to clean myself up afterward. Not that I cared.

But *he* did.

I raked back my tousled hair. "Always the planner."

He looked at me, his fangs still descended. Lust glimmered in his eyes, and he gave me a fervent look that said he'd be ready for another round if I kept riling him up with that sharp tongue of mine.

I shivered, suddenly wishing we had a warm bed to snuggle up and sleep in. "I'm not sure I'm ready to flash across town after that."

He stepped close and encased me with his arms. I flattened my hands against his vest, thinking how handsome he looked in the historic little getup that I'd so gleefully mocked.

"Better?" he asked.

I tilted my head up, his whiskers tickling my lips. After a short journey, my mouth found his. Instead of going in for a kiss, I relished the feel of his soft lips touching mine. They brushed together, and that innocuous gesture was more sensual than I could have imagined. My heart did a quickstep, and a funny feeling came over me.

Especially when his arms held me tighter, and most especially when his eyes gently closed. We swayed for a moment in the darkness, and it occurred to me that his embrace was what beckoned me in the wee hours of the morning. Not for sex, but I craved that indefinable connection that transpired between us in quiet moments.

Without warning, a dull pain struck my temple. A lost

memory, reminding me that something was missing. Regret and bitterness filled me as I stepped away. Also fear. In the back of my mind, the absence of memories always left me in doubt. Without them, I didn't know my own true intentions. Especially if I was the one who'd asked Houdini to remove everything that tied me to Christian. Those fucking gaps in time messed with my head in more ways than I thought possible. And worse, I couldn't get them back. Christian said Houdini probably had a keyword or phrase to unlock everything, but only *his* voice and *those* words would lift the spell. I couldn't remember the words, anyhow. With my luck, he hadn't made the mind wipe reversible.

Christian cupped my face, his thumb stroking my cheek. "I know that look. Someday I hope to never see it again."

I chortled when his other hand gripped my ass. "I bet you can't stop touching me."

He leaned in and whispered against my ear, "That's a bet I'll never take, Miss Black."

I glanced toward the street. "We need to go. There are too many juicers out here, looking for an opportunity."

He stepped back and studied the tear in his sleeve. "Stay close to me, you hear? If I have to slow down in a lit area, then you will as well. I won't be able to catch up if a Mage takes off after you."

"Since when did you turn into a chivalrous knight? I don't need saving, Mr. Poe."

A crooked smile touched his lips. "Who said anything about saving you? I just want to watch the action."

"You say all the right things to make my heart go pitter-pat." I gave him a quick kiss on the lips before lifting the collar of my coat. "Be right back after I pull my stunner out of that asshat."

He waggled his brows and followed behind. "A girl after my own heart."

Chapter 10

CHRISTIAN AND I NAVIGATED THE streets of Cognito on foot and made it to Ruby's Diner in no time flat. We snagged my favorite table in the back and split an entire pecan pie between the two of us. Betty was off duty, and the staff kept the place lit with candles on every table. It was kind of romantic. Humans were taking precautionary measures against becoming a victim of crime and just staying home. Most who had night jobs couldn't work, so the usual crowd was thinner than normal. Hot coffee and pastries were ours for the taking.

Christian pinched a pecan from his plate and devoured it. "That's gorgeous."

"I don't think I've ever seen you eat this much food," I said, pointing my fork at his empty plate.

He gave me a wolfish smile. "You know how to work up a man's appetite."

"Why don't you ever eat?" I set down my fork. "And don't give me that business about going to the toilet."

He unbuttoned his sleeves and began rolling them up. "That's part of it. When I worked as a guard, it was night and day. There wasn't time for breaks. That's another reason Vampires are best suited for that line of work. We don't require food, sleep, or bathroom breaks, and we're unfazed by the weather."

"But you're not a guard anymore."

"Old habits die hard."

"You can't tell me you don't enjoy food. You looked at that pie like you looked at me earlier in the alley. The only time I ever see you eat is when you're either being polite or on the job and trying to blend in."

Christian wiped a napkin over his mouth and beard before wadding it up and dropping it on his plate. "I don't know that I've given it as much thought as you have."

"Maybe you don't experience hunger in the same way everyone else does, but your taste buds aren't dead."

He smoothed his beard while looking out the window. The candlelight brought out all the angles in his face. Features that might have intimidated some were genuinely handsome to me. His skin had warm undertones, complementing his brown hair and intensely black eyes. There were faded lines in his forehead from arching his brow, and though his nose looked as if he'd broken it once in his youth, it was unnaturally straight for a man who had been in as many fights as he had. If Christian were still human, he'd look like a train wreck of broken bones and scars.

"To a Vampire, food is a drug," he began. "It has no real purpose... except to fill the emptiness. Or perhaps induce false feelings of joy."

"False?"

"Haven't you seen how women melt over a chocolate-covered strawberry? That's not *real* joy."

I chuckled. "Speak for yourself. Maybe you raise the bar too high on what qualifies. Just because joy doesn't come from love or sex doesn't diminish the effect. If food brings comfort, it's not a false emotion." My eyebrows knitted as I tried to decipher what Christian was implying. "Are you saying you don't want to feel joy, even from the smallest of things?"

"You're not a full Vampire, so you can't possibly understand. You have to eat, or else in time, you'll wither and become weak. That's not the case for me. I can go an eternity without food. My body will never weaken, my muscles will never vanish, and my belly will never ache for it. It's just a reminder of a life we once lived, of a person we once were. Food doesn't fulfill us in the same way that it does you. The pecans are nutty, the sugar is sweet, but the feeling of satisfaction is never quite there."

I gave it some measured thought before responding. "Lots of women have sex even though they can't have orgasms."

Christian nearly spit out his coffee before setting down the cup.

"Look, all I'm saying is that maybe food isn't something you need to survive, and maybe you don't get that full satisfaction like everyone else, but it still feels good, doesn't it? There were plenty of times I hustled for food. Mostly, I went for meat and carbs— maybe vegetables if I was lucky enough to find a sensible eater. But if Betty hadn't given me a slice of pie with ice cream every time I showed up here, I don't know if I would have made it through those rough years. Eating to survive isn't the same as indulging in a treat. That Angus burger made me feel like a human being again after I'd spent a week sleeping in an abandoned garbage bin to get out of the rain. Don't underestimate the power that one small fraction of joy can give you, no matter where it comes from."

Christian took another sip of his hot coffee and sighed. "You're a peculiar woman."

"And you're a peculiar man."

He smirked. "That's a compliment, you know. Better than being a dry shite."

"So all this time, your insults were compliments?"

One brow arched sexily as he finished his coffee. Nothing smelled better on a cold night than fresh coffee percolating in a diner.

My gaze drifted around the dark room. It looked like a different place with the lights out. Intimate. The red vinyl seats were muted, and my eyes weren't drawn to the flashy pictures of classic cars on the walls. Only three other people were in here, though I couldn't see around the corner toward the front. I had my back to the bathrooms, which gave me a view of the entire diner and parking lot.

I folded my arms on the table. "I can't believe this many people are running the streets to cause trouble. I don't mean looting but all the other stuff."

"Nothing warms cold hands like a raging fire."

"What do they hope to accomplish by burning down those shops? The owners will just rebuild."

"Will they? Now that they know things aren't as normal as they seem and their enemies are lurking around the corner, they might not feel as safe. Prejudice doesn't die with immortals. Some of them are old enough to have fought in ancient wars with the man living up the street from them. Even the younger generations of Shifters hear tales from their fathers about how a Mage once shackled them and used them to pull their carriage. They're not stories of generations past. Imagine looking into the eyes of a Mage who works just around the corner, knowing that he used your mother as his personal whore before Shifters were emancipated."

"We have laws now. Times change."

"People don't. Jaysus, look at humans. They've barely made strides among their own kind with people who don't share the same skin color or religion. Breed—we're over that. Every man is equal, but every Breed is not. We all have rank on the totem pole, and believe it or not, Vampires are near the bottom. No one trusts us, and they've been trying to exterminate our kind for thousands of years."

"I thought it was Shifters. Why Vampires?"

"Because we're deadly. We have the power to erase memories and manipulate behavior. We're not easy to kill, and not even a Chitah can pick up our scent. Best you keep your fangs in your mouth until this blackout has ended."

I pinched my bottom lip, deep in thought. A glimmer of a theory touched the edges of my mind before the side door opened, yanking me back into reality.

"*Brrr.* It's nippy out there." Claude bustled inside and sat next to Christian.

When Shepherd came in behind him, I scooted toward the window to make room.

"What the hell happened to you two?" I slid a stack of napkins across the table so Claude could wipe the blood off his face.

He dipped the napkins in Christian's glass of water and cleaned his mouth and jaw.

"We had an altercation with a group of assholes," Shepherd said nonchalantly as he lit up a smoke. "Nothing we couldn't handle. You been here this whole time, eating pie?"

Christian's black eyes snagged on mine before he split his attention between Shepherd and Claude. "Do you see my Honda anywhere in the parking lot?"

I tossed back my head and laughed. Couldn't help it. Christian and that damn Honda.

He glared. "Your laugh is infectious… like gonorrhea."

I lifted my coffee cup. "Can't help it. That car has been a hex."

"Maybe you're the hex."

"What's with the getup?" Shepherd jerked his chin at Christian's old-fashioned vest and button-up.

"Laundry day."

Claude turned his head and wrinkled his nose at Christian. "You smell like garbage… and blood… and…" He leaned in and drew a deep breath.

"And sex," Christian finished, just as cool as could be. "Aye. It was a gory scene at the brothel on Fifteenth. Nothing but fists and fannies as far as the eye could see."

Claude twisted his mouth as if someone had told him a brainteaser he couldn't figure out.

And that brainteaser was why the both of us smelled like sex. I snapped my knees together beneath the table and blew the steam from my cup toward Claude. "Lots of juicers out there tonight," I said, switching topics. "A group of them came after me."

Claude's golden eyes briefly pulsed black. "Did they touch you?"

Christian pinched his chin. "Worry not, lad. She touched them back."

Once home, Shepherd dropped us off at the front door before heading to the garage to park his Jeep. I gazed up and saw Niko standing on the interior balcony on the third floor. He wasn't paying attention to us but staring off in the distance. As soon as I opened the door, warm air touched my cold cheeks. An orange glow emanated from the study to the right of the stairs. We didn't have central heating, but the fireplaces provided all the warmth we needed. But it was unusual to see them burning at three in the morning, especially when no one was around. Kira also hadn't extinguished all the candles in the main foyer.

"Sleep well," Claude said, yawning as he trudged up the stairs. His bloody shoelace from one sneaker dragged along the steps.

I gave the winged statue by the door a cursory glance before deciding not to throw my coat over it. It drove Viktor crazy. Since I was scantily clad and not wearing panties, it made more sense to leave my coat on for the time being. My boot heels knocked against the floor on my way to the dining room, Christian shadowing behind me. Odds were that if anyone was up, they were sitting in the gathering room. I wanted to see if Viktor was awake and dispel any suspicion he might have about why Christian and I were hanging out alone all night. Since we hadn't had a chance to celebrate closing our case, that was going to be our alibi.

I passed through the empty dining area and headed into the gathering room, where a fire was roaring.

In one of the chairs facing away from me, a familiar Irish accent made me freeze in place. It wasn't brooding or full of textures like Christian's, but melodic, friendly, and dominating the conversation.

Viktor rose from his wingback leather chair and circled it to greet me with a reserved grip to the shoulder. "I am glad to see you're safe on a night such as this."

Patrick Bane rose from his seat and bowed, his pale-green eyes flicking between Christian and me with hesitation.

I wondered why a member of the higher authority would come knocking at this ungodly hour. Someone else must have died. "Were we assigned the murder case?"

"I'm afraid not, lass," Patrick began. "I'm here on behalf of the higher authority."

I blinked in confusion. "But you *are* the higher authority."

His nervous laughter didn't go unnoticed. "I'm only one member of a larger group."

Viktor folded his arms. "Every organization has emergency plans, and due to the circumstances surrounding the blackout, one has been set into motion."

Christian rested his hands on the back of the empty chair. "What circumstances?"

"We're not able to determine the cause of the outage," Patrick answered. "I led the investigation the moment the power shut down. We have insiders at key locations. Police departments, FBI, hotels, mental institutions, nuclear power plants—you name it. Any major infrastructure you can think of, we have a man in place. But our contact wasn't on-site, and we can't get him back in to see what's happening. Either this is an unfortunate accident, or some fella set the wheels in motion to destroy our city."

I shifted my stance. "That's a little exaggerated, don't you think? We saw street guardians moving into action on our way home. People go berserk when it's dark, but it'll be a different story tomorrow morning."

Patrick tilted his head to the side. "Come now. Are you really that dim-witted?"

Christian stepped between us, his tone slightly menacing as he said, "She has a valid point, Mr. Bane. People settle down in the light of day. And I'll ask you nicely to watch your sharp tongue and not cast aspersions on my partner. Next time I won't ask nicely."

I pinched Christian's vest and tugged at it. Asshole or not, Patrick Bane was still an authority figure who could throw our asses in Breed jail for any reason he so desired.

"Forgive him," Viktor said. "Christian does not mean to threaten you. It has been a long night for us all."

I took a step left between Christian and my boss. "Naive is the word I think you were looking for," I said to Patrick. "And I'm not that either. I'm just practical. If the power doesn't come back on, things will get wild by sundown. But you'll have a certain amount of order on the streets in daylight. I was just saying that it's not the end of the world as long as you can control half the day."

"Nevertheless," Mr. Bane said, rocking on his heels, "we still have to follow protocol. I'm not pleased with it any more than you are."

I looked at Viktor. "What does Keystone have to do with protocol?"

Viktor shared a look with Patrick before answering. "My contact has requested our assistance. They are calling upon a few trusted organizations such as HALO and Keystone to locate and transport members of the higher authority to safety."

Christian put his hands on his hips, and the curve in his spine made me want to look at his firm ass in those pants again. "Why would they need us when they have Regulators?"

"They've disbanded," Patrick answered. "Most are Chitah, and they're receiving threats from their own kind about protecting those who are not."

I shook my head. "In what time period are they expecting this to be done?"

Viktor stroked his beard as if he'd already considered that fact. "Twenty-four hours."

"Feck me," Christian muttered.

I gave an exasperated sigh. "If there are over a hundred names on your list, it'll take more than twenty-four hours. Have you seen the traffic situation out there?"

"Without knowing how long the outage will last, we cannot waste time," Viktor continued. "It's a paid assignment, but it's also a matter of survival."

"What's wrong with them staying home and hunkering down?" I asked. Seemed like the logical choice.

Patrick put his hands in his pockets, looking like a debonair James Bond, except with thinning hair. "No power means no alarm systems. Some guards went home to protect their own families because of the violence spreading across the city like a rash. It's a volatile climate, and I don't mean the weather. We've recently implemented new laws that have some people upset, and there have been vitriolic attacks against city officials. There are plenty of factions who use every given opportunity to overthrow the powers that be."

Well, this added a whole new level of fuckery to our evening. There were probably over a hundred of these officials spread all over the city. I wasn't familiar with every street and section of town, so it would take a while to find each address unless I relied on the phone GPS.

"Can we tell everyone where to meet?" I asked. "Just give them the address of where we're taking them and we'll pick up any stragglers who don't have a ride."

Patrick chortled. "They won't even tell me. Only two men know the safe locations, and they keep that information confidential in case someone compromises our security by revealing it to a third party. That's how emergency plans function. We can't even alert everyone on the panel. Security reasons and all that. I only know the plan's underway because I was working on the outage situation." Patrick sighed and shifted his stance. "The Regulators were supposed to assist with the transport. Everyone knows that."

Something occurred to me. "If Viktor's contact is the one who alerted us of the plan, then what are you doing here?"

Mr. Bane drew in an audible breath and sighed. "I came for a favor as well. The operation doesn't allow family members. Only representatives receive rights to sanctuary."

Tiny footfalls sounded from the far end of the room, and a little boy emerged from the shadows.

Chapter 11

WHEN SHEPHERD STEERED HIS JEEP into the parking space in their garage, his headlights illuminated the dark space. He looked at the other side and noticed a black car. Not one of theirs, unless someone had bought it in the past few hours. The van was running in tip-top shape, so that was unlikely. The plates weren't new, either. Shepherd eyeballed it before heading up the ramp and outside. Luckily, they had solar panels to operate the door for just such occasions, so he closed it before heading toward the house.

Despite the frigid air, he unzipped his leather coat and took it off. His blood was running hot after all that excitement, and he'd never felt more alive. But something else had been pressing on his mind all evening, and that was leaving Keystone. Before the skirmish, when Claude was riding on the hood, Shepherd should have been more alert to his surroundings. But consumed with all his personal issues, he'd put a brother in danger.

With each step he took toward the mansion, Shepherd knew what he needed to do—give Viktor his resignation. Keystone was his life, his saving grace. But unless he could harness his wandering thoughts and get his shit together, he would only pose a liability. These people deserved better. He didn't think he could live with someone's death on his hands, all because he lacked focus.

It broke his fucking heart. Viktor had scooped him up during a bleak time in his life when he had no purpose or direction. Shepherd had fallen in with the wrong men, but Viktor saw something in him and gave him a shot at redefining his life. And

Shepherd redefined it in every way, including changing his name from Samuel to Shepherd. He was no longer Samuel—never would be again. That man died the night he saw his baby cut from the womb of the woman he cherished.

Shepherd pulled a cigarette from the hard pack in his coat. He stopped for a second to strike a match and light up. That was when he glimpsed a shadow moving on the lawn. With his coat draped over his arm, he cupped the end of the cigarette, puffing slowly as he scanned the property. He couldn't see a damn thing in the dark, only four shadows that didn't belong. His Sensor gifts worked better while touching objects, but when the emotions were ripe, he could pick them up in close proximity.

After heading inside the house and hanging up his jacket, his ears perked up. Though as tired as fuck, he gravitated toward the dining room, where the voices were coming from.

"Who are the four douchebags hanging around the front property?" he called, swaggering into the gathering room with the cigarette between his lips.

Christian, Viktor, Raven, and Patrick Bane turned to look at him.

"Raven, let the others know," Viktor said. "No sleeping in today."

Raven moved past Shepherd and gave him a shrug, Christian following behind.

Every time Shepherd saw Patrick, all he wanted to do was wrap his hands around the man's pasty throat and squeeze. Since Shepherd didn't want Christian picking up on his racing heart, he kept his cool, patiently waiting until they left the room so he could release the breath he'd been holding.

"What's going on?" he managed, wedging the cigarette between two fingers.

"We'll have a team meeting soon," Viktor informed him.

Shepherd wasn't looking at Viktor. Wasn't even listening, for the most part. All he could focus on was the little boy standing by the fireplace.

Patrick clasped his hands in front of him and slowly approached

Shepherd. "The situation is more dire than we could have anticipated. I'm leaving my boy in your care until this blackout blows over. I have no options as he can't come with me, and there's no one else to speak of I'd trust more. No one knows I'm here, which means no one knows *he's* here. I realize your group will be spread thin over the next day, but Viktor assures me he'll be safe in your care. Your home is secluded, secure, and built like a fortress."

Viktor glanced at his watch. "Will you excuse me for just a moment? I should wake up our help so she can look after the boy."

Both men waited until Viktor was no longer in the room.

Patrick stood before Shepherd, a twinkle in his eyes. "I have the utmost confidence that you will protect the boy. If my life is in danger, so is his." Patrick lowered his voice. "If you do anything foolish, Keystone will be dismantled and locked up for treason. You have more to think about than just yourself."

Shepherd could scarcely breathe. The boy... staying here? Shepherd had been two seconds away from packing his bags, but now he couldn't go anywhere. Not with the boy under their watch. Not if his life was in danger.

"I don't like this situation any more than you do," Patrick admitted. "But it's the best strategic move to protect my assets. Keystone has orders under my authority to make sure the boy is kept safe and returned to me when this is all over. If that doesn't happen, I promise you I'll do everything in my power to see your entire team executed for being an accessory to a crime against an official. The stakes are higher now. I'm a benevolent leader among my peers, and they won't take kindly to someone stealing my child after I entrusted them with his safety." Patrick held up his index finger. "Don't trifle with me."

Viktor returned. "Patrick, let me invite you for a drink before you go. Come. I keep the good stuff hidden away in the kitchen."

Patrick gave Shepherd a pointed stare before leaving the room. Moments later, Kira tiptoed through the dining area and entered the gathering room. It appeared Viktor had whisked Patrick away in an effort to protect Kira's privacy. Patrick was the sort of man who would barrage her with questions if he knew she would be the primary caretaker. Shepherd didn't know exactly what was going on, but it sounded as if Keystone had a mission that might take him away from the boy.

His boy.

The kid was still in pajamas. Grey with white stripes... like a prisoner. They were inadequately short, as if he'd outgrown them months ago. Shepherd wondered if the kid even knew how old he was. He probably didn't celebrate his birthday. Not that it was a big deal among Breed, but it wasn't uncommon for parents to honor their child's birth if they chose. At five, he was no longer a baby. But he still looked so damn little.

Shepherd's eyes shifted to Kira. She wore her red hair pulled back in a messy braid. Her blue V-neck nightgown was neither revealing nor silky. It reached her ankles and did nothing to frame her body type. She dressed as modestly as she behaved. Kira hustled over to the little boy and squatted in front of him, a smile widening across her face. She had kind features, and her smile warmed the room as much as the fire.

The boy observed her closely. Sensors didn't always trust facial expressions, so he touched her cheeks. When he did, he grinned. He must have sensed her genuine amusement.

Curious, Shepherd quietly watched their interaction. Kira had never spoken English. Hell, the woman barely spoke at all. So he wondered how this exchange would work. She pointed at the boy and then used her index and middle fingers to mimic legs walking. Then she pointed toward the door before crooking her finger, gesturing him to come.

He nodded and took her hand.

As easy as that, Kira led him away without having said a word. It unnerved Shepherd to witness how easily a stranger had gained the boy's trust. Jesus. Anyone could walk up in a public place and snatch him. Shepherd suddenly felt a surge of protectiveness and wanted to give him a lecture about the dangers out there, but this wasn't the time. And a mercenary like him had no place giving this kid life lessons.

Kira held the boy's hand and kept a steady eye on him as they moved through the room.

Shepherd glanced down and briefly met eyes with the boy, who waved at him. Not the short wave you give a total stranger, but the kind you give someone you know. His sleepy blue eyes held a look of recognition, and that filled Shepherd with unexpected joy.

"Hey, little man," he said, greeting him with a sideways grin. Shepherd probably looked as scary as hell, and he was certain there were still bloodstains on his white T-shirt, but he didn't care.

Kira and the boy scurried through the dining room and into the outside hall. Shepherd stepped into a shadowy corner, suddenly feeling a renewed sense of purpose.

Viktor and Patrick finally emerged from the kitchen, half-empty glasses in hand.

Patrick gripped Viktor's arm firmly. "I appreciate the favor," he said. "You're a good man, and I trust he'll be safe in your care. Can I have your word on that?"

Viktor nodded. "Keystone will look after your son as if he were our own."

"I'll hold you to that, Mr. Kazan. He's precious cargo. He's the most important possession in my life. 'Twould be a crime if you broke your promise."

"You have nothing to worry about. I trust my team, and he is safer here than anywhere else. We have miles of land surrounding us, and someone will always be watching him. He will not leave our sight for a moment."

As the two men walked out, Patrick glanced over his shoulder. Shepherd wasn't certain if Patrick saw him standing in the shadows, but he felt his look just as certainly as he saw it on his smug face. It was a stern warning. To be a member of Viktor's organization, loyalty played an important role. Patrick took advantage, knowing Shepherd wouldn't do anything selfish if it meant sacrificing the lives of people who trusted him. A decent man couldn't live with that on his conscience. Patrick also knew that no one else would protect that boy like his own father.

He had Shepherd by the balls.

Thoughts of leaving Keystone miraculously vanished. It became a moral imperative to stay for the duration of the boy's visit. The blackout made things dangerous, even if they were far the fuck out of the city.

But another thought rolled through Shepherd's head in those quiet moments.

For whatever short period they kept the boy, Shepherd would have an opportunity to know him. Maybe it would only prove how unfit he was to parent a child. Maybe the boy would hate his guts. Maybe Shepherd would realize his only place was with Keystone, and that his pipe dream of having a son died the day Maggie did.

Or maybe… he would learn to love again, and that terrified Shepherd more than the thought of losing his child.

Chapter 12

AFTER AN ICE-COLD SHOWER TO rinse off the blood and sex, I changed into a pair of clean panties, jeans, and a long-sleeve black shirt. Ripped jeans weren't the warmest things to wear in winter, but this pair was easy to move around in, and I liked being flexible. I also had on black leggings beneath them for added insulation.

Christian volunteered to wake everyone up and assemble them downstairs for an impromptu meeting. In case Viktor wanted us to leave straightaway, I grabbed my leather jacket and hustled to the first floor. My Converse sneakers were untied, the laces slapping all over the place as I jogged and stumbled toward the dining room.

Out of breath, I waltzed in and slung my jacket onto one of the empty benches. Everyone was seated at the table except for Gem and Christian.

Wyatt rubbed his eyes. "Can you fill us in now? Her Majesty is here."

I cut him a sharp glare. "Poor baby. Are you going through video game withdrawal?" I scanned the bowls of food on the table, none of which required refrigeration or heating. "Breakfast already?"

"I'd hardly call it that," Claude grumbled. "I'd kill for sausages."

Blue stabbed a pineapple chunk with her fork. "All the meat's in the trash, unless you want to dig it out and get worms."

Claude rubbed the dark circles underneath his eyes, having not slept but maybe an hour or two, by the looks of it. The candles were still burning even though it was already light outside.

When I sat down, Viktor spooned a medley of chopped fruit onto my plate. Without argument, I ate every bite. The lack of electricity had not only limited our food options but made showers unbearably cold. The few luxuries we had were now gone.

"We could have built a spit outside," Claude said. "Don't we have a grill?"

Blue swallowed her fruit. "Without a way to properly store meat, what are you going to cook?"

"I used to hunt squirrels back in Tennessee," Wyatt remarked. "Hey, don't look at me like that. As Hank Williams Jr. once said: a country boy can survive."

Niko choked on his water and quickly set the glass down. "Apologies. I thought you lived off french fries. This must be like a famine for you."

"The frypocalypse," I quipped.

Wyatt glared at Niko, but I could see the amusement dancing in his eyes "You're real funny over there. A regular George Burns."

Niko ran his finger around the rim of his plate until he found his fork handle. "Kira's domestic experience is not as limited as ours. Perhaps she can find a large kettle and make hot vegetable stew."

"We have no time for such comforts," Viktor said. "Eat what is here, because each of you has a long day ahead. An evacuation of the higher authority is in place to protect them during the outage. They're no longer able to keep tabs on all their representatives. Some of the cell phone towers have backup generators, but others are inoperative. Regulators have left their posts, and—"

"They did *what*?" Blue's eyes rounded.

Wyatt stroked his chin. "That's a plot twist I didn't see coming. Does that mean we're going back to the Dark Ages?"

Shepherd continued eating his protein bar and cheese cubes. There was something different about him, but I couldn't put my finger on it.

"What's the emergency plan?" Niko asked, leaning forward so Viktor would hear him. "And how do they know this is a long-term outage?"

"Our sources cannot pinpoint a cause; therefore, we can make no assumptions." Viktor sipped his orange juice and then set down his crystal glass. "We have a list of names, and our job is to transport those individuals to sanctuary. Alarm systems are down, and bodyguards are abandoning their positions. As you may or may not know, many crimes took place last night. No one could have predicted we would see such anarchy." Viktor leaned forward, a pensive look on his face. "The future lies in your hands. Perhaps the power returns today, but if not, it is our job to ensure that every name on that list is protected."

Wyatt's brows knitted. "We're not bringing them here, are we?"

"*Nyet.*" Viktor slipped into speaking Russian before stopping himself and rubbing his eyes. "Forgive. It has been a long night. There are six key locations, each beneath a church. No one knows these places exist, so you cannot reveal our plans to anyone. That includes those you're assigned to transport. Do not let the officials use their position to make demands. This order is above their rank. They cannot refuse. They cannot bring anyone with them, and that includes pets. No children, no wives, no husbands, no dogs."

"Fish?" Wyatt joked. "Sorry. They can hardly be considered a real pet."

Viktor's jaw set. "If you want to inadvertently transport a Shifter in animal form, jeopardizing lives, then by all means, take the fish."

Wyatt held his palms up. "Kidding. Kidding."

"Anyone with pets, write down their address, and someone will look after the animals while they're gone."

I felt a sudden tug on my shoe and peered under the table. Patrick's boy was sitting Indian-style, tying my shoelaces. I smiled at him. "What's your name?"

He said nothing.

When I sat up, Viktor was looking at his weathered hands. "I did not think to ask Mr. Bane the child's name. How rude of me."

"He doesn't talk much," I said, realizing Viktor must have already informed the team about the kid before I came down. "I don't think I've ever heard him say a peep, but he sure knows how to giggle."

Just then, a small giggle sounded from beneath the table, making everyone smile.

I set down my fork. "Was Patrick on our list?"

"Nyet."

"Why couldn't he have just stayed and come with us?"

"They have separated the members onto different lists for a reason."

I lowered my eyes to my plate. "Are they separating them by Breed?"

When Viktor didn't answer, I lifted my eyes to his. "If we're only assigned one location, we're going to figure it out."

Viktor leaned back and sighed. He remained quiet, pretending to brush lint off his charcoal sweater.

"Six locations won't cover everyone," Wyatt pointed out. "Not unless they group together the ones who don't pose a danger to others because of their gifts."

I held out my hand, lifting a finger for each Breed. "Vampires, Chitahs, Mage, Shifters... Sensors?"

"That's the way I'd do it." Using his hands, Wyatt gobbled up the rest of his strawberries. "You can't group Sensors with anyone else. So that leaves Gravewalkers and Relics. They're pretty harmless. No snazzy powers or venomous fangs."

Blue snorted. "Like anyone's going to kill each other beneath a church."

"You never know." Wyatt grabbed a napkin and wiped his sticky fingers. "Didn't you ever watch those old *Twilight Zone* episodes? People get paranoid when you put them together in groups during a crisis."

"What about the other Breeds you didn't mention?"

Wyatt laughed. "Do you think they'd put a Gemini on the panel? Nope. And as for any others, it wouldn't matter since they're the minority. They only put majority members up there to represent their people."

"I cannot answer specifics," Viktor said. "You can draw your own conclusions, but we have a task to perform. We are not responsible for the whole higher authority, only a defined list, and we are to adhere to that list."

"Who else is helping?" Claude asked. "Please say it's HALO. They're the only group I trust."

"HALO will handle their own list. Since they have more men, they will have more officials to transport between multiple locations. I have the names of other groups involved, and I'll give those to you."

I looked around the table, comforted that everyone looked as nervous about this as I felt. Hauling around members of the higher authority was a huge responsibility. One fuckup, and that was the end of Keystone. Maybe even civilized life as we knew it. Without the laws in place, some of these nut jobs would tear the city apart. And I felt especially protective of humans. They were the innocents in all this.

Wyatt picked at the buttered bread on his plate. "How do we move them?"

"That is for you to figure out," Viktor said. "Create no suspicion. You must not cause neighbors to take notice."

Wyatt's eyes lit up like a computer switching on. He loved working out problems. "I've still got leftover decals for dry cleaning we can slap on the van. We'll just stuff our precious cargo into an oversized bag and haul them off."

Shepherd pushed his plate away. "You need electricity to dry-clean, dum-dum. They don't just spray your shirts and magically wipe away the grime."

"We could move a few that way," I agreed. "Some people like to continue feeling normal even when things aren't. Do you have any decals for garbage services?"

Wyatt rubbed his scruffy chin. "Maybe. I keep all kinds of stuff like that around for our jobs. Anyone else got ideas?"

"Storage," Niko offered. "Immortals are moving old furniture to second locations or storage facilities all the time."

Blue patted his shoulder. "That's a good one, amigo. Nobody

will blink twice at a few big boxes moving out with a couple of chairs."

"We don't have room in the van for chairs," Wyatt pointed out. "Not if we want to fill it with as many warm bodies as we can."

Shepherd sat back, one arm hooked over the back of his chair. "Then we dump the furniture in a ditch somewhere. Fuck 'em if they complain."

Wyatt gestured to Shepherd. "Point to Shep."

I looked at Viktor. "What if we get someone who won't cooperate? Exactly what authority do we have over them?"

"You have all the authority you need to ensure they are transported to the safe location. *Alive.*" Viktor gave me a pointed stare, his grey eyes not showing any hesitation. "They are not expecting the evacuation, but they are aware that Regulators are the ones who would round them up. So bring weapons if you must."

"What if some of them suspected an evacuation might be coming and split?"

"Do not hunt down those people who have already left. We have no time for such nonsense."

Heads turned when Gem entered the room. She looked more rested than before, but her mood was dejected. She hadn't done anything special to her hair, and the wavy locks hung limp on her shoulders. Her oversized black sweater stood out since she usually wore colorful, fun outfits. I barely noticed her white leggings. Her crystal necklace didn't hold the luster it usually did, and neither did her violet eyes.

Gem sat in her chair between Claude and Shepherd and drew up one knee, locking her fingers over it. "Christian filled me in, so you don't need to hit the rewind button."

Claude rubbed her back consolingly, but no one said anything since it might upset her.

Blue laced her fingers together. "Viktor, which Breed are we covering? Please tell me it's not the Vampires."

A shudder went through me. I felt the same as everyone else did about Vampires even though I was half.

"You will do the job regardless of which Breed you are assigned to protect."

"Viktor, we need to be prepared," I said. "Are they all the same Breed? Same church? What weapons should we take?"

Viktor stretched his arms. "The names had to be divided up based on how many people are on each team. One of you will remain at the church, and three will ride in the van. We have less than twenty-four hours to deliver twenty-five names. Because you may be doing heavy lifting, I need muscle."

"Can we take the Jeep?" I asked. "Shepherd's got tinted windows."

"Nyet. We have one inconspicuous vehicle. We have to be discreet. If you wind up dealing with an uncooperative individual, people will take notice if you shove them into the back of a Jeep or pickup truck. Your passenger might break the windows, knock out the driver, or jump out. You have more control and privacy in the van."

Niko used a band to tie his hair back. "You said one church. That means one Breed. Which one?"

"Do you think you can all handle one of your own kind?"

Relief swam through me.

Claude yawned. "A Mage I can handle, but I need to crash for another hour."

Viktor got up and circled behind his chair. "Sleep in the van if you must, but you're going. I want Claude, Raven, and Wyatt first shift. I realize I'm splitting up teams, but this task requires that you all work together as one. Second shift is Blue, Shepherd, and Niko."

Claude rubbed his eyes. "Can I swap with Niko and go second shift? I won't be any good if I'm sleepy. I don't mean just picking up the bags and boxes to haul, but if we have trouble, I won't be on my A game."

Viktor scratched the back of his neck with a look of frustration. "Very well. Claude and Shepherd, I want you to go to your rooms immediately and sleep for as long as you can."

Gem blinked. "What about me?"

Viktor walked behind her chair and placed his hands on her shoulders. "You, my dear, should rest."

"I don't want to rest. The team needs my help."

He sighed. "I have a special assignment for you. One I trust no other with."

She frowned. "Meaning you don't trust me to help the team."

"I am entrusting you with an even greater responsibility. I need you to guard the property."

Her shoulders sagged, and she looked defeated. Gem was in no frame of mind to come along, and despite her balking, she knew it.

"I have much to oversee," Viktor began. "As long as the phones are working, I'll be making calls all day to confirm delivery of each member with my contact—from the moment they're collected to the moment they're dropped off at the safe location. I will also remain in close touch with leaders of the other organizations who are working this assignment. If one completes their duties, then they must help the others. I am tasked with coordinating which names to shift around. I do not have time to watch."

Gem tilted her head back. "Watch what?"

Shepherd knocked on the table as he stood up.

A few seconds later, a tiny knock sounded back.

Gem jerked her head back, her eyebrows drawing together.

Shepherd leaned against the wall behind him, arms folded and feet crossed at the ankle.

When the dark-haired little boy poked his head out and stood up, Gem gaped.

She cocked her head to the side and didn't seem to recognize him. "Who are you?"

Viktor put his hand on the boy's shoulder. "You remember Patrick's little boy? I have given Patrick my word that we will look after his boy's safety. Kira will be his primary caretaker, but she will need assistance, and you two can share that responsibility. But I also need someone who will patrol the house and check all the windows and locks. I was going to do this myself between phone calls, but if you insist on working, I could use the help. Keep your Mage senses alert in case someone enters the property. If anyone compromises our safety, you have my permission to blast them with a fireball."

Blue snorted. "Are you sure about that, Viktor? Those incendiary fireballs can get bigger than you've probably seen. Gem's got a good pitching arm, and she might leave a hole the size of Kansas in your backyard."

He pursed his lips. "Just don't burn down my house with all that power you have."

Gem smiled at the compliment. She reached out and pinched the boy's cheek. "You're a handsome little devil. Did you bring any toys?"

The boy looked up at Viktor, eyes brimming with uncertainty.

Viktor mussed his hair. "Nyet. This was a last-minute decision. Mr. Bane left a change of clothes. There is much here to explore and keep him occupied, but I want eyes on him at all times. Never a moment out of sight. I've relayed this to Kira, so you will only do your security check when she has taken over watching him. I do not want him outside, even in the... trees and benches," he struggled, pointing toward the windows in the gathering room.

"Courtyard," Gem said, suggesting the right word.

Viktor widened his eyes. "*Spasibo.* Do not let him out in the courtyard. Is this clear?"

"Crystal." She straightened her back like a soldier receiving orders. "You can count on me."

Gem appeared content with her important assignment of guarding a child's life. This was no simple task of babysitting, not in the current climate with all hell breaking loose in the city. It might also provide her with a much-needed distraction. But that girl was going to be okay. Something had broken her long before, and it wasn't Hooper.

Viktor rubbed his face. "Kira will have to find a way to make coffee, or I will not last another hour."

"There's instant in one of the cabinets," I reminded him. Poor guy. He needed sleep more than I did and was under a lot of pressure. "She can heat water in the fireplace."

"Are we ready to get this show on the road?" Christian asked from across the room.

When I swung around to look at the doorway, nothing could have prepared me for the tantalizing visual. Christian was leaning against the doorjamb, as he often did, but my jaw dropped at his priest outfit. It ranked somewhere between hysterical and as sexy as hell, and not knowing whether to laugh at him or lick him left me wondering if I needed a confessional.

His gaze caught mine and held on for a moment before dashing across the room to the boy, who hid behind Viktor when he got a look at Christian's black robe.

"Where on earth did you get that?" I managed to ask. "And why?"

He tugged at the white collar. "Viktor's idea. I already tried to talk him out of it."

Wyatt leaned around to get a good look before he belted out a laugh. "You look like the punch line to a joke."

"You would know," Shepherd grumbled.

I shook my head. "Do you have outfits like that just lying around?"

After Wyatt wrapped up his laugh with a snort, he grabbed his slouchy beanie off the table and pulled it over his head. "We never throw things away. It's left over from a costume party we had before you came on."

I looked between everyone. "Who the hell dressed as a priest? I usually see historical outfits at those fancy parties, not Halloween costumes."

Wyatt smiled handsomely. "Shep wanted to go fully armed. It was his first party."

Shepherd widened his stance. "Button it up."

Ignoring him, Wyatt continued. "He already looks like a marine gone rogue, so just imagine Shep in a priest outfit with bulges all around his waist."

I grinned at the mental image. "Then maybe Shepherd should be the one to stay at the church, not Christian."

Blue chortled. "Nobody would buy that."

Christian lifted his robe, revealing his black boots and bare legs. "And they'll believe a Vampire is a man of the cloth? The robe was custom made for Shepherd. I say *he* wears it."

Shepherd flashed an unapologetic smirk. "Ain't a chance in hell."

"Let's not be dramatic," Viktor cut in, defusing the situation. "We've already laid out the plan, and I need someone with good ears inside the church—someone powerful enough to thwart an attack. Besides, I've already tailored the robe to fit you perfectly. There's no going back."

I tilted my chair back, balancing on the rear legs. I couldn't wipe the smile off my face. What a shame I'd miss out on making jokes about Christian's new look.

Niko rose from his chair with an elfin smile. "I'll drive."

I loved Niko's subtle humor. He'd probably be a better driver than Wyatt.

"Fine with me," Wyatt said, giving me a playful wink. "I call shotgun."

"As long as I get dibs on the radio station." I rose to my feet and scooted my chair in. "I'm not about to listen to Bread's greatest hits for the next twelve hours."

Wyatt stood up, singing "Baby I'm-a Want You."

Everyone suddenly paused to look down at Patrick's boy. He was sitting at Shepherd's feet, tying the laces on one of his boots.

It might be nice having a kid around to lighten the mood, and he seemed like a quiet little tyke.

"Go to sleep," Viktor ordered Claude and Shepherd with a snap of his fingers. "Go on. Wyatt, I need you to set up a new phone for Christian."

Wyatt flexed his fingers that had SOUL tattooed on them. "Again? You people lose phones like I lose sleep."

Gem frowned. "That doesn't even make sense."

Wyatt shrugged.

"Give him whatever phone you have available before he leaves," Viktor continued.

"I also need you to track down my car," Christian added. "I can give you the location where it was stolen."

Wyatt shook his head. "No can do. Not until the power comes back. My outlets don't work, so keep all your phones charged in the car. Wyatt's World is temporarily closed for business."

Shepherd cleared his throat. "If you three got any time to spare, swing by Patrick's place and get this kid some gloves."

Viktor patted the boy's head. "No need to worry. We have blankets, and we'll keep the fires lit."

Niko circled the table. "I think Shepherd makes a good suggestion. The boy is in our care, and while we've grown accustomed to the temperature within the mansion, I'm certain Patrick keeps theirs at a warmer degree. The child should have something to cover his hands."

"Very well," Viktor agreed. "Only stop there if you have time. Gem, you have small fingers—you can lend him a pair of mittens in the meantime."

"Sure," she said, the sparkle in her eyes dulling.

That was probably how I looked for a few weeks after my rescue. I had moments where my emotions switched on and off. While gregarious by nature, she needed more time to sort things out in her head.

I neared Christian, my smile widening. "Come on, Vamp. You ready to save some souls?"

He waggled his eyebrows. "Won't be the first time. I can't count how many women have found God in my presence."

I smothered a laugh.

"What was that?"

"Nothing. I just had a tickle in my throat. If you're such an expert at saving souls, then you can start with mine."

Christian gave me a crooked smile. "You can't save what's already been sold."

"What's the matter? Can't perform miracles?"

"Not unless you get on your knees."

"Don't let the collar go to your head. They're still not letting you through the pearly gates."

"Now, is that any way to speak to a man of the cloth?"

"No, but the only thing holy about you is your sweater collection."

His eyes narrowed slightly but glinted with humor. "You have a tongue that could clip a hedge."

Christian and I were back on form. I could have kept going with the banter, but eyes were lingering on us just a little too long, so I turned to Viktor.

"I'm going to grab some weapons before we drop off a Vampire dressed up as a priest at the church. I hope we have a benevolent God. If not, I'll pick up a few handbaskets on the way home for our trip to hell."

Viktor pinched his chin, his brow furrowing. "You better take a lightning rod, just in case."

Chapter 13

"VIKTOR'S A FUNNY GUY." I jolted when the van hit another hard bump.

Wyatt slowed down at the intersection and tossed his aviator sunglasses on the dash. "He must be if he put Christian in a priest outfit."

"Maybe it'll do him some good."

We had already dropped Christian off at the church. The building had tall ceilings and decorative windows with elaborate paintings. The priest was a trusted human in the Breed world, which I found hilarious. Weren't immortals the epitome of evil in the eyes of the church? They'd spent centuries trying to eradicate our kind. Perhaps now they thought it was better to work with us than against. Or maybe they thought they could save our wicked souls.

Even with the heater blasting in the van, I shivered. The temperature had been dropping steadily, and a light mist coated the windshield.

I looked over my shoulder at Niko, who was sitting on the bench behind Wyatt. "You look cute in those."

Despite his golden-brown complexion, his cheeks reddened. We all had on dark-blue coveralls with a logo on the back that matched the decal on both sides of the van. Since they were thick and warm, I didn't need to wear a jacket. They were also customized for undercover work, so we had special pockets with easy access to our weapons. I had a few push daggers on me that were easy to grip and use in tight spaces.

I checked the double knotting on my shoelaces to make sure they were tied. "Shepherd was acting weird this morning."

"Yeah. Not his usual dickish self," Wyatt agreed. "And all that fuss over the kid needing gloves. It's not like we live in an igloo."

Niko chimed in. "Igloos are warm. Patrick left him in such a hurry that he didn't think about basic necessities, only his safety. It would be neglectful if we didn't go above and beyond what Patrick expects from us. After all, our charge is just a frightened little boy."

I adjusted my fingerless gloves. "We can swing by Patrick's later. Hopefully, nobody on our list gives us any trouble."

"I brought rope," Wyatt said, his smile widening.

"Great. Let's hog-tie the most powerful politicians in the city. That'll go over well."

"Hey, Viktor said whatever means necessary to get them to the church alive. You think I want to mess with a Mage zapping me unconscious or rendering me incapable of fathering children? I say we tie them all up... just in case."

Our van passed by a juicer stealing light from another man in broad daylight.

I swallowed hard, my nerves taking over. "What's the plan if someone fights? Stab and bag?"

Niko scooted to the end of the bench behind Wyatt's seat and joined in the conversation. "The officials weren't alerted that an evacuation order was in place, so they will likely answer the door. Those who don't wish to cooperate might simply slam the door in our face, but that will be at their own peril."

"What if we skip them?" I suggested. "We could waste a lot of time on problem children when those precious minutes could be spent hauling the cooperative folks back to the church."

Wyatt slowed the van to a stop. "I like that idea." Instead of a slouchy beanie, he wore a tight blue one to match our outfits. His wavy brown hair poked out of the edges and covered his nape. "We'll do the math to see how many out of our twenty-five resist. Since they're spread out all across town, I drew up a route based on their locations. The map is in the glove compartment. We can highlight anyone we skip and pass it off to the second shift."

I cut him a sharp glare. "That doesn't seem fair. If we have trouble with almost everyone, Viktor will send all of us out on the second shift. We need to rethink this. Twenty-five isn't as bad as over a hundred, but we still have to haul ass in case another group runs behind and needs help."

Wyatt cut off the engine and huffed. While he mumbled to himself, I stared out my window at the brownstone and scanned the mostly empty street. Neighbors knew they were living next to a member of the higher authority, so we had to play this cool.

Niko rubbed his chin. "Let's stick with the original plan and make every effort to convince our targets to comply. If someone takes up too much of our time, we'll leave and come back to them. But something tells me we won't have trouble transporting them back to the church. An uncooperative party might calm down when placed in the van with his peers."

I unbuckled my seat belt. "Or cause a mutiny. What if they convince everyone else to bail?"

"That's why I brought rope," Wyatt said, messing with his front zipper.

I opened my door, the cold air sneaking into the van. "Enough with the rope. We don't need rope. This isn't a rodeo."

"Would you rather go directly to plan B?"

"Which is?"

"The machete."

We both got out while Niko opened the back doors. Instead of going under the guise of a dry-cleaning service, we'd gone with a storage facility. Immortals were moving shit all the time, and a storage company didn't need power to stay in operation. The downside was we couldn't walk the officials out to the van. Someone might see. People need their leaders. It gives them a sense of security that everything's all right, even if it's not.

Wyatt jogged up the steps and rang the bell. When I reached his side, I knocked on the door, reminding him that doorbells probably didn't work if the power was out. Not unless they had those old-fashioned bells rigged up in the foyer.

I leaned back and looked up to the third story. "Nice town house. I bet they cost a fortune."

"Two million in this neighborhood." Wyatt looked nervously over his shoulder at Niko, who was hanging out by the back of the van. He had on a pair of aviator sunglasses and behaved like a bored worker taking a break.

The second time I rapped my knuckles on the door, the locks turned.

When the door opened, a bearded man in a black robe answered. I stared down at his hairy toes and back up to his bald head.

Wyatt thrust our business card in his hand before he could say a word. The card had a special message printed on it so we didn't have to explain ourselves out loud in case Vampires might be nearby.

Wyatt switched on his Southern accent. "Mornin', Mr. Favreau. We're here to collect."

The man flipped the card over and stepped back. "Come inside." He had an accent that I couldn't place after only hearing two words.

As soon as the door closed, I stepped through a cloud of aftershave and looked around. "Are you alone?"

"*Oui.* And you are?"

"Your taxi service."

He pinched his fat bottom lip, looking between us. "And we go where?"

Wyatt put his hands in his pockets and rocked on his heels. "I'm afraid we're not at liberty to say."

"You might want to put on some clothes," I suggested, steering my eyes away from the opening in his robe, which revealed a thick bed of chest hair. "Don't make any phone calls. No one can know what's happening or who we're affiliated with."

He curled the end of his mustache with his finger. "And exactly who *are* you affiliated with?"

"The card is proof of identification. We're not here to explain things. That comes later. We're on a tight schedule, so why don't you grab some clothes and let's get a move on."

Mr. Favreau inclined his head before turning around and heading up the stairs.

"Tick-tock!" Wyatt yelled. He grabbed a vase from a pedestal and tossed it back and forth between his hands. "That was easy."

"Someone needs to acquaint that man with a razor."

"That's too much manscaping. He'd have to hire a team of professionals."

I walked across the marble floor and studied the paintings on the wall in the quaint foyer that spilled into the living room. Just beyond that was another doorway that probably led to the kitchen.

"Do you see why they need protection?" Wyatt's boot heels clacked against the hard floor. "Here we are, in the middle of a blackout, and that nimrod opens the door for just anyone. Doesn't ask who's there, doesn't even peek out a window."

"I'm beginning to hate this idea."

Wyatt kept tossing the oriental vase between his hands. "Why's that?"

"First of all, that crate takes up a ton of room in the van. Secondly, we were anticipating average-size people. That lumberjack isn't going to fit in it."

"Everyone fits. It's the same size as an eternity box."

"A what?"

Wyatt set the vase down on the pedestal and crossed his hands over his chest like a dead person. "One size fits—"

The vase toppled over and crashed on the floor. Shards of ancient pottery scattered all over the place.

"Real smooth. That vase is coming out of our paycheck."

Wyatt swung his eyes up. "What vase? I didn't see a vase."

"Back to what I was saying, the crate is a decent size for most, but he's tall."

"We've got the dolly. If we can't get the lid on, he'll just have to bend his knees, and we'll wrap it with cellophane."

"Why not put him in a giant duffel bag?"

Wyatt licked his finger and rubbed at a smudge on the wall,

making it even worse. "It's easier to handle an object when it's stiff than when it's limp."

"Well then, I hope you did all your push-ups this week, because we're going to be hauling that damn crate down who knows how many stairs and lifting it into the van."

"Would you rather we put him inside a piano?"

I put my hands on my hips and paced in a circle. "I think I've got a better idea. Do you have an extra hat lying around in the van?"

"No, but there's an old ski mask in the glove box. It covers up the entire face except for a rectangular hole over the eyes. Shepherd's worn it on a few of our missions to creep me out."

I bit my lip. *Could this work?* "What if we dress him up in a pair of coveralls? We've got extra pairs in the van for the second shift, all different sizes."

Wyatt cocked his head to the side, his eyes brightening. "You're a genius, Einstein!"

"Anything I can do to get out of heavy lifting. Why make it harder than it needs to be? Neighbors might poke their head out for a minute or two to see what's going on, but if we keep moving in and out, they'll lose track of how many workers we have. We'll load a few chairs or a painting in the van—something he doesn't care about—and then dump it before our next pickup. Let's try that and see how it goes. The full-head mask is a better idea, because it'll hide his beard."

"It's cold enough for it. We're supposed to fall below freezing by noon."

"Run outside and stuff Claude's coveralls and the mask in the crate. We'll have Favreau change, carry something out to the van, and climb in the back. Then you and I will carry the empty crate back."

Wyatt kicked a shard of pottery against the wall and scratched his neck. "I hope that ugly thing wasn't worth millions."

"We'll soon find out."

After he dashed out the door, I collected all the broken pieces I could find. Mr. Favreau was a Mage who was at least a hundred years old, so everything in his house was probably antique and worth a lot of money. I hurried toward the back, passing through a deep-blue room with baroque chairs, more vases, a caddy for alcohol, and large paintings of naked women.

When I entered the kitchen, I dumped the broken pottery into a trash can. To further hide our expensive mistake, I wadded up a few paper towels and put them on top. Maybe after our shift, I'd come back and tidy up. The idea of a million dollars coming out of our paychecks made me sick. Viktor would kill us.

I lifted my head and gazed through the window over the sink at the patio garden. "Must be nice," I said, admiring the wooden fence that enclosed the property. None of the plants were alive, thanks to the winter, but I could only imagine its splendor during the summer. Not everyone in the city had their own yard, and this one had all the privacy a man could afford. Not to mention a hot tub.

I blinked in surprise when two legs dangled in front of the window.

Mr. Favreau dropped to the ground, and when he stood up, we were eye to eye. He was dressed and ready to haul ass, but not with us.

"*Shit.*"

As soon as he turned to run, I bolted to the back door and fumbled with the locks.

"Raven?" Wyatt called out.

"We've got a runner! Get the van!"

I flung the door open and stumbled down three steps, my arms windmilling as I regained my balance and sallied forth.

Favreau scaled the fence at the far end.

"You idiot! We're trying to help!" I jumped over a bush and climbed the fence with ease.

As soon as I landed on the other side, I caught sight of him sprinting down what appeared to be an alleyway. I was hoping we would have wound up in someone's backyard, blocking him in.

Once again, destiny screws me over.

I flashed after him, but being a Mage, he stayed ahead of me.

Favreau had the advantage since he knew this neighborhood better than I did.

When he turned left, I followed.

As soon as we crossed an intersection, I unzipped my coveralls enough in the front to retrieve the large stunner sheathed inside the lining. His energy would run out eventually.

Favreau kept running in a straight line, but when he neared a burning building, he made a sudden left turn.

I glimpsed a few men by the fire, beating someone up.

Not my concern.

Not today.

I halted in my tracks when he led me down an alley littered with cardboard boxes and discarded furniture.

"Will you just stop?" I yelled out. "Do you want all your friends to know you're nothing but a big pussy?"

He briefly looked at me before taking off again. "I don't know you!"

"Really? Is that what this is about? Holy shit, just stop before I throw a stunner into your back!" I tripped over a pipe and fell to my knees. Undeterred, I sprang to my feet in pursuit. "I get it. You're paranoid. But can you just stop and think for a second? If we wanted to kill you, why the hell would we let you go upstairs to get dressed?"

When he finally quit running, I bent over—hands on my knees—struggling to catch my breath.

"Why are Regulators not picking me up? That's in the procedures. I don't recognize you."

Rubbing a stitch in my side, I straightened up and widened my stance. "Because most of them abandoned their posts. Haven't you heard?"

"*Mon Dieu.*"

Shit. Maybe I wasn't supposed to blurt that out.

"The phones do not work," he countered. "How am I to know this is true?"

"Look, we can't do this out in the open."

Tires screeched behind me. When I looked back, I glimpsed

the tailpipe of a van moving out of sight. It backed up, and Wyatt rolled down his window.

"You all right?" he yelled.

"Give us a minute." I held up my dagger and tried to resist throwing it at Favreau. "I'll put this away. Unless you're good at scaling a ten-foot wall, you've got nowhere to go. I *promise you* that we're the good guys."

His breath clouded the air in front of him, and he wiped his sweaty forehead. "What would you do in this situation if you were me?"

I looked over at Wyatt, who was backing up into the alleyway. Niko had the rear doors wide open.

I tucked my hair behind my ears and faced Favreau. "If I were in your shoes, I'd run. But that's me. You're a representative of the higher authority, and you know all about these emergency protocols. You also know that if you deviate from the plan, they could revoke your position. I'm a good thrower. If I wanted you dead, I would have struck you in the heart already and finished you off. I'm asking you nicely to get in the van, or else my friend is going to hog-tie you."

He got that cocky look all men who think they're important get. "You would not dare."

I heard the whistle of rope whirling against air, and when I turned, Wyatt was approaching with a lasso twirling around him.

"Ask me how many years I spent rounding up wild horses," he boasted. The only other time I saw him that giddy was whenever we had a new shipment of candy. "I've wrestled hogs bigger than you."

"Wyatt!" I hissed. "I've got this."

When I looked back at Favreau, he was attempting to scale the concrete wall behind him.

"Great job, Spooky. You scared him."

Wyatt winked and strutted past me, lasso swinging high. When he spoke, he switched to that Southern drawl I'd heard him use on rare occasions—the drawl he was probably born with. "Y'ain't seen nuthin' yet."

Chapter 14

I T TOOK US EIGHT HOURS to load the van for our first drop-off at the church. So far, we had six out of twenty-five. Driving between homes took up a lot of time, especially with the traffic signals out and accidents at intersections. But so did chasing after three officials. One woman had even gone so far as to sic her poodles on us. I didn't even know you could train poodles to be attack dogs, but I had a hell of a time getting them away from Wyatt. After an official throat punched me, I started carrying a machete to the door to persuade them not to run. Between Mr. Favreau hog-tied in the crate and a woman we had to tie up after she blasted Wyatt, we didn't have any more room in the back.

Two of them were squabbling nonstop. Since Wyatt was still recovering from electric shock and a few dog bites, I'd taken over driving.

"How are you holding up?" Niko asked from behind my seat.

"Fine," I said quietly. "But I don't have a good feeling about this. Viktor said one of the other groups handling Vampires was having serious issues, so I don't know how we're going to get them all in."

"We can only do what's possible."

I turned my head toward the window so I could speak privately over my shoulder. "Thanks for chasing down the last guy."

"You should level down when your adrenaline spikes. We talked about that in the training room. If you lose control of your energy, it'll turn on you. We still have several hours before the second team takes over."

"Gotcha."

Leveling down was something every Mage had to learn. Uncontrolled energy spikes had a nasty way of turning into a reverse vacuum and sucking the energy out of you for days if you let it. The flashing I'd done when chasing down a few officials helped burn off some of that excess energy, but it also made me anxious that everyone might run. I got energy spikes each time we showed up at someone's door.

Now I was wiped out, missing a dagger, and my shoulders were sore.

Since there were a few cars in front of the church, I pulled up to the side and saw a door up ahead where the building extended.

I shut off the engine. "Niko, can you jump out and have a look around?"

There were bushes and trees on the outskirts of the parking lot that made it difficult to see if anyone might be hiding. Niko had the gift of seeing energy, so I hopped out of the van to let him climb out through the front. The crate covered the floor in the back, and our passengers were resting their feet on the edge of it, much to the dismay of Mr. Favreau, who was still inside.

While Niko circled the van, I heard a door open and turned to see Christian and a priest emerging. I tried really hard not to laugh at Christian's getup.

Tried and failed.

"Raven, this is Father Martin."

"Nice meeting you." I smiled at Christian. "And you are... Father Poe?"

He dipped his chin and gave me a thorny look. "We have a door in the back for deliveries. You'll need to go around."

"No need to trouble anyone," Father Martin said, his feet dancing back and forth to stay warm. "Are the keys in the engine?"

My brows popped up. "Do you know how to drive?"

"I live in the rectory and gave up my license years ago, but I miss driving."

Christian clapped him on the shoulder. "Keep her under the speed limit, Father."

The priest chuckled as he climbed into the driver's seat.

"Niko!" I called. "Step out of the way. We're backing up."

He approached us from the opposite side of the van, his pace sedate.

"It's all clear," I assured him. "None of those concrete parking bumper things or poles are on this side of the building."

He picked up speed until he reached me, the wind blowing his long black hair. "I smell snow."

"Aye. We might get a flurry or two, but the ground's been too warm this past week for it to stick on the roads."

"Bridges might be a problem," I added, stuffing my hands in my pockets. "Has anyone checked the weather report?" It was a rhetorical question since no one in our house knew what the weather would be from one day to the next.

Both Niko and Christian stood relaxed, neither man affected by the cold temperature, which was making my teeth chatter.

"Are there drinks inside?" Niko asked. "We should take a short break before we start again."

"There's wine in the back," Christian said, humor edging his words. "What's ailing Wyatt?"

Niko reached up, his fingers running across the logo sewn into his coveralls. "One of our passengers knocked him out. I can heal injuries, but I can't do much for the aftereffects of an energy attack. With him out, it's going to slow our progress."

Christian's eyes swung to mine. "How many did you bring?"

"Six," I said, combating the wind by turning against it. "And it wasn't easy. They know emergency plans exist for different situations, but they were expecting Regulators. Some of them took one look at us and freaked out. They thought we were part of an organized faction trying to overthrow the higher authority. So you can imagine how easy it was to convince them to get in a black van."

Christian scratched his neck. "Call Viktor and find out if any of the others are ahead of us. Have you been using the crate?"

"No," Niko said. "Raven came up with a clever plan to dress them in coveralls and a mask and pretend to be workers. Only two were forcefully restrained—the others we managed to convince or capture. I'll speak to Viktor while Raven gives you the update."

We headed to the door and entered a narrow hallway. After a short walk, he stopped at an intersecting hall.

Christian gripped Niko by the shoulders and turned him to the right. "Straight this way goes to the vestibule. The fourth door on the left is a private office you can use to call Viktor. There's also a water fountain in the front. If you don't find us first, we'll find you."

Niko reached out until his fingertips touched the wall, and he used them to count the doors as he passed each one.

Christian grabbed my hand and led me into a room with candles burning on two long tables.

I looked around at the cabinets and appliances along the wall. "I didn't know they had kitchens in churches."

"Where do you think they cook all those potluck dinners?"

As the door shut behind me, Christian went straight to the fridge. The light didn't come on when he opened it and pulled out a bottle of green Gatorade. After twisting off the top, he handed the warm bottle to me. "Drink it. You're an awful sight."

"You really know how to woo a girl with compliments."

I chugged down half the bottle and gasped to take a breath. Man, did that hit the spot. I drank the rest, not even caring that I probably had a green mustache.

Christian set the bottle on the cabinet and examined me closely. "Your heart rate is weaker than normal. And the blood vessels on your face are flushed."

"Stop looking at my vessels." When I licked my upper lip, his eyes smoldered.

Christian stepped closer, the heat between us rising at least ten degrees.

I devoured the sight of him from head to toe. His dark hair was wild from the wind whipping it around, and the scruff on his neck disappeared beneath the white collar. Because the robe was formfitting, he wore the hell out of it. Damn if he didn't look dashing and formal. There was a moment when it felt as if he might be out of my league, but then I remembered this was Christian Poe and not a Jane Austen character. Maybe Christian was right about modest clothing. The less I saw of him, the more I wanted to unbutton that robe and discover what was underneath.

"Your pupils are dilating," he informed me.

"Maybe you shouldn't look so damn hot in a dress."

"It's not a dress, it's a cassock. Now shut your gob and give me ten Hail Marys."

I reached around and grabbed his ass. "Don't wield that power of yours, or I'll smite you."

"Mmm, that sounds like something a sinner would say." His lips brushed against mine.

When I felt my sex pulse with desire, I backed up. "No, no. I'm already going to hell in a handbasket, but I draw the line at having sex in a church with a Vampire dressed as a priest."

His brow furrowed. "Why do you keep rubbing your neck?" Christian pulled the zipper halfway down on my coveralls and swept my hair back.

"Nobody bit me," I assured him, stretching my back. "I had to do a lot of running and a lot of climbing, and I think I pulled something out of whack."

"Turn around."

I gave him a warning look as I faced the door. Instead of sliding his hand inside my coveralls, he pulled the material away from my shoulders. Before I could ask what he was doing, his strong hands were on my neck.

I moaned when his thumbs pressed against my spine. Those hands had the power to crush bones, but instead they kneaded my sore muscles.

"That feels good," I breathed, crossing my arms so my heavy coveralls didn't drop to the floor.

His cheek rested against the side of my head. "I'm not just good for one thing."

I tilted my head. "I know that."

Christian's remark was bereft of humor, and suddenly, this felt very wrong. Neither of us had made any declarations on where our relationship was heading, yet that hadn't stopped us from having sex. Did he think I was using him? I wanted to feel the same emotions he did, but someone had taken me out of the race and put me at the starting line again. Sometimes I thought my heart would leap out of my chest when I saw him walk into a room, but I didn't know *why* I felt that way. With no recollection of intimate conversations between us that would have elevated us to that level, how could I trust a raw emotion?

And yet guilt consumed me as he silently rubbed my shoulders.

I stepped away and zipped up my coveralls.

Christian averted his eyes before going into the fridge and grabbing two more bottles of Gatorade. "Wyatt better wake his arse up."

"I'm coming here when our shift is done."

He slowly strode past me. "And why is that? Viktor might need you at the house."

"Viktor's getting an update from Niko. I think it's a good idea if one of us stays in the city in case Shepherd's crew runs into trouble like we did. You could also use some help guarding the church."

Christian approached the door and half turned. "I'm concerned about that. The rooms are downstairs, but there's no escape tunnel. Back in olden times, escape tunnels were commonplace. An extra measure of security should someone set the building on fire. I wager when they devised this plan, they expected Regulators to be guarding the doors."

I folded my arms, my eyes downcast. "That's a huge flaw in their plan they didn't account for. Are most of the Regulators Chitahs?"

"Aye. It fluctuates over the years, but the job attracts Chitahs. Besides the fact that they can kill a Mage, they're incredibly fast and have a sharp sense of smell when it comes to emotions."

"I thought they were men of their word."

"Perhaps their families are more important than guarding their mortal enemies. If anyone's going to rise up against the higher authority, it'll be now. Every day that passes without power increases the odds of war."

"All because the lights went out."

"It's the small things that govern our actions. If any more cell towers go down, we'll have no way of knowing what's happening."

A chill ran down my spine when I thought about my father. What if Fletcher came out of hiding and went after him? It wouldn't be hard to do since there weren't any Regulators around to keep the peace. He could come after me, but Fletcher was too smart for that. He knew how to push buttons by finding a person's weakness, and my weakness was family. We needed Regulators, but how could we possibly talk them into working the positions they so casually abandoned?

"What's going on in that head of yours?" Christian asked. "I can see the wheels turning."

Christian could read me like a book, so I left the room before I showed him my hand. He enjoyed telling me what I should and shouldn't do, forgetting that he was my partner and not my boss. Christian wasn't always right, and that was a flaw I had to be careful of. I had an idea nestling in my head to visit the Overlord. It would never have entered my mind had I not met him in person. If Quaid held more control over his people than the higher authority, then Regulators would never refuse his orders. Not only would they be able to help us finish this job, but their presence would restore a little order. It was a shot in the dark, but I tucked the idea away for the time being and decided to tell Christian later. He needed to keep his mind on guarding the church, not on me.

We entered the main chapel, my eyes drawn to the lofty ceilings. Afternoon light illuminated the colorful windows, and tall candles brightened dark corners. I was approaching the steps to the altar when Christian snagged my sleeve.

"The chancel is for clergy and choir only. I'm afraid you'll have to find a pew."

I looked around, having never been in a Catholic church. It was an older one with wood beams curving around the arched ceilings. The statues were sublime and the silence welcoming. I glanced on either side of the altar near the back. "What are those armoires for?"

Christian led me down the aisle, and we sat on the second row. "Those are confessionals." He spread his arms over the back of the bench. "The secrets people tell in there would make a prostitute blush."

"You shouldn't eavesdrop."

Christian's laugh reverberated off the walls, and he quickly stopped. "Who do you think they were confessing to?"

I glared at him, keeping my voice low. "You're supposed to be guarding the church, not working the confessional."

He put his hands in his lap. "I got tired of people asking me questions, so I went in there for a moment of privacy. It's a perverted job they have, listening to all those sins."

"And you were willing to oblige."

"To be sure." He lowered the kneeler in front of us with his foot.

A rustle of clothing from behind made me turn my head. A woman rose from her seat, making the sign of the cross while pulling her purse strap over her shoulder. Her eyes locked on the back of Christian's head, and a smile touched her lips as she left the church.

Something told me that Christian was the one who'd brought up sexual fantasies and fueled the conversations. He had a smoky voice that could make knees quiver.

"What exactly did they say to you?" I asked.

"*Jaysus wept*. If you only knew. Some of them just want to confess their dirtiest fantasies."

After a long silence, I elbowed him. "And?"

"I listened to every explicit detail before giving them their penance."

"What did the blonde with the red lipstick say?" I asked, jerking my thumb toward the back where the woman had been sitting.

He twisted his torso, his heated gaze melting me in my seat.

"What's revealed to me in that confessional is confidential. I'm merely the Lord's instrument to listen."

"You're not an instrument. You're a tool."

Wyatt lumbered in, his hat askew and eyes half closed. He plopped down on the pew in front of us and grabbed the drink Christian handed him.

"Now I know what it feels like to get hit by lightning," he said between sips. "My chest hair singed."

I snorted. "What chest hair?"

"The chest hair I used to have before it was singed off."

I sighed and stared up at the cross. "We'll need a miracle to get the rest of these officials in. I had to talk a lot of them into cooperating, but something tells me Shepherd won't be so nice."

Niko came up the aisle behind us, his hand touching every bench he passed. When he found our row, he sat on the other side of Christian. "Another team's having trouble," he informed us. "So it's not just the ones moving the Vampires. Viktor's concerned we won't be able to transport them all in the given time frame."

I leaned forward, my arm resting on the bench in front of me. "What happens after twenty-four hours? It's not like the world blows up."

"The church doors lock. They can't risk extending the time since every hour increases the likelihood of someone noticing what we're doing. Churches have business hours and close up at night. What will that look like if our van is dropping people off every night? It's dangerous to lead anyone here, so the fewer trips we make, the better."

Christian kicked the kneeler back up. "Niko's right. The priest is keeping the doors open today to throw off suspicion."

"But what if the people downstairs start making noise?" I asked.

Christian handed Niko the drink. "Only humans come to this church. Besides, it's farther down than you think. We've confiscated their phones, just in case someone gets the bright idea to blab their location to a friend."

"What happens when the lights come on?"

Niko laced his fingers together. "That, we don't know. The Regulators have abandoned their posts, and that doesn't instill a lot of confidence for those who require their services."

"Seems like gathering them all up in one place makes them a bigger target."

"Churches are safe havens," Niko explained. "Most criminals will honor those rules, or they'll lose respect of those that follow them. But you're right. I suppose Viktor will have us assemble here once we've finished transporting everyone. A well-guarded location is more impenetrable than a hundred unguarded ones. Strength also lies in numbers, and few will storm a church filled with fifty Vampires or Chitahs."

I tugged on my earlobe. "Unless they have nothing to lose."

Christian locked his fingers behind his head and gazed at the ceiling. "If that's the case, we're in for a long night."

Chapter 15

AFTER OUR SHIFT, WE DROVE back to Sacred Heart Church to wait for our team. Claude and Blue arrived together in his red Porsche, and Shepherd showed up a few minutes later in his metallic-grey Jeep. We brought them up to speed on the most efficient methods we'd employed to round up our list and warned them of the trust issues. Since Claude was a Chitah and his word was his bond, Niko suggested that he be the one to ring the bell and win their trust.

I would have loved to tag along with a bag of popcorn and watch Shepherd do all the talking, but I had other pressing matters on my mind.

Bone-tired, I shucked my coveralls and threw on my leather jacket. After Niko and Wyatt headed back to the mansion, I had a private conversation with Claude about my plan to visit the Overlord. He gave me a couple of addresses but had reservations about lending me his Porsche. I reminded him I wasn't good driving a stick and would probably strip the gears on Shepherd's Jeep, so he reluctantly handed over his keys, apparently deciding my visit to the Overlord was worth a shot. At this point, we were running out of options.

Before throwing myself at the mercy of a Chitah, I made a pit stop at Patrick's place to pick up gloves and maybe a few toys for the kid. None of the clothing stores were open after dark, not that I wanted to go shopping when people around me might be having sex with the mannequins. Hopefully the madness would end tonight, but just in case it didn't, I let Wyatt off the hook and volunteered to go.

I pounded my fist against Patrick's door for the second time. "Hello? Anyone in there?"

The other team must have already picked him up, so I decided to check around back. The property looked uninhabited. No security, no lights, no personal guards, and no cars. Not wanting to draw attention, I'd parked down the street a ways and walked back. No wonder the higher authority put all these security measures in place. You couldn't count on guards in a time of crisis. After all, they were just paid employees.

When I reached the back of the house, I noticed they hadn't boarded up the hole blasted in the wall from the Valentine's party. A large plastic sheet hung over it, debris littering the patio. I pulled the plastic away and ducked as I stepped inside.

"Hello? Mr. Bane? It's Raven Black. If you're still here, say something."

No reply came, so I crossed the kitchen. The smell of charred flesh still lingered in the air even though the cleaners had cleared out the bodies.

"I'm coming in! Just in case you're waiting around the corner... with a giant sword," I ended in a murmur. I flared my energy so he'd feel my presence even if he was out of earshot. "Mr. Bane?"

The house offered no warmth or light. My Vampire eyes allowed me to navigate up the stairs to the second floor. None of the rooms looked like a kid's room, so I kept searching until I wound up on the third floor. My night vision was good but not *that* good. I took a small flashlight that I'd found in Claude's glove compartment out of my jacket and shined it into each room.

When I passed a room with a small bed, I halted in my tracks and went inside.

"Poor kid," I said, shining the light around a room bereft of color. There was nothing whimsical about it. No painted walls, no pictures of animals, not even a cartoon bedspread. Just a bed, a dresser, and a small desk.

I rifled through the drawers and stuffed clothes inside my

jacket, including a pair of mittens. We didn't know how long the outage would last, and it didn't seem right to have him wearing the same clothes for days on end. I got on my hands and knees to search for toys beneath the bed, but there were none. Patrick had always struck me as a neat freak, but this was ridiculous.

"What an asshole," I said, finally getting up. "There better be a playroom."

Out of curiosity, I searched the rest of the rooms on the floor, only to turn up nothing but storage rooms for furniture and paintings. When I reached the open balcony at the top of the staircase, memories of Patrick's masquerade ball came flooding back. Even though it had all worked out, I still couldn't shake the image of seeing his boy getting thrown over the banister. It occurred to me that he was around the same age as I was when I'd survived a fire and lost my mother. Kids should never have to experience that kind of terror. Their chief concerns should be which cartoon to watch or how high they can stack their blocks.

I tucked the flashlight in my coat pocket before approaching the center banister on the top balcony that joined the two staircases.

That kid would have died from this height had Shepherd not caught him. When I bent over to look down at the first level, a mitten sprang free from my jacket and dropped to the floor. Not wanting to lose anything else, I zipped my coat all the way to the top.

When the lock suddenly turned on the front door, I sucked in a sharp breath and backed up into the shadows.

"Come in," a man said, but it wasn't Patrick's voice.

"Are you sure we're alone?" The woman sounded uncertain. "Whose house is this?"

"The boss is away on business, and my companions have been instructed to stay away so that you and I can have privacy."

I moved a little to the left to peer through the gaps in the banister. From my vantage point, I saw a husky man with short black hair. Their faces weren't clear from my angle, so I watched as he attempted to take the woman's coat.

"No," she insisted. "It's cold in here."

"Very well."

"Are you positive we're alone?" She looked around, so I kept my light concealed in case she was a Mage. Luckily, neither of them was a Vampire or a Chitah, or else they would have sensed my presence.

"Worry not. We have this house to ourselves. Is my deceased friend with us?"

"No. After he gave me your information, we parted ways. It's possible he moved on to the next life."

"Let us go somewhere comfortable."

"Keep in mind I won't share any valuable details until I'm paid. Gravewalkers get stiffed all the time by the living, and your friend didn't have any hidden money to speak of. He said you were the one who handled his finances."

"He's correct."

"And just so you know, I always withhold additional information until I'm in a safe place. If everything goes smoothly, I'll call you with the rest. Well, as long as the phones are working."

As they moved out of sight, I tiptoed quietly down the stairs, thankful I'd chosen to wear sneakers instead of boots. Patrick had a grandiose double staircase on the main level that curved on both sides, joined by an upper balcony on the second floor. The open area below was spacious, and while it was usually empty during parties, Patrick had moved his statues and chairs back in.

Who the hell was coming into Patrick's house with a Gravewalker?

When I reached the bottom of the staircase, hinges on a door squeaked. I flashed between the stairs and hid behind a large statue.

The man crossed my line of vision as he headed toward the other staircase, and after a few moments, he returned holding a candle. The light illuminated his face, and I recognized him as Cyrus—Niko's nemesis.

I ducked out of sight when he suddenly stopped and looked my way. The black mitten on the marble floor had caught his attention, and I listened to the sound of his footsteps drawing nearer as he walked over to it. Ignoring my racing heart, I trained my focus on concealing every drop of my light. One energy leak, and I might as well tap-dance my way to the front door. Though I had a better shot at fighting him without his goons around, Niko's grim warning made me reconsider any notion of fighting an ancient who was a master swordsman. This guy had assassinated his own Creator.

Oddly, we had something in common, as I wouldn't have minded killing my own.

After a moment, I heard the soft pat of the mitten hitting the floor and Cyrus's footsteps growing distant. I waited until he and his guest resumed talking. As I reached down and swiped the mitten off the floor, a small voice in my head suggested I eavesdrop. Was Cyrus working for Patrick? If so, Patrick had *no* idea what kind of man he was employing to guard him. Cyrus didn't strike me as a man who took jobs in the kitchen, so that ruled everything out but guard or chauffeur. Either way, he had no business getting that close to a member of the higher authority.

I hauled ass out the door, not caring if they'd heard me leave. I had bigger fish to fry.

Niko shifted his balance, his full weight bearing down on his wrists. He was in a planche position, his body horizontal with the floor and only his hands holding him up. Because his body had to work harder to support his full weight and keep his feet off the ground, it strengthened his muscles in his arms and abs. These endurance exercises required skill and balance, and he went through a number of different positions to train his body and mind. He'd slept well the night before, so after returning home from his shift, Niko decided to work on muscle strengthening for a while.

It had been a rough day transporting officials to the church. Wyatt suffered a nasty gash on his leg while scaling a chain-link fence, so Niko had to use his Healer magic since Shepherd wasn't around to patch him up. Jobs like these were especially frustrating for Niko since he couldn't run or flash in public. He could follow energy trails with ease, but that didn't eliminate obstacles like poles or curbs. So on chases, he helped Wyatt navigate the streets and then aided Raven in loading them into the van.

His thoughts drifted to what Wyatt had revealed to him on the way home. Plato, the ghost who'd been following Niko around, had gone along with them. Wyatt said the specter had pulled a vanishing act after the first drop-off at the church. He suggested something spooked the ghost but thought it worth mentioning since it was the first time that Plato had left the mansion.

This news troubled Niko. Plato wasn't a religious man, so the church wouldn't have sent him running. The only reason he was probably hanging around Niko was to get information on the book Niko was hiding, and Niko had taken great care not to reveal its location. So why would Plato leave the mansion, knowing he might never find his way back?

Unless while out, he found someone to convey a message to Cyrus. Maybe it was nothing, but Niko couldn't stop thinking about all the possible scenarios. What if Plato had overheard information he thought might be useful as blackmail? What if there was a window somewhere in the mansion that was unlocked? What if he had somehow found that cursed book?

Niko heard the door open, and after a quick glimpse at the faded amethyst light, he lowered his legs and sat down. "Gem, what an unexpected surprise."

"It's dark in here."

He chuckled. "I've been saying that for years." When she didn't laugh, he rose to his feet. "Apologies. Stay where you are, and I'll get a lantern."

Sighted people were helpless in the dark. He strode past the exercise equipment to where they kept a spare lantern and matches.

After lighting the candle inside, he closed the tiny door and latched it. "Does this help?"

"It's spooky in here when the lights are out," she said, her light floating like a ribbon to the center of the room. It lacked its usual shimmer, and he sensed she was still processing her grief.

Niko lifted the lantern and walked across the room. When

he reached the thin mat, he set the lantern down at the edge and swept his hair out of his face. "Come join me."

She strolled over, and he couldn't quite read her emotions.

"Do you actually like working out?"

"Why do you enjoy swimming?"

"It calms me," she said decidedly. "It's peaceful, and I feel like I'm the only person in the world."

"Positive sensations come in many forms. Working out creates temporary pain, but the effect is the same. Your body is an instrument. When I strengthen my muscles and meditate, I feel focused and confident."

"I feel the same when I wear the right gemstones."

"The crystals you collect harness energy, and it's good to use them when your spirits are low. But don't rely on them as a source of strength."

Gem must have grabbed the climbing rope, because her energy swirled in a circle. Niko had learned to find joy in pain and persistence, but Gem relied on external things to make her feel good. Roller skating, gemstones, musicals, and even people.

"The body and the mind are connected," he explained. "When the body is relaxed and playful, so is the mind. But when you strengthen your body, you also strengthen your mind."

"I'm too little to be strong."

He gave a small grin and walked toward her, gripping the rope between his hands. "A pebble can cause an avalanche. My sensei taught me valuable lessons on survival that have nothing to do with acquiring money. So much emphasis is put upon power and wealth to sustain."

"Without money, we can't eat. That's why we have these jobs. We're going to be alive for a long time, Niko. A long, long, *long* time."

"Not unless you learn basic survival skills. Money won't protect you from all the dangers in our world. Did your Creator impart any wisdom on you?"

Gem rarely spoke of her life before Keystone. They all cohabitated without any stipulations that they share the details of their past. That knowledge wasn't required to determine who was competent or trustworthy. Those traits revealed themselves with each moment spent together, with each mission.

"She was the parent I never had," Gem answered, her light pulsing. "She taught me how to use my Mage gifts and how to survive as a woman. My training didn't require sit-ups."

It warmed Niko to know that she'd had a Creator who cared for her. There were far too many stories—including his own—that didn't have happy beginnings. "She sounds like a good woman."

"She was."

"I'm sorry for your loss."

"Someone... killed her. Was your sensei your Creator?"

"No. Sometimes there are better men out there than the ones who make us." Gem was inquisitive by nature, so he didn't want to invite questions by admitting that his Creator was also murdered. "Your Mage gifts as a Wielder and Blocker give you confidence, do they not?"

"Yes."

"You can find that same reward by testing your limits. Not just limits of your gifts, but also of your mind and your body. See how high you can climb the rope."

"Um, I don't know. Claude's the climber. Besides, Viktor hired me for my brains."

Still holding the rope, Niko circled around Gem. "Your playful spirit is unique, but I worry for the flower in the storm."

Gem was vivacious, but she lacked confidence when it came to her own abilities. Viktor often coddled her and discouraged her from using those powers. He wanted to utilize her Relic knowledge, and protecting that asset meant suppressing her true potential as a Mage. But Niko also understood how coveted her gifts were by nefarious men who would use her for their own gain. Most especially Stealers who could pull core light and gifts from another Mage. Stolen gifts would naturally disappear, as the body would eventually reject foreign light, but not if an Infuser permanently sealed it.

"Indulge me," Niko said, letting go of the rope. "See how far you can go."

She snickered. "Alas, probably two feet."

"Don't let your arms do all the work. Use your feet to anchor yourself, and when you feel like you can't go on, pull yourself up another few inches."

"What if I fall?"

"The mat doesn't hurt too much." When she made a peculiar snort, he chuckled to let her know he was teasing. "You won't fall. That only happens when you give up on yourself."

Gem drew in a deep breath and sighed. "Well, here goes nothing."

Niko watched as Gem's light moved upward. It was a beautiful sight to see the colors going vertical instead of their usual horizontal rhythms. He listened to her labored breath and her shoes scraping against the rope.

"Learn to control your breathing," he instructed her. "The most important thing you can do is breathe."

"You're funny," she said, her voice much higher.

"Don't look down."

"Now you tell me."

"If you think about falling, you'll never climb. Stay focused."

Suddenly, Niko was nervous for her. Gem occasionally came into the gym to goof around, but she didn't work out unless you counted roller skating. Her leg muscles were probably stronger.

"Rely on your feet if your arms get tired," he said, coaching her. "Find your balance."

"I'm scared," she squeaked. "I don't think I can get down. I'm so high up."

Niko gripped the rope to hold it steady. "You can do anything you set your mind to. Don't think about falling. Don't think about what happens afterward. The only thing standing between you and the top of that rope is self-doubt."

The rope jostled, but her light continued its ascent. After a few breathless seconds, Gem shouted, "I did it!"

She glowed, and he could read the happiness in the textures. "Well done!"

"It's beautiful up here. The room looks so different."

Niko reveled in the fact that he'd made her forget her pain, if only for a moment. Young immortals had much to learn about processing their grief. If they didn't have effective coping mechanisms to endure the tragedies that lay ahead, they would never survive. Creatures like Gem were rare, precious things that came along once every thousand years. You knew it the moment you were in their presence. They were special souls who had suffered and yet were destined for something greater in this world.

"I'm coming down now."

Niko heard her struggling, and the deep-blue flutters of light revealed she was anxious.

Gem shrieked, and the rope suddenly jerked.

"Take it slow," he said, his heart quickening. "Don't rush or slide down."

Now she sounded out of breath. "My arms are shaking."

The rope fluttered as Gem continued her descent. Niko kept a close watch on her light, measuring the distance between them. The thought of her falling suddenly terrified him. He wouldn't know which way she was landing to catch her. Gem wouldn't die, but she could snap her neck or break a bone.

When her shoes scraped against the rope, he reached out, bracing to catch her. But Gem held on, and she wasn't even halfway down yet.

Without hesitation, Niko gripped the rope and pulled himself up. "Hold on, Gem. I'm coming for you."

Niko didn't need to use his feet or legs to climb. His svelte muscles were conditioned, his mind focused.

When Gem's shoes touched his shoulders, he pulled himself higher and then used his feet to anchor himself. "Wrap your legs tightly around me. Don't let go of the rope until they're locked around my waist. Do you understand?"

Gem didn't say a word. He felt her slim legs struggle before they snaked around his waist.

"Maybe we can walk down the rope together," she said unconvincingly. "We'll both fall if you carry me."

"Let go," he said. "Trust me."

He took on her full body weight when she let go of the rope and clutched his shoulders, quickly wrapping her arms around his neck. After a brief period of adjustment, she hooked an arm beneath his right one and locked her hands in the front so she wouldn't choke him.

Niko began a slow descent. He had to be especially careful since he couldn't see the rope each time he let go to change his grip. Memories of his formative years after escaping Cyrus came flooding back, how a wise warrior had taken him under his wing. Climbing down a rope with a woman's weight on his back was nothing compared to the slabs of stone his teacher had placed on his back while he remained in a push-up position. Niko's training had been about endurance and testing his boundaries. Testing his willpower. Testing his breaking point.

The moments when you feel the most pain are the ones where you doubt yourself the most—when all your failures in the past rise to the surface.

Gem suddenly let go, and Niko reached out with one arm to catch her.

"It's okay," she said from just a few feet down. "You can let go."

Relieved, Niko dropped to the mat and lay beside her.

"That was so great," she said, still panting. "I make fun of Claude and his prowess, but he makes it look so easy. Blue can't match his speed, but she always reaches the top. I didn't realize how hard it really is."

He drew up his knees. "You should challenge yourself more often. You're capable of great things."

"I'm a petite woman who can't even open a jar of pickles. It was fun, but physical endurance is not my forte."

Her modesty was endearing. Even Wyatt had failed to reach the top of the rope.

"Fear holds people back more than anything else," Niko said, his heart rate finally slowing to a normal rhythm. He turned his head to face her. "You conquered a fear today, braveheart."

She glowed, her light radiating with contentment. "I miss Hooper."

"I know."

"He wasn't perfect, but he deserved a long life. Why are good people always the ones who suffer the most? Sometimes it seems like only the villains win."

Niko rolled onto his side and propped himself up on his elbow. "May I touch your face?"

The silence between them was palpable.

Niko knew her height and approximate weight, and he'd also felt how lean and strong her legs were. But what he was most curious about were the things others could see that he could not. Was her hair silky or coarse? Did she have any dimples? Were her cheeks plump or carved like stone? Did she have long lashes or were they sparse? He had never learned the shape of her face.

"Would that be all right?"

"Well... I, um... I don't know what you think you'll—"

"I just want to have a better sense of you."

Niko reached out and lowered his hand until he found her ear. Her soft hair slipped between his fingers. It wasn't straight like his but had stubborn waves. And it was longer than he imagined, just to her shoulders. When his fingertips brushed along her face, he froze. Her skin was dry and cracked like leather. At first, he couldn't believe it, but when his fingers reached the slope of her nose, that had an even stranger texture.

Gem rolled away and bubbled with laughter.

Niko sat up, overcome by a maelstrom of emotions. Was she scarred? Burned? The thought horrified him, and he felt anger rising for someone who would have inflicted that kind of pain upon such an innocent soul. He felt even worse for invading her space and taking the liberty of touching her scars.

"I'm sorry," she said, still giggling. "It was just the look on your face." Her laughter died in her throat, and he felt her hand on his knee. "Oh, Niko. I'm sorry. I should have warned you, but you moved in before I could say anything."

"Apologies," he said, bowing his head. "I didn't realize you were scarred."

Her light dimmed. "Now I feel just awful. I'm not scarred, Niko. I'm wearing a face mask. It's the kind you peel off after it dries." She sighed, and it sounded like she was touching the mask. "I feel like such a monster."

He smiled at his misunderstanding. "I'm not offended. Now I know why you sometimes smell like cucumbers."

"I don't always think before I speak. I didn't mean to be cruel. It's hard for me to tell when my jokes have crossed the line until it's too late."

Gem's jokes were often the highlight of his day. Even the pink shirt she'd placed in his closet had become a secret source of amusement for him. Niko had trouble relating to people, but since joining Keystone, the younger ones in the house reminded him of the simple pleasures in life that he took for granted. They had so much to teach him.

Gem nervously cleared her throat. "When I was a little girl, they used to keep me locked up in a room that kind of looked like the rooms in this mansion. I didn't have toys, but there were lots of books in the room. I taught myself how to read. I guess it's innate since my Relic gift is language. I used to tear out the blank pages of those books and write my secrets in another language. I didn't know at the time that was my gift; I just somehow knew how to speak in ways that others didn't understand. I used to write down all my wishes and dreams on these tiny pieces of paper. Then I'd fold them up just as small as I could and slip them between the cracks in the stone walls."

Niko thought of a room filled with nothing but her wishes and dreams pressed between stone.

"I don't know why I'm telling you all this," she said apologetically. "I guess I just want to explain why I'm not always good with recognizing when I've done something to make someone feel embarrassed or hurt. I wasn't around people who taught me that, so I just said whatever I wanted, albeit I said a lot of it in archaic languages they couldn't understand. But it was the only way to get out all that anger I had pent up inside. So if I ever say anything cruel, call me out on it. Okay? I should know these things at my age, but sometimes I struggle with how to interact with others. Please accept my apology, Niko. Please."

"Only if you accept that I too have a sense of humor. I'm not offended easily, and you don't have to walk on... pins and needles for me."

She giggled. "You mean eggshells."

Niko smiled. He spoke many languages but found English one of the most challenging. From simple words that made no sense to where to put the emphasis—it had all been a struggle to learn in the beginning. And just when he felt he had finally grasped it, ever-changing slang and colloquialisms would frustrate him. It was just one reason why Gem's mind fascinated him. Language to her was like breathing.

He watched her light rise as she stood up and moved around.

"Do you think the power will ever come back on?" she asked.

"Yes."

"I hope it's soon. All this darkness gives me the heebie-jeebies. When I was doing my last patrol of the property, I kept thinking about what would happen if the whole city just went savage. If the bad ones take over Cognito, what's to stop them from doing the same everywhere else? I don't like hiding from humans either, but they wouldn't understand what we are. There are more of them than there are of us, and they have all those bombs. They're the reason why we all went back into hiding in the first place. I'm not sure if I'm more afraid of the outlaws in our world or the human scientists who would dissect us like frogs. They'd use us to find some way to transfer our immortality or gifts to their own DNA."

Niko rose fluidly to his feet. "You have been through so much, and it's late. Perhaps we shouldn't worry about an unknown future and focus on the troubles at hand."

There was a subtle lilt in her voice. "Like Patrick's boy. He's a mischievous little guy. Escaped from Kira twice, and it took forever to find him. He likes exploring. I think we need to put a bell around his neck."

Niko tossed back his head and laughed.

"I have to go peel my face off now."

Niko laughed even harder, tears welling in his eyes.

"Thanks for making me feel better," she said in earnest.

He settled down and wiped his wet lashes. "Would you like me to accompany you on your next security check?"

She hooked her arm in his, leading him toward the door. "By the time I finish washing my face, you'll probably be zonked out. Get some rest. You've had a busy day. I'll protect the castle."

"As you wish, little flower. As you wish."

Chapter 16

I SPED AROUND THE CORNER, HOPING to dodge the anarchy unfolding between two Chitahs and a Mage outside a bakery. I kept my foot on the gas so I wouldn't look as if I were rubbernecking. After leaving Mr. Bane's mansion, I unzipped my jacket and put all the kid's clothes in the passenger seat. Due to the late hour, I had concerns that the Overlord wouldn't accept visitors. There was also the strong possibility that he'd left the city shortly after the outage occurred.

Claude had given me three possible addresses, so I started with the closest. The Overlord resided in a historical building in the busiest section of town. The architecture was reminiscent of a castle, with pointed peaks at the top of the seventh floor.

Chitahs were lined up outside the entire building like soldiers standing guard. They were armed with swords and unforgiving expressions. And every single one of them eyeballed my car as I slowly drove past in search of a place to park.

"Here goes nothing," I said, parking in front of the main doors.

When I got out, four Chitahs rushed me.

"Hold on," I said, my hands in the air. "I'm here on business."

One man craned his neck down, his four canines on full display. "What's your Breed?" His nose twitched, and his voice sounded villainous.

"I'm a Mage."

"And what business do you have with the Overlord, *Mage?*"

Who does this guy think he is, flashing his fangs at me?

I slammed the car door and lifted my chin at him. "That's

above your pay grade. Instead of breathing all over me, why don't you pop a breath mint in your mouth and tell your boss that Raven Black is here to talk about important business. Tell him we met at Patrick Bane's party."

Another guard shook his head at the one speaking to me.

I backed up a step and gazed at the dark windows above. "I need to speak to the Overlord!"

The Chitah with the foul breath opened my car door and gestured for me to get in and go back where I came from.

So I slammed it.

"It's an emergency! My name is Raven!" I flashed to the rear of the car and climbed onto the roof. Waving my arms, I shouted, "It's a matter of life and death! Please let him—"

My words were cut off when some asshole grabbed my ankle and tried to jerk me off the car. I fell to my knees and kicked him in the head. "You asshole. You just made me dent the car."

I was used to Chitahs being passive with women, but these guys weren't taking shit from anyone when it came to protecting their leader.

"Let her go," a voice boomed.

Every guard stepped back and bowed his head.

"Send her in."

I slid off the car and eyed the entrance. A figure was standing in the shadowy space of the revolving door, and I approached cautiously.

"Watch her car," he commanded.

A guard bowed. "Yes, Sire."

When I reached the dark-haired man, I recognized him. "Thanks, your, uh… Overlordship."

He chuckled softly as we entered the building. "You can call me Quaid."

Inside, a number of guards were standing at key locations— entrances to rooms, hallways, and elevators. Quaid led me across the carpeted lobby, lit by a few sparse candles, to a set of wooden doors with gold handles. One of the guards opened it for us as we entered the empty room.

"Would you like a drink?" He walked up to a massive liquor cabinet and turned over two glasses.

I looked at the fire roaring in the fireplace. "Tequila, if you have any."

"I don't make cocktails."

"A shot glass is fine. Or the entire bottle. Either way. I like the burn, so don't worry about salt or anything like that. I'm sure you buy the quality stuff anyway." When I heard myself rambling, I sat down in a plush chair by the hearth. If this place had once been a hotel, this must have been one of those rooms where men came to smoke cigars and brag about their investments and properties.

Quaid handed me a glass of tequila with a lime wedge. "I put club soda in there since you're driving."

"It hardly matters these days with everything going on outside. Thanks." The drink was weak, but I still refrained from gulping it down in one go.

Quaid sat in front of me and crossed his long legs. Thankfully, he wasn't wearing pajamas, or this might have been incredibly awkward. Just dark slacks and a grey cotton sweater. He sipped his drink and set the glass on the flat armrest of his chair. "To what do I owe this honor?"

"Maybe someone higher up has already talked to you about this, or maybe I'm not even supposed to be here. But we're in danger of losing control of the city."

He gave a noncommittal shrug. "Until power is restored, there isn't much we can do."

After glancing at the closed doors, I lowered my voice. "You're the Overlord. I'm guessing you might be aware that there are certain... emergency evacuations underway? Because of your high-ranking position, I'm just guessing that you might be privy to things that others aren't."

He nodded. "I am."

"Then you're aware that the Regulators are supposed to oversee these evacuations. There's something else going on that I can't talk about, and the blackout makes the situation even more urgent. The higher authority is taking precautionary measures to ensure everyone's safety, but they hired outsiders like me to do the job. Why? Because the Regulators decided to take a sick day."

Quaid drew in a deep breath and uncrossed his legs. "That's not entirely true. The city is divided, and many Regulators are receiving death threats for guarding their mortal enemies. These are family men."

"So are the officials. Well… probably. That doesn't really matter. What do you think will happen to this city if someone gets to the officials? Leadership is the only thing keeping order, because it instills fear in outlaws. Believe me, this is something I know a lot about. Criminals won't stop what they're doing, but they still act within the parameters of the law. They have to limit their crimes—plot and plan—because they know that someone might turn them in or blackmail them. Without leaders, this city will fall like dominoes."

Quaid sipped his drink, his eyes pensive.

"You have a lot of influence," I continued. "People follow the higher authority because they have to, but Chitahs follow you because they want to. We have a short amount of time to complete this job. The longer it takes, the greater the risk to the whole operation." I downed the rest of my drink and set the glass on the armrest. "I'm here to ask you to order the Regulators back to their posts. We can't do anything about the ones who aren't Chitah, but we don't need every single body. We just need enough familiar faces to pull this thing off. Officials are running from us."

Quaid laced his fingers and slowly rubbed his thumbs together. "It's a difficult task, asking a man to walk away from protecting his family. Chitahs hold their family above all else."

"Their sacrifice is for the greater good. We're supposed to be done by morning, but some of the other teams are doing worse than we are. Especially the ones trying to negotiate with the Vamps. I get that this puts you in a bad position, but maybe you can tell them it's just until tomorrow morning. That's our deadline. That shouldn't pose any unnecessary risk to their families. No one will even know that they're gone."

"Will this evacuation end if the power returns?"

I shrugged. "I don't know. Right now, nobody's security systems work. Personal guards are vanishing, and phones are unreliable. You've got a nice view from this building. I'm sure you've seen what's going on. People are losing their minds out there. Humans are looting, but we've got bigger problems in the Breed district. Lions roaming the streets, businesses burning, juicers on a binge, and some crazy Vamp running around naked on Fourteenth Street. If we don't protect the leaders who keep everyone in line, this place is going to become a zoo."

A smile touched his lips. "You're a tenacious woman."

"If you command the Chitahs working as Regulators to help us evacuate, you'll have a favor in your pocket from me."

Quaid tilted his head to one side. "You can keep the favor if you promise me this: continue fighting battles you believe in. Strength of character isn't a common trait in young Learners such as yourself. I'll be curious to look you up in five hundred years and see where you are."

"Probably flipping burgers if I get fired for this."

Quaid smiled warmly and rose to his feet. "You have nothing to worry about, female. I know Viktor Kazan, and I'm certain he'll recognize your good intentions for what they are."

"Thanks again." I stood up and worried my lip. "I'm not sure how to organize this—the Regulators won't know who we've already picked up."

"I'll have two men follow you discreetly and offer assistance. After you give them a brief update, they'll contact one of my associates to coordinate with those who have given us their commitment to help."

The Overlord wasn't such a bad guy, for all the money and power he had. Then again, that cynical part of me couldn't help but wonder why he was so easy to convince.

"Can I trust you?" I inquired and almost instantly regretted the question. Maybe it was the dark rings that pulsed in his eyes, or maybe it was the fact I might insult him enough to rescind his offer.

He inclined his head. "On my word as a Chitah. Good night, Raven. Leave now before your foot gets trapped in your mouth."

I smiled sheepishly. That was what I did best.

During the drive back to Sacred Heart, I spied a car following me with their headlights off. The Overlord had said two Regulators would follow me back, but I was also paranoid about someone tailing me who wasn't supposed to. Trusting a man I didn't know proved difficult.

When I pulled up to the side of the church, the other car parked beneath a large tree. After I scooped up the clothes in the passenger seat, I noticed Christian lingering by the door. He must have heard me drive up. What a relief. If these guys tailing me hadn't been sent by the Overlord, at least I'd have backup.

I kicked the door shut with my foot and turned to face the men. Well, well. If it wasn't Merry and his quiet friend. They were out of uniform but still armed with katanas. I wondered how those two got paired up considering how opposite they were in looks and personality. Merry looked like a catalogue model and Weather his bodyguard.

Merry bent down, collected a shirt that had fallen to the ground, and placed it back in my arms. "We meet again."

"You two," I said. What a strange coincidence.

Merry glanced at Weather. "We're the primary investigators on the murder cases. The Overlord knows we've met, so perhaps he thought you would trust us more than a stranger."

I raised an eyebrow. "You divulge personal information relating to cases to a third party?"

"I'd hardly call the Overlord a third party. He's the only one outside of the higher authority who's aware, and we weren't the ones to give him that information. That would be our boss."

"You were at each crime scene?"

"Yes. We collected evidence and handled the cleanup as

discreetly as possible. Unfortunately, that wasn't feasible at Mr. Bane's party."

I shifted my weight to my other leg. "Any news?"

"Another murder today. HALO sent word that they came across a body."

"Exactly who did they tell? We're in the middle of transporting everyone."

"The Overlord. A Chitah runs HALO, from what I understand, and because the victim was a Mage, he wanted to make sure the Overlord was aware. I suppose he was afraid the deed might be pinned on his group, so he was covering all bases."

"Who was the victim?"

"We haven't been able to investigate."

"Because you and all the other Regulators bailed? Nice move, by the way. You've put this entire operation in jeopardy."

Weather's eyes narrowed, and he widened his stance. "Chitahs are receiving death threats. When someone threatens your family, you don't have time to decide if it's a hoax or not."

I looked between them. "Why would anyone do that?"

Merry's eyebrows popped up in surprise. "There isn't a Mage in this country who wouldn't want to see our population diminish."

"And that'll happen for sure if we don't have any leaders running this place."

I stalked off and approached Shepherd's Jeep. After leaving the kid's clothes in the driver's seat, I slammed the door and breezed by Christian on my way inside. "We need to talk."

"What are those shitebags doing here?"

"That's what we have to talk about. I went to see the Overlord, and—"

"You did what?" Christian stepped back, eyes fierce.

"Unwad your panties and listen. Daylight is coming soon, and there's no way we're going to get everyone here in time. Not without someone spotting one of our vans and following us. I don't know what the other teams are thinking, but they're probably feeling the same way—that we've failed. We've got too many runners, and the main reason is they're not expecting *us*. They're expecting *Regulators*."

Merry and Weather walked in just then, but I ignored them.

"I asked him to order those men back to work. I don't care if they stick around afterward, but we also need someone to collect these officials so we can lock down the church."

Christian folded his arms. "And he just said yes. No favors."

"I offered him one, but he didn't take it. Well, not really. He just gave me some advice."

"Not to visit Chitahs after midnight?"

"He's not a gremlin. Look, we need to get Merry and Weather up to speed. They'll be the liaison between the Regulators and us. I'll let Viktor know as soon as possible so he can reach out to the other teams. These two will coordinate between all the groups and assign Regulators according to how many more pickups there are. Can we fight about this later? We don't have time to waste."

He dipped his chin and lowered his voice. "I'll take a rain check on that quarrel." After a beat, he snapped his fingers. "You two, come with me."

Merry and Weather followed Christian down the dark hall. I went in the other direction and cut straight to the main chapel. This time, it was empty. The priest must have been downstairs, handling demands from his unexpected guests. Christian said that each official had his own room and that the living quarters were quite nice for being small. As much as I wanted to go down and check out their accommodations, it probably wasn't a good idea considering I'd manhandled some and stabbed others of them.

I sat down in the front pew and savored the silence. It wasn't even the silence so much as an overwhelming sense of peace.

"May I sit?"

I jumped. The priest had given me a start. "Hi, Father."

He sat next to me, one arm resting on the bench, his head propped in his hand. "You can call me Tony."

I crossed my legs. "Don't you have rules about that?"

"I have immortal beings sleeping beneath my feet. I'd say I'm fairly progressive. Besides, I can tell it makes you uncomfortable."

"I didn't grow up going to church."

"There's no sin in that. We all have our own path to God."

"Maybe God doesn't want everyone showing up at his house."

He tipped his head. "Is there a question you want to ask?"

I looked down at my black nail polish and picked at it. "Do you think we're evil?"

"Breed?"

I glanced up at the cross. "I mean… where do we fit in? Are we the demons you talk about in your sermons?"

He pursed his lips and sighed. "God doesn't create evil. Man is his own demon. I can't deny what I see with my own eyes, and if God created Breed, I have to believe in a divine purpose."

"What if our purpose is to give you an enemy?"

"The journey to understanding begins with a leap of faith. I'm willing to extend a hand of friendship. I grew up reading about monsters, just as you did."

"But I chose to become one."

He put his hand over mine and leaned forward. "I can see you're doing some soul searching, but there aren't easy answers for the most difficult questions. We're all in the dark, searching for the light. But maybe we should stop looking and start listening." Father Martin stood up and snorted like a man with allergy problems.

I struggled to contain my laughter as it reverberated off the walls. "Thanks for the chat, Tony. You would have made a good father for real."

A smile lit up his face. "You think? I don't know if I could have survived the diaper stage," he said, strolling away.

I got up to stretch my legs and walked to the water fountain in the back. When I looked for a button to push, I realized it was holy water. What did people do? Wash their hands in there? If it really cleansed the soul, I probably needed to bathe in it.

Christian entered through the wooden doors in the rear and spied me leaning against the wall. I flicked water in his face, and he gave me a bemused look.

"Just checking," I quipped. "Where are the Regulators?"

"The two Tweedles are on the phone with Viktor. Did you let him in on your plan?"

"No. I'll worry about the repercussions later. I figured if anyone could get those guys back to work, it was their leader. Not their boss, but their Lord."

"Lords govern territories. You went to the Almighty." The way Christian folded his arms, I could tell he was peeved that I hadn't filled him in on my intentions.

I shrugged tiredly. "We were running out of time, and since I recently talked to the Overlord and got along with him, I thought I might be able to persuade him to help. We've literally got just hours to finish the job. You haven't been on the front lines, so you don't know what we had to deal with. How many of those officials do you think took one look at Shepherd and fled? I know Viktor said to detain them by any means, but I'm pretty sure we can kiss our careers goodbye if Claude bites someone." I closed my eyes. "None of us want to walk out of this a failure."

Christian gripped my jacket and led me forward. "Follow me."

Candles flickered as we walked past them. He lifted a tall one encased in glass and headed toward the hall to the left of the altar. When we reached the end, Christian turned right and opened the second door.

"He wouldn't let us have the sacristy or his personal office. There's another room where they hold classes, but it's not carpeted."

I stared down at the maroon carpet. "What is this place?"

He set the candle on a small desk, the light reflecting off robes hanging on a rack and a large armoire. "It's the vestry. The priest sleeps in the rectory—that small building on the right side of the church." Christian reached inside a wardrobe closet. "But I found out he likes to secretly take naps in here."

I watched Christian unfold a small cot and place it in the left-hand corner. He dragged a red chair beside it and then reached for one of the robes.

"No, don't mess with those," I said. "I have two pairs of pants on, and I'll just use my jacket for a pillow."

I unzipped my jacket and threw it onto the cot. Then I toed off my sneakers and sat down.

"Stay here," he said, briskly leaving the room.

I kept my socks on since the room was frigid. Luckily there weren't any windows. The small desk in front of me was pristinely kept, and a small bookshelf behind it contained leather-bound books, some with gold lettering on the spine. The room looked like storage for robes and books. I stared at the opposite wall and wondered what Father Martin used the sink for. Mounted on the wall above it hung a large wooden cross.

I tucked my hands beneath my armpits to warm them and leaned forward. How can anyone believe in a benevolent God when evil men like Fletcher exist? Men who get a thrill from using people to satisfy their own needs. Guys like Hooper die, and his killers get away with murder. How is that a fair world?

And where exactly did I fall in the spectrum?

Christian returned and closed the door behind him. He handed me a tall thermos before taking a seat in the chair.

I wrapped my hands around the tumbler and drew in a deep breath. "Where did you get coffee?"

"Every man has his secrets."

"Thanks." After sliding the tab, I took a few sips to warm my belly.

Christian casually crossed his legs and ran his hand through his disheveled hair. "HALO dropped off two more men while you were out. They had three others who were assigned to a different location. I really wish we'd been tagged with another group."

I picked up on the annoyed look on his face and the way he scratched his beard as if it were the enemy. "Wanna share?"

"I have a history with one of them."

"Did you piss him off?"

Christian answered with an arch of his brow. "I don't think he'll ever really forgive me, and nor should he."

"Sleep with his woman?"

"Jaysus, no. Sometimes a man needs to leave his past behind and start over, but it's not easy to do when you keep running into the same people who remind you of the mistakes you made. That's why a lot of us have traveled over the years, to have a fresh start."

I drew my knees up and tucked the thermos between my chest and my thighs. "I know what you mean. I never made any besties in the immortal world, but I sure made a lot of enemies. It makes the city feel smaller and smaller."

"Trust me, friends make it worse. They place their trust in you, and if you let them down or lie—no matter how good your reason—they won't forgive you. And even if they do, they won't forget."

"But you've got new friends now."

"I'd hardly call what we have friendship. Shepherd's the only one who's given me a fair shot. Everyone else tolerates me, but they don't necessarily trust me. Especially Blue. And probably you, for that matter. You didn't trust me from day one, and I sometimes wonder if you still question my motives."

I tilted my thermos, steam escaping. "I question my own motives more than I question yours, so don't flatter yourself."

After a few more sips of coffee, I found myself getting sleepy instead of waking up. Apparently, my body was ignoring the presence of caffeine, probably due to all the flashing I'd done earlier that day.

"Do you need to be somewhere?" I murmured, my eyelids dropping like anchors.

"I can hear everything from in here," he said, his voice hushed. Christian sounded far away, as if he were standing at the end of a long tunnel.

Memories of the day swirled around like a kaleidoscope of images. Running down streets, scaling fences, loading people into the van, reassuring frightened officials. The people downstairs were safe because of me, and that was a good feeling. I was used to bringing down criminals, but saving lives brought its own special reward.

I shivered, my eyes still closed. "Turn on the heater."

Someone moved me, and I opened my eyes. "What are you doing?"

Christian held me on his lap as he sat down on the cot. "There's no heater, lass. It's warmer this way. Now close your eyes and get some rest."

"But you don't get cold," I muttered sleepily, not understanding his intent was to warm *me*.

My ears latched onto the sound of his beating heart, and it lulled me with its persistent rhythm. Christian was warm-blooded, and since his arms were intimate and inviting, I stopped dissecting my feelings about it and nuzzled against his chest. I could rationalize lust and sex but not so much all the other stuff that crept up from time to time. Like the irrational belief that Christian was my protector. Not just as a partner, but something more. Something I couldn't put my finger on.

In a nebulous fog, I remembered the fire I'd survived as a child. Faces in the streets watched but never helped. I could still recall the visceral fear in my bones as the smoke thickened and the heat intensified. I was a little girl who knew she was about to die.

And then I remembered the stranger who appeared out of nowhere and rescued me. Who scooped me up in his arms and shielded me from the flames. How could he have heard me? Where did he go afterward? I recollected him passing me off to someone else, and sometimes it seemed possible to glimpse his face in my dreams. I spent a lot of time measuring the meaning of my life because of that stranger. Why had he risked his life for mine? Why had he left without ever coming back? Did he ever think about me? Did he expect me to accomplish great things because of the sacrifice he'd made?

A dull pain lanced through my temple, and I let go to the serenity and rocking tide of sleep.

Chapter 17

THE NEXT MORNING, I WOKE up alone. Christian had draped a thin white robe over my legs. I remembered falling asleep in his arms, and I wondered what that must have looked like to an observer. A Vampire dressed as a priest, rocking a woman to sleep in his lap. I'd always assumed men felt emasculated by tender affections since most steered away from them in public. The men in my past were nothing like Christian, so I had no one to compare him to.

After I located the bathroom and washed up, I went to the kitchen. There were two camping lanterns on the table, but I decided not to use up their batteries since the indirect light from the hall was good enough to see by. The smell of breakfast sausages hung in the air. Since the kettle on the gas stove still had hot water in it, I opened up the giant can of instant coffee and put three scoops in my cup before adding water. Then I sat down to gather my thoughts. At least my neck didn't hurt anymore.

Instead of thinking about Christian, I wondered what my father was doing. Was he taking care of himself? Had the blackout forced him to shut down the garage? I hadn't made any clandestine trips out to his house in a long time, especially not with Fletcher still on the loose. I wanted to call him to see if he was okay.

But I couldn't, because he believed I was dead.

After I finished my coffee, I went out in the hall and followed the sound of a commotion coming from one of the rooms. I stopped at an open door and looked inside.

Hunched over on his knees, Shepherd had his back to the door.

His movements were hurried as Claude handed him something from a medical bag.

"What's going on?" I walked around them and saw Blue laid out on the floor. Her coveralls were unzipped, her shirt cut open down the center. Blood pooled around a small wound in her belly. "What can I do to help?"

Shepherd jerked his chin at a bloody towel beside her. "Press that over the wound."

I stanched the bleeding while Shepherd held up a vial and extracted the contents into a syringe. "What happened? I thought the Regulators were supposed to help."

"They did," Claude said, his shirt stained with blood. "But not before this happened."

"Did an official stab her?"

"No. We were chasing down a runner. I sprinted after them, and Blue joined the pursuit. She took another route to cut him off since it looked like he was heading for the subway. I caught the male and slugged him, but Blue never showed. I thought maybe she got lost, but I couldn't go searching since I had to wait for Shepherd to find me and collect the cargo. When I picked up her scent, it led me to a dead end. She was unconscious and alone."

"Probably juicers," I said. "She's lucky she's still alive. It's easy to drink too much light from someone who isn't a Mage."

Claude pinched the bridge of his nose, his eyes fixed on the blood. "It was dark, so I didn't see the blood at first. She didn't have her axe, but by the marks on her knuckles, she put up a good fight."

Blue had a serene look, her sable hair spread across the cheap carpet like an angel. Her beauty was always overshadowed by her tough personality, and it was the first time I'd really seen her shell without the contents. She didn't even look like herself.

I jerked my chin at the syringe. "What is that?"

Shepherd flicked it and pushed air bubbles out with the plunger. "Something to wake her ass up."

"She should have shifted."

He shoved her sleeve up and stuck her with the needle. "Blue never runs from a fight."

Seconds after he pushed the plunger, her blue eyes widened, and she gasped.

Shepherd gripped her chin and made her look at him. "Shift!"

I fell back when Blue morphed into a peregrine falcon. She flapped her impressive wings languidly before shifting back to human form. On her knees, Blue lowered her hands and touched the unsealed wound on her belly. Blood no longer seeped from the wound, but it looked grotesque.

Claude leaned in. "Once more, female. You're almost healed."

"So tired," she whispered.

Yep. Someone had juiced her. Light from a non-Mage was weak, but it didn't stop juicers from stealing it.

When she shifted back to a falcon, Shepherd hurled the syringe. It skittered across the floor and hit the wall. He sat back, one leg bent at the knee. Sweat glistened on his forehead as he panted. "Fucking hell. Only alphas can pull another Shifter from their sleep. I was lucky I had that on me."

"Why didn't you give her that at the scene?" I asked.

He wiped his forehead. "I didn't know she was cut. She had a big fucking knot on the back of her head, and we just assumed someone had knocked her out. It wasn't until halfway home that Claude scented something wasn't right. It was too dark to see the blood on her coveralls."

"Her chemistry changed," Claude said.

Blue's falcon flapped its wings, but the only place to perch was on the back of a chair. Normally Blue could remember her entire shift, but I had a feeling she was resting in there.

I stood up, the outside light flooding the room from a window in the hall. "Is the power still out?"

Shepherd gathered up the bloody towel, syringe, and clothes before tossing them in the tiny wastebasket. "Yep."

"What's it like out there?"

"A clusterfuck." He cracked his knuckles and then gingerly lifted his black bag. "I'm going home. You want a lift?"

"No, I think I better stay," I said. "Are Wyatt and Niko here yet?"

"No need. The Regulators helped us finish the list."

My eyebrows nearly touched my hairline. "So fast? What about the other teams?"

Claude stood up and stretched his long arms. "I wouldn't be surprised if they're almost done. Enough Regulators showed up that we could have assigned one to each name on the list." He clapped my shoulder. "Good thinking, Raven. I would have never been ballsy enough to go to the Overlord. Tell me, why is it you didn't go to the Mageri instead?"

I shrugged. "Too much red tape. And there are more Chitah Regulators than Mage. It was a numbers game. What does Viktor want us to do now?"

"Guard the church," Shepherd said gruffly.

I clutched his wrist as he turned. "Wait. I forgot to mention I went to Patrick's house. I got the kid's clothes and put them in your Jeep."

Shepherd gripped my wrist in return and gave me a peculiar stare. "What else happened?"

I wrenched my hand away when I realized he was reading my emotions. "*Don't* do that."

"Can't help it."

"Patrick wasn't there."

"But?"

"Someone else was. I think one of his guards. Nothing to report," I said, deciding Shepherd didn't need to get involved. "If you come back, bring a change of clothes for Blue. It's probably a good idea if she's not running around naked in a church."

Claude crossed the room to a metal folding chair and sat down, the legs squeaking beneath his weight. His blond curls were flat at the top where he must have been wearing a hat. "I'll stay in here in case she shifts back. Close the door on your way out. I don't want her attacking the priest."

"If she does, there's a confessional just around the corner," I said, making a brisk exit into the hall.

I walked a few paces and leaned against the wall, watching Shepherd head to the side exit. I breathed a sigh of relief knowing we'd transported every single name on our list. The power outage and continued attacks were causing a firestorm out there. In my old life, I would have been one of those troublemakers. I smiled wistfully at the idea of taking down thugs on every corner without anyone to stop me.

In fact, with all the officials accounted for, what was stopping me?

"Raven, I've been looking for you."

Sucked out of my fantasy, I turned my head to the blond male heading my way. "And why would that be, Merry?"

"I have a murder to investigate, and I'd like you to accompany me."

Merry looked strange out of uniform. He had on tan winter boots with sherpa lining on the cuffs, and a cable-knit sweater in the same shade. Less like a dangerous guard and more like a catalogue model, ready to hit the Aspen slopes after making maple pancakes.

I watched him latch a leather belt and scabbard around his waist. "What have you been doing all night?"

"Guarding the church," he said, fastening the belt. "My men made several loops before dropping the targets off, just to make sure no one followed them back to the church. Did your team do the same?"

I folded my arms. "We did the best we could under short notice. Maybe you should have given us the procedure manual before you abandoned your duties."

A smile touched his lips, and he pulled a knit hat over his head. This one had thick weaves, like something his grandma knitted. "Would you like to accompany me?"

"Is it another official?"

"Yes." He glanced down at my feet. "Where are your shoes?"

I turned toward the room where I'd slept and went to retrieve them.

Merry followed and leaned against the doorjamb while I sat

on the cot and tied the laces on my sneakers. He folded his arms and tipped his chin. "How much loyalty do you have to the higher authority?"

"Was there an oath I missed?"

Merry tapped his chin. "Let me rephrase that. Do you believe in what they do?"

Deciding not to answer him, I threw on my jacket and stood up. Something about his question gave me the chills. Or maybe it was the way his nose kept twitching. I didn't like people reading my emotions, so I thought about my father just to throw him off. "Are we the only ones going?"

"No. My partner will ride along."

"Then I should get mine."

"No need." Merry stepped away from the doorway. "We've already spoken, and he's unable to leave the premises. Your boss ordered him to stay."

I zipped up my jacket and fished my fingerless gloves out of the pockets. "We drive in separate cars. I'll follow."

He tilted his head to the side. "You don't trust me."

"Nope. But if it makes you feel better, I don't trust anyone. Unless you want to give me your word as a Chitah that you don't plan to kill me."

Merry never gave me his word.

As we left the church, I ascertained there were Regulators standing at key locations inside the building. Outside, I spotted two dressed in street clothes. One was sitting in his car, and the other stood by a stop sign, smoking a cigarette. When I asked Merry about it, he said the Regulators weren't in uniform. It would call attention to them, so they had to be discreet. Until they received further orders, all the assigned churches were under their protection. Our location afforded ideal cover, allowing his men to spread out and cover more ground.

I followed their black SUV, mist coating the windshield of

Claude's Porsche. The dents on the hood stood out in the light of day, and that was coming out of my next paycheck.

Or three.

Would it kill him to drive a cheaper car?

Merry parked in front of a charming house with a wrought iron fence all around it. A cobblestone pathway led to the front, but first you had to get past the two German shepherds that were barking their heads off.

Weather squatted in front of the bars and showed the dogs his fangs, which incited them to bark more ferociously. One bounced back and forth in front of the gate, but he didn't seem as aggressive.

"Who called this in?" I asked, approaching the front door.

"No one," Merry said. "One of the teams discovered the body last night. They left the scene untouched before relaying the information." He stared down at the dog guarding the gate. "This will be a problem."

I reached for the gate and wrenched it open. "Hi, sweeties! Are you hungry? Do you want a cookie?"

The dog cocked his head, ears perking up. I casually strolled toward the house, the other dog still barking at Weather.

"Come on," I said. "They can smell fear."

Dogs always liked me. I wasn't sure if that applied across the board, but when I was growing up, we always had stray dogs that looked like huskies or wolves running around. Some left me alone, but others were friendly. Most animals sensed Breed, so the key was showing them you weren't a threat. No eye contact, pay attention to body language, and go about your business. Tail position also indicated their mood. The one barking at Weather held his high, but this fluffy guy had a low, swinging tail and a smile on his face.

When I reached the door, I said, "Let's go find you a cookie."

Clearly, he knew exactly what that word meant, because he darted inside excitedly, his toenails clicking against the wood floor. I followed him to the kitchen. Noticing the bowls were empty, I filled them with the bag of kibble sitting in a pantry closet. The dog treats were in a drawer, which he happily barked at to show me. I gave him plenty, tossing a few on the tile before heading back outside.

I whistled a few times and tossed the rest onto the grass. The second dog snapped his gaze at me and decided eating was more important than harassing Weather.

"Put your fangs back in," I called out. "Either come inside now, or stay out there."

Weather flashed me a thorny look before turning his back to the gate.

"Where did you learn to do that?" Merry asked.

I shrugged. "If a stranger came to your house, would you be more threatened by the one offering food or the one showing you his weapons? I'm really surprised you guys aren't better with animals given you got all those catlike instincts."

He chuckled. "Cats and dogs, you know?"

"Right."

We went in search of a body. The house was small in comparison to some of the other officials we'd visited. It felt more like a quaint English cottage. A stone fireplace to the left, two couches facing each other. No leather or big sectionals, but dainty with floral patterns. Wood beams ran along the ceiling, the same type of wood as the bookshelf and coffee table. Merry checked a door beneath a staircase on the right as I ventured up.

The sound of the dog crunching on kibble faded as I reached the top landing. I'd heard stories about pets devouring deceased owners within hours, and the thought of finding *that* revolted me.

The upstairs was just as small as the downstairs. Maybe smaller since walls closed it off. There was an empty bathroom to my immediate right. Straight ahead, a door, and another to the left. I chose the one in front of me and flipped on the nonfunctioning light out of habit. It smelled like old roses and cedar. The drapes weren't blackout curtains, so I could see just fine. The white bedspread had patterns woven in and knotted fringe along the edges. The room was as neat as a pin, including the dresser. Personal effects such as hairpins, old-fashioned perfume bottles, and a silver hairbrush each had their own place. There wasn't even dust on the mirror. Someone took pride in this place and loved it.

I stepped out of the room and approached the other door. It was slightly ajar, and the hinges creaked when I swung it open. Merry's footfalls sounded from the staircase as I entered the bedroom. The curtains were drawn open, and on the bed to the right, a woman lay motionless beneath the covers, her eyes closed.

For a moment, I wondered if she might be sleeping. She looked so peaceful, and I'd never seen a dead person look that alive. That thought quickly faded when I noticed the red line across her neck where her head was severed. Drops of blood puddled on the floor; undoubtedly, most of it had pooled into the mattress.

Merry entered the room and drew in a deep breath. "It's been too long, and other scents are mingled here."

I stepped back to give him room. "Probably the other team. At least she didn't know what hit her."

"Interesting," Merry said.

"What?"

"The dogs are still alive."

I looked out the window at the foot of the bed. Aside from the porch, most of the yard was visible. The second dog was still barking at Weather, who had moved closer to the curb. Because of the outage, people were probably ignoring things like dogs barking and car alarms since it was happening with greater frequency. I sat down in a green chair with gold trim, a dozen scenarios running through my head.

Merry pinched his nose. "She's been deceased for two days."

"How can you tell?"

"The smell. And the body begins to change with time. Bulging eyes, discoloration, maggots, their tongue—"

"Okay, I get it."

Without heat, the temperature inside was as cold as outside. Perhaps cold enough to have preserved the body since I didn't smell anything as strong as what Merry did. The fireplace in the corner had an open flue, the air whistling against the chimney pipe.

"Whoever did this came at night," I said. "And he snuck into the house. The dogs would have woken her up if he'd kicked in the front door." I crossed my legs and drummed my fingers on the armrests. "Do you think she died around Valentine's Day?"

"Likely."

I sprang up from my seat and turned down the covers. That was when a stronger smell hit me, and I covered my mouth and nose.

Merry folded his arms, watching me peel the bloody sheet back.

"Scratch the intruder theory," I said. "She had a guest."

"How do you know that?"

I pointed at the negligee. "Single women don't wear sheer black with no panties in winter, not unless someone else is there to appreciate it. Do you think we can find out if she had any regular lovers?"

"My sources say no."

Nauseated, I flipped the sheet and blanket up to her neck. When I was human, I'd always imagined myself dying in my sleep. Suddenly it had lost its appeal.

Merry pulled off his hat and stuffed it into his coat pocket. His messy hair covered half his face, making it difficult to see his expression. "Valentine's Day is an easy holiday for a woman to take a new lover."

"Maybe we need to drill it down," I suggested. "Do you remember seeing her at Patrick's party? It was the day before Valentine's, but that would fall within the timeline of her death. It's possible she met someone and invited him back to her place."

He pinched his bottom lip and eyed me. "My understanding is that every Mage on the panel was present. So we can assume she was there."

"She—an official of the higher authority—let an armed man inside her house. That's a huge show of trust." I steered out the door and jogged down the stairs.

"Where are you going?" he shouted.

"To check something out!"

I found a door in the kitchen that led to the garage on the

right side of the house. The driver's-side door was open on a white Rolls Royce. *Nice car.* Unfortunately, the deep-orange leather seats reeked of bleach.

"Someone made an effort to get rid of fingerprints," I said, hearing Merry come up behind me.

"Fingerprints aren't effective since we don't collect them."

"I meant emotional fingerprints. That includes smells." I ran my finger along the sleek exterior. "I can see how it might have been easier to have sex and wait until she fell asleep, but I bet they never got that far. Otherwise, he would have burned the bed or the entire house. Maybe they came inside, had a glass of wine, she went to slip into something more comfortable, he followed, asked her to get in the bed, and then put on a striptease so he could get the sword off. That's even worse, because it means she wasn't asleep."

"That's quite a vivid imagination you have. Perhaps she offered someone a room for the night."

I strutted past him. "And decided to slip into her sexiest negligee, just in case he mistook her bedroom for the bathroom in the middle of the night?"

The dog was still gobbling up kibble that had scattered on the tile, so I gave him a refill, pouring excess on the kitchen floor so he wouldn't go upstairs and eat his owner.

"You've been working on this case and have more information than I do," I pointed out. "What *aren't* you telling me? What did the victims have in common?"

Merry lifted an empty wineglass from the sink and smelled it. "We called the Mageri to speak to the record keeper. They document every legal Mage and store their information. He said the victims were all ordinary men and women with no past criminal history. Well… to their knowledge. Each was at least one hundred years old, had served with the Mageri at some point in their career, were staunch supporters of human rights, donated to charity, and had different Creators."

"Why would their Creator matter?"

"Nepotism."

"And you believe him? Maybe he was conspiring."

Merry laughed haughtily. "To do what? I trust Novis, though we've only met the one time. Everything he said was the truth. No man can conceal a lie from me."

I scratched the dog's ear when he nuzzled my hand. "Was every victim confirmed a Mage?"

"Yes."

"Did they have similar gifts? Were they all Creators?"

"That was the very first thing we eliminated. We're way ahead of you, Raven."

"Don't be such a cocky asshole."

"A good investigator leaves no stone unturned."

"Except for the one that reveals what they all have in common. Whoever's killing these people had plenty of opportunities to take out more than one official. Every victim is a Mage, so that narrows it down. But Elaine's death is the big monkey wrench. If someone wanted to kill every Mage official, it would have been easier to attack her at home and kill her husband. Instead, they skulked in the shadows and followed her to a secret retreat that she shared with her lover. Why didn't the Mageri take over the case?"

"It's out of their jurisdiction. Aside from that, the higher authority doesn't communicate all their affairs to them freely. This is a delicate situation, so divulging the truth without facts would turn the Mageri against us."

"This is why I will never join politics."

"My dear, you are already involved in politics. Just of a different kind."

"Maybe."

He unzipped his coat and rested his hand on the pommel of his sword. "If you don't believe in politics, why are you protecting politicians? Because your boss told you to?"

"The system we have scares me. The Mageri has the power to destroy Learners they see as unfit. The higher authority executes without due process. Simply collect enough evidence and cut off their heads. That's a lot of power they're wielding. But even though it's barbaric and differs from the legal system I grew up with, the higher authority serves a purpose. Fear keeps people in line, even the criminals." I kicked a piece of kibble across the floor, and the dog trotted after it. "People aren't just committing crimes because of the power outage. They're not receiving any communications from officials. They don't see Regulators keeping order on the streets. They don't have that sense of security that everything's going to be okay. That lack of visibility has thrown this city into turmoil. So to answer your question—yes, I'm putting my life on the line to protect these officials because that's my job. But I'm also doing it because without them around, my job would get a lot harder. Don't you think? I don't have any loyalty to these people, but I have one to mankind. Without the higher authority in the picture, what's to stop people from organizing groups to hunt down and kill humans?"

Merry turned around and put his hands on the edge of the sink.

Our conversation was too deep and making me uncomfortable, so I switched back to the matter at hand. "Did you question Elaine's husband, or are you still concealing her death from him?"

"We ruled him out as a suspect."

I walked a few paces, kibble crunching beneath my sneakers.

Merry turned to face me. "Perhaps the human government is behind this."

"That's a wild conspiracy."

"So is accusing Elaine's husband when we have proof of his whereabouts. We have to look elsewhere."

Merry and I weren't on the same page. Couples knew private things about each other, and even if Elaine's husband wasn't a suspect, he might have useful information.

I brushed my hair away from my eyes. "Were any of the other victims bonded to someone?"

"No."

"What was this victim's name?"

"Does it matter?"

I gave him a cross look. Maybe it didn't matter, but she deserved to be more than a pronoun.

"Mathilda."

I wrestled with whether or not I should tell Merry what I was thinking. Mathilda invited someone into her house that she trusted, someone armed with a sword. Most people didn't bring large weapons to elite parties. Daggers maybe, but someone with a sword would stand out.

Unless they were a Regulator.

Walter, Elaine's lover, had opened the door for an armed person and turned his back on him to get a drink. Either he knew that person, or he automatically trusted them. Who could be trusted more than a Regulator? While this was an important epiphany, it wouldn't be in my best interest to reveal such an accusation to someone who was now on my suspect list.

Though a mortal enemy to a Mage, a Chitah would have been forbidden fruit to Mathilda. Interbreeding was frowned upon, but that didn't stop folks from doing it in secret.

"Something on your mind?" he asked.

"I think we need to call someone to collect the dogs."

"I'll take care of that. Weather and I have to stay behind and clean up the crime scene."

"Don't send them to the kill shelter, okay?" I backed up a step, suddenly unnerved by his enigmatic gaze. "Did the higher authority request my presence here?"

"No."

"Then why did you ask me to come?"

He slowly removed his jacket and held it between two fingers. "Weather isn't one for conversation, and I thought you might make better company."

"If I were a Chitah, would I scent a lie?"

Merry bowed. "We'll see each other again."

When I left Mathilda's house, the dogs were still barking at Weather.

What the hell was that scene about?

Maybe Merry invited me to see if I was holding back any information related to the case, but my gut told me something wasn't right.

Could I trust Merry? I was the one who'd asked the Overlord for help, but what if I'd just invited the enemy to have unlimited access to every Mage official in Cognito?

Chapter 18

"AND WHERE HAVE YOU BEEN all morning?" Christian blocked the entrance to the church, his squinted eyes glaring down at me. He looked tortured when the sun poked out from behind a cloud and shined on his face.

Leaves rustled nearby where either a Regulator or a squirrel was hiding.

"Merry said he talked to you about a murder case, but you had to stay here."

His dark eyebrows slanted down in the middle. "Is that what he said?"

I shouldered past him to get inside. Not that we had any heat in the church, but it was a hell of a lot better than standing out in the wind. The sun warmed things up, but it had been playing peekaboo most of the day.

He slammed the door and locked it. "I thought you went back home to speak to Viktor."

I peeled off my gloves. "I plan on doing that a little later. How do you get downstairs?"

When I veered down the hall, he caught my arm.

"I'm ready for our quarrel now. Tell me where you've been, because that shitebag lied."

I turned, realizing that Christian wasn't playing around. "He said he invited you to come along to look at another murder, but you had to stay."

Christian slowly shook his head.

The hairs prickled on the back of my neck. "Another team

found a dead Mage. Merry and Weather are the ones handling the murders. He invited me along to check it out."

"Why?"

I shrugged. "I assumed to be helpful since we were called in on the last one."

"We weren't called in to solve that case, Raven. They hired us to verify the identity and give an outside opinion on the matter."

"We're not consultants. Anyhow, whoever's doing this is good. I think the victim was at Patrick's party and took someone home with her. She has a standout car that would be easy to spot on street surveillance, and we know the time that everyone left because of the explosion. She could have taken off before, or even after since some people were detained, but we have a rough window of time to work with. But until the power comes back on, I can't get Wyatt to confirm my suspicion."

Christian's black robe swished as he stepped closer. "You think the killer lopped off the heads of two men, set off a bomb, and went home with the girl?"

"More than that." I looked down the hall and then lowered my voice. "I think he's a Regulator."

Christian's jaw went lax, and he gripped my arm firmly. "You can't make that kind of accusation, lass. They'll take your head for slander."

I raised my chin defiantly. "She let someone into her house who was armed with a sword. Nobody at that party was in costume or wearing a long coat to hide a blade. They were dressed like penguins. It's possible he kept it in his car, but they went back to her place in *her* car. He poured bleach all over the seats."

Christian pinched his chin. "Erasing evidence."

"Exactly. Regulators were at that party. Who else would be more trustworthy? Elaine's lover opened the door and let someone into their apartment. If a Regulator appeared at your door, you'd invite him in. Nobody wants to piss those guys off. I know it's a wild speculation, so that's why I'm only telling you. I don't want this coming back to bite me in the ass if I'm wrong."

"What does your gut tell you?"

I leaned my back against the wall and shook my head. "I don't know. I can't figure out what the motive is. Do you think you could charm Merry and see if he knows anything?"

"Fecking *not*. Are you stark mad? There's a law against charming a Regulator."

I gave him a dubious look. "So you've *never* done it?"

He lightly poked my forehead. "I didn't say that. But the risk is too great if you're not prepared to kill them, and we're not in a position where that's an option. This church is under guard, and we have at least fifteen men who won't hesitate to dice me up into little cubes if I so much as cast a lingering gaze toward one of them." Christian flattened his hand on the wall above my head and leaned in. "Did you give him reason to suspect anything? Think carefully, lass. The man can smell your past."

"I don't think so. He might have sensed my suspicion, but that's not a crime. If he's guilty, he'll see me as a threat. And that's fine. I've got a blade with his name on it."

"We'll keep this between us for now. I'll make sure Father Martin doesn't let the Regulators near the basement no matter how much they threaten him."

"Going somewhere?"

"I'll be going where you're going."

I reached out and pressed my finger against the white square of his collar at the base of his throat. He dipped his chin and kissed my hand, his lips warm against my cold skin.

"Is Elaine's husband here?"

He kissed my knuckles. "Aye."

"Give me five minutes with him."

"No one's allowed downstairs," he murmured, still kissing my hand.

I traced my fingers down every button on his robe. "How do I make you feel?"

"Hard."

"Is that all?"

I caught a look on his face I couldn't peg.

Christian held my gaze. "Are we having a serious chat? Because this is neither the time nor the place."

I gathered his robe between my fingers and pulled him closer. "Then maybe you should take me out on a second date."

His breath hitched when I curved my hand around his side. "Whatever you desire, Precious."

Our lips almost touched before he retreated and raked his hair from back to front. "Someone's coming."

I folded my arms and grumbled, "Someone will always be coming."

Christian clasped his hands over his groin and bowed when the priest appeared. "Father Martin."

Vampires had a reputation that preceded them, but Father Martin never spoke to Christian with disdain. In fact, he seemed like a man with a lively personality rather than one with a funeral procession marching behind him. Perhaps that was why Christian showed him a measure of respect.

"I never thought I'd be cooking for so many people," Father Martin said, his cheeks rosy and hair curled at the nape from sweat. "I came up to put the beans on the stove."

Christian gave him a wry grin. "Do you really think beans are a good idea in that confined space? They might blow us to smithereens if someone lights up a cigar."

A flurry of laughter erupted from the priest's mouth that sounded more like a cackling old woman. Christian winked at me, clearly amused by his new partner.

I lowered my arms. "Father, can I speak to you for a minute?"

Father Martin placed a hand on Christian's shoulder and reeled in his laugh. "Why don't you go put the beans on. The extra pots are beneath the sink."

Christian flicked a glance between us before walking away, and I couldn't help but admire his commanding walk in that outfit, which I still found sexy on him.

Yep. I was going to burn in hell.

"What is it, child?"

"Father, I need to speak to someone you're keeping downstairs.

It's related to a case I'm working on, and I just want to see if he has any information that might shed some light and help us track down a killer."

Father Martin's fuzzy eyebrows arched. "Have you no faith that God will find the killer?"

"God may get him in the end, but here on earth, his ass belongs to me. Please? It might save lives."

He clasped his hands, and I guessed him to be around forty-five. Somewhere on the cusp of middle age, but he hadn't relinquished his youthful personality.

I could tell he was struggling with a decision. "Christian's going to update you in a little bit about locking the door and not letting anyone down there, including Regulators. I'm sure you agree that's the best idea. Right now, we need to ensure their safety by trusting no one. Well, except you, since you have the key. You can walk down with me. I'd feel better with you there. I stabbed a few of them, and they might be holding a grudge."

His lip twitched. "Come with me."

I stuffed my hands into my coat pockets and followed Father Martin across the chapel. He stopped in a short hall and retrieved a set of keys from his pocket. After unlocking a heavy door, he switched on a small flashlight and said, "You go first."

I peered into the dark stairwell and took a few steps down. It was significantly cooler with a musty smell, and the steps were made of stone instead of concrete. "How old is this place?"

Once he finished locking the door, we continued our descent.

"The church was rebuilt after a fire in 1908. The lower levels didn't sustain any damage, so they look just like they did two hundred years ago. Well, except for the plumbing we installed. And electricity. Oh, and the furniture."

"So basically, the walls look the same?"

He moved past me, the bright beam guiding our way down the curved stairwell. "The higher authority paid for everything. Since this church has always been one of their chosen safe havens, they've given us everything we've ever needed. It's been a real blessing in times of struggle. Just last year, they sent a check to cover the cost of adding the rectory. Before that, I had to take a bus. Though, to tell you the truth, I often slept in one of the spare rooms. There's a lot to do around here, and public transportation isn't always timely."

"Why don't you drive?"

"Too many tickets. Who is it you wish to speak with?"

"His name is Henry. Bonded to Elaine Sanders."

The stairs seemed to go on forever. I imagined a dungeon with officials eating gruel out of wooden bowls and sleeping in hay.

"Are there rats down there?" I asked.

"We've never had a problem with rats. I guess they haven't found a way in. But we haven't been able to evict the spiders. We call an exterminator twice a year just to keep them from taking over."

I shuddered at the thought.

When the priest unlocked the second door, warm air hit me in the face. The sound of a loud motor came from a room on the left.

"It sounds like you've got a motorcycle in there!"

"That's the generator." Father Martin locked the door behind us. "It's in a room with a large ventilation pipe that leads outside, and we keep the door sealed off when it's running. It's not as if the fumes will kill our immortal guests, and it was at their insistence. We're only running it for brief periods anyhow." He led me away from the door and stopped. "We weren't prepared for an outage. Christian was good enough to have someone deliver us the generator, but the man couldn't come downstairs. We were lucky that one of the officials knew how to wire things up."

"It doesn't work upstairs?"

"There's no need. The gas stove works just fine, and we never run out of candles." As we continued our walk, he did a lot of speaking with his hands. "I'm useless with repairs. Sometimes we have volunteers fix small issues with the heating and plumbing. We've warmed things up in here with space heaters, and the walls will do a good job holding in the heat. We have excellent insulation."

Candles flickered behind the glass sconces on the wall, but

that was the only rustic thing about the enormous room. The pillars and oval-shaped, recessed ceiling reminded me of a hotel lobby, and doors to each room spanned the outer walls. The center had massive red-and-gold rugs covering the marble floor, which absorbed light and brightened the room. Black leather sofas, coffee tables, and plastic plants decorated the middle, and between each doorway was a religious painting. Candlelight reflected in the prisms of two crystal chandeliers and on the walls painted gold. The higher authority spared no expense, then or now.

I noticed numbers above the arched doorways.

"We barely had room to spare," he said. "There aren't any rules about how many of each Breed serve on the panel."

"Maybe they should have stuck to equal representation."

He clicked off his flashlight. "The evacuation plan was formulated a long time ago, and I suppose no one has really looked at it in over fifty years. It's not uncommon. People put emergency procedures in place but never test them. Sometimes they don't even think about them until it's too late."

"How did you get involved in all this?" I asked, truly curious. "In the church?"

"No. With Breed."

He chuckled and flashed his green eyes at me. Father Martin kind of looked like an Italian cook I used to see at a local pizza place. Except cuter, in a nerdy, priestly kind of way. "There's a selection process of who they bring in as trusted humans, and it's all under the guidance of the clergy who have been working with Breed all their lives."

"It seems like finding out about immortals would make you question your faith."

"If a chosen human isn't willing to accept the truth and learn more, they simply scrub them, and their life goes back to normal."

"Nice."

"They give us a choice. I prayed about it and decided that God would want me to accept all his children. Even the ones with fangs."

I pointed at the doors we passed. "Are you locking everyone in their rooms?"

"Goodness, no," Father Martin said, holding in his laugh. "They used the couches early last night, but some of them don't get along well with others, so they retreated to the privacy of their rooms. Once we got the generator running, most of them wanted to watch the news."

"They have TVs?"

"The higher authority decided it was a necessary expense. They installed them, oh… about twenty years ago. They're the older models. They used to have cable running down here, but five years ago, a crew came out to connect them to the internet. I don't watch television, so I don't know how that works."

It made me think how rapidly technology changed in just five years.

He stopped at door number twenty and knocked.

"Come in."

Father Martin opened the door. "Sorry to interrupt, Mr. Tate, but I have someone here who wishes to speak with you."

The man reading in his chair looked up at me. "I thought you said no visitors were allowed down here."

"This is an exception. She works for Keystone, the group who brought you here. Shall I step into the hall and let you two speak alone?"

Without waiting for our answers, the priest walked backward and closed the door.

I scoped out the room. Sconces lined the walls in here as well, but it looked less formal than the main room. The television sat atop a dresser to the right, and across from it, a sofa and chair. To my immediate right, a short counter had all the basic necessities a person could want: a coffeepot, creamers, mugs and drinking glasses, bottles of water, and a basket of snacks. I wondered if Father Martin had recently brought down those goodies or if they'd expired five years ago. Nightstands flanked the bed, which was opposite the door. The red lampshades on the lamps matched the color of the bedspread.

"Why don't you turn on the lights?" I asked. "The generator's working."

"He suggested using as little electricity as possible," Henry replied, closing his book. "It's mainly so we can run our space heaters and catch up on the news. He doesn't want to leave it running all the time since there's no ventilation down here." Henry rolled his eyes. "As if we could die. I'm sorry, have we met?"

"I'm Raven Black. I investigated Elaine's murder."

"You're not a Regulator. How do you know about her death?"

"My partner and I were assigned to research something on her case. Are you familiar with Keystone and what we do?"

"I am." Henry uncrossed his legs and set the book on a small table before walking away. "Did you find the killer?" He closed the bathroom door on the other side of the dresser and returned.

"No."

"Then you're here for your own amusement?"

"Is your last name Tate?"

He chortled and sat back down in his chair. "Some investigator you are."

"Your name wasn't part of my job," I retorted, sitting on the sofa beside him. "I don't like ambiguity."

"Sanders was Elaine's surname, not mine. What Breed are you?"

I shifted in my seat. "I don't see how that's relevant."

"If you know anything about Mage bonding, then you'd know that most of us don't change our last names. Some like the old custom, but most women prefer to keep the name of their Creator. It generates more problems with record keeping when you change it."

"You don't seem upset she's dead, Henry."

"I'm also not hosting a party in my room and drinking champagne. How is one *supposed* to look when his wife is found murdered in an apartment that she shared with her lover?"

"Point taken. I'm sorry for your loss."

Henry crossed his legs. "No, you're not. You're only saying that because it's the civilized thing to do. People should say what they mean."

"Fine. I think you're an arrogant asshole."

"Is that what you came to tell a widower?" He rested his head against his fist, every strand of his brown hair perfectly in place.

I shifted to face him, searching for the best way to broach the topic. I was still certain Henry Tate hadn't killed his wife, but he had to know something. "Did you love your wife?"

He considered the question for a long while. "When we first bonded, yes, I loved her. If you're asking me if I knew she was having an affair, then no. I suspected it, but I didn't want to rock the boat."

I furrowed my brow. "What do you mean?"

Henry pinched his chin. "Elaine and I were a power couple. It made more sense to stay together. We were so compatible, even if it was obvious that we'd fallen out of love with each other a long time ago. It doesn't mean you can't still be friends with a person, but I suppose that's why most immortals don't bond. Forever is a long time. Those feelings of newness and love fade, and if you don't enjoy the company of the person you're with, you'll never be happy."

"If you got along, why would she cheat?"

Henry didn't look comfortable with our conversation and gave me a stern look.

"I'm just trying to get a better sense of who your wife was. Maybe they told you this, or maybe they didn't, but she wasn't the only victim."

"I'm aware."

"The victims might have something in common."

"And you think asking about my sex life will capture the killer?"

I felt my face flush. "The devil is in the details."

He sighed and looked away. "Elaine and I stopped having sex years ago. It's not easy to feel passionate about someone you've fallen out of love with. Maybe she wanted to feel that newness all over again, or maybe she had carnal needs like everyone else.

Regardless, she wanted us to stay together and do whatever it took to work out our problems."

"What kind of problems? For the record, I don't think you did it. I probably shouldn't tell you that, but you're the one who likes honesty."

Henry uncrossed his legs. "If Elaine were alive today, she'd be organizing an army of people to get the lights back on. I'd rather sit here and let whatever happens... happen."

"That's an odd remark from an official. Aren't you worried about all the crimes underway? And what if rogues decide to go after the humans?"

"While the higher authority has laws in place that protect humans, not all of us agree with them. That's why we have a diverse panel."

"I guess I didn't consider you guys had party lines like Democrats and Republicans."

A smile touched his lips. "It's more complex than you could ever imagine. We have an open vote every year on exposing our secret to humans. Those votes are compared to the higher authorities in every city across the nation. You would be surprised to learn just how many cities out there are ready to expose our world and risk war."

"I guess that makes it important to get more people like your late wife on the panel."

"That was the one thing we always disagreed on. I couldn't care less if we discovered a supervirus to exterminate them all, but Elaine didn't feel that way. Her vote could never be swayed. She helped to create some of the laws that protect human rights and punish Breed who violate those laws. She said it was the only way to keep order, but you can imagine how many felt like she was betraying her own kind by valuing the lives of humans above our own. Anyhow, it's just as well things ended the way they did. Seeing what's happening to our city would have crushed her."

Funny, Elaine hadn't struck me as especially sensitive to people's needs when I'd met her. But you couldn't judge a book by its cover or a woman by her $4,000 pair of shoes. I sat back and looked across the room at the black television screen. I remembered the conversation I'd had with Merry earlier about the victims. The Mageri official had said they were upstanding people on the right side of the law. He'd also mentioned how each of them was a staunch supporter of human rights.

All of them? Could it be as simple as someone wanting to clear out the dissidents?

"Do you think you could give me a list of every official who supports human rights?"

Henry frowned. "Do you think someone targeted her for that reason?"

"I don't know. I'd have to compare the names on the list with the deceased."

"It's not as long a list as you might think." He rose to his feet and grabbed a notepad and pen from the counter. "With most policies, we have a certain number of members on each side of the issue. It's not always even, but that's irrelevant. Then there are a larger number of swing votes. It's not like human politics. People sometimes change their vote from one year to the next depending on how the debate goes and how convincing the speakers are." Henry continued scribbling as he spoke. "There's nothing confidential about this list, but I would advise you not to spread your theory around. You have no idea the level of disruption this could cause, especially if it isn't true." Henry tapped his chin with the pen and glanced up at the ceiling before adding another name.

"Trust me, I know all about your slander laws."

Henry closed the distance between us and handed me the paper. "These are the names of every official in this city who is unwavering in their support for human rights. Every single one of them has participated in the annual debates."

I stood up. After folding the paper, I stuffed it into a pocket in the lining of my jacket. "Thanks for your cooperation. I can't give you any updates, but I'll do what I can to find her killer."

He inclined his head. "I appreciate your help, Miss Black. Or is it Mrs.?"

I snorted. "That'll be the day."

After he showed me out, I zipped up my jacket and wondered what to do with this newfound information.

"Miss Black!"

I turned swiftly, expecting someone to be running at me with a giant steak knife. Instead, I saw Patrick Bane in a long red robe, rushing from his room to greet me.

"I didn't expect to see you here," he said, his accent just as jovial as ever. "What a pleasant surprise."

I scratched my neck. Few people had ever said those words to me. "I thought you were on someone else's list. What are you doing here?"

"I believe this is where I'm supposed to be. Are you familiar with HALO? Fine lads. They dropped me and another man off not long ago."

"How do you like your accommodations?" I asked, the generator still grinding away.

"One can hardly raise a complaint when your host works for the man upstairs," he said, making the sign of the cross. But the way he did it was irreverent. "While I have you here, how's the boy?"

"He's fine. Someone's keeping an eye on him and watching over the property."

"Good to know. If you don't mind my asking, who's watching over him?" Patrick gave me a guarded look, but he wasn't an easy man to read. "Is it a woman?"

"Yes," I said tersely.

A smile relaxed his face. "That's what I like to hear."

My jaw set.

"Only meaning that I wouldn't want any able-bodied man to be babysitting when he could be helping with the evacuation."

I bristled at the implied insult. "All the able-bodied women were already working the assignment. We just happened to have an extra person to spare."

He chuckled. "I'm an old-fashioned man, Miss Black. Do forgive me."

"By the way, I went by your place to pick up some clothes for the kid. What's his name again?"

Patrick frowned. "You went to my home?"

"Yep. You didn't think we had children's clothes lying around, did you?"

He tightened the belt on his robe, which was already tight.

"Don't worry. I didn't go through your things. Did you get new guards? I noticed a couple of new guys at the Valentine's party."

"Yes, you can never have too many."

"How much do you know about them?" I didn't want to disclose what little I knew about Cyrus since Niko tied into that story. "I'm just curious how someone goes about hiring new people. Seems like it's hard to find someone you can trust."

"Why do you ask?"

"When I went to your house, your guard was there."

Patrick wobbled for a moment before his fists clenched. "My guard?"

"Yeah, the Samoan-looking dude. Nobody else was on the property—just him. It didn't feel like he was supposed to be there, so I thought I'd alert you that you might want to keep an eye on him. He had someone with him. Don't know who, but it just felt like he was up to something."

"Did he say anything?"

"No, he didn't see me. Who was his last employer?"

Patrick's nostrils angled in such a way that his nose looked like an arrow pointing to his mouth. I hadn't really noticed it before until they were flaring with tempered anger. "He came with glowing recommendations."

It sounded as though someone had duped Patrick, and I wondered whom Cyrus had paid off to get those references. "Well, just thought I'd let you know."

He reached out and captured my wrist. "When do you think we'll be getting out of here?"

"I don't know. I guess it's up to the guy in charge of this operation. We still have a murderer on the loose."

"That's hardly a reason to lock everyone up." Patrick put his hands on his hips and gazed at the ceiling. "I finally know what jail must feel like."

I snorted. This place was a five-star hotel in my eyes. These rich snobs didn't appreciate the basic things in life, like a bed and four walls. Maybe this experience would humble them.

"I've gotta split," I informed him.

Patrick bowed courteously before strolling around the open room.

Father Martin led me back to the stairwell, and as we began our ascent, I realized Patrick hadn't told me his son's name. In fact, it seemed odd that he didn't have a message to pass along. Maybe what he was doing was out of obligation and not love, but wouldn't he at least want me to tell him to be a good boy?

Ah well. What did I know about being a parent? Kids weren't exactly in my future.

Chapter 19

S HEPHERD SWUNG HIS LEGS OVER the edge of the bed and set his bare feet on the cold floor. He rubbed his face repeatedly, erasing the exhaustion that still lingered. It had been a long night rounding up the remaining names on the list, and thank fuck the Regulators had taken over to finish the job. Not a moment too soon, especially after what happened to Blue.

Shepherd grabbed the box of matches he kept on the bench next to his bed and lit a candle. He flexed his fingers, lacerations and bruises accenting the brutal landscape of his scarred hands. Despite the injuries, he cracked his knuckles. He didn't know what time it was without a clock or window in his room, and because he'd fallen asleep after dawn, his internal clock was on snooze.

Banged up and tired, Shepherd decided to skip exercises on the green-and-gold carpet in front of his bathroom entrance. His knee still hurt when he bent it, so he put more weight on the other leg when he stood.

Shepherd limped to the bathroom to drain his pipe, his gait stiff. In addition to candles, he kept a battery-operated lantern in there for quick trips. Living without electricity hadn't turned out to be such a big deal. A man learned to acclimate to his surroundings. After he finished and washed his hands, he caught his reflection in the mirror... and it was rough. Dark stubble covered his jaw, and the circles underneath his eyes didn't do much to improve his appearance. Too tired to shave or brush his teeth, he walked just outside the bathroom doorway and gripped the pull-up bar he'd recently installed overhead.

He leaned his head against his bicep and hung there for a moment. His room looked like a prison cell compared to everyone else's. Upon move-in, they'd each received the same rustic bed, which was too low to the fucking ground, and an armoire. The rest was up to them. Shepherd never bothered buying a new bed or a chest of drawers. He didn't like forming attachments. Nothing good ever lasted in his life.

He let go of the bar and strode to the bed, lifting the candle from the bench before it dripped wax on his clothes or set them on fire. Not that he had a lot of clothes to begin with. It made more sense to own a few T-shirts, good jeans, and a jacket. There was plenty of storage in the armoire, but that was where he kept his weaponry. The only things Shepherd needed in life were guns, knives, clean clothes, and a pack of smokes.

He circled the bed and set the candle down on his desk to the left of the door. His papers were neatly stacked on one side, a rock serving as a paperweight. Not that there were drafts since he didn't have a fireplace or vents, but once in a while—especially on windy nights—a draft crept into the room from beneath the door.

He rubbed his bare chest and returned to the bench by his bed. Since he wasn't the kind of guy who walked around in his boxer briefs, Shepherd put on jeans and then grabbed a white T-shirt before heading out the door.

When he turned down the hall, shirt clutched in hand, he crashed into Kira.

She gasped, staggering backward and windmilling her arms to keep from falling. He reached out to grab her wrist and steady her, but she wrenched away.

Why the hell is she so afraid of me?

Granted, he had a formidable appearance, but why didn't she have the same reaction around Christian? Most people didn't like the idea of sleeping under the same roof with a bloodsucking Vampire, even if she had gotten used to his presence back in Bulgaria. Besides, Shepherd always cleaned his plate no matter what she served for dinner. It was all delicious, but for some reason, he didn't want her to see him as a monster. So he'd flash a smile when she collected his empty plate from the table. People used to say he had a charming smile, but maybe he was so rusty that it looked villainous.

Shepherd studied Kira, her fear still clinging to the palm of his hand like sticky gum. Her emotions were never mixed with surprise, shyness, or even anger. Always fear. He'd first noticed it a while back when she dropped a pan after he walked into the kitchen. He picked it up and felt her emotional imprints all over it. To be honest, it pissed him off. Over the past few weeks, she'd been good about keeping her emotions off his plate at dinner. Maybe she set the table with gloves, knowing he'd feel it.

"Didn't see you," he said, breaking the silence. "Where's the kid? I thought you were watching him."

She wrung her hands, clearly hoping he'd lose interest and move on.

Shepherd held his hand around the height of his waist, palm flat. "The boy?"

Kira wore a kerchief over her head, knotted in the back. It held together all that beautiful red hair, but now all he could notice were her flushed cheeks, darting eyes, and the way she was worrying her lip. She was taller than Raven but shorter than Blue, which put her at around five-nine. Her shoes were flat, so he always got a true sense of her height.

"Never mind," he grumbled, shaking his head. "I just thought someone was supposed to be watching him."

When he walked past her, he couldn't help but notice her gaze fixed on his tattoo.

Strange woman. At least she stayed out of their business.

Shepherd pulled the T-shirt over his head and tucked it into his jeans. It was a little tight from excessive washings. Either that, or he'd put on some muscle. He rubbed his whiskery jaw, wishing he'd grabbed his smokes on the way out. Because Shepherd's room was on the first floor, he didn't have far to walk to the dining room. He'd chosen his room for that very reason, as well as the necessity of locating himself close to the medical room, which had to be by the front door.

When he entered the main foyer, the dim light outside the

windows gave him a good idea about the time. It would be dinner soon. Had he really slept that long?

Shepherd swaggered into the dining room and halted in his tracks.

The kid was sitting alone in Viktor's chair, his chin resting on the table. His black hair was unkempt, but someone had given him the change of clothes that Shepherd had left on the dining table earlier that morning. He must have slipped away from Kira.

The candles in the chandelier glowed brightly, as did the sconces on the wall. Shepherd only took notice of one thing: the mittens. He'd thought the kid would refuse. Kids were capricious, unpredictable, and combative. They didn't like adults telling them what to do. But there he was, wearing those gloves. They weren't the kind Shepherd would have bought for him. The best gloves for Sensors were made of a thin, breathable material that didn't make the hands sweat. It didn't matter what they wore in winter, but the Sensor variety was preferred since they were flexible. For some, gloves dulled the sensory emotions on people and objects, and for others, they completely masked it.

He wondered how strong this kid's abilities were.

Shepherd approached the table and sat in Wyatt's chair. "I like those gloves," he said. "Do you know what makes them awesome?"

The boy's blue eyes glittered with curiosity. They were beautiful eyes, rimmed in black and filled with so much innocence Shepherd would never understand.

"Because gloves have magic powers for people like you and me." He noticed the skeptical look growing on the boy's face. "Want me to show you how they work? Go on. Touch my hand."

Shepherd stretched out his arm, and the boy gaped at all the scars.

"I dare you."

The boy reached out cautiously and traced his gloved finger along one of the fresh marks. Shepherd glanced over his shoulder to make sure no one was listening. As far as they were concerned, the kid was a Relic.

"See that? You can't tell what I'm feeling, can you?"

The boy shook his head and then touched more of Shepherd's hand. His fingers were so damn small in comparison.

"Sometimes those things you feel are yucky, aren't they? Especially when you go to the store... or a party."

The boy frowned and put his hands in his lap. Shepherd wished he could understand how much Patrick's rules had damaged the child. Using a Sensor that young to read people was dangerous and irresponsible.

Shepherd folded his arms and gave the boy a curt nod. "I think they make you look like a superhero or something."

That roused a smile. But then the kid reached up and ran his fingers along the scar that hooked across his own face. It was deep and wouldn't fade with time. In fact, Shepherd feared as the boy grew and his skin changed, it would become more noticeable. It was in a place he wouldn't be able to cover with whiskers or a beard.

Fuck Patrick. Making that kid wear a mask at the parties to hide identifying marks had given the boy a complex. And what comforting words could Shepherd possibly have to offer? That scarred people were special? What was so special about his own scars? They were wasted attempts at saving the woman he loved.

They were a constant reminder of his failure.

So Shepherd said the only thing that made sense in that moment. "All true warriors have marks... like yours. Sometimes we win battles, and sometimes we lose, but we're stronger than everyone else. Don't let anyone ever tell you different. You got me, little man?"

It shattered him that he couldn't even call him by a name. Patrick denied him everything that would give him an identity, hoping to brainwash the kid from an early age. But that time at the grocery store, when the kid had defiantly run away from Patrick so he could ride a mechanical horse, had revealed his unbreakable spirit. Deep down, the kid must have sensed something was wrong with his life. He had no sense of normalcy to compare it to, and Shepherd was certain the boy had never watched television a day in his life. Did he know what a father was?

"When you get older, you won't need to wear the gloves

as much. You learn tricks, like how to tune out all those shitty emotions. Uh... I mean sticky emotions."

The boy giggled and covered his mouth, delighted by Shepherd's tacky attempt to fix his swearing habit.

Or maybe Patrick never cussed around the kid and Shepherd had just taught him his first swear word.

Great.

Shepherd laced his fingers together and tried to hear Maggie's laugh in there. Sometimes he caught a flash of her in the boy's blue eyes or the way he would smile.

It didn't take but a minute for the kid to settle down, and when he did, Shepherd couldn't help but notice how he'd put his arms on the table, lacing his fingers together.

Shepherd pointed one finger up.

The boy smiled, copying the gesture.

Shepherd put his finger down.

The boy did the same.

Finding amusement, Shepherd stretched all his fingers out. When the boy mirrored his movements, it became a game. And this went on for several minutes.

By the time Niko walked in, Shepherd and the kid had their thumbs in their ears, wiggling all their fingers. At least Niko couldn't see how ridiculous the scene was, but he must have picked up on something.

"He likes you," Niko said, taking a seat on the opposite side.

"I thought Kira was supposed to be watching him at all times."

"Gem said Kira takes him exploring every few hours so he'll behave when she's doing chores. He's a bright child."

"Yeah," Shepherd said, feeling a heavy weight on his chest.

"His presence has healed you in some way."

Bored with the conversation, the boy hopped out of his seat and skipped into the gathering room. Shepherd kept an eye on him through the entryway and open archways in the wall.

"Maybe the fates have brought him here for a reason," Niko offered. "To remind you where you're most needed."

"What kind of cruel joke is that? Dangling the kid in front of me like a carrot, showing me what I'll never have, isn't a lesson I need."

Niko's hair slipped forward when he lowered his head. "I'll never know the joy and heartache of creating a life, but one thing I've learned is that sometimes we need others more than they need us. Even if you were to raise him, you'd only have him for a short while. No matter what that boy's fate is, he will soon grow into a man who will make his own decisions. You needn't worry about Patrick's influence. I have no doubt he'll brainwash him long enough to get what he needs, but one day, the boy will take a long look at his reflection in the mirror and question who he is and what he believes in. Every man faces the reflecting pool. Trust that no matter the outcome, he'll have enough of your bravery and his mother's goodness to choose the right path, even if you have no part in that choice. Have you told Viktor?"

Shepherd shook his head even though Niko couldn't see. His silence was answer enough.

"Would you give up everything for the boy?"

Shepherd clenched his fists. "I'd die for him."

That kid was the best thing that Shepherd had ever done—the result of two people loving each other so much that they created another life. Shepherd didn't know the boy, but he felt a strong devotion to him unlike anything he'd ever known.

Niko sat back and lifted his gaze. "Enjoy the time you have together. Maybe this gift is an opportunity to show him what a real home is like—what having a father is like."

Shepherd rose from his chair and abruptly left the table. As much as he wanted to bond with his son, it would only make the separation worse. Niko was right about one thing: even if he kidnapped the boy, he'd only have him for a short while. Children grow up fast, and living on the run was no life for a child, especially if Shepherd couldn't get work and make enough money to pay for their next meal.

He entered the foyer, heading for the opposite side of the stairs.

Raven burst through the front door. "Hey, Shep."

Shepherd ignored her. He needed to clean his weapons and wait for Viktor's orders, because Keystone was all he had.

Chapter 20

W HEN I ENTERED THE MANSION, I caught sight of Shepherd passing through. Just the man I needed to see.

"Hey, Shep."

As the door closed behind me, he stormed off as if I didn't exist. Shepherd didn't walk like most men; he had a mean stride with a heavy gait. But something had lit a fire in his ass as he hustled behind the stairs and toward his room.

"Fine," I muttered. "I'll just tell Claude that you refused to fix his car." After I shucked my jacket and slung it across the winged statue, I headed for the dining room.

"What are you doing in here alone?" I asked Niko.

He turned his head, but his body remained facing the entryway to the gathering room. "Watching the little one."

I peered through one of the open archways into the next room and saw Patrick's little boy skipping around in front of the roaring fireplace. It looked as if someone had dressed him in the clothes I brought home, but man, did I do a piss-poor job at selecting them. The little tyke's red sweatshirt and green pants made him look like Christmas.

"I couldn't find any toys," I said, still bitter about that. "Unless Patrick keeps them hidden in a basement, there were none in the rooms I searched."

"A child's imagination is the best toy there is."

"Is Viktor around?"

"Downstairs office." He studied me for a moment before approaching. "What troubles you?"

"When I went to Patrick's house, I saw Cyrus. Is he really working for Patrick?"

Niko took a deep breath and clasped his hands behind his back. "I'm afraid so. They were here when Patrick brought the boy."

I jerked my head back. "I didn't see them."

"They parked in the garage and then roamed around the property. Viktor wouldn't allow them inside."

"Not much of a bodyguard."

"It appears they have a special arrangement to work as a sentinel but not as a personal bodyguard. Their business relationship makes no sense to me. Cyrus would never work for someone else, especially a white man. Not unless he wanted something out of it."

"Money?"

Niko shook his head, his back ramrod straight. "He's trying to find a way to get to me."

"Why go through Patrick? That's so random."

"I have no idea," he admitted, but Niko's answer seemed disingenuous.

"I caught him talking to a Gravewalker at Patrick's house."

Niko drew in a sharp intake of breath. His neck turned red above the crewneck collar of his long-sleeve shirt, and he teetered before widening his stance. "Are you certain that's what you saw?"

"Yep. He had a secret chat with the lady, but I was out of earshot. They slinked off to another room, and I got the hell out of there."

"You made a wise decision. Cyrus is not a man to trifle with, and if he knew you'd witnessed something you weren't supposed to, he wouldn't have stopped hunting you until your head was away from your neck."

"Do you think he's conspiring against Patrick? I was thinking how easy it is for servants and guards to overhear things they're not supposed to. The only thing I can't figure out is why he'd involve a Gravewalker."

"I would caution you against sharing this information with anyone."

"Too late. I already gave Patrick a heads-up. If Cyrus is after you, he might be taking advantage of Patrick's trust and using his power. He knows Patrick and Viktor are friends. Better that we warn him now before Cyrus starts planting ideas in his head."

Niko turned sharply when the boy stomped his feet on the floor. "Are you jumping on the furniture?"

Niko had apparently assumed what I could see with my own eyes—that the kid was repeatedly climbing onto the chair and jumping off.

I rocked on my heels. "You want me to find Kira on my way out?"

"No need. He's a spirited child but no trouble."

"Well, he's in the right hands if he gets hurt. By the way, how's Gem doing today?"

Niko crossed one arm over his chest and rubbed his shoulder. "She's still recovering from the loss."

"I just hope someone's taking food to her room even if she's not hungry."

I wondered if people were casting judgment because I hadn't gone knocking on Gem's door to offer consolation. I'd probably make her feel worse by saying the wrong thing. My father hadn't raised me to be sensitive, let alone cognizant about how I spoke to people, so I'd always had a difficult time bonding with other women on an emotional level.

"Are you going back to the church?" I asked.

"Viktor wants me to stay here and help him make calls. We haven't had trouble with our cell phones like some people, so he's trying to stay in touch with everyone involved."

"I better go talk to him."

I turned on my heel and headed through the short hallway that led to the grand foyer. Viktor had a study on the other side of the stairs, one he used for private meetings and phone calls. Viktor had lots of studies within the mansion, and each one had a different purpose for his business affairs.

I rapped my knuckles on the door. "It's Raven. Can I come in?" When no one answered, I pressed my ear to the door and heard low talking. "Viktor?"

The second time I knocked, he opened the door. I stumbled inside, my cheeks heating as I shut the door behind me.

Viktor had the phone to his ear and held up one finger to signal he would be with me in a minute. "That is correct," he said. "Their church is insufficiently guarded. We can spare two Regulators."

I moseyed over to the small table on the right and flipped the chair around to straddle it.

"I could really use a drink," I murmured, dreading the conversation we were about to have regarding my trip to see the Overlord. Merry had already reached out to him, but I was fairly certain that Viktor assumed the Regulators came back on their own. Everything had worked out fine, and even though Viktor liked us to think and work independently, I worried that he would take issue with my going over his head.

Viktor glanced at me. "Da, that was Raven."

I furrowed my brow. "Who's asking?"

Ignoring me, he turned away and grumbled. "Then let *them* decide who to send to the other church. I cannot spare my time with such frivolous details, Christian."

I tapped my hand on the table to get Viktor's attention. "Is the church a Mage location?"

Viktor shook his head.

"Tell him to send Merry and Weather."

Viktor continued listening to Christian, and it made me wish I had Vampire ears. "No, I have no need of her. She can return... What detours?"

When Viktor slanted his eyes toward me, I knew Christian was filling him in on how I'd spent my free time with the Overlord. He'd probably assumed I'd told Viktor all about it by now.

"See you soon." Viktor hung up the phone and slipped it into the pocket of his chinos. One of his shoelaces on his leather shoes had come untied, but he either didn't know or didn't care. After taking a seat across from me, he moved the candle between us and used it to light a second.

"Is our assignment done?" I asked. "Is that why Christian's coming home?"

"Nyet. Shepherd sent him a message that he's on his way to take over watching the church. Christian deserves a break."

"Vamps don't need breaks, remember?"

"He may not need sleep, but a man needs to rest his mind." Viktor stroked his silver beard, and his eyes crinkled at the corners. "I heard you went to see the Overlord."

I rested my chin on the back of the chair I was straddling. "That's why I came in here to talk to you. I should have asked permission, but I was afraid—"

"I would say no. Did we not have a discussion about doing things behind my back?"

"We also had a discussion about how you trusted us to make our own decisions."

He folded his arms. "Are you trying to twist my words against me, little one? Do you understand the repercussions if you had insulted him?"

"I'm just pointing out that either we do as you command, or we have freedom of choice. I used common sense, and I wouldn't have done anything that would jeopardize whatever relationship you have with him. The worst he could say was no, but it wasn't as if speaking to him would be the downfall of Keystone."

Viktor chuckled, his eyes lit with a mixture of amusement and terror. "Sometimes you do things that make me want to take up smoking. But... you were able to get the Regulators back."

"You're not mad it might make us look incompetent?"

He wagged his finger at me. "Protecting our leadership is more important than protecting my ego."

I scratched the waxy candle with my fingernail. "How long are they going to keep them underground? I couldn't have predicted there would be so much resistance from officials, so it worked out for the best."

Viktor scratched his cheek. "The murders complicate things. Perhaps it's in their best interest to stay where they are."

"Speaking of which"—I pushed up my sleeves—"I think Regulators might be responsible."

Viktor blanched. "And why do you say that?"

"All the victims were beheaded with a long blade. Walter, Elaine's lover, let someone he either trusted or knew into the apartment. Someone carrying a weapon. And the latest victim invited a man who was also armed back to her home. There was no sign of a break-in, and someone erased all the imprints left behind in her car. It looks like they came directly from Patrick's party. When the power comes back, I want Wyatt to look at surveillance video along her route home. She would have passed through the human district, so we might catch something."

Viktor didn't like that revelation at all. He looked as if he were trying to rub the lines out of his forehead as he stared down at the grooves in the table.

"I might be wrong, but it just makes sense," I continued. "I know it's not our case, but after going to one of the crime scenes earlier with the two lead investigators, I got a weird feeling. He's never given me bad vibes until that conversation." I drummed my fingers on the table.

"Why would Regulators target the higher authority? Their loyalty runs deep. They have sworn an oath to protect them."

"An official gave me a list of names." I retrieved the paper from my pocket and set it in front of him. "Don't worry. I had a good reason to be talking to him. He was bonded with one of the victims. He mentioned his wife was vocal about supporting human rights. On a hunch, I told him to write down everyone who shared the same unwavering view. I don't have a list of all the previous victims, but the ones I know about are on that paper. Do you see any more?"

Viktor ran his finger down the paper, mumbling to himself. "All the victims are on this list."

I sat up straight. "Two on there are Vampires. I recognized their names, thanks to all those swanky parties you take us to."

Still holding a frown, Viktor stood up and crossed the room. When he returned, he had a pencil in hand. I watched him studiously place a mark next to certain names on the list until he reached the bottom.

He turned the paper toward me. "Every name I marked is a Mage."

My eyebrows arched. "That's a lot of officials."

"That list does not contain the name of every Mage on the panel."

"That's what Henry said. He told me he was only writing down those who led some of the debates, because everyone else could be a swing vote."

"Those swing votes are typically those who have been with the higher authority longer. You would think it to be the opposite, but they have been around long enough to know the game. The newer ones have stronger opinions."

"Because of the selection process the Mageri has?"

Viktor squinted and looked at me like an equation. "How do you know this?"

"I pay attention when people are talking."

"Ask yourself what gain a Regulator has in committing these acts. There is a motive behind every crime."

I held up my hands. "I don't know enough about politics to come up with motive. It seems pointless to get rid of the people who support human rights if the next batch of replacements will share the same views. So you've made no progress. Maybe I've got an overactive imagination and this is nothing more than someone targeting every Mage on the panel so they can fill those seats with Vamps or Chitahs."

"They'll be replaced by another Mage," he said. "Most likely."

"Most likely?"

"If too many die, the Mageri might not have enough qualified candidates."

I rubbed my eyes. "I'm starting to think you should just give me the dogcatcher assignments. This is too much conspiracy."

"The murder case is not ours to solve. They only wanted us to identify the body and give our unbiased opinion."

I leaned in. "Why is that? Why would the lead person on this investigation hire an outside party when they've got two Regulators working the case? Do you think your contact suspects them and that's why he really called us in?"

Viktor steepled his fingers. "If you are right, that means we've given the murderer a key to the castle."

"I don't think the killer will try anything with all the other Regulators around. Everyone in the basement can hear and see one another, so there would be too many witnesses. If all the Regulators were behind it, the officials would be dead by now. You know the names I mentioned earlier when you were on the phone with Christian? They're my top suspects, which is why I suggested they be the ones who transfer to the other church. Better safe than sorry."

"A great investigator examines every piece of evidence before making accusations. You must never have doubt. It is so easy to be led down the wrong path by our own, uh... blinders? I am too tired to remember the right word." He leaned back in his chair and stretched, his biceps visible below his shirt. While older, Viktor kept fit. Sometimes I saw him jogging outside. "If only the outage would end."

I stood up and rested one knee on the chair, my hands gripping the back. "You should get some sleep."

"There is no such luxury for me."

"Want me to put a kettle on and make you some instant coffee?"

His lips set in a grim line. "I miss my espresso. Whoever is responsible for this blackout should be locked up ten years for each day I go without coffee."

A smile touched my lips. I rubbed my neck, amused by how even Viktor couldn't live without the amenities of electricity. "Why would anyone intentionally knock out the power in winter? It's too damn cold."

"Whoever did this had no clear purpose, or they would have

galvanized people into action. They probably wanted to create a little chaos."

My gaze darted off as the word resonated.

Chaos.

This was exactly like something Houdini would orchestrate. No real reason behind it other than to watch what happened. Like at Club Nine when he had me switching out the lights to each room. He could have charmed people to do his bidding in order to pull this off. After all, he was part of an underground network, not to mention he lived in the Bricks with all the crazy people.

"I gotta go," I said tersely.

After abruptly bouncing out the door, I hurried upstairs as fast as my feet would carry me. Out of breath, I made it to the third floor and sprinted down the hall before bursting into my bedroom. The sun had just gone down, but there was enough ambient light for me to see with my Vampire eyes. I grabbed the silver cube off my desk and turned it in my hand.

The devil lies within.

Those were the words Gem translated from the enigmatic symbols etched into the metal. I'd spent so many nights staring at the key inside, wondering what it opened. Whatever it led to would expose Houdini and end him—that much he believed, whether it was true or not.

I turned it in my hand. There was no way to be certain if Houdini was behind this blackout, but it felt like him. It felt *exactly* like him. No one could seem to make sense of it, let alone fix the problem. No organized groups had claimed responsibility before wreaking havoc. It couldn't have come at a crazier time—right in the middle of a murder spree.

The streets were getting more dangerous by the hour, and I worried for my father's safety. He lived on the outskirts of town, and because of all the land, there might be packs or rogues looking for trouble. The sooner this blackout ended, the sooner the higher authority could get back to business.

And I held the key.

Chapter 21

GRAND FUNK RAILROAD PLAYED "SOME Kind of Wonderful" on the radio while I sang along, my window halfway down, my hands slapping the steering wheel to the beat of the song. I hadn't touched the dial since getting Crush's truck back. Some local radio stations were probably down, anyhow.

With absolutely no clue on how to locate Houdini, I drove straight to the one place I knew he might be—the Bricks. I had an inkling he might be keeping tabs on me. After all, he'd been following me for years, and in retrospect, none of the encounters seemed random. Perhaps I was his greatest experiment of all.

The streets were drenched in darkness with only a slice of moonlight to guide the way. I'd never seen the Bricks so desolate. Either everyone was protecting their property, or they were stirring up trouble elsewhere in the city.

The truck jolted when a man jumped into the back, so I hit the gas, attempting to knock him off-balance. He was two seconds from busting through the back window when three loud pops sounded. The man pirouetted right out of the truck and onto the street.

I slammed on the brakes and searched every corner, every car, and every window for the gunman, but it was too dark for me to see beyond the shadows of my headlights. The engine rumbled like a waking lion. Seemed as if the shooter would have shot me too, but I had a feeling it wasn't a random act of heroism.

"I want to make a deal," I said. "Meet me at Arrowhead."

When I reached for the silver puzzle box beside me, I held it up and then drove to Arrowhead Bridge.

Knowing Houdini would never follow right behind me, I took a longer route to give him a chance to jump ahead. By the time I reached the river, "Wherever I May Roam" was playing on the radio. I drove across the two-lane suspension bridge and turned off the truck when I reached the center. It must have been a spectacular view on any other night when there were lights twinkling along the shore, but tonight, only the moon iced the waters below. I zipped up my jacket and hopped out, leaving the door ajar.

The wind blew relentlessly on the empty bridge, so I walked to the right side, where it would be against my back. My black hair rippled in front of my face before settling on my shoulders. Leaning against the railing, I turned the silver puzzle box in my hands.

I glanced left and right—no sign of headlights or anyone walking toward me.

What the hell am I doing here?

I felt like an idiot. This guy probably had better things to do than stalk his youngling. He was in all likelihood taking advantage of the outage by finding more young women to sell on the black market. I had no way to reach him—no address, no phone number, not even a full name. Houdini was an alias, and in many ways, Houdini was a ghost.

Untraceable.

Untouchable.

And most of all, unpredictable.

"You better be out there," I said. "I need to cut a deal with you." The wind battered my back for a moment before easing up. When it was quiet enough, I continued. "I've got your key, but I need you to turn the lights back on. You've had your fun. You told me you don't do these things maliciously, but now you see what it's doing to this city. People are dying, and that blood is on your hands if you let it continue. The higher authority is in peril, so why don't you flip on the lights and see what happens next?"

The cables on the bridge creaked. I looked around but saw no movement in the darkness.

"This is what you wanted." I pulled back my arm and then pitched the box into the air. It hurtled forward, moonlight glinting off the steel as the wind carried it farther than I could see. I listened for the sound of it hitting the water, where it would sink to its forever home.

I wasn't certain if Houdini needed the key or just didn't want anyone else to have it. Maybe it was just an excuse to stay in my life.

"Are you a man of integrity?" I returned to my truck and gripped the open door, looking around one last time. "Turn on the damn lights."

When Christian called Viktor, he was already on his way home in a borrowed car. After he ended the call, he reached out to Merry with instructions that he and his companion switch locations. One of the churches didn't have enough guards. Christian was glad for the reprieve and also wanted to check on Raven. If she had any other ideas going through that inquisitive head of hers, he wanted to be there.

Along the way, he spotted her truck barreling toward him. So he turned and tailed her. Wasn't hard to do with her monstrosity of a vehicle. The motor sounded like thunder in Christian's ears even from two blocks away. She was probably on her way back to the church, but he kept a safe distance just in case she had something else in mind. When she steered toward the Bricks, he cursed under his breath. That girl had a penchant for trouble.

And it was sexy as hell.

Christian had always been attracted to dominant women. It was his weakness. It was also his downfall.

She drove through the Bricks as if she owned it, oblivious to the men spying on her from windows and dark alleyways. Christian switched off his headlights and fell back far enough that she couldn't see him but he could see her. When a plonker jumped onto the bed of her truck, Christian nearly blew his cover. Raven hit the gas, but the man held on and reached back with his fist to punch through the rear window. Gunshots fired. While the man was flopping across the road like a fish on land, Christian trained his ears on a vehicle parked on a side road up ahead. He heard the distinct sound of a window rolling up but nothing else.

Raven suddenly spoke, saying she wanted to make a deal. She wasn't talking to Christian, nor was anyone else standing near her truck. Those words were meant for Vampire ears.

Raven was here searching for her maker.

Christian's heart pounded against his ribs like a war drum, so he took a deep breath, forcing it to slow down. This might be his big chance to see the one and only Houdini. While he'd noticed him in a bar shortly before Raven's abduction, he hadn't put the man's face to memory, thinking he was just another patron. As Christian tailed behind Raven, he neither saw nor heard a second vehicle. It was dark enough that a Vampire could shadow walk after her, and if Houdini was out there, he knew Christian was following.

Raven approached a bridge, her speed slowing until she stopped in the middle. After parking his vehicle, Christian treaded lightly across the grass and stood next to a tree, watching her from a safe distance as she got out and approached the edge. She was a vision to look at, her gorgeous black hair whipping around like tassels. After she said a few words, he realized what she was doing there. Raven was giving up something in exchange for saving the whole damn city.

As she threw an object into the water, she appeared confident that Houdini was listening and would accept her offer. That made Christian's blood boil. Despite the gaslighting, Raven and Houdini shared the intimate bond between maker and youngling. All Vampires had experienced that powerful connection. It made younglings more trusting of their makers, no matter if they were good or evil. It was innate and one of the great mysteries of immortality. Even Christian had struggled with those feelings with his own maker, and Ronan was a decent man. It made severing the connection difficult—probably nature's way of protecting the elders. Because of that, it was hard to know if Raven had reason to trust this man or was blinded by the blood they shared.

After her truck sped away, Christian readied himself for a confrontation. "I need to speak to you," he ground out, shadow walking up to the bridge. "Still hiding like the coward that you are? I know what you're doing to Raven." Christian stalked to the center of the bridge, tuning out the wind so he could hear the Vampire's heartbeat. He'd heard it all along. It had pounded faster when Raven asked him for help, and Christian realized just how much Raven excited the man.

The figure standing at the far end approached, his pace steady and confident. Christian could make out his bleached-white hair and narrow eyes. His dark eyebrows were perfectly shaped and sloped down in the middle, but the serious expression came across as forced. He was Christian's height but with a slimmer build. Body type hardly mattered when determining a Vampire's strength.

Houdini could have shadow walked to close the distance between them, but he continued at a leisurely pace. As he neared, his light eyes reeled in Christian's attention. It wasn't easy to tell from the distance their exact shade, but they definitely weren't black.

Raven had been keeping a secret: Houdini wasn't a full Vampire. Either that or he was defective.

It was common knowledge that Vampires had black eyes due to their fully dilated pupils. Their irises ceased to exist. Christian remembered him from the bar the night Raven went missing, but he'd always just assumed that Houdini was wearing contacts. Up close, it also appeared he didn't have the same complexion as a Vampire. It was pale, like a man who lived underground, but there were far too many imperfections. Houdini had angled features like those of a well-bred aristocrat and hands that had never seen a day of manual labor. Christian was turned at thirty-one, but lower-class men like him were seasoned from experience and hardships. He guessed Houdini to be in his twenties.

"Nice night," Houdini said, the collar on his grey coat standing straight up. "Since you've already seen my face, I'll make this one exception."

"What makes you so certain I won't murder you?"

A smug smile touched the Vampire's lips. "Surely a man of the cloth wouldn't commit a mortal sin."

Christian folded his arms, his robe flapping in the wind. "I wouldn't hold your breath."

"You also make an assumption that you could overpower me. Maybe you can, but maybe you can't. Do you want to risk losing? And what might that mean for Raven?"

Christian's fangs punched out. He lunged at Houdini and gripped him by the lapels. "If you ever hurt her, I will destroy you... even in death."

"Then it seems we're at a stalemate." Houdini shoved Christian off and stepped back. "I do tire of assumptions. If I wanted to harm Raven, don't you think I would have done it by now?"

"Haven't you? She's without her memory."

Houdini played with the black stud in his ear. "You should thank me for that. You know as well as I do that whatever infatuation you have with her will never last. Raven only interests you because she's different."

"Aye. But answer me this: how many of your other younglings do you follow around? Do you meddle in their lives too, or do you just sell them on the black market like cattle?"

Houdini's eyes narrowed.

"Your infatuation with her is unnatural. She's your *youngling.*"

"She has my blood, and I have hers, but you act as if it's incestuous."

"You're abusing your power!" Christian fired back, no longer able to control his anger. "If the Elders knew what you were doing, they'd lock you up for manipulation and gaslighting. Raven's not herself. She doubts her memory and doesn't even know her ideas from yours. Mind control is forbidden. Of all your crimes, that is the most heinous. Worse than selling your younglings on the black market. You and I both know it."

A look of acknowledgment flashed on Houdini's face, and Christian was certain that he recognized his crimes. The question was how much he cared. The more trust he built with Raven, the harder it would be for their relationship to sever naturally, as was the custom between a maker and his youngling. A Vampire must be able to go out into the world and make his own decisions without influence. Houdini was still the finger resting over her trigger.

"You erased me from her memories so you'd have more control," Christian said sharply. "She trusts me, so that makes me a threat in your eyes. But why should you care? You obviously don't want her, or you wouldn't have thrown her away like trash when she turned."

Houdini snarled, and his fangs punched out. "Never speak of what you don't know!"

"You're a clever fella, but you don't seem to recognize your own insecurities." Christian squared his shoulders. "This was never about Raven; it was about your sense of entitlement and ownership to what she's become. You want her to bow down at your feet and worship the ground you walk on. Charm her all you want, create a fictional life in her head that doesn't exist, but there's something deep down that neither of us can touch."

Houdini tossed his head back and gazed at the universe. Christian watched closely, wondering if Houdini could see every celestial body that traveled across the heavens as he could. Raven had less-than-average vision for a Vampire. Had she inherited that trait from her maker?

"I'm aware of her free will," Houdini admitted.

"Then give her back her memories."

Most Vampires didn't erase everything forever, not when it came to large chunks of memory.

Houdini quirked a brow. "Having trouble winning her heart?"

Christian locked his hands around Houdini's neck, squeezing hard enough to kill an ordinary man.

Houdini's lip curled in a snarl. "Kill me, and she'll *never* be whole."

"You're a weak, insipid little man. Raven told me all about your little experiments. You've managed to convince her that you don't have ulterior motives, but I don't buy it—not from a man who tips the scales in his favor by selectively scrubbing her memories. You're a coward. You hear me? You're so afraid that she won't subscribe to your beliefs that you've erased pieces of her to ensure that never happens."

Houdini's eyes slanted to the side before returning to meet his gaze. "Everything comes at a price."

"And what is the price of her mind?"

"If you wish to bargain, you'll know when the time comes."

After a brief struggle, Christian let go. The wind battered the two men, who stood impervious to its frigid temperatures.

"Are you certain this is what you want?" Houdini asked, a fiendish smile touching his lips. "You make a valid point. It's never a good idea to forget your past, is it, Mr. Poe?"

Christian felt uneasy about the implied meaning behind those words. "You'll give it all back? I have your word?"

"You make a compelling argument that I can't in good conscience ignore. I'm not the villain here, you know."

"No. You're the devil incarnate."

Houdini laughed, and he sounded like a young man without a care in the world. Christian finally understood why it was so easy for Raven to believe him. Her maker came across as genuine and affable, and those were the most dangerous men of all.

"Do we have a deal?" Christian pressed. "You'll give Raven her memory back? All of it?"

Houdini tucked his hands in his pockets and casually shifted his stance. "I'd shake on it, but that's such a human thing to do." He gave Christian an inscrutable gaze, but behind it lurked a secret. "Careful what you wish for."

Before Christian could nail the fanghole with a right hook, Houdini shadow walked out of sight.

Christian knew that favor would come back to bite him, but it was a risk he was willing to take. Raven had soldiered on, despite the violation. But she didn't deserve this.

Would her restored memory change her feelings for him?

Perhaps. But for the first time in a long time, Christian was putting someone else's needs before his own.

And that revelation surprised him more than he could have possibly imagined.

Chapter 22

AFTER LEAVING ARROWHEAD BRIDGE AND the puzzle box behind, I made my way back home. Because of the Regulators, Viktor didn't need me at the church. We'd successfully moved all the officials on our list, so our job was done. When I pulled into the garage to park my truck, all the cars were accounted for, including the van. Curious how Blue was doing, I headed up to the second floor and heard chatter coming from Wyatt's office. It sounded like a party going on in there.

When I poked my head inside the room, I caught Wyatt rolling across the floor in his leather chair. He had one knee on it, hands gripping the back, and a look of jubilation, as if his team had just won the Super Bowl.

"Put it back on the other channel!" Blue demanded from Claude, who was standing up with the remote control in his hand.

"*A River Runs through It* is a good movie," he argued. Claude switched on another floor lamp and sauntered back to the L-shaped sofa.

It was surreal to see the lights and television working again. Wyatt's vending machine was lit up inside, and he had several laptops and monitors switched on. All the colorful pillows on the black sectional were scattered, some on the floor and the rest in the corner. Blue was in the black beanbag chair, facing the TV, and she glared back at Claude to get his attention.

"No, go back one," she said. "To the news."

Claude turned his mouth to the side and reluctantly switched stations.

"I see the power's back on," I said from the doorway. "When did that happen?"

Wyatt rolled in my direction and startled me when he gripped my head and kissed me on the lips. "Ten fantastic minutes ago."

I wiped my mouth with the back of my hand.

Wyatt rolled to his desk to check everything. "All systems are go."

I strolled farther into the room. Viktor was also sitting by the desk, and he and Niko were engaged in a quiet conversation. Claude sat on the couch across from the television while Shepherd claimed the side facing Wyatt's desk. He was putting his cigarette out in an ashtray, his hands battered from whatever had happened during their shift. The room felt warm because of all the electronics running and warm bodies. Though Wyatt had a space heater beneath his desk, he hardly ever used it.

"Those people have no idea what it's really like to live without power," Wyatt remarked, replying to something the news reporter had just said. He peeled the wrapper off his candy bar. "All hell breaks loose because they can't use their blow-dryer. It's like people have no idea how to function."

I snorted. "Says the man who's always glued to his computer."

He spun around in his chair. "Hold your ponies. This is my *job*. I can live without electricity."

"That so?" Shepherd asked, a smile winding up his face. "'Cause I don't see how the TV and vending machine are part of your job."

Wyatt narrowed his eyes and turned to face him. One of his socks had a hole with his toe poking out. "If you put one finger on my shit, I'll put all your smokes in that vending machine and charge twenty a pack."

Shepherd spread his arms across the back of the sofa. "You do that, Spooky. See what happens to that windup toy you call a car."

"Touch my car, and I'll donate all your weapons to a museum."

"All right, enough!" Blue said, cutting through the bullshit. "I'm trying to hear the news."

When I approached Viktor's chair, he reached for my hand and patted it.

"I was just telling Niko how proud I am of each of you. Because of the important nature of this assignment, I was able to negotiate generous pay. My contact assured me they'll send payment once the officials are released."

"Are they doing that now?"

"Nyet. The power only just came back. I believe they're still looking at the most recent murders before they proceed."

"Is your contact also in one of the churches?"

He smiled with his eyes. "I cannot tell you who my contacts are, little one. But rest assured, you will receive payment. It will just arrive later than usual."

"That's fine. It's not like I had anything on layaway."

"Lay a what?"

"Never mind." I squeezed Viktor's shoulder and then pushed up my sleeves. "How's Gem?"

"I am not without compassion. I have taken her off assignments for at least two weeks."

Viktor was a good man. Work or not, he was concerned about our mental health and didn't push us beyond our limitations. We were people with emotions, and sometimes we needed a mental vacation, or the stress would bleed into our work and put others at risk. There were enough of us to go around, so taking someone out of the game for a few weeks wouldn't cause any irreparable damage.

"Did I hear my name?"

Everyone turned to Gem, who lingered by the door. Not a stitch of makeup was on her face, but her colorful hair and violet eyes more than made up for it. Her long grey duster floated past her black leggings, and she wore a bright-pink shirt beneath it. What also caught my eye were her roller skates.

Claude rose from his seat and glided toward her before lifting her off the ground into his arms. "How are you feeling, female?"

"Can't you smell it?" she asked, her heavy skates dangling off the ground. "Put me down, Claude. I don't want to make a scene."

He did as she asked and stepped aside.

Wyatt used his feet to walk his chair up to her. "How's it shakin', Rollergirl?"

She mussed his hair. "I heard the television all the way from my room."

He rolled back to his desk and resumed work on his computer. "I've been monitoring the surveillance cameras around the city, and the good news is the looting has stopped."

She rolled past Claude and sat on the arm of the sofa. "What's the bad news?"

"McDonald's still isn't open."

I was curious about Christian's whereabouts but didn't want to draw attention to the fact I was interested. "Where's the kid?"

"Sleeping," Viktor replied. "He's a good boy. Kira has had no trouble with him. Well, except for the sleeping arrangement."

"What about it?"

Viktor picked a few pieces of lint off his sweater. "Young children are often frightened of strange new places. He does not want to sleep alone."

"I don't blame him. You decorate this mansion like a haunted castle."

He pursed his lips and looked prepared to go on the defense.

"Don't even try," I said. "You probably gave him a room that still had spiders under the bed."

"Shhh!" Blue raised her arm and snapped her fingers. "Everyone, look at this."

I hurried to the sofa and sat beside Gem. The news reporter clutched her microphone, the wind obliterating the hairspray that had once held her hair perfectly in place.

"We don't have any confirmed totals, but police have stated there *are* casualties," she went on. "Witnesses reported seeing flames, but because of the widespread crimes and looting, it appears that the fire department didn't have enough resources to put out the fire."

"Lindsey, are there any confirmed deaths?" the news anchor asked.

Lindsey looked over her shoulder at a policeman setting up crime tape, and when the camera panned back, the gutted remains of a church came into view. "We don't have information at this time. Residents are *stunned* as they look at the charred remains of what was once a beacon of light in this neighborhood. According to one gentleman, this church has a long history dating back to the eighteen hundreds, and his family has been coming here for generations. The chief of police has a live update scheduled in one hour, and hopefully, they can provide us with information on whether this was an accident or arson. Lindsey Fernandez reporting live from outside St. Anthony's. Back to you."

I grabbed the remote from the armrest and turned down the volume. "Are you guys thinking what I'm thinking?"

But Viktor was already thinking it. With his chair turned away, he spoke quietly on the phone. Claude took a seat to my left and spread his long arm behind me. No one spoke, because we were all sick to our stomach with the idea that we could have lost officials.

Blue stood up, smoothing down the flyaways in her hair from static. "Churches are neutral ground. Everyone knows that."

Niko sat on the desk. "Someone isn't playing by the rules."

"What made you think they would?" I asked. "Breed bars are neutral ground because the consequences are getting blacklisted. People like their beer. Not everyone cares about church."

"Maybe we should have hidden them in a bar," Wyatt offered.

Claude hitched up the leg on his sweatpants and crossed his ankle over his knee. I looked at his giant foot, the sole slightly dark from walking on dusty floors.

Still straddling the armrest, Gem rolled the back wheels of her skates on the floor. "It's probably a coincidence. There was so much looting going on last night."

"Fuck coincidence." Shepherd reached for his smokes on the table next to him and lit up another. "Did you see that cop in the background? I know that guy. He's a Sensor. We used to work together until he got a job as an insider for the police department. Now he investigates Breed crimes."

"How do they cover up what they find?" Claude asked.

Shepherd took a drag and blew out the smoke. "Vamps. No offense," he suddenly said, looking at me. "Vampires work in every department, and when they collect evidence that points toward one of us, the Vampires begin the scrubbing process. They have a system so that nothing ever leaks. Everything's clean. Witnesses usually leave statements with their names, and they know which cops worked a scene. It's easy to track down everyone and erase memories. Anything in the computer system is either altered or deleted. As for evidence, that's destroyed or moved by the guy who works in that department. Trust me. We're everywhere."

"Like fleas," Wyatt added, rolling his chair toward the center of the room.

I crossed my legs and reclined my head on Claude's arm. "Before you left the church, did Christian fill you in on the change of plans with sending Merry and Weather to another location?"

He nodded. "Yes. He called."

"Was it *that* location?" I asked, gesturing at the television.

Claude shrugged. "I don't know. Why?"

Heeding Viktor's stern warning about unsubstantiated accusations, I quickly said, "I'd hate to think we sent them to their death."

"Listen up." Viktor stood from his chair, his cheeks flushed and eyes alert. "I have confirmation that the church fire was one of our safe locations. My contact is working on clearing the scene of media, though there is little they can do about the information being public knowledge."

Wyatt shook his head. "Son of a ghost. That's a lot of damage control."

"Which group was it?" Shepherd asked. "How many?"

Viktor folded his arms, his eyes downcast. "That location housed the remaining members of the higher authority who didn't fit in a populated group. Two Gravewalkers, Three Relics, and one Gemini."

Blue's eyes widened. "A Gemini? I didn't think you could kill those guys."

"You can kill anyone." Wyatt spun his chair around before stopping it with his toe. "Immortal is kind of a loose term. I mean, everyone can die. But since some of you special people don't get old, in theory, you could live forever. Well, so long as you stay away from fires and guillotines."

A cold chill ran down my spine. "Someone knows what we've been doing."

"Maybe they just followed one of the teams," Blue suggested.

I wrung my hands. "That's a huge assumption. If we're wrong, someone could target the remaining five churches. Then what?"

Shepherd flicked his ashes into an ashtray, a few of them scattering. "They'd bring in replacements. It's not like we'll be without a body of law, but that'll take a shitload of time to get organized."

I looked back at Viktor. "What did your contact say?"

"He is the man in charge of contingency plans, assigned to overrule the officials. Yet he wants to make the officials aware of the risks so he can weigh their thoughts. I sent Christian a message to spread the news in our church, and the other teams will be notified to do the same."

I felt a rush of adrenaline as I stood up. "They're safer spread apart in their homes. The power's back, and now they can call their bodyguards."

"It is not up to us. After all, it is *their* lives we are protecting, and they have a right to decide their fate."

Shepherd held his head in his hands, a long tendril of smoke rising from the cigarette wedged between his fingers. "They gotta stay put. They don't have anyone on the outside to protect them, not until they locate their bodyguards. They're easy targets."

Blue put her hands on her hips. "What if someone knows all the locations? They're sitting ducks."

"You can't let 'em out."

"We will do whatever is ordered of us," Viktor reminded them. "This is not our battle."

Shepherd's head remained down. "They might have done this to drive the officials out into the open. What about the boy? You gonna send him home with Patrick when there could be an assassination attempt?"

"The kid's not our problem," Blue informed him.

"The hell he isn't!" When Shepherd slowly raised his head, his brown eyes were savage.

Claude shot forward and threw his arm protectively in front of Gem and me.

Shepherd stamped out his cigarette in the ashtray. "I got something to say, and you ain't gonna like it."

No one could silence a room like Shepherd. The bomb he'd dropped on us months ago about his pregnant girlfriend's murder was shocking enough, but learning that his baby was still alive *and* in Patrick Bane's care took the cake.

"You *caught* him," Gem repeated, still in a stupor. Of all the people at Patrick's party, it had been Shepherd who saved the boy from a perilous fall. She drew up her knees and wrapped her arms around them. "Did you know then?"

Shepherd leaned back on the sofa. "No. Maybe if I'd gotten to hold him when he was born, I might have been able to tell, but I had no fucking idea. Not until I saw the picture with the scar on my phone and confronted Patrick."

Viktor stood before Shepherd, his arms folded and eyebrows sloped down. He hadn't spoken a word since Shepherd had laid it all out on the table about his son. This kid was also a crossbreed, except a mix between Relic and Sensor. Shepherd reminded us how most mixed Breeds couldn't have kids. Those who did had babies with gifts canceled out. It deterred people from procreating outside their Breed. It was extraordinarily rare for a child between two different Breeds to retain all his gifts. And for that reason, the murder and abduction made sense. Patrick wanted a child with fused gifts. And this boy was especially dangerous because of his innate knowledge of human physiology and viruses.

Shepherd ran his hand over his bristly head. "Patrick wants to use my kid, and he's brainwashing him. Do you understand why I have to stop this, Viktor? If we sit back and let it go, my son will end up on one of our lists someday. I can't let that happen."

"And what does this mean?" Viktor prodded. "You kidnap boy?" Viktor's anger was rising just as certainly as his words were dropping.

"He threatened to destroy Keystone if I try. He's backed me into a corner. I thought about leaving. I didn't want my distraction to put your lives in danger. But you want to hand over the kid to Patrick while there's imminent danger, and I'm not down with that. There was no way for me to explain why that's not gonna happen without telling the truth. He's safer here, with us. We don't know what'll happen if we let the officials out too soon."

"Patrick's keeping him because of his Relic knowledge?" Claude asked. "Not because of his Sensor abilities?"

Shepherd shook his head. "He's using him for that too. Ever notice at the parties how he gives the kid glasses and dishes that some of his business companions have touched?"

"Bastard," Claude growled.

"Yeah. And when he gets older, that son of a bitch is gonna use my kid to destroy the world."

Blue had returned to the beanbag chair and, by the look on her face, was mulling over all the information. "Why tell us now? Why didn't you just tell Viktor... or leave?"

"I was thinking about skipping out, but that would put me on your hit list, and you need to know what my motives are. Maybe it'll change things, maybe not, but this fucking secret is eating me up. I can't pass that kid in the hall without thinking about everything I stand to lose." Shepherd suddenly dropped his head into his hand and pinched the bridge of his nose. A tear escaped, and he quickly wiped it away with the heel of his hand. After a quiet moment, he leaned forward, arms resting on his knees. "If this means I gotta leave Keystone, then I'm asking you not to wipe my memory. I know you have to erase everything during my time working for you, but I'm *begging* you to leave me the memory of my son." His eyes locked on Viktor.

Viktor sighed. "I will ask you again. Do you plan to kidnap the boy? I do not want to hear about Patrick's threats or your guilty conscience. I want to know the truth, and Claude will tell me if you're lying."

Shepherd rose to his feet and stood like the Rock of Gibraltar. "I always thought of Maggie like a shooting star because I knew I wouldn't have her for long. A Relic has the life expectancy of a human. She was beautiful and went out in a flash of light, but maybe what I need in this life is something steady—something true that I can count on always being there. Maggie was my shooting star, but my son will always be my North. I don't know him. I didn't get to change his diapers or rock him to sleep, but I'll do whatever it takes to make sure he isn't dealt a bad hand because I wasn't strong enough to protect him. So to answer your question, no, I'm not gonna kidnap my own son. That would put his life in danger, and I'll die before that ever happens."

We could all hear the resignation in his voice.

"Then I will not ask you to leave," Viktor promised.

Shepherd cleared his throat. "Thanks. And now that you all know, just be sure that Patrick doesn't get suspicious. If he thinks I told anyone, there's no predicting what he might do."

Gem sprang from her seat and rushed Shepherd, wrapping her arms around his neck. He recoiled. Shepherd wasn't a guy who smiled much, let alone showed public affection toward anyone.

"All right," he said, pushing her away. His neck and face were beet red as his gaze darted about the room. "Time to pack up all those feelings."

She wiped her tearstained cheeks. "You're still a big grump."

A few of us chuckled, breaking the awkward silence of not knowing where Shepherd stood with our team anymore. Poor guy. I couldn't imagine what he must have been going through all this time, being dragged to those parties and continually running into Patrick and his kid.

Wyatt rolled back to his desk. "This cowboy has some work to do."

"Can you look at the surveillance footage from that night?" I asked, still wanting answers about the last murder victim.

"That's exactly what I'm doing now, buttercup."

Blue stood up. "How many Regulators were at the church?"

Viktor glanced at his phone. "*Chetyre.*"

"In *English*," Gem said. "He means four."

I blinked in surprise. "Only four?"

"Da. We only had a certain number of Regulators show up. They were divided based on how many heads they had to protect."

My thoughts drifted to Merry and Weather. Would they have murdered their own kind just to get to their targets? Were all the officials in that church on the list that Henry Tate had given me? I could easily see Relics being more supportive of human rights, but I wasn't sure about the others.

Viktor's phone rang, and he turned away to answer.

Deciding to return to the church, I stood up. Maybe it wasn't our job to protect them anymore, but those men and women were in imminent danger, and I suddenly felt responsible for all their lives, including the asshole who'd body-slammed me against the concrete in a futile attempt to escape.

Viktor lowered his arm. "The attack was deliberate. I have confirmation that the Regulators and the officials were all beheaded. The fire was to burn away evidence."

I felt sick to my stomach. Once the guards were taken out of the picture, the officials downstairs probably hadn't even known what hit them. They were unarmed and defenseless.

"I'm heading back," I said, veering out of the room.

I clenched my fists, my heart thumping against my ribs. I thought switching on the lights would fix all our problems, but now it seemed as if we were in an even worse predicament. Since everyone now had access to the news, the media would be all over another church fire. Did we have enough manpower to cover them all up? What if I had just inadvertently created an opportunity for humans to discover Breed?

Perish the thought.

"Wait up!"

I twisted around and wondered why Shepherd was jogging toward me.

"I'm coming with you," he said.

"Why? I thought maybe you'd want to hang out here and, um…"

"Bond with a kid who doesn't know who I am?"

"Is that such a bad idea?"

He shook his head. "What does it matter? He'll just go back home and forget me."

My gaze drifted downward. "You'd be surprised how one person can leave an impression on a child. When I was a kid, a stranger saved me from a fire. I grew up wanting a better life because of him. I didn't want to let him down. Weird, huh?"

"And then you went and let a Vamp suck on your neck."

I smiled. "Life doesn't always work out like you planned. He seems like a good kid. I'm real sorry all that happened."

Shepherd turned, and we walked together.

"I suck at advice, but maybe you should tie sandbags to Patrick's feet and drop him off in a lake somewhere."

Shepherd chuckled. "The thought crossed my mind. He's got too many guards, and I'd never get away with it. Then what? The kid winds up in an orphanage."

"Look at it this way: Patrick only gets him until he's an adult. Believe it or not, kids rebel. It won't take long for him to realize Patrick's manipulating him."

"He doesn't even have a name."

I blanched and stopped in my tracks. "What?"

"It's part of erasing his identity. Patrick wants to raise an obedient little soldier, so he just calls him *boy*."

"Then you need to give him a name. Fuck Patrick and his rules."

"What if that name I give him ends up on our list someday?"

I clapped his arm. "If he's your son, I wouldn't expect anything less."

His lip twitched. "I guess you're right."

"Kidding aside, you would have made a great dad."

He shook his head, eyes downcast. "I smoke, I drink, I cuss, and I kill."

"So did my father. Well, except for the killing part. I think.

Unless war counts. He was textbook crazy. Didn't even know how to pack a lunch. You know what he did the first year he had me? Drove up to my elementary school every day on his Harley and brought me fried chicken from KFC."

"Sounds like a good man."

"Crush is one of a kind."

Chapter 23

EFORE LEAVING THE MANSION, I changed into a comfy beige sweater and left my leather jacket behind. My truck had a heater, and with the power restored, the church would warm up in no time. A jacket was one less thing to lug around.

"What's in the bag?" I asked Shepherd.

He patted the plastic sack between us. "Christian's clothes. That robe is creeping me the fuck out."

"Not a religious guy?"

"Not when it comes to Christian."

I chuckled. "The irony of his name."

"Maybe hiding these knuckleheads in a church is just asking for it."

I turned down the radio. "Are you going to behave around Patrick?"

Shepherd crossed his heart, but I wasn't confident that taking him along was the wisest idea. Now that the cat was out of the bag about his son, he might follow through with one of his deranged fantasies about killing Patrick. He'd gotten his revenge on the men who'd killed his pregnant girlfriend, so whatever Patrick had coming was going to be exceedingly worse. We had enough dead officials at the moment.

"If you kill anyone, we don't get paid," I reminded him.

His leather jacket creaked when he folded his arms. "Feels good to get that shit off my chest. Niko was right."

"Niko knew?"

Shepherd didn't answer.

Knowing that Niko hadn't divulged such a secret made me feel better about confiding in him. Niko must have encouraged Shepherd to tell the group, but I could understand Shepherd's point of view. It wasn't easy laying out all your dirty laundry for the world to see, especially when it could affect your position in the group. Keystone was all we had.

"I could really go for a bacon sandwich," I said, pulling into the church parking lot.

"Inside a warm roll," he added. "With hot coffee."

"If this job doesn't pan out, I might open up a joint that serves bacon with everything."

"Keep it open twenty-four hours, and I'll be a regular."

"What the hell are they doing?" I muttered, noticing two men poking around in the bushes by the building.

I parked and switched off the engine. When one of the men turned around, I recognized his face and shot out of the truck. Pulling a long dagger from the strap on my leg, I flashed toward him, weapon drawn. "What are you doing?"

Merry bowed, his gaze affixed to my blade. "I would advise you to put the weapon away, lest I have to kill you in self-defense."

"Not until you tell me why you're snooping around in the bushes. Weren't you reassigned?"

He squared his shoulders, his expression blank. "Are you aware of the mass assassination?"

Shepherd appeared at my side, a gun drawn but aimed at the ground.

Weather stood up when he caught a whiff of tension culminating behind his back. He brandished his katana, and we were suddenly in a standoff. "Put down your weapon, Mage."

I scowled at Merry. "Are you planting a bomb?"

Merry slowly moved his hand over the pommel of his sword, his blond hair tied in the back. "That's what we're here looking for."

"Why here and not the location where we sent you?"

He stepped forward, eyes still on my blade. "Because the other location was burned to the ground."

I glowered. "You were at the church, and it just so happened to burn down? Shepherd, call Viktor."

Weather raised his sword. "Touch that phone, and I'll cut off your hand."

Shepherd raised his gun and aimed it at Weather. "Can you run faster than a bullet?"

Merry blurred as he rushed at me, and two fangs sank into my shoulder. Incensed, I blasted him with energy, and down he went. I heard a gunshot but ignored it as I straddled Merry and shocked him again. His eyes glazed over, but he still looked confused as to why his venom hadn't paralyzed me. I pulled the collar of my sweater off my shoulder and looked at the two bleeding puncture marks. He hadn't meant to kill me, or there would have been four. After unbuckling Merry's belt, I rolled him onto his stomach and tied up his hands while he was still unconscious.

"Stay down, motherfucker," Shepherd snarled.

He shoved Weather's face against the concrete while tying him up with a nylon cord.

"Where the hell did you get that?" I asked.

He cinched the knot tighter and then looped it around Weather's feet. "You think I don't got pockets in the lining of my coat?"

"I thought you put cigarettes in there. Who knew you carried an arsenal of survival gear?"

"You're going to regret this," Weather growled. "Just wait until the higher authority hears you've attacked a Regulator."

Shepherd kicked him, and I blasted Weather with enough energy to silence him.

"You attacked first," I spat. "And who's out here planting bombs? Huh? Yeah, the same guys who burned down the church."

Shepherd walked over to the bushes and performed a search. I sheathed my dagger, still out of breath.

"Jaysus wept. Is that who I think it is?"

I turned to Christian. "They were up to something."

"Aye," he said, approaching me and lowering his voice. "They were searching the grounds for bombs and hidden weapons. I sent them out here."

"They're not supposed to be here in the first place!"

"They never made it to the other location before the attack."

"Is that what they told you?"

Shepherd eased up to our huddle and wiped the sweat from his brow.

Christian pinched the bridge of his nose. "They didn't have to. The attack happened ten minutes after they left. Now, unless they have wings stuffed in the back of their trousers, they weren't at the scene of the crime."

Shepherd wiped his forehead. "Didn't find anything in the bushes."

Christian cut him a sharp glare. "Of course you didn't, you big numpty. Did I hear a gunshot?"

Shepherd shrugged. "Nobody's dead. It's just a flesh wound." He glanced worriedly over his shoulder and then back. "This looks like something we'll have to deny later."

Shortly after untying Merry and Weather, we cordially invited them inside for a "Please don't have us executed" cup of coffee so we could explain.

I finished the last sip of my drink and slid the cup across the table between Merry and me. "Look, we're all here for the same reason. You have to admit it looked suspicious."

Merry rubbed his chest where I'd shocked him. I averted my eyes to Weather, who was sitting at the end of the table with his shirt off while Shepherd stitched up his arm with a needle and thread the priest had given him.

"Why didn't the other Regulators step in to help you?" I asked.

"Each is assigned to guard a location," Merry answered. "To leave his assigned post creates a breach. It's a common divisional tactic. Our priority is to protect the officials, not each other." He gave me a long look that made me uncomfortable. "You suspected us all along, didn't you?"

I glanced to my left at Christian. "No."

Merry leaned forward and drew in a deep breath. "You lie."

Christian pointed a finger at him. "I'll thank you kindly to get your nose out of her face."

"I didn't suspect you the entire time," I explained. "So it's not a lie. But why does my suspicion come as a surprise? The victims let the murderer into their homes—someone with a long sword that they trusted enough not to use it. Who carries swords?"

"Lots of people, I might add."

"Yes, but let's take a hard look at the last victim. She invited a man back to her house. She drove him. Everyone at the party had a car, so why didn't he follow her? Because maybe he didn't have a car. I've seen the way you guys pile into one vehicle for these events, and one of your buddies would've noticed if the car went missing. She invited an armed man back to her house. There's only one form of protection women want men to carry when they invite them into their bed, and it's not a sixty-inch sword."

Christian chuckled and sat back.

When Merry lifted his coffee cup to his lips to blow the steam, it drew my attention to a scratch on his cheek where I'd shoved his face into the concrete.

"You're still not convinced of our innocence," he said to me. "Even after your partner confirmed our whereabouts."

A knock sounded at the door, and Father Martin stepped in. "Christian, I need your assistance."

Christian rose from his seat and squeezed my shoulder before leaving the room.

Merry set down his cup. "Would you two gentlemen give us a moment of privacy?"

Weather wrenched his arm away, and Shepherd grumbled a curse as they gathered their things and left us alone.

When the door closed, Merry wrapped his hands around his coffee cup. "What has you so convinced that I can't be trusted? I smell your emotions, female. Don't lie."

I scooted back. "Why did you invite me to the last crime scene?"

"You were involved with the previous."

"Yes, but we were called in as a third party to verify the identity. We weren't hired to work the murders, and you know that. Viktor's contact didn't ask me to go with you, so why did you invite me? Why did you lie and tell me you already asked Christian, knowing I'd find out the truth? Maybe I don't have a Chitah nose, but I can smell bullshit a mile away."

His lips pressed into a mulish line before he let go of his cup. "This evacuation wasn't by the book. I had apprehensions about your team staying within the church. I looked you up, Raven. I'm aware of your sketchy past. Let me allay your fears by explaining that I have no intention of killing you."

"But you did."

"Correct. I invited you to Mathilda's house because I wasn't certain of your motives. I wanted to draw you away from your partner and get you alone."

"To kill me."

He raised his palm, signaling me to slow down. "Let me explain. The purpose was to speak with you alone. You said you had no loyalty to the higher authority, and when someone makes a bold statement like that, it's a red flag for treason. I had every right to question your intentions. But you also said something that changed my mind—about your loyalty to mankind and the necessity for law to exist. You recognize the value of our agencies even if you disagree with our methods. You care about humans, and perhaps it's because you're still connected to their world." He leaned back in his chair, his fingers laced together. "What made you suspicious of me in particular?"

"Because you asked me how loyal I was to the higher authority. And that's a red flag in *my* book. I wondered if you were fishing to see if I might be willing to join your rebellion."

Merry laughed, a dimple pitting his cheek. "The very question that saved your life was one that risked my own. I merely saw Keystone as a threat to the lives I'm duty-bound to protect. I understand your organization has aided in the capture of many outlaws, but you each have questionable pasts that make you untrustworthy in the eyes of a Regulator."

"If you killed us, you would have suffered the consequences."

"Killing you would have been for the greater good, protecting the lives that save us all. That alone is worth my life and freedom. I will admit that my concern wasn't with you directly harming them."

I folded my arms. "You thought one of us would leak the location or sell it to the highest bidder, didn't you?"

"One church is destroyed. Should I still be concerned?"

"Why would we betray the people who fund one of our revenue streams?"

"Because maybe an organization unconcerned with ethics doesn't care where their money comes from. If someone offered one of you a substantial bribe, I don't see what would stop you from accepting it."

"Criminals want nothing to do with us. We're the ones who hunt *them* down, and we don't just do it for a paycheck. I don't know what you dug up about me since I'm not in any records that I'm aware of, but my past has nothing to do with who I am."

"On the contrary, it has everything to do with who you've become. You can't understand a man's present frame of mind without looking at his past."

"There are men out there with squeaky-clean records filling your jail cells. You can't make assumptions based on someone's past; you have to look at their motives. What motive would Keystone have for putting our lives at risk to save these idiots just so we can have them killed? Money? The higher authority hires us because they trust us. I thought you guys would respect that, but now it appears you were going to execute me for nothing more than suspicion."

"No one is above the law. No one."

"Good. Then we're on the same page. Do you trust your comrade in arms?"

"All Regulators have been accounted for. We watch each other closely. No one could have left their station to pull off an attack."

"What about the ones who aren't Chitahs? They're not on the job. Do you think one of them might have leaked information?"

"Only those who showed up are privy to the locations and details. When a man is assigned a task, he doesn't divulge the information to anyone who is not part of the assignment, not even his brother. It's the code we follow."

I rubbed the bite marks on my shoulder. "Before you start assuming all your guys are clean, maybe you should do some sniffing around."

"I agree," he said, rising to his feet. "May I ask you a question?"

"Sure."

His eyes lingered on my shoulder, and he drew a breath. After a beat, Merry blinked a few times and looked me in the eye. "Did you report me to anyone?"

"No one outside my team. But that's not what you were going to ask me, was it?"

He wanted to know why his bite hadn't paralyzed me but likely decided that asking the obvious wasn't worth the effort if he wasn't going to get the answer.

Merry drifted toward the door, hands in his pants pockets. "Let no Regulator inside the church. Except for the two I trust, I'm issuing an order for them to remain outside. Can you have the priest back me up?"

"Sure. You should put someone by the road to look for suspicious cars or activity. Now that the lights are on, we can see who's coming."

"If our location was compromised, this was all for naught."

When we stepped outside, Merry sauntered off to organize his men. I still had reservations about how much we could trust these guys, but if Merry and Weather were the killers, they wouldn't have come inside for coffee.

Then again, maybe they *were* the killers but had nothing to do with the church assassination. What if that was unrelated? It didn't fit with how the previous murders were connected.

I rubbed my temple. "What the hell did you sign up for, Raven Black? Political conspiracies? Serial killers? Black marketeers? I miss the good old days when I could just single out an asshat and suffocate him in the bathroom."

When I neared the door to the subterranean Mage motel, it opened, and Christian lingered in the doorway.

"Come with me," he said.

Curious, I followed him down the spiral stairwell, my hand touching his back to keep me from tumbling in the dark.

"I heard you out there," he said. "If you're having second thoughts, maybe you should go back to your scavenger life."

"Could you please tune me out when I'm talking to myself?"

I stumbled and flew into Christian. To keep from falling down the stairs, I wrapped my arms around his waist and held on.

Christian stood motionless. "I know my arse is sublime, but can't you restrain yourself?"

I clawed my way up to my feet, and we continued our descent. "What's this about? I thought we weren't letting anyone down here but the priest."

Overlapping voices grew louder as we approached the bottom and emerged through the door. Christian had the key, and he locked the door behind him.

Officials in the main room were engaged in noisy discussions that sounded more like debates.

"I broke the news," Christian quietly informed me.

"What's the vote?"

"They wanted to stay. But Patrick Bane, our illustrious rabble-rouser, is riling them up."

"He probably wants to see his kid," I said facetiously. "By the way, you missed the big news."

Christian turned his back to the crowd and cast his gaze downward. "And what news is that?"

I leaned in tight. "That boy doesn't belong to Patrick. He made up that entire story about the mother working for him and getting killed. That's Shepherd's kid."

Christian's eyes rounded. "Don't be telling me fibs."

"I'm dead serious. Shepherd said they had a confrontation at one of his parties. Shep saw a picture on my phone of the kid not wearing his mask. There's a scar on his face just like the one the baby would have had because of the knife. It didn't take him long to put two and two together. Anyhow, Patrick admitted it, and he threatened to ruin Keystone if Shepherd tried to come after him. You can't say anything to him—not yet. He's still got a lot of power, and Shepherd wants to protect his kid. If Patrick thinks we're all in on his little secret, he might do something—"

"Ruinous," Christian finished. "You mean to tell me he was behind murdering the child's mother, or he coincidentally ended up with the boy?"

"What Mage coincidentally ends up with a child? He orchestrated the murder, and he has plans for this kid. It's a long story, but don't even allude to it."

"That infernal little shitebag."

I watched the animated crowd. "I agree with him on letting everyone out. They're sitting ducks."

"Aye. And Daffy wants a word with you."

"Why me?"

"Because I told him to feck off when he asked for my phone. He threatened to dismantle Keystone if I didn't get someone down there who would listen to reason."

"Aww, that's so sweet. You need my help, don't you?"

He dipped his chin. "Maybe I just wanted your help hiding the body."

I circled around Christian and headed for Patrick's room. By the sound of all the dissention, he'd managed to convince enough people to vote on leaving.

"What's this all about?" I asked, storming into his room.

Patrick quit his pacing and stalked toward me, this time dressed in black slacks and a white button-up. "Give me your phone."

I folded my arms. "Give me your mansion."

"Don't be daft," he growled, holding out his hand. "Give it to me!"

Christian swaggered into view, his arms also folded. "Do you see what I've had to endure? Wyatt rings me with an update, and this one goes ballistic."

"What update?" I asked.

"Street surveillance outside the burning church caught four men running out."

"You hear that?" Patrick snapped. "It's an assassination plot. You're going to get us all killed."

I'd never seen Patrick this flustered, and after tonight's news, I enjoyed watching him squirm. "Go out there and have a debate, but make it quick. Our contact wants a vote by the majority."

"Let me speak to Viktor. I'm not letting another man vote on my life."

"That's not how democracy works. If only four men are responsible for the attack, we've got you covered. There are more Regulators guarding this church than there were the other one, and besides," I said, gesturing to Christian, "you have us to protect you."

Patrick lunged, and I lunged back. I rammed my left arm against his throat to shove him back and reached for the dagger on my belt.

Christian wedged between us and gripped my wrist. "There'll be no penetration in the holy temple, and that includes your blade."

I let go of the grip. "Fine. But if he touches me again, you'll need Father Martin down here to give him his last rites."

Christian shoved Patrick, putting more distance between us.

Sweat beaded on Patrick's pasty brow, and it wasn't hot down here by a mile. Sweat stained his armpits, and he was behaving erratically. "I'll pay you. Leave the others here if you want, but let me out."

"And what makes you think the killers won't follow you out of here?" Christian asked. "You'll be on your own. No Regulators, no bodyguards—"

"I'll take my chances," he bit out.

Christian's jaw clenched. "Why are you so paranoid? Did you leave the door to your porn stash unlocked?"

"Don't trifle with me, boy. I could have you executed with a snap of my fingers." When Patrick snapped his fingers for emphasis, the tension crackled.

Christian's stare went ice-cold.

I pushed the sleeves of my sweater up. "Let's just cool down for a minute. You've convinced a few people out there to change their minds. I have my opinion on the matter, but we have to follow orders. The person overseeing this operation wants a vote from every church location before he makes a decision."

"Bloody hell!" Patrick threw his hands up in the air. "*All* the locations? So ours is just one part of the larger vote? That's just grand."

"I think you guys should separate, but it's not up to me. Chances are slim that someone knows about all the locations. How could they? Nobody knew about the evacuation in advance."

The muted television to the right flashed cell phone video of the church ablaze. Flames licked the outside walls from the shattered windows, and the red banner that ran at the bottom of the screen displayed the words: Breaking News. The film looped once more while the camera zoomed in on the shadowy images of four hooded men sprinting from the front door. It was too dark and grainy to make out their faces.

Patrick sat down on the sofa, his hands trembling as he shielded his face. "We're going to die down here."

Christian pulled out his phone to check his messages. "Don't get your knickers in a bunch."

I noticed him staring at the phone with a bemused look. "What is it?"

He turned away from Patrick and lowered his voice. "Wyatt has an update on one of your murder victims."

"Why did he send it to you?"

Christian tilted his head to the side. "Is your phone turned off?"

I looked down at the leather jacket I wasn't wearing. "I must have left it at home when I changed clothes."

Christian handed me his phone.

"Is that a gas station?" I asked, studying the image.

"Aye. He said there's video, but that's a still image of the best shot. The license plate matches your last victim."

In the picture, Mathilda was holding the gas pump. I used my fingers to zoom in on the passenger seat of the car since the image was a front view of the vehicle. The man's face was nondescript due to distance and video quality. Wyatt was crazy if he thought this picture could provide a positive ID, but as I looked closer, I noticed the man's arm resting on the car window. I zoomed in as far as it would go. "I think I know who that is."

"That's a shite picture," he pointed out.

Still keeping my voice low, I pointed at the screen. "See that tattoo on his bicep? That's Cyrus, the guy who fought Niko outside Flavors. He's one of Patrick's personal guards. I'm sure of it."

"That could be anyone's ink. You can't even make out the pattern."

"But you can tell it's tribal."

"That's not enough to convict a man."

"How many inked men did you see at the party? Most of them were politicians. And besides, he's not even wearing a suit."

"You think arseface over there has something to do with it?"

"I don't know. These guys might have their own agenda."

Christian's gaze drifted to the ceiling. "He'll never talk."

"Maybe you can threaten him with holy water."

Christian snatched the phone and strode toward the sofa. He leaned forward and held the phone in front of his own face. "If I give you this, do you swear to behave?"

When Patrick's eyes lifted, his expression went blank.

"Now that I have your undivided attention," Christian began, taking a seat beside him, "I want you to look deep in my eyes and trust me. I'm a friend you can confide in. A man of the cloth would never lie to you, now would he?"

"No."

"Raven, lock the door."

Panic swept over me. "Christian, don't do it. It's treason."

"Do as I say, lass. There's no turning back now."

After locking the door, I hurried over to the leather chair. "If you're wrong, they'll execute us."

Christian held his gaze. "Tell me about Cyrus."

"I don't know a Cyrus."

"He's lying," I said.

Christian turned the onyx ring on his finger. "Do you have personal guards?"

"Yes."

"Are any of them Asian?"

"No," Patrick said flatly, caught in Christian's charm.

"Jaysus, Raven. Are you sure about this?"

"Yes. I even saw him inside Patrick's house. Maybe they weren't really hired as his bodyguards."

Christian sighed heavily. "Do you employ a man of Asian descent?"

"Yes."

"But he's not your guard."

"No."

"What do you pay him for?"

Patrick was caught in a dreamlike state, and his pale-green eyes showed no indication he comprehended what was happening to him. "I hired him to do as I ask. They are not my guards."

"This is like pulling teeth," Christian growled. "What are their names, and what specifically do you pay them to do?"

"Their names are Tom, Dick, Harry, and John."

I snorted.

"The less I know about them, the better," he continued. "They are assassins for hire."

"Now we're getting somewhere." Christian shifted in his seat. "And who are you hiring them to kill?"

"The officials who support human rights."

I stood up and put my hand on Christian's shoulder. "Ask him why."

"Why?"

Patrick tilted his head to the side. "To destroy humans. That is our ultimate goal, and the first step toward freedom is to tip the laws in our favor."

"The higher authority exists in many cities," Christian pointed out. "How is changing one city going to make a difference?"

"It's the domino effect. I'm not the only one."

Chills ran down my spine.

Christian stood up and severed the connection. "You little shitebag. I should have known."

Patrick blinked a few times, and the visceral look on his face when he stood up made me reach for my dagger. "You have the audacity to charm a man of the law? How *dare* you!"

Christian nonchalantly folded his arms, a smug look on his face. "Go ahead and turn me in."

Patrick's gaze flicked back and forth between us, his lips pressed thin.

We were at a stalemate. Neither Christian nor I could use his admission as evidence to turn him in. Charming a member of the higher authority was treasonous. And Patrick Bane could gripe all he wanted about our conniving behavior, but he wouldn't risk turning us in. They would question our motives, and if someone charmed Christian, they might discover Patrick's confession. Funny how the law worked. I was kind of hoping Patrick would turn us in, but even if they convicted him, Christian and I still wouldn't escape the charges of treason.

So there we all stood, helpless to the facts.

I let go of my dagger. "What do you have against humans?"

Patrick looked at me with disdain. "Something you'll never understand, lass. You're too green and attached to their ways. I lived in squalor until I met my Creator. He gave me a chance at a life of comfort, but when humans beheaded him for treason against their king, where do you think that left me? I lived for centuries as a vagabond, and I hid the fact I was a Mage so they wouldn't execute me for witchery. It took me years to acquire money and status. Do you think I'm going to waste my life protecting humans when they've done everything to upend and destroy my liberties?"

"You think they haven't done the same to me?" Christian lowered his arms and glowered. "Pull up your britches and stop your sniveling."

I shook my head. "I don't get it. So you kill everyone who supports human rights. I know firsthand that the Mageri now recommends those who are supporters. It looks like they have their own agenda."

Patrick barked out a laugh and strode to the counter to pour himself a glass of Chartreuse from a half-empty bottle. "Since you'd be fools to turn me in after committing treason, I'll tell you. I have clout with the Mageri. I'm the one who reviews their recommendations for preapproval. There are those who support my vision—*our* vision—and are willing to lie to claim a chair on the panel. We've been grooming people for years to fill these seats and tip the scales in our favor when it's time to vote on new laws." Patrick took a long gulp of wine and smiled ruefully at his glass. "The blackout ruined everything."

I leaned against the door, my mind racing. What the hell were we going to do with this information? If that was the clearest shot Wyatt could get from the surveillance video, we were screwed. Patrick didn't even know Cyrus's real name, and that posed an additional problem if they were to charm him. Patrick knew exactly what he was doing.

I put on my best poker face. "We have surveillance video."

He swallowed his wine audibly, fingertips turning white around the wineglass as he gripped it tighter. "If you had evidence, you wouldn't have charmed me."

"What do you even know about those guys?" I asked. "You have to be the dumbest person I've ever met to blindly hire men off the street to do your dirty work."

He finished his wine and set down the empty glass. "Don't be daft. Uneducated criminals are the easiest to dupe. Never hire a smart man to do your bidding. That simpleton didn't even negotiate a higher pay. I don't plan to keep them around for long. Once you're done with the trash, you take it out."

I shared a furtive glance with Christian, and we read each other's minds. Patrick confiding in us had nothing to do with trust; he planned to kill us. Maybe not tonight, but he was a powerful man who could pull it off, and we would never see it coming.

I thought about the crime scenes and my debunked theory

about Regulators. "How did you get those people to open the door for your men?"

Patrick strolled across the room, hands in his pockets. "Easy. I was with them. All except for the last one. Mathilda's desperation made her an easy target."

"You killed Hooper."

He pivoted on his heel. "Who?"

"The second victim at your party."

Patrick reclined his head, searching his memory. "Ah. The bartender. He was the only way we could get the target outside alone. Your friend sold sensory magic on the side, you know."

"He didn't deserve to die for it."

Patrick shrugged. "One could say the same about Elaine's lover. My sources told me he wasn't usually the first to arrive at the apartment on their designated nights, so we weren't expecting him. When he answered, I simply told him I needed to speak to Elaine about a life-and-death matter. Can't be too careful about lying to a Chitah. Your friend and Elaine's lover are what you might call collateral damage. Wrong place, wrong time. I can't afford witnesses." Patrick pursed his lips and looked toward the television. "Things were going so well until the blackout thwarted my plans. You see, a blackout makes people more reluctant to answer their door. Neighbors are peeking out windows at the sound of every barking dog and car passing by. Even now, once we're released from this godforsaken hole in the ground, my colleagues will be on high alert."

Christian swaggered toward him. "My deepest apologies that your killing spree was interrupted."

Patrick stumbled backward. "Stay away from me, Vamp."

Christian grabbed a fistful of Patrick's shirt and yanked him close. One of the buttons popped off and clicked against the floor as it went skittering underneath the sofa. "You're gonna tell me where we can find your henchmen."

Patrick looked at me instead of Christian. "I'm not that stupid."

Christian's lips peeled back. "No, you're a fecking eejit. Tell me now, or I'll rip your tongue out and shove it up your arse."

"I don't know their names, and I don't know where they sleep at night. I call them at a throwaway number when I need them. You can't prove my involvement in any of this. They won't question me based on your accusation alone. It's inadmissible. Slander laws prohibit investigations against us without hard evidence."

"Aye, that's why I need your henchmen."

Patrick laughed haughtily. "I left the scene of every murder. I wasn't even there. I didn't actually see anything."

Christian shook him. "But you ordered the hits!"

"Says who? You have nothing on me, Vampire."

Christian shoved him so hard that Patrick flew against the sofa, hitting his head on the wall before slumping over. "Entitled bastard," he murmured.

I looked down at Patrick's unconscious body. "How's your temper tantrum going to help?"

Christian stared daggers at me. "He's got connections everywhere. He'll have those men killed before we ever get our hands on them. We have just enough evidence on them to open an inquiry, and if we can get the higher authority to approve legal questioning about the church attack, they'll charm those shitebags to find out who they're working for. Patrick will be implicated, but not directly because of us. It's the only way to save ourselves."

I rubbed the healing wound on my shoulder from Merry's bite. "Save ourselves from what?"

"How long do you think it'll be before he pins the murders on Keystone? He won't just come after *us*, Raven. He'll see our entire team as a threat. A man in his position can create evidence out of thin air."

My lungs filled with oxygen as his words sank in. "I hadn't thought of that."

Patrick sending his goons to kill Christian and me was a given, but he was too smart to think we'd keep this information all to ourselves and not include our boss. To be on the safe side, he'd come after Keystone. If Christian and I were out of the picture, it would be even easier to pin the crimes on us.

Christian walked over and rested his shoulder against the door.

"I've been around, and I know how men like him think. He aims to see us six feet under."

"So scrub his memory of this entire conversation."

Christian shook his head. "It's too dangerous. If anyone notices a lapse in his memory, they'll use skilled Vampires to pick his mind. If they're not able to undo the erasing, they'll question us since we were seen entering this room by everyone outside. We can't do anything impulsive that would dig our graves even deeper. Perhaps he won't do anything asinine to call attention to himself now that he knows we're onto him."

"Don't tell Viktor what you did," I warned him. "He doesn't like secrets, but he'll flip his lid if he finds out about this. And Patrick will *know* if we've told him. They spend a lot of time together at parties, and you can bet your ass that Patrick will be using that boy to find out the truth."

Christian's head thumped against the door.

I stretched my collar with both hands. "We should pull Niko in on this. He's got history with these guys. Give me your phone."

"I'd rather you not use the phone. Someone might intercept the call." Christian's dark eyes met mine. "You can't tell him what I've done. No one can know, or they'll execute me. Have you ever gone to the courts and witnessed a trial? They perform the execution right then and there, Raven. Your head rolls right in front of a live audience."

My stomach turned. "Fine. I'll drive home and fill him in. He might know where to find these guys. Promise I won't be long." I tugged the sleeve of his cassock. "Shepherd brought you a change of clothes. I want to see you out of this dress by the time I come back."

He stroked my cheek with his fingertips, but the humor was absent from his eyes. "Aye, Precious."

The tenderness in his touch pinched my heart unexpectedly. It was in that moment I realized I needed to let go of the past and stop doubting his intentions. It was a losing battle.

"Are you going to be okay in here?" I asked. "What if he tells everyone you attacked him?"

Christian tucked a lock of hair behind my ear. "He's had too much to drink. More than half the wine's gone. Poor bastard slipped and hit his head."

I wanted to fold into Christian's embrace. I wanted to forget all these problems and go back to our date night beneath the stars.

I wanted him to take off that damn robe so I wouldn't be scarred for life for having sexual fantasies about him in a priest outfit.

"Go on with you, lass. Better we find his men before he gets out of here."

"I'll call and let you know the plan."

"No diversions," he stressed, tapping my nose with his finger. "I'll not have you going into Patrick's mansion alone. Promise me you'll have someone with you if you get another hunch."

"Yes, sir."

"Mmm, I like that."

I got all warm and tingly between my legs from the way he growled and ran his hand down my back. Christian's gaze was molten, his lips hungry for mine as he licked them in anticipation of a kiss.

Just as he leaned in, Patrick moaned.

"Better go," Christian breathed against my lips. "Before I have to knock him out again and take you against this door."

"Promise?"

Chapter 24

AFTER LEAVING PATRICK'S ROOM, I held a neutral expression as I passed Shepherd in the hall upstairs.

He pressed a bloody rag against his elbow. "What's the plan?"

"I'm heading back. They're still debating downstairs, so I don't know how long it'll be."

He grimaced. "We're not gonna be the ones driving them back home, are we?"

"I'd rather go home in a body bag. What are we? A taxi service?"

He chuckled. "Nobody's got time for that."

"If the other churches vote to leave, their opinion won't matter anyhow. Father Martin should probably get their cell phones and other personal items ready to return. I have a feeling our job is done."

Shepherd walked alongside me as I journeyed to the back door. "Three people already tried to break in."

"Who?"

"Probably some pissants who stole a TV and want forgiveness before they go home and watch Netflix on it."

"The Regulators let them get all the way to the door?"

"We can't barricade the parking lot entryway from the street—someone might call the cops. They're scoping out suspicious cars and using their noses. Two Regulators are guarding the inside doors."

"Let me guess, Batman and Robin?"

"I heard that," a man said from behind me.

I turned, not surprised to see Merry. The scabbard hanging from his waist tapped against his leg as he headed toward us.

"Miss me already?" I asked.

He tucked a loose lock of blond hair into the elastic hair tie that held it all together in the back. "What's the plan?"

Shepherd folded his arms. "I feel like there's an echo in here."

I shrugged. "You'll have to check with Father Martin for updates. I'm outta here."

Merry reached in his pockets and put on his leather gloves. "I'll walk you to your car."

"I'm a big girl."

"You're also unpredictable, if I might add. Maybe I want to make sure you don't put a knife in one of my boys."

"Rest easy, Tony the Tiger. I'm impulsive, but I'm not crazy."

"Wouldn't Chester Cheetah have been a more suitable reference?"

"Jesus," Shepherd said, biting back a laugh. "I'll leave you two alone."

After he disappeared, I gave Merry a thorough appraisal. "How do I know *you're* not the one who's going to put a knife in *me*?"

He stretched his fingers in his gloves. "Let's walk."

When we stepped outside, the humidity felt sticky against my face. But it wasn't uncomfortably cold, especially since the wind had died down.

"That little incident earlier won't be going in my report," he assured me. "I'm hoping you'll do me the same courtesy?"

"We don't file incident reports."

Merry straightened his collar so it was vertical. "No, but I would appreciate it if you kept it between us and didn't discuss it with your contact. I'm a seasoned Regulator who specializes in murder investigations, but I'm relatively new to this district. Despite my references, it would ruin my reputation if my boss found out someone had gotten the upper hand on us, especially while we were guarding officials."

I curled my hands beneath my sweater sleeves. "I get it. You're afraid of the ridicule when people find out a girl took you down in ten seconds."

He stopped and lightly gripped my arm. "That's not it, female. You're a tough adversary."

I glanced around. "Your buddies might say something."

"The men I work with have a code of honor. I trust them with my life. Teasing, I can handle, but a disparaging remark from my superior, I cannot. Incidents like these tarnish reputations and might prevent me from future promotions."

"Don't worry. I'll make sure my team doesn't talk about it. But a word of advice? Never attack someone unless your weapon is drawn and you're ready to fight to the death. What if I had disarmed you?"

He inclined his head. "Duly noted."

"I used to be terrified of you guys, but it's hard to be scared of a man who won't draw his sword."

"I only draw it when I intend to use my weapon."

"Your friend drew his. Is it because I'm a woman?"

He blinked and quickly shook his head. "A Mage usually poses no threat to me. Besides, it was just a misunderstanding."

"I threatened a Regulator with a weapon. I'm pretty sure you have rules about no mercy when it comes to that kind of thing. Weather was ready to take Shepherd's head, but not you." I folded my arms and tried to hide my amusement. "You only bit me with *two* fangs—enough to paralyze but not to kill. I'm not sure what your code of conduct was up in Canada, but down here, it's every man for himself. I lived on the streets for years, and people here will take advantage of mercy. They see it as a weakness."

"Are you saying I should have killed you?"

I dropped my arms at my side. "Do you really think you could have? I know Chitahs revere women, but that will always be your weakness, and one of these days, a woman is going to be the end of you."

He rocked with laughter, a hand over his stomach and eyes tearing up.

I turned away and headed to my truck. "You need help."

His laughter died down. "Come now. Haven't you heard? A woman will be the end of us all."

I rolled my eyes as he started laughing again. It sounded like something Christian would say. Why did all men think that women would be their ruin? My life had been exclusively ruined by men, not women.

When I reached the front of my blue pickup, I ran my hand alongside her frame and got in. I loved the interior smell—it wrapped around me like a security blanket of memories. I'd even found a candy bar wrapper wedged between the seats when I was fumbling around with the lap belts the other week. Little things like that made it paralyzing to get through the day. I was the reason I couldn't see my father, and that was a heavy burden to carry. I missed him. I missed all the years I'd never have with him because of all these fucking rules.

Packing up the past was a necessary evil, and it wouldn't be fair to involve my father in a world of immortals when he hadn't asked for it. He deserved a normal life, and it was selfish to want otherwise. But sometimes, late at night, when I was tossing and turning in bed, I heard Fletcher's voice creeping into my worst nightmares: "I'm going to find him, and I'm going to kill him."

My stomach knotted as I turned the truck in a circle and exited the parking lot.

"That's just great. I've finally become the stereotypical brooding Vampire. Maybe I should just wear all black and lament the death of my mortal soul."

A Regulator loitering on the curb lifted a bottle of alcohol wrapped in a paper bag to his lips, but he had his eye on me the whole stretch of the turn. It yanked me out of my thoughts and reminded me of our current situation. Christian had just blown the lid off the murder mystery, and now that Patrick saw us as a threat, it was a race against the clock to locate Cyrus and his men before Patrick devised a plan to destroy Keystone. He wouldn't do anything just yet—not as long as we had the kid.

A pickup truck passed me going in the opposite direction, and I took notice since not many people in this city drove trucks.

Through the rearview mirror, I observed several men in the back with what looked like baseball bats.

"Nah, couldn't be. They're just out celebrating… with bats."

My gut instinct told me they weren't touring the city or driving home from a baseball game. I gripped the wheel, annoyed that I didn't have my phone to call Christian and give him a heads-up just in case.

They can handle any trouble that comes along. No need for me to intervene.

Christian was counting on me to get home and touch base with Niko. If we could just capture one of Cyrus's men, it would help us build a solid case against Patrick. There were plenty of Regulators outside the church. Shepherd could handle himself.

"Dammit."

I jerked the wheel, and the tires screeched as I spun in a circle and sped back to the church. I instinctively reached in front of the seat toward the floor where my father always kept his gun. The holster was still there, but he'd taken his weapon before selling the truck. I already knew that, but occasionally, I lost sense of time.

I blew through an intersection and turned the corner before slowing the vehicle down. The church was up ahead on the right, and I wanted to check out what was happening before charging in like a madwoman and getting my head taken off by sleep-deprived Regulators. After parking by the curb, I strolled up the sidewalk, my hand gripping the T-shaped handle of my push dagger. On the upside, I didn't hear the sound of alarms, screaming, or someone getting their skull bashed in with a baseball bat.

"You're paranoid," I muttered, stepping onto the sidewalk.

These couldn't be the same attackers as the first church, not if they were going to rush Regulators with nothing more than sporting equipment.

When I neared the parking lot turn-in and didn't see the Regulator with his bottle of booze, I sharpened my light. As I curved around the bushes, I noticed a black boot poking out. It didn't move when I nudged it.

The hair on my arms stood on end from either fear or the

staggering amount of static I'd built up from nervous energy. I leveled down, containing the power before it spiraled out of control. Bushes and trees bordered the outer edge of the parking lot, so I walked alongside those bushes instead of cutting straight through the open area.

Where the hell is everyone?

Instead of going around to the side entrance on the left side of the building, I headed right and cut between two buildings. The rectory and a small youth center were on my right, and a winding sidewalk separated them from the church. It wasn't until halfway through that I heard a ruckus. I jogged across the dead grass to the end of the building and gripped the corner wall, peering around back. Two Regulators were engaged in a spectacular swordfight with men who wielded identical swords. I was willing to bet those men had lifted the weapons off the Regulators they'd knocked out.

One Regulator impaled a man straight through his gut, but the guy backed up and freed himself. Blood seeped between his fingers where he held his stomach, and seconds later, he shifted into a massive leopard and lunged at the Regulator.

My eyes swung to the right. Three Regulators had a Vampire surrounded, but none of them had impalement wood. While they could decapitate him with their swords, it was risky to get too close. Only certain types of wood could paralyze a Vampire. Cedar was one I knew about. The amount was also important, as a single toothpick couldn't bring down a Vamp. I searched the property and flashed toward a tree before snapping a branch off.

As I flashed by a Regulator, I shoved the branch in his hand. "See if that works."

He gave me an incredulous look. After giving the wood a quick sniff test, he lunged at the Vampire from behind and stabbed him in the back of the neck. The Vampire had just enough energy to turn and swing, striking the Chitah on the shoulder and knocking him down. The poor man bellowed in pain, his bones broken. The Vamp, on the other hand, fell like a dying cyclone.

I did a quick scan of my surroundings. Two were entangled in a swordfight, but farther behind them, I witnessed two Chitahs knocking down a Regulator. They'd overpowered him, stolen his sword, and sliced his throat. I winced at the savagery. The Regulators on my right were too distracted by their screaming friend to notice.

I flashed toward the Chitahs and aimed for the tallest guy. The second my dagger found a home in his neck, I jumped onto the other one and sank my fangs into his jugular. My legs locked around his waist, and I did what I did best. He attempted to shove me off, but I was in my zone. I drank fast and hard, enough that his steps faltered. I tried to think of his blood as medicine, but the repulsive flavor made me want to expel every drop in one heave. Someone beat on my back several times, knocking the wind out of me. When I felt warm liquid trickling down my back, I realized the other Chitah had stabbed me with my own dagger. I let go and stumbled backward, putting distance between myself and the armed man.

The guy I'd attacked cupped his neck, swayed, and then hit the ground with a sickening thud.

One of the Regulators from the far end of the parking lot caught sight of us. He ran at Chitah speed and tackled the armed man from behind.

My next instinct was to protect the entrances. With five attackers in sight, I calculated there were more on the property. I'd seen at least that many in the back of the truck.

I jogged alongside the wall until it cut left into an alcove that led to the back door. Inside, the lights were off. When I neared the doors, I caught light glinting off a sword from inside. The Regulator inside neared the door and stared at me.

I pounded my bloody hand on the glass. "Open up!"

He shook his head.

I tugged on the locked handle. "We need help! Christian!"

If Christian was downstairs, there was no way he could hear what was going on up here, not with that many feet of earth between us.

Someone slammed into me from behind, and I smashed against the glass door like a bug on a windshield. The weight of him was crushing, so I used my hands to push back with all the force I could muster.

"Get... off... me!" I growled.

He used me like a battering ram, hauling me back by my sweater and shoving me against the door again.

"Now you've pissed me off," I muttered against the glass.

I charged my light and spun on my heel to blast energy into his shoulder.

When the jolt surged through him, he recoiled for a moment and grinned. "I thought you were a Vamp. *Interesting.*"

My assailant was about three hundred pounds of muscle and looked like some Ukrainian weight lifter named Igor on steroids. Based on his reaction to my light, he was definitely a Mage. *Fucking hell.*

But I was a Stealer, and that meant I could pop his little cork and render him mortal. How hard could pinning him down be?

"Come to papa," he said, wiggling his fat fingers in a come-hither motion.

Ignoring the blood trickling down my back and the throbbing pain, I flashed my fangs at him. Since he knew I wasn't strong like a Vampire, I reeled in his gaze and stepped forward. "Look into my eyes," I whispered, pretending I had the ability to charm.

He blinked rapidly and averted his eyes. I seized the moment and tried to flash through the small gap between him and the wall, but Igor swung his thick arms and wrapped them around me. I'd heard of tree huggers, but now I finally knew what it was like to be hugged by a tree.

"You're not my type," I growled, wriggling to my knees and loosening his hold.

He gripped the waistband of my pants and hauled me off the ground. This reminded me of the first time Crush had taught me self-defense. I was twelve, and while walking home from school, an older man had offered me a ride. He was actually a neighbor who lived a few streets over, and he made me feel guilty for saying no, as if I'd done a bad thing. I told my father, and he said a woman should never do anything a man wants her to do. Then he called his boys over, and they took off and left me with a babysitter. Three hours later, the sound of motorcycles filled the yard, but they never talked about where they'd gone. For the rest of the night, they showed me how to claw, bite, and kick my way out of anything. But I'd also learned a few other tricks.

While dangling upside down from Igor's grip, I quickly untied his bootlaces. "What do you plan to do to me?" I asked, trying to stall him so that he'd stay still. "That guy inside will slice off your head."

"He hasn't yet."

I quickly tied a lace from each boot together and made a tight knot. When I finished, I put my hands flat on the ground and twisted. The button snapped off my jeans when I gripped the edge of the sidewalk and pulled myself toward it.

Igor had to step back to keep from losing balance, and when he tried, his knotted shoelaces caused him to trip and let go. He hit the ground with a bone-crunching thud.

I scrambled to my feet, straddled him, and sank my teeth into his neck. I tried to reach for his palms, but his arms were too long. My stomach churned at the taste of his blood, the dark poison just as black as the one I'd tasted before him.

When he came to, he grabbed my head and shoved me back. So I spat blood all over his face before punching him in the nose.

Igor groaned with revulsion and flipped over so fast that I couldn't escape. Pinned between the concrete and three hundred pounds of stupid, I had no room to breathe.

He palmed my hands, pulling my light before I had a chance to even think about pulling his. I was too busy trying to breathe, trying to get away. But now my light was escaping, and he was on a juicer's high. I fought hard against it, but once the stream was open, it was impossible to reverse.

First my arms tingled, then my feet.

I jolted when a loud bang went off, and Igor started gasping and choking. His eyes bulged, and blood poured from a hole in his throat onto my neck and chest. I swung my head away and saw Shepherd fast approaching.

With a gun in hand, he nudged Igor off me with his boot.

I stared up at him. "You missed."

He extended his left hand. "A head shot would have been messy."

I took his hand, and he hauled me to my feet. "And this isn't?" I asked, my sweater soaked and my neck and chin drenched in blood.

"You would've been picking brains out of your hair for a week. A throat shot is cleaner."

I grimaced at the thought.

Shepherd caught his breath and straightened his back.

I noticed his fat lip, bloody hands, and swollen eye. "Did you come from inside?"

He holstered his gun and looked around. "Other side of the building. Took out a Shifter. Looks like two Chitahs flashed around the perimeter and clubbed the guards. When the Regulators got wind of what was going down, five ran inside to guard the doors." Shepherd wiped his lip and looked at the blood on his wrist. "It happened fast, but I think we've got it under control."

"I saw them driving this way when I was leaving. I would have called, but I don't have my phone."

When the door behind me clicked, we both turned to look.

Christian was tucking his black shirt into his pants, eyes down. "I thought you'd be gone by now. We have news from Viktor. It looks like the order is to release the officials, and— Jaysus wept!" Christian jerked his head back when he got a good look at Shepherd and me. Then his eyes swung down to the oaf bleeding out in the weeds. "If you wanted a snack, I would have made you a plate in the kitchen."

I wiped my face on my sleeve and gave him a cocksure grin. "He insulted my truck."

Christian put his hands on his hips. "I'll be sure not to be making the same mistake." His head tilted to the side as he listened to what was going on around the building.

I walked up and patted his shoulder. "Don't worry. We saved

the day." As I moved inside, I turned to look at the Regulator who'd watched it all go down. "Enjoy the show?"

Before he could answer, I punched him in the jaw. I would have aimed for the eye, but he was too damn tall.

When he tilted his blade, I stepped back.

Christian moved between us. "If you raise that sword any higher, I'll remove your spleen with my bare hands."

The man's eyes grew stony. "You don't frighten me, Vampire."

Christian kneed him in the groin, and the man's eyes bulged. No doubt Christian had put a little extra force in that maneuver, hopefully not enough to prevent the man from fathering children in the future.

Shepherd had taken off, so I hurried down the hall toward the front. "What's the news?"

"Everyone goes home immediately," Christian said, matching my pace.

I swayed and hit the wall before straightening myself.

Christian gripped my sweater and stopped me. "You all right?"

And there it was, that look of concern. His onyx eyes weren't as cold and distant, as if a fire burned in their depths for only me.

"I just feel sick. Gulped down some dark blood, and Igor out there juiced my light."

I didn't bother to mention the stab wounds on my back. Since I could breathe fine, none of them had punctured a lung. Two of them were in my shoulder, so I didn't suspect any major organ damage. My push dagger was only two inches long, anyhow.

"You look better," I noted, glancing down at his dark jeans and tight-fitting shirt. Christian had a nice shape. Broad shoulders, a narrow waist, and a crooked smile that was making its appearance.

"I like the way you look at me," he said softly, leaning closer. He even smelled good.

Too good.

I swayed before resuming my pace. "You better get everyone out of here. Apparently, the word's out that they're holed up in these churches, and that truck of idiots might be the first of many."

"Hold up."

I stopped and wanted to spit out more blood. I could read the blood inside me, and those men had intended to kill everyone inside. Their intent was burning my throat.

No, Raven. Not on the church floor.

"Viktor wants you to take Patrick to pick up his son. I told him you left, but now that you're here…"

I turned around. "I'd like to drive him off a cliff. What makes you think he won't kill me?"

"He'd be a fool to try. We have witnesses outside who will testify to you risking your life to protect this church, so if he wants to put a spin on it that you attempted to assassinate him on the way home, no one would believe it. They'd question him, and he's too smart a man to create an implausible crime."

I reclined my head and sighed. "Fine."

"I have to move fast and organize a convoy to get them out." Christian turned on his heel and stalked down the hall. "Wait in your truck. I'll send him up."

Chapter 25

P ATRICK AND I DIDN'T SHARE a word the entire ride home. He fiddled with his coat sleeve and buttons, and I tried to keep from passing out. The wounds on my back were sore, but drinking from Christian wasn't something I wanted to do on the regular. To constantly rely on him felt like a weakness, and besides, Vampire blood still made me nervous. It held tremendous power, and I hadn't learned enough about that power to trust it. Drinking during sex seemed harmless enough, but making it a regular habit wasn't a wise move.

I distracted myself during the ride with fantasies about plowing the truck into a gas pump or off a cliff. But there weren't any cliffs in the city, and blowing us up would kill me too. As much as I despised Patrick, I felt like sticking around for a few more years.

Instead of pulling into the garage, I drove through the main gate and circled the front driveway before parking outside the door.

The first thing I planned to do the next morning was wash the blood out of the truck. The second was to get Father Martin to sprinkle holy water across the passenger seat where Patrick had defiled it with his mere presence. I should have made him ride in the back.

Patrick reluctantly waited at the front door for me to get out before he tapped the door knocker.

I lumbered along, my eyelids heavy.

"Ah, Patrick. It is so good to see you." Viktor should have won an award for how genuinely pleased he sounded considering he now knew about Patrick's devious past with the boy.

Patrick clapped his shoulder. "It's been a hell of a week, my friend."

Viktor scanned me from head to toe as I crossed the threshold. He muttered something in Russian that was likely a swear word. "What is this?"

I glanced down at myself. "O positive."

Wyatt jogged down the stairs, and his eyes rounded. "Holy Toledo! What happened to you, Bloody Mary?"

I slammed the door behind me. "Can you get me one of your energy drinks? Something with a lot of flavor."

He gave a dashing smile and shuffled down the hall to the left, his socks swishing against the stone floor.

"Let me fix you a drink," Viktor offered as he took Patrick's coat and hung it on a tall coatrack by the window.

"Brandy, if you don't mind," Patrick said, but it sounded more like a demand.

While they headed to the study by the stairs, I veered left into the dining room.

Wyatt emerged from the kitchen, his arm extended in the darkness. The dimming embers of the fire in the next room provided just enough light for me to see him but not vice versa.

I held out my hand to take the drink. "I'm here."

"Kira put out the candles already," he said, stating the obvious.

Each night, she'd extinguish all the candles in the main rooms and leave one or two burning in the hallways where our bedrooms were located.

I took a box of matches from a short table on the right and lit a fat candle. The flame was long since the wick hadn't been trimmed. I moseyed over to one of the booths and set the drink and candle on the table before sitting down.

"Did you get my message?" he asked. "I sent it to Christian, and when I tried calling you again, I heard your phone ringing in the house. Tsk tsk."

"Christian showed me the picture," I confirmed. "Hard to make out a face. Can't you do some computer magic?"

He sat across from me and scooted against the wall so he could put his back to it and rest his foot on the bench. "Just because I can work magic doesn't mean I'm a magician."

A wand joke felt appropriate, but I was too tired. After I cracked open my drink, I guzzled it down and slumped in my seat.

"You're injured," Niko said as he crossed the room.

"Well, if it isn't Captain Obvious." Wyatt chuckled and gestured toward me. "She looks like a Popsicle made for a Vampire."

I scooted over to let Niko sit. "You think Christian will want a lick?"

Wyatt shuddered. "That's a therapy session I ain't got time for. I just hope that's not the blood of an official."

Niko sat and tilted his head to look at my back. Not only could he see light, but he was able to identify imperfections. Injuries were apparent to him.

I chugged the rest of my drink, hoping it would restore some of my stolen energy. My core light would replenish in time, but that combined with blood loss had left me battered.

"So Patrick's here to pick up the kid, huh?" Wyatt shook his head. "That smarmy little buzzard. What did Shepherd say?"

I shrugged. "We went our separate ways back at the church. Besides, there's nothing we can do. It's probably better this way." I pried the top off the can and flicked it across the table. "I'd hate to think Shepherd would do something stupid and snatch the kid. Patrick would declare him an outlaw, and we'd have no choice but to hunt him down. I don't want to be in that position."

"Shepherd's considered his options," Niko said. "He understands that Patrick keeping the boy is the only way to guarantee the child's safety. It would be an egregious mistake to abduct him. We live in a small world, and Patrick is an influential man with resources, money, and time."

"Nothing's changed," Wyatt remarked as he removed his hat and twirled it around his finger. "The most dangerous criminals are the ones in power. Even back in my day, men like him kissed enough ass and paid off enough people to control entire towns. Street criminals get locked up, but guys like Patrick get promotions.

At least in my day, we could round up a posse of men to shoot them down."

"Didn't they end up on wanted posters?" I asked.

Wyatt blew out a breath that flapped his lips together. "Nobody paid attention to those except bankers and bounty hunters. Now we've got all these methods to investigate crime scenes and track people down. It makes it harder to pull off something like that and get away with it. So much for vigilante justice."

Niko folded his arms on the table. "Perhaps it's not up to us to decide Patrick's destiny."

"Yeah, but what about that boy?" Wyatt pointed out. "He's a good kid. Smart, funny—you'd never know he belonged to Shepherd. Well, except that he doesn't talk." Wyatt flipped his hat back onto his head and straightened it. "Maybe Shepherd isn't fit to raise a child, but Patrick sure as hell isn't."

"Keep your voice low," Niko hissed, admonishing him with his tone. "You forget Patrick is unaware that we're privy to his crimes. Should that change, it would be dangerous."

I rubbed my eyes. "That ship has sailed."

When Niko gave me a questioning look, I tapped my hand on the table to get Wyatt's attention. "Can you leave us alone? I've got a stab wound I want Niko to look at."

Wyatt shuddered. "I'll be upstairs, reviewing security footage, if Viktor needs me." When he cleared the threshold of the door, his voice rang out. "And wash that seat you're sitting on! People like to eat in here, you know."

I turned to Niko. "Do you know about the still images that Wyatt sent us?"

His crystalline eyes searched my light. "I'm the one who asked him to send them to you specifically."

"I thought so. Christian showed them to me on his phone."

"Wyatt mentioned a tattoo. Is it who I think it is?"

"It's Cyrus. There's no doubt in my mind."

Niko glanced at the doorway before lowering his voice. "Cyrus isn't just a rogue. He's a masterful planner—one who strategizes his every move far in advance. But the attacks are too random."

Please, Niko, be smart enough to put the clues together so I don't have to say it.

Niko propped his elbow on the table and stroked his lower lip. "Working for Patrick is out of character, and I considered at first he might be trying to obtain information. But Patrick wouldn't be careless enough to discuss sensitive matters in front of his guards. Why would Patrick hire a man like Cyrus, who has no documentation or references? Unless Patrick is behind the murders," he said on a breath. Niko glanced at the doorway. "We can't even utter the accusation. It's treasonous without evidence."

"How can we find Cyrus? He always seems to appear wherever you are. If we capture him, we might have enough evidence with Wyatt's video to have Vampires question him on behalf of the higher authority."

Niko closed his eyes. "And what *else* might he confess?"

I hadn't thought of that. We couldn't turn in Cyrus if it meant inadvertently implicating Niko in a conspiracy against his Creator. I drummed my fingers on the table. "If Patrick's behind the murders, he won't be able to complete his mission with Cyrus out of the picture. God knows why he trusts those men, but why don't we go after them? We'll deal with Patrick another time."

"I've spent my entire life evading my Mage brothers," Niko said. "I'd hoped they would have fallen victim to the ravages of war and time. Cyrus was always a braggart, and that brought him much trouble in his youth. Perhaps he's curbed his temperament, but I was foolish to think I'd never face my enemies again."

"I only *wish* I could face mine," I said. "Fletcher, in particular. Especially before he goes after those I care about. You're not a helpless young man anymore, Niko. I've never met anyone who can handle a sword like you, see like you, strategize like you. What could you possibly have to fear?"

"Only the end of the world," he said obliquely. "Lean forward and let me assess your injuries."

I folded my arms on the table and rested my chin on top of my hand while he reached beneath my sweater. His warm palm grazed my skin, slender fingertips deftly searching the area until they located the beginning and end of each gash.

Instead of lending me his healing light through our palms, he healed me the way he would Wyatt or Shepherd. Light crackled and popped as the skin warmed, and healing energy soaked beneath the surface of my skin.

"Are you ever going to tell Viktor about Cyrus? If they're the killers, we have to find a way to build a case against them. One way or another, Viktor's going to find out that you have a history with them."

"It would seem my options are limited."

Warm light permeated my skin, and another loud pop sounded.

"Do you miss your old home?" I asked, thinking about how long Niko's journey to America must have been.

"I've had many homes."

"I meant your first one. Not the house itself, but your first life."

"Do you miss yours?"

"Sometimes," I admitted.

"That longing fades with time. My beginnings were a mixture of good and bad memories. My family struggled, and I could do little to contribute."

"So what's been the best time of your life?"

He lowered my sweater. "I don't know, Raven. Sometimes I wonder if I'm still waiting for it." He cupped his hands, one inside the other. "Perhaps you shouldn't waste time comparing one point of your life to the next. It's a continual path, and there's no going back. Even if you do go back, the scenery has changed. The past will always beckon you, but do not heed its call. Its embrace is a promise of happiness and comfort, but all it gives you is regret and sorrow."

"But the past catches up with us."

"True, and we must keep moving forward down our path. Think of people you've known. What becomes of a person who can't stop looking back?"

I thought of my father. "They drink their sorrows away until they have something to live for again. At least, that's how it works in my family."

"You often speak fondly of your father. It sounds like you have rich memories of a good life. Not all perfect, but learn the difference between holding a memory and grasping for it. Your life has only just begun. You have many centuries ahead, filled with things you cannot imagine."

"Flying cars?"

Niko tossed his head back and laughed. "I hope so, Raven. Then maybe I could cross the street without fear of becoming a pancake."

Viktor rapped his knuckles on the wall as he entered the room. "Mr. Bane wishes to leave."

"Don't let the door hit him in the ass," I said, sitting up.

"And as he is without transportation or guards..."

"I'm indisposed."

"Would you rather he stay with us?"

I rubbed my eyes, sensing I was in a losing battle.

"I would advise you to be on your best behavior," he said tersely.

That was code for: "Don't stab Mr. Bane in the eye with a pencil."

"May I go along?" Niko asked. "With the child, we should take extra precautions."

"Agreed." Viktor yawned, and I wondered what kept him going. "Use Shepherd's vehicle. The windows are tinted."

My shoulders sagged. "You know I hate driving a stick."

He bowed. "Forgive me. You can take down an army of men, but heaven forbid you have to drive a manual transmission. My deepest apologies. Christian's motorbike is available."

I snorted. Viktor had a dry sense of humor I could appreciate. "Fine. But I'm not paying for any damages if I strip his gears."

Niko rose from his seat. "I'll drive."

Chapter 26

L UCKILY, SHEPHERD'S JEEP HAD ONLY stalled twice. I'd never bothered learning to master a stick shift, but Viktor had a point. With all my learned talents, it seemed ridiculous to avoid familiarizing myself with a manual transmission. Maybe one day, I'd be able to drive one without putting it in the wrong gear.

If anything, the kid had a giggle about it. Patrick remained quiet despite the lurching and sudden stops. He must have had too much weighing on his mind about our newfound knowledge. No doubt he was plotting. It didn't seem fair that powerful men were so protected, but it now made sense why corrupt men sought political positions. It allowed them to create laws that offered them more protection than the average Joe.

Patrick had packed a travel bag for his stay below the church, and when we arrived at his mansion, he told me to grab it.

"If only I had my dagger," I grumbled when he got out of the Jeep.

Niko touched my shoulder from the back seat. "Careful, Raven."

"Do I look like a bellhop?"

I flung open the door and jumped out. While I opened the rear door to get the bag, Niko slid out the other side with the sleeping boy cradled in his arms. Something sloshed around inside the bag—probably ten bottles of fancy wine.

I wondered how Christian was faring with organizing everyone's safe return. Electricity instilled a sense of normalcy. It threw lights on dark shadows and made people feel secure. What worried me were the remaining names on the list Henry had given me.

I let the suitcase drag on the concrete as I neared the front door.

"That bag is worth more than your salary," Patrick informed me while checking his phone.

"Quit your bellyaching. Hauling luggage isn't in my job description."

"Now is that any way to speak to an official of the higher court?" He spun dramatically on his heel and looked at Niko. "Your obstinate friend will get you in trouble one day."

Niko stared vacantly toward the door. "Apologies, Mr. Bane. It's been a long night, and Raven is weary and not thinking straight after risking her life for countless officials."

Niko delivered that statement in earnest, but I was certain that Patrick read between the lines and felt the full meaning.

As soon as the door opened, Patrick switched on a lamp. "The bag goes upstairs to my room. Second floor, third door on the right."

"Where are your guards?"

He cocked his head, probably using his Mage ability to tell the time. "They should be here within the hour. Otherwise, they can look for a new job." He set down the keys on a small table and looked around.

Niko carefully navigated over the threshold and took slow, careful steps inside. "What shall I do with the boy?"

The kid was knocked out like a light. He looked adorable as hell in Niko's arms, and it made me sad this innocent little child would never know what it was like to have someone truly care about him.

"The servants usually handle him," Patrick said, staring at the boy as if he were an inconvenience. "I need to make sure all the rooms are secure since I still have a hole in my kitchen. The boy's bedroom is on the third floor. It's the fourth door on the left, but you need to take the hallway on the west wing. Do you know which side that is?" Patrick noticed the way Niko never met his gaze. "Can you even climb stairs?"

Niko's face tightened, and he made a slow and defiant walk straight ahead. We'd been in Patrick's house enough that he knew there were two curving staircases on either side of the room, so he veered left.

I grabbed the suitcase and hurried to his side, noticing he wasn't going far enough to the left and would miss the stairs. "Hey," I said, lightly tugging his sleeve. "Follow my trail."

Since Niko could see energy, I moved ahead of him and stopped as soon as the stairs began. This would be his cue. The bag thumped on every step as I dragged it up.

When we reached the top, I led him to a central staircase that ascended to the third floor. "Are you good from here?"

"I can manage stairs," he said. "Have you seen the boy's room?"

"Yes. It's exactly where Patrick described. The bed is on the left side of the room, but I can't remember which end the pillow was on. If you can't figure out which way the covers turn down, just cover him up from the sides like a burrito. There aren't any toys on the floor you'll trip over. It's an open space."

He blew out a breath. "Good. I would never drop him, just so you know."

Niko didn't need to explain. He would probably use his ninja skills to spin around and take the brunt of the fall, but I could tell that Patrick had rubbed him the wrong way by questioning his abilities.

We parted ways, and when I located Patrick's bedroom, I slung his suitcase inside without switching on the light. I had no urge to see if he had tassels on his bedspread or a chamber pot for the servants to empty each morning. Nothing about him interested me. That aristocratic monster had ordered a child to be ripped from his mother's womb. It didn't even matter that it was Shepherd's kid. Shit like that would have earned Patrick a spot on my hit list back when I used to take down men for fun.

I jogged down the stairs, eager to head home and relax. I couldn't remember the last time I'd eaten a decent meal, and I still hadn't washed up since taking a bath in Igor's blood. Just thinking about it had me reaching in my pocket for an elastic band so I could tie up my bloody hair and get it out of my face.

When I reached the marble floor, I cocked my head to the side. At first, I thought Patrick was on the phone, but the longer I listened, the more certain I was that at least two people were speaking. It could have been his guards, but I concealed my light just in case. With the house unguarded and the giant hole in the kitchen, anyone could have broken in.

Unarmed, I grabbed a small marble vase. The voices came from the back, but they were distant.

I moved down the rear hall and turned left before taking another right toward the kitchen. My sneakers allowed me to move around stealthily, and when I reached the kitchen entry, I peered inside.

The plastic tarp covering the hole flapped from a gust of wind, and the outside chatter grew louder again.

I tiptoed through the room and dodged the windows over the sink before positioning myself by the back door. The wind carried their voices inside, but I couldn't tell how many were out there. Through the glass in the door, I counted two figures. Patrick was easy to identify with his pale complexion and slim figure, but the other I couldn't see.

Patrick set a candle on a glass-top table and faced the man standing to his right. "You killed good men."

"Says who?"

I squinted, trying to identify the other man, but the beveled glass created distortions.

"You deviated from the plan," Patrick chided.

When I heard the rustling of clothing behind me, I turned sharply and shushed Niko. "Stay low," I whispered, setting the vase on the counter.

Niko ducked, one arm extended as he crept toward me. I led him to the other side of the door.

"That's Cyrus," he said matter-of-factly, staring through the glass. "I recognize his light."

"Do you see anyone else?"

Niko gripped the pommel of his sword and turned sharply.

"We meet again," a man said, announcing his presence.

I looked over my shoulder at three familiar faces, each man holding his sword on the offense.

Niko anchored himself in front of me. "Kallisto, Arcadius, Lykos. We're here by invitation."

"We know," one of them replied.

"You don't get paid for mistakes," Patrick continued, seemingly oblivious to our presence. "There are a dozen other men who would gladly do the job."

"Is that so?" Cyrus countered. "Let us call them and see who is interested. You hired us without regard to our past. Do you think we're street trash who will do anything for money? You're not the one who holds the power in this situation—I am. You know this to be true."

"You're wasting time! I want them gone. We'll discuss this later. Hurry, before they leave."

One of the men facing us smiled. Patrick didn't intend for us to leave alive. The longer Christian and I drew breath, the greater the odds we would divulge his secret plan to assassinate parties of the higher authority. I bet he'd plotted this whole thing while I drove him home from church, afraid I'd tell Viktor. No wonder he was so damn quiet after sending messages on his phone.

"Outside," one of the men ordered, raising his sword. "Three against two, and your girlfriend doesn't even have a weapon." He clucked his tongue.

My best weapons were my gifts, but I kept that to myself. I reached to open the door, and we moved outside.

Patrick looked startled but quickly regained his composure. "I see you've found our guests."

"You won't get away with this," I promised him. "Viktor will never believe your lies."

"But you protected me against vagrants. You'll have a hero's funeral to honor your bravery."

I shook my head. "Christian won't let you live. He's a man who doesn't give a fuck. If you kill me, he'll plaster your secrets on every billboard in town."

"What makes you think I'm not already taking care of him?"

Cyrus laughed, his slim eyes curved like crescent moons. Just like the other times I'd seen him, he had on a regular T-shirt. I suspected he might be a Thermal. Either that, or he loved showing off the bold tattoos on his brawny arms, regardless of the weather.

Patrick steered his attention back to Cyrus. "*Only* the names on my list. That was the agreement. *I* pay *you*, remember? Your sophomoric mistake has put me behind schedule."

"We have killed those you have asked us to," Cyrus replied, his tone as apathetic as his expression. "Why should I care about the others? Why should one name be any different from the rest? You are all the same in my eyes."

I looked between them, confused.

"Because, you fool, not only did you kill my allies, but your attack on the church heralded a change that will now offer *more* protection to all the officials. They're assigning each member a Regulator, and that includes me!"

I stared, slack-jawed. "*You're* the one responsible for the church attack?"

"No," Patrick snapped. "It was this moron!" He raised his arm and pointed at Cyrus.

With a move so swift I barely saw it happen, Cyrus swung his blade and severed Patrick's finger. It fell to the ground and jutted out of the dead grass.

Patrick recoiled, his eyes wide with shock before he moaned in pain.

"I cannot respect a man who disavows his role in a plot of his devising," Cyrus declared.

Niko suddenly flashed in front of Patrick and faced Cyrus. "He doesn't realize who he's dealing with, Cyrus. But I do."

Cyrus cocked his head to the side. "You would protect a man who was going to slaughter you? Time has changed nothing. You are still the fool you always were, Nikodemos."

"Death is not punishment," Niko informed him. "It's a means

to an end. Humiliation is the best revenge. Wouldn't you rather watch your enemies suffer?"

Cyrus considered it for a moment as Patrick clutched his bleeding hand. "His capture will implicate my men."

"He doesn't know your real names," I reminded him. I wasn't sure why, all of a sudden, I was Team Patrick, but despite my hating the man, Niko had a point. I wanted to see this guy jailed and publicly shamed. Not to mention he hadn't revealed to us the names of those working with him, plotting against the higher authority in cities nationwide.

Cyrus gave Niko a loaded look. "Bane has connections. Even in jail, he will pay bounty hunters to track us down. I do not wish to spend my life looking over my shoulder. He will extend his life by making deals. I know his plans. He has access to facilities that experiment with human viruses. Did you know his goal is to create a supervirus to wipe out all humankind?" Cyrus belted out a laugh. "It is what weak men do when they fear battle. If they cannot assemble an army to fight for them, they create an army of microscopic organisms. I care nothing for his plans. He was simply a means to get more information on you, my friend. And then I seized an opportunity to eliminate your leaders. It doesn't take long for chaos to erupt in this pathetic kingdom of yours. Is this the life you prefer?"

Niko never wavered, his sword ready to strike. "You will never have what you came for."

Cyrus lifted his chin. "I will baptize your city in the blood of innocents until you bow before me. And you will."

He nodded in my direction, and I suddenly felt a pinch at my throat and nape. Flanked by two of his men, each with his blade positioned against my neck—one in the front and the other in the back—I had no way to escape. One wrong move, and their swords would remove my head like scissors snipping a label off a new jacket.

Niko looked my way. Maybe he couldn't see the position of the swords, and maybe he could, but he sensed my life in peril.

Cyrus straightened his shoulders and lowered his sword. "Step back and allow a man to negotiate with his boss."

Niko backed away slowly.

"It's not too late to prove what kind of a man you are," Patrick said through clenched teeth.

"You're right," Cyrus agreed. "How much is your life worth to you?"

Patrick was doubled over, but he managed to stand up straight and look Cyrus in the eye. "I'm an official of the higher authority. If anything happens to me, you'll have men hunting you down for the rest of your life. I'm giving you an opportunity to be a part of something bigger."

Cyrus approached him and shook his head. "You mean nothing to me. You're just another rung on the ladder."

The whistling noise I heard next made my skin crawl. It was the sound of Cyrus's sword cutting through the air. He executed the maneuver so swiftly and with such incredible precision that I initially thought he'd missed.

Until I saw a ring of blood around Patrick's neck. He actually reached up for his head as his legs gave way, and I shut my eyes before I saw something that might give me nightmares for the rest of my life.

When it was quiet, I risked a glance and quickly averted my eyes from the body slumped on the ground.

Cyrus wiped the blood from his sword onto his pant leg. "Never underestimate how far I'm willing to go to get what I want. Plato was a loyal brother, which is more than I can say about you. Even in death, he served me well, relaying information to a Gravewalker about your plans. Only one church had enough weaknesses for us to conquer; the rest were impregnable. Had I received their locations sooner, I would have shared that information with more people."

"Have you no respect for what the authorities do to protect us?" Niko asked harshly.

Cyrus studied his sword. "How can you serve leaders who care nothing about you? The only thing they protect is their ever-growing wealth. Do you really believe you're one of the good guys? You're only one thread away from lawlessness."

The blade across my throat pinched my skin, and blood trickled down my neck. Their shaky hands weren't doing me any favors.

"Join us," Cyrus offered. "This world won't be for long. War is coming. Maybe in a few centuries, a few months, or a few days. But it rides toward us with the fury of a thousand wild horses."

Niko looked toward the house. "Someone's coming."

Cyrus tapped his sword against Niko's. "Another day, brother. Another day."

I clutched my neck when the blades moved away, afraid they might have pulled the same stunt on me as they had Patrick. The men flashed off, and I breathed a sigh of relief when I found that my head was still attached. A small bit of hair from my ponytail had been sliced off and was lying at my feet.

Niko sheathed his sword and hurried toward me. He cupped my neck in his hands, his shoulders sagging. "You're all right."

"I can't believe he was going to kill us."

"If Cyrus wanted us dead, it would have happened."

"I meant Patrick. How stupid can he be?"

Niko furrowed his brow. "Why would he give that order? Why was it so imperative it happen tonight?"

I worried my lip. "He might have suspected that Christian and I knew he was behind the murders."

"And what gave him that idea?"

"He saw the picture of Cyrus on the phone."

Niko's eyes hooded the way they sometimes did when he was reading my light. "I won't ask anything more on the matter."

"Best you don't."

The plastic tarp ripped away, and we both turned as Merry strode outside, brandishing his sword. When his eyes tipped down to Patrick's body and then to Niko's sword, I froze. I couldn't imagine this looking any more damning.

Merry approached so unhurriedly that his energy rippled. "Who perpetrated this dastardly deed?"

I tried not to laugh at his flair for the dramatic. "It wasn't us."

"I can see that. Your friend's steel is pristine."

"He hears that a lot."

Merry's lip twitched for a moment before his expression went grim. "I assume you drove Mr. Bane home since he left with you. I was assigned to guard him until they closed the investigation on the murders."

"I heard Mr. Bane confess to the crimes," Niko blurted out. "Raven was inside, putting the boy to sleep."

I stared up in confusion at him.

Merry looked genuinely startled. "Are you referring to the plot against the higher authority?"

"Yes. I can give you a full account of everything I overheard between him and his hired men."

"They're responsible for this?" Merry asked, gesturing toward the body.

"I tried to protect him," Niko said truthfully. "Raven came out, and his men put blades to her neck."

"I can see that." Merry's golden eyes examined the base of my throat. I was already covered in blood, but the fresh wound was probably glistening.

Touching my neck, I cleared my throat. "How long will this take?"

"Have a seat, Miss Black. Once I take your statements, you're free to go. If we need you for additional questioning, we'll be in touch. I heard what you did outside the church. Weather and I were guarding the doors to the basement. You should be commended for your bravery."

"Thanks." I tugged on the collar of my bloodstained sweater. "Think this'll come out in the wash?"

He winked. "Red looks better on you anyhow."

Chapter 27

MERRY WAS THOROUGH AND QUESTIONED us separately to make sure Niko's story was corroborated by my version. It was easy to go along with Niko's twist in the facts. I was convincing enough that Merry didn't ask me too many questions, especially since Niko had given him more than enough information. Patrick's death had me rattled, and I couldn't stop touching my neck and reliving those tense moments when I thought those men would take my head as well. It wasn't easy to lie to a Chitah, so I used some of that emotion to dance around the facts.

Niko had left out personal conversations between him and Cyrus. He explained that because of Merry's sudden arrival, the men didn't have time to take us both down. They just got the hell out as fast as they could.

Now we were in a quandary. With Patrick dead, the boy had a one-way ticket to the Breed orphanage. Shepherd wasn't going to like the news. Not one bit. Merry asked if we could take the boy home for the night. The cleaners would be arriving to collect the body, and it didn't make sense to expose the kid to something that traumatic. Aside from that, he wasn't safe with killers on the loose.

Poor kid. I searched his bedroom for anything personal of his he might want, not certain if he'd ever have a chance to return and collect his life. But I found nothing aside from clothes, shoes, pencils, and paper. Not even a tiny plastic soldier. So I stuffed his clothes into a bag, and Niko carried him over his shoulder to the

Jeep. He slept through everything, even when the Jeep lurched and died after I took my foot off the clutch too soon.

Niko called Viktor on our way home to bring him up to speed. When I parked in the garage, he was waiting. We spoke candidly, telling him every detail and leaving nothing out. Well, except the part about Cyrus and Niko's past.

After we wrapped up the briefing, I stumbled to an empty room downstairs and shut the door. I lit a candle, poured myself a glass of vodka, took my hair down, and curled up in a fat leather chair. I figured Viktor might have more questions and come looking for me, but the longer I waited, the more difficult it was to stay awake. I was battered, bruised, and still feeling incredibly sick from feeding on that Mage. His dark blood had worked its way through me, and it was cold, like a snake slithering around my insides.

It only seemed like minutes had elapsed since I'd nodded off, but when I opened my eyes, the glass was no longer in my hand. I leaned over to see if it had fallen on the floor, and that was when I noticed the dying embers of a fire in the hearth beside me.

The door opened, and I heard footfalls.

Niko set a tray of food on the table beside me. "I knocked, but no one answered. I was going to leave this here for when you were hungry."

"I just woke up," I mumbled. "Did you light the fire?"

"No. After we cleared the table, Viktor asked me to bring you a plate."

Still disoriented, I stared at the pot roast and French bread.

"You've been asleep for fifteen hours."

I rubbed my eyes and then stretched my sore neck. "Thanks for not disturbing me. Sometimes I just have to sleep it off."

Niko dragged a smaller chair across from me. "You're referring to the blood?"

I stabbed a potato with a fork and bit into it. "Dark blood is hard to ingest. The more sinister the person is, the worse it feels. Those guys were bad, but they weren't the most devious men I've encountered."

"So… some men, you can stomach, and others you can't."

I smiled. "That's one way to put it. A Mage also juiced my light, so I think that's why I crashed for so long." I set down my fork. "Why did you blame Patrick and give the Regulator all that info? Weren't you afraid he would call a Vampire to charm you?"

"Yes. But we'd already placed ourselves at the scene of the crime. You had the telltale marks from a sword on your neck, and if they called in a Sensor, they would have picked up our emotions all over the place. Sometimes you're better off going with a truthful approach. Well, within reason." He turned his left palm up and created a ball of green light the size of a marble between his fingertips. As it turned in a circle faster and faster at his command, it changed to bright orange. "There's something else you want to ask me."

"Why did you implicate Patrick in the crimes? Why not just say we walked in on a robbery? We have no solid proof outside of his alleged verbal confession."

"Plausible motive." The light changed to yellow and crackled. "People saw him as a luminary in his profession, so they deserved to know that he was a blight on humanity. Duplicitous men are rarely exposed for what they are. Besides, we have to follow a code of honor. If Patrick was a conspirator in a larger plot against all higher authorities, we have an obligation to shine a light on his deeds. Doing so will open up an internal investigation and expose others involved. Turning a blind eye wouldn't stop the wheel that's already in motion."

I reached up to scratch my head and noticed how matted my hair was with dried blood. The log on the grate split apart, revitalizing the dying fire. Lost in my thoughts, I absently picked at my tangled hair.

When Niko flicked the ball of light toward the fire, it fizzled out. It wasn't constructed the same as Gem's energy balls. It didn't hold the same kind of power but just seemed like an extension of his light.

"Now that Patrick's dead, I don't know how they're going to

find out who was part of his circle," I said. "I mean… assuming he wasn't working alone."

An imperceptible smile touched Niko's lips. "No need to cover your tracks, Raven. If there's anything that would get you in trouble, keep it to yourself. Sometimes secrets keep us safe."

I definitely didn't want to reveal what Christian had done to Patrick, but since Patrick had confessed, there was no harm filling Niko in on the rest. "One of the officials gave me a list of names based on a hunch I had. We don't have much else to go on, but maybe the higher authority will share the conspiracy with the other groups around the nation. They might be keeping news of similar murders under wraps, and that list could help uncover who's responsible."

"It's not our concern how they smoke them out, but rest assured, they'll have the most skilled investigators working on it. Our job is done—not that solving the murders was ever our job. We coordinated the evacuation and identified flaws in their system. Hopefully they'll never have to use it again, but if they do, I believe they'll be better prepared."

I sat up and looked at my plate, but I had zero appetite. "Is the kid still here?"

Niko turned his head to the fire. "Yes. He was confused when he awoke, but he doesn't know about Patrick. The child might not have had love for his guardian, but Patrick was the only life he knew. The stability and routine he once had is now gone, and that will create a lot of uncertainty for him. Children cling to the familiar."

"I know all about that." I had grieved the loss of my mother, but I had also missed everything about my old life. My room, my bed, my toys, the way Mom used to cut my peanut butter sandwiches into the shape of a butterfly, and I even missed my neighbor's dog that she'd sometimes let me pet. I loved Crush, and he took care of me, but that first year of transition was rough.

Immersed in memories, I drew in a deep breath and looked at Niko. "What are the orphanages like?"

"Most of the children live their lives there. Adoption isn't a common occurrence in the Breed world, especially when you don't know anything about the child's background. It's a far more complicated issue than with human children. And because they're Breed, it's against the law to let humans adopt them. That's why Viktor donates his money to the orphanages. Many of them sleep in open rooms with no privacy. They are truly the lost children, and society has forgotten them."

"Out of sight, out of mind. Maybe they should invite the kids to one of those fund-raiser parties, don't you think?"

The door opened, and I heard the familiar sound of rubber wheels gliding across the floor.

"Messenger girl!" Gem sang. She sounded livelier than I'd heard her in the previous few days. She skated around my chair and skidded to a stop before raking me over with wide eyes. "Jiminy Christmas! Wyatt wasn't exaggerating. You look like a horror movie."

I glanced down at my chipped nail polish. "I guess I *am* overdue for a manicure."

She giggled. "That's the Raven I know."

I stood up and regarded her for a moment. "And that's the Gem I know."

She leaned back. "Don't hug me. I don't know who you've been sucking on."

"I get that a lot."

"I meant whose neck..." Her cheeks flamed. "You're all bloody."

"I'm just messing with you. I woke up a few minutes ago and still don't know what day it is."

Gem skated toward the door. "Viktor wants us in the dining room *pronto*."

I followed Gem, watching her slim figure swing left and right as she weaved instead of skating in a straight line. She had on a cropped black sweater and purple ombré leggings that faded to silver at the bottom.

"It's so nice to have the power back on," she said cheerfully. "I finally had a hot shower this morning." She fell back and performed spins in the open space.

"I hope Viktor's revealing that our next job is finding a runaway wolf," I said to Niko.

He chuckled. "Trust me, Raven. That's no picnic either."

"I'll just have to take your word for it." I glanced down at my red sneakers. At least I'd chosen the right color shoes.

When we entered the dining room, there was a collective gasp from those who hadn't seen me.

Shepherd sighed. "Guess that means I'm gonna have to torch the seats in my Jeep."

"Don't be such a germophobe," Wyatt said, the humor in his voice thinly veiled.

Shepherd gave him an icy stare.

"Sorry, I didn't have time to brush my hair," I said flatly as I took a seat next to Viktor.

Wyatt waggled his brows at me from the kitchen doorway but cringed when Gem rolled over his foot—probably intentionally— before taking her seat. He limped over to his chair across from me and sat down.

Viktor swirled his glass of red wine, his eyes on the empty chair beside me. One of the last things Patrick had said was that he was taking care of Christian, and the impending announcement filled me with dread. So much so that I didn't ask about Christian, afraid that talking about it might make it real.

The smell of pot roast and fresh bread lingered in the air. A pan clanged from the kitchen, and Kira uttered a strange word that made Gem perk her ears.

"I bet that was a swear word," she said to herself, probably filing that word away in her mental drawer. Gem hadn't lost interest in learning the language that Kira never spoke in our presence.

Christian swaggered in, his dark hair wet and combed back. I tried not to sigh out loud at the sight of him, tried not to notice the way he smelled like soap. When he sat down, he pushed up the sleeves on his grey Henley, his dripping hair wetting the shoulders of his shirt.

After a moment, he looked over at me. "What are you gaping at, lass?"

"I thought Patrick sent someone after you."

His gaze darted around at my messy hair and bloodstained sweater, but it briefly stopped on the cut across my throat. "An incompetent little fecker showed up."

"Who?" It couldn't have been Cyrus's men.

"Didn't ask his name, but the fanghole now resides in a narrow sewer pipe. It was a tight fit," he said, adjusting one of his sleeves.

Viktor laced his fingers together. He looked more rested, the dark circles beneath his eyes much diminished and the color back in his cheeks. His whiskers were trimmed short and evenly along his face, longer around the chin and lip.

His knuckles whitened. "First, I begin with news. A high-level investigation is underway to identify those conspiring against the balance of the higher authority. You are all aware that Patrick was murdered last night, but we have reason to believe that he was involved in the assassination of several officials in an attempt to control votes."

Shepherd pulled a final drag from his cigarette and pressed it into the ashtray. "What about the bomb at his own house? That was sloppy."

Gem scooted down in her chair, eyes downcast.

Viktor's eyes swung over to Christian and me. "The bomb was a diversion to create panic and erase evidence. The threat against the higher authority will be ongoing, but they have implemented plans to..." Viktor said something in Russian and looked at Gem.

Her eyes swung up for a moment. "Smoke them out is a good way to say it."

"Spasibo. So while we lost one of the men we were charged to protect, things miraculously worked in our favor. Sometimes I think the fates are on our side."

Blue set down her wineglass after another swallow. "Do they still have Regulators assigned to the officials?"

Viktor nodded. "Not only to protect, but they are observing patterns. They will monitor those who are outspoken against human rights. I have heard two men resigned already. They claim it was the events of the past week and attacks on the church, but there is no way to know. Guilty conspirators will probably follow their lead, and they are already bringing in immediate replacements who have been properly screened. There are many changes coming."

Shepherd circled his fingertips on the table. "That's not what you want to talk to us about. I can feel your anxiety skimming across the surface."

Viktor sat back and put his hands in his lap. "Let's not be dramatic."

"I see it too," Niko added.

Viktor cursed and stood up. "Will everyone stop reading me? It is rude." He lifted a bottle of wine from the cabinet behind him and topped off his glass before sitting back down.

"It's our pay, isn't it?" Wyatt folded his arms, covering the wording on his T-shirt, which said: HAVE A NICE AFTERLIFE. "They're stiffing us because it didn't go smoothly."

Viktor tipped his head from side to side. "That is not entirely false."

Everyone groaned and sat back.

"Cheap bastards," Shepherd muttered. "They busted up my face."

"Your face?" Blue exclaimed. "I almost died!"

"Quiet down," Viktor commanded, banging his fist on the table. "Much has happened this week. Many unexpected revolutions that have weighed on my mind."

"Revelations," Gem said, staring at her fingernails.

His eyes swung over to her. "Gem has suffered a personal loss, and though I have given her an important task, she came to me and said she wanted no part of the money. This was a group assignment, and you know I am generous with paying all a share, even those who do not participate. Her share was meager, but I had to recalculate that amount toward everyone else's check."

My gut instinct told me that Viktor wanted to donate the money to charity. It would be the right thing to do, under the circumstances. We'd busted our asses and put our lives on the line, but we'd also lost so much, and with Patrick dead, it felt like a hollow victory.

Viktor sipped his wine and studied the glass as he set it down. "The boy will be leaving our care tonight. They will send out someone to collect him."

Shepherd rubbed the old scars on his hand.

"I have spoken to the higher authority about the child's welfare and what will become of him. They will transport him to the orphanage and try for adoption. But you see I am concerned. The boy is not a defect but has two gifts that will make him a target. Someone in the orphanage might leak that information for profit."

Shepherd's chair creaked when he sat back hard, his hands clenched into fists. "What about Maggie's family? Can someone track them down?"

Viktor steepled his fingers. "We can look into it, but it would require much explanation. Not every family wants a child with mixed gifts."

Shepherd's brown eyes squinted, and the lines etched in his forehead deepened as he glowered.

"They will never legally adopt him out to a man with your record," Viktor informed him. "If you snatch him from the orphanage in a vain attempt to protect him, they will hunt you down."

"I didn't like Patrick having him," he admitted. "But I could deal with it. Now what? He goes off to some fucking orphanage where kids are abandoned and neglected? You think a Sensor will want him when they find out he's also a Relic? And do you think a Relic wants to raise a kid with Sensor abilities? They like to work closely with clients, and nobody will trust him because he's a crossbreed. No family will want both halves. The wrong person is gonna find out what this kid knows about human genetics. I can't let that happen."

Viktor's lips pressed into a thin line. "You must leave Keystone. You will always be a liability." He looked at the stem of his wineglass. "I have no choice but to scrub your memory. We cannot guarantee what the end result of the scrubbing will be. You know too much—have seen too much. You will pose a constant threat to those you have worked with."

"Aye," Christian agreed. "There's always a risk when you start Swiss cheesing someone's mind. I can't promise you'll remember all of your past, including your son. Removing that much is time-consuming and complicated. I know what you're thinking, Shepherd, but don't run. It'll be far worse if you run from this."

Shepherd propped his elbows on the table and cupped his hands over his mouth as if blowing heat into them.

"I see how much this place means to you," Viktor continued. "So I have a proposal. I have spoken to my contact, and they agreed to let us keep the boy in lieu of payment."

A thunderstruck silence fell across the room.

After a long stretch, Wyatt muttered, "Now that's a twist I didn't see coming."

Viktor moved his glass forward, his fingertips gripping the stem. "There is a catch. Everyone in the group has to agree to give up their paycheck to allow the child to live within Keystone." Viktor's eyes moved about the room. "That is a lot to consider, but each and every one of you must be in agreement. A group like ours is not a home. It's a refuge—a safe haven for dangerous people. A child living in our care will always be at risk. With Kira, we are more capable of leaving him in her care while we go on assignments. But make no mistake—this is a huge change that not everyone may be in agreement with, and that is why whichever way you vote, it must be unanimous. It is the only way to maintain harmony as a team. The higher authority has compensated us very well this time. You would each see two more zeroes on your deposit than usual, so that is a lot to give up."

Shepherd blanched, his eyebrows drawn tightly together. He looked like a cat caught in a rainstorm.

"We will discuss and vote."

Shepherd rose to his feet. "I have to think about it." He opened his mouth as if to say more but ducked out, the heavy tread of his boots sounding all the way down the hall.

Blue circled the table to sit in Shepherd's spot. "Is this a good idea, Viktor? Think of what that child will see. Just look at Raven. That's enough to give him nightmares for a month."

All eyes turned to me, and I slumped down in my chair.

"We could traumatize him." She freed a wisp of hair that had tangled around her feather earring. "What if your wolf attacks him? What if Claude flips his switch and—"

"I would *never* harm a child," Claude snarled, rising to his feet. All four canines punched out, and his eyes darkened.

Blue rolled her eyes. "You can't even sit at this table for more than five minutes without flipping. Some of us have short fuses. And what about injuries? He'll be exposed to seeing some horrific things."

"Like your dirty panties lying on the floor next to your hamper?"

She gave Wyatt a hawkish stare that made him swing his green eyes back to Viktor. "We don't even know much about each other. What if someone at this table hates children or has abused them in the past?"

Viktor sighed and sat back. "I have extensively researched each of you, but you make a valid point about safety. Christian can charm each of you to admit the truth, and I will supervise with Niko's assistance. He can read light."

Wyatt rumpled his hair. The light-brown locks were wavy and messy, but that was his signature style. "Maybe Shep doesn't want to be a daddy. He obviously wants his kid in a good home, but taking him in? That's a lot to consider."

Viktor folded his arms. "I want to give Shepherd a choice in the matter. He cannot legally adopt the boy. Shepherd is good for Keystone and has a future here, but this distraction will ruin him if he allows it. I could scrub his memory and send the boy away, but Raven once remarked on all these empty rooms. Not long ago, this house was full of life and laughter. All my brothers lived here with their mates and children. They are all gone now, but maybe this house has room for the laughter of one child. I can make that room. Can you?"

"I agree," Gem chimed in. "We can all help."

Niko leaned forward into view. "Is the idea for Shepherd to take on a fatherly role?"

Viktor stroked his chin. "I do not know if Shepherd will even accept that, based on his reaction, but that is up to him. I have no… stipulations?"

Gem nodded at his word choice. "Plus we have Kira. He's already taken to her, and I think he likes it here. Lots of room to run around."

"I just wonder if the boy won't be confused," Niko said.

Viktor jerked his neck back. "What is confusing?"

"Apologies. I should be clearer. He's living in a house with… hunters, for a lack of a better word."

Wyatt tilted his head to the side. "I prefer maverick. Or what about agent? I like the sound of Agent Blessing."

"And I prefer assassin," Blue said. "File a complaint. It doesn't matter what we call it. Niko's right. How are we going to explain what we do for a living? And not only that, will his loyalty be automatic as he grows up? He might overhear or learn things he shouldn't."

"We could tell him we're superheroes," I suggested.

Wyatt snorted. "Who are you? Captain Carnage?"

"I like Red Plasma better," Christian quipped.

Claude scooted in his chair and folded his arms over the back. "What about a trial period? It'll give Shepherd the chance to know his kid. We'll take care of him until there's a candidate for adoption. That way, Shepherd won't feel so locked into a commitment, and he'll have control over who will raise the boy if he decides to let him go."

Everyone's gazes crossed, and we nodded in agreement.

"I like that idea," Viktor said. "But you will still be giving up your pay for what might be a temporary arrangement."

Blue's soft brown hair shielded half her face as she lowered her head. "I think Shepherd will discover it's too late for him to be a father. But this way, he won't have any regrets." She looked around the table. "If we send the kid off, he'll leave. One way or the other, I have a feeling he's out the door. But say the kid stays. Shepherd might be overwhelmed by the idea of raising a child and decide to send him to a good home. No regrets. Viktor has connections, and Shepherd could screen the candidates."

Gem's purple lips turned to a frown. "What if Shepherd wants him to stay? Is everyone going to complain?"

"Gem is right." Viktor pulled his collar away from his neck. "We must all be in agreement with both possible scenarios if we allow the child to stay. It cannot be one or the other."

"I'm in," Claude said.

Gem smiled. "Me too."

The rest of us raised our hands, all but Blue.

She looked around the room and held a poker face.

"You hold the power," Viktor said. "If we're not all in agreement, the boy goes to the orphanage in two hours, no matter what Shepherd decides."

Blue rested her arms on the table. "Here's my concern: we all chose to be here, even Kira. But this boy doesn't have a choice. He's too young to know what he's getting into. What if, down the road, he doesn't want to associate with us? We'll have no choice but to scrub him. And how many years will Christian have to erase? Five? Ten? His whole life erased! He'll wind up a babbling idiot on a park bench who won't accept the fake identity Christian implanted in his head—empty memories with no tangible connection to the real world. Are you all willing to accept that responsibility? This is a child we're talking about, not a puppy."

Blue made a valid point, and it gave me pause.

"What if we send him off in the world and find out later he was abused and murdered?" I asked. "Or what if he grows up and decides to use his knowledge to destroy the human race? Look, he's got a better shot with us than anywhere else. And besides, there's no way to predict what'll happen. Maybe he'll want to work for us, or maybe he'll want to be a priest. A lot of us didn't have a fair shot in life, but here we are. Who could have predicted our lives would have led us here, even in our darkest hours? There's no way to guess what'll happen, no matter which way he goes."

"Shepherd has a chance to know his son," Gem said softly. "Is it our place to deny him that right? None of us have children, so we can't understand what his heart feels. If we send the boy away, we're keeping a father and son apart. We could ruin two lives. It's only fair that we give him the opportunity. Decisions can be made later, but let's make the one that counts."

Blue's shoulders sagged. "You should have been a lawyer, Gem. I think everyone knows my position, and I've outlined the risks you're all accepting. Shepherd's an asset to this team, and sending the boy away will mean his departure." Blue sat back and shook her head. "I agree, but only on the condition that we tell Shepherd all the risks. If the kid ever betrays us, he'll receive a memory wipe. Because of that, we need to keep confidential files out of reach. Wyatt should have password locks on all computers. Shepherd can change his mind at any time and place the boy in a home, but maybe the sooner, the better. Less to erase. If he wants to make it a permanent arrangement, I have no problem with that."

"*If* he wants," Wyatt emphasized. "He ran out of here faster than a groom getting cold feet at his own wedding."

Gem stood up and skated toward the door. "I'll go find him and bring him back."

I noticed the light dimming outside as it neared dusk. When I rose from my chair, Viktor ensnared my wrist.

"I want everyone here when he makes the decision. Hurry back."

So much for showering.

Chapter 28

SINCE I DIDN'T HAVE TIME to shower, I made a quick visit to a downstairs restroom and washed up. My nape and scalp were itching from clumps of dried blood where the Mage had bled out all over me from a gushing gunshot wound to the jugular. With the boy running around, I became self-conscious about looking like a poster for a Wes Craven movie.

What a strange turn of events. Having a kid around was unexpected, and I understood why it made Shepherd anxious. Were we fit to raise a child? Or would a few years with us scar him for life? Couldn't be worse than the suffocating life Patrick would have given him. Patrick would have bulldozed that kid until he didn't know good from evil.

I dried my face with a towel and stepped into the long hall on the east wing. The beautiful blue-tinted windows colored the floor and walls each morning, but now they were a dim shade of indigo. While passing an alcove that led to Gem's secret room, I glimpsed something outside. When I approached the glass and peered out, I gasped and stepped back.

That was no shadow or stray cat. Houdini stood not one foot away on the other side of the window. He made no gesture, but I knew he wanted to speak to me as he turned toward the back of the house.

I walked alongside him, standing higher than he was. When I reached a heavy steel door in the back, I slid the bolt and walked down two steps before my shoes flattened the dead grass. I hugged my middle as he approached.

Houdini had his hands in the pockets of his grey coat, the high collar leaning stiffly against his jaw. His whitish hair seemed multifaceted, with dark roots and subtle hints of silver. He looked so fresh-faced and casual, his hazel eyes not taking notice of how nightmarish I looked in contrast.

He licked his lips before speaking. "I like that you don't ask the obvious questions. What am I doing here? Where did I come from?"

"If you're here, I'm guessing you'll tell me why."

He cocked his ear toward the door, probably listening for anyone else. But we were utterly alone. There were far too many walls between us and the rest of my team.

"I'm curious where you parked your car, though."

He smiled, lines marking the sides of his face. "Too much time passes between our encounters. I see you've been busy with all the chaos ensuing around the city."

"Nice word choice."

Blackbirds cawed and flocked in the grass just behind me. Sometimes Niko fed the animals that roamed our land, and the birds weren't shy about badgering us for food. One of them strutted up to my foot and flapped its showy wings.

"Should I thank you for turning on the lights?"

Houdini took a step forward. "Is this a conspiracy?"

My heart thumped in my chest. "Huh?"

He gestured toward the birds and me. "That's what they call a group of ravens." He tapped his chin. "Or maybe I'm wrong and it's an unkindness."

I lowered my arms. "To be determined. You're good at deflection, by the way."

"You're not so bad yourself." He watched one of the birds give up and take flight. It landed in a barren tree across the open ground. The stars were already twinkling as the sky changed as subtly as a mood ring. "I sometimes question if I'm really living the life I want. I suppose you think you have it all figured out, but one day, you'll be more lost than when you started, and you'll wonder how the hell you got there. I do tire of the repetitive nature of life."

"I think the blackout was about as much unpredictability as I can stand."

He rocked on his heels. "Evil thrives in the dark. You can't see the cockroaches in the daytime."

I slid my jaw to the side. Patrick was definitely a cockroach, but I didn't want to admit to Houdini that his little blackout had actually aided in exposing a major conspiracy. But I guessed by the way he was looking at me that he probably knew something about it. Could Houdini have known about Patrick's secret? Had he orchestrated the outage to either expose their flaws or stop the murders? I wasn't sure what to believe, and Houdini would never give me a straight answer.

"Would you like to come in for tea?"

"Yes, I suppose I should be getting right to the point," he said. "I promised to return this to you, and I'm a man of my word." Houdini raised his hand from his pocket. Dangling from the silver chain was the heart-shaped pendant Christian had given me before a masked ball. I'd worn it all the time until Houdini took it from me. The glass sparkled even in the disappearing twilight.

"I never understood why you wanted it. What's the occasion? Or maybe you're feeling guilty about kidnapping me."

"I never abducted you, Raven. You came willingly."

I rubbed my temple. I *had* gone with him. I'd sat right in his car. "You charmed me."

"A man attacked you in the parking lot, and I came to your rescue. You act as if I planned it, but you know that isn't true. A selective memory won't serve you well in the job you're in." He stepped forward and opened the clasp. "May I?"

Houdini fastening the necklace behind my neck felt oddly intimate and tender. He held the heart in the palm of his hand and shifted it.

I lifted my chin. "I'd rather have my memory back than a cheap necklace."

"Are you certain that's what you really want?"

"You had no right to take it. That wasn't part of our deal, and I want it back."

"Careful what you wish for, Butterfly. Someday you might wish you hadn't."

My breath caught. "Say again?"

He reached out and cupped the back of my neck with his hand. His fingers could snap my vertebrae in one swift movement, so I found myself paralyzed. Houdini leaned in, and his lips brushed softly against my ear. "I put a spell on you…"

When he whispered the rest, images flashed through my mind like a slide show, and it felt as though a floodgate had opened. My breath quickened, my heart raced, and I suddenly remembered everything.

My first kiss with Christian. Every intimate conversation we'd had. Tender things he'd said, and the way my heart had grown to feel something more than desire. And then I remembered the one piece of the puzzle that made everything fit.

The fire.

Christian was the stranger who'd saved me from an inferno when I was a child. I remembered our conversation in an abandoned building and how we'd both come to the shocking realization that we'd met once before. I remembered drinking from him, feeling sexual thoughts, our conversation at my mother's grave about seeing where our relationship would go. I remembered choosing the onyx stone for his ring and how it filled me with such joy to see him put it on right away, because the necklace he'd given me wasn't made of glass. I teared up thinking about all the pieces of my heart that Houdini had locked away. He had intentionally put Christian at a disadvantage.

I finally lifted my eyes to his. "Why did you give it all back?"

"Let's just say I'm a generous man and leave it at that." Houdini's hand slowly moved away from my neck and touched the rare Burmese ruby. "I'm surprised you wanted this back," he said obliquely.

"Why?"

Houdini let it go and stared at the red tinge on his fingertips from where he'd touched my neck. "It was purchased for another woman." His eyes flashed up to mine and caught my confusion.

"He didn't tell you that? Seems like an important detail to leave out when giving such a precious gift."

There he was, trying to stir the pot again. "And how would you know something like that?"

"Because I was there." Houdini unfastened the only button holding his coat closed. "Christian's not the man you think he is. Ask him who he bought the necklace for, Butterfly. Ask him."

With the last two words, Houdini raised his arms and transformed into a white owl. Awestruck, I watched as he flapped his wings and disappeared into the night.

"Holy shit," I whispered.

I'd seen him as a white panther, but an owl? My mind reeled. Shifters shared their body with only one animal. Then again, I'd never actually seen him shift into that panther. Maybe I'd imagined it.

I touched the necklace, wondering if maybe this was a hallucination, an aftereffect from all the blood. Whether it was a dream or a nightmare, my memories were restored.

And now that I had my heart again, I didn't know what to do with it.

Shepherd could hardly breathe. He'd heard stories about people going into shock, and for the first time, he knew what it felt like. He'd come close to passing out at the table when Viktor made the surprise announcement that keeping the boy was an option. The possibility filled him with terror, and he fled the room before they could vote.

After finding a window overlooking the courtyard on the second level, he sat down. His hands were so shaky that he couldn't even light his cigarette, so he tossed the unlit stick onto the floor and rested his head in his hand. Now that Patrick was dead, the unknown fate of his son's life left Shepherd confused. Would he be better off in an orphanage? Would anyone there bond with him? How would Shepherd be able to check on his welfare? Would they educate him? How long would it take before others found out about his gifts?

That part gave Shepherd nightmares. Not many kids from interbred relationships retained gifts on both sides. The wrong person could find out and use him just as Patrick had intended to. And they could be far more sadistic. They might even take him to another country.

"Thought I'd find you here."

Shepherd jumped, so lost in his thoughts that he hadn't heard Gem roll up.

The pink wheels on her skates had collected dirt from the floor, and when she sat down, she crossed one ankle over her knee and brushed them off. "Viktor really dropped a bomb, didn't he?"

Shepherd pinched his bottom lip. "Yeah."

Her violet eyes flashed up. Gem had twisted her hair into two knots on top of her head, purple strands weaving together with silver ones. She looked like a character out of an anime cartoon. "I'd give you advice, but alas, I'm a childless Mage who can't begin to understand your dilemma. That's not sarcasm, by the way."

"What does Viktor expect me to do? Raise him? I can't be the father he needs. The kid deserves better."

Gem studied her silver nail polish before she resumed picking at the wheels on her skates. "Maybe it's not really about what's better... but what feels right."

"I don't know what it takes to be a good father," Shepherd admitted. "I'll fuck him up."

She crossed her legs and then leaned back, her finger briefly touching the tiny black mole below her eye. "I know what it's like to be in his shoes. I was... sold on the black market."

Shepherd's eyes flashed up. Gem rarely mentioned her childhood.

"I know what it feels like to belong to others and never yourself. Now that he's away from Patrick, he has a chance to figure out who he is. I know he's just a little kid, but all these life experiences are leaving an indelible mark. I don't think anyone here expects you to be a superdad, but your son deserves to know he's loved and isn't just a possession. All of us love him a little bit, and in time, we'll love him even more. But you already loved him before he was born."

"Love ain't enough."

She tapped her foot in the air, the heavy skate rocking her entire leg. "Locks and bars don't make a prison. Even a palace can be a cage. If we make Keystone a place only for business, we'll have made our own prison. I think we need this as much as you do. We all came here for a new life, but what's a life without family? You all are the closest thing I have to family. I don't know what it's like to have parents. Do you want that to be something your kid says when he's my age?"

"We could lose him in this place. What if he falls down the stairs?"

Gem giggled, and it reminded him of little bubbles rising to the top of a champagne glass. "I think the little monkey knows how to climb without falling. I watched him climb on top of that statue by the door."

"And you didn't stop him? He could have been hurt."

She pouted. "Maybe that's your job as a father to know those things. Do you think anyone at the orphanage will pay him close attention? And what if he gets in trouble? We don't know how they punish kids. This isn't about giving him the perfect life. I don't even know what that is. Maybe all we can do is just give him the best life we have to offer and hope that's enough."

Shepherd fought back hot tears. "What am I supposed to tell him about me? About his mother?"

Gem shrugged. "In time, the truth is always best. But for now, he doesn't need to know all that. Maybe he just needs to know that he has a dad who would do anything to give him the best life. Viktor said we can keep him either permanently or until you choose his adoptive parents. But wouldn't you rather him stay here than an orphanage? What if he grows up and learns you had the chance to love him but were too scared?"

Shepherd leaned to the left and rubbed his forehead.

"We've already voted. No one cares about giving up the money. We made the choice out of altruism. It's up to you now. I can't tell you what to do. All I can do is shine a little light on my own experience as an unwanted child. I used to dream about my family finding me and coming to my rescue. I didn't care if they were perfect or rich. I just wanted someone who was willing to love me unconditionally. I never got that, Shep. Never in my whole life. Even my Creator didn't love me. She cared for my well-being and had compassion for my plight, but I don't know what it feels like to be loved. I thought I had that with Hooper, but now I'm not so sure even *that* was real." Gem stood up and glided a few feet to the right until she touched the wall and turned around. "You'll never have this opportunity again. Never. Once they collect him, chances of your seeing him again are slim to none. You can't have a life with him outside these walls, but Viktor's giving you a chance to have them within." She skated off in a huff. "Don't blow it!"

He leaned forward and stared at his hands. Gem always got right to the point, and her words resonated. Shepherd could never be the dad his son deserved. He didn't know how to give hugs or read bedtime stories. That version of him died the night Maggie lost her life. But maybe the others in the house would make up for his shortcomings. Gem's playful spirit and demonstrative personality, Viktor's wise words and storytelling, Wyatt's love for video games and technology, Blue's determined spirit, Niko's fighting skills and balanced temperament, Claude's protective nature—each of them had something to teach the boy. Well, except for Christian and maybe Raven. Those two were fucking nuts. He still liked them, but could he trust them all? What did he really know about their past?

Before he knew it, he was downstairs, heading to his bedroom. Once inside, he squatted in front of the armoire and opened a bottom drawer with a key. There were a few items he'd bought at pawnshops, like throwing stars and a set of handcuffs. When he reached far in the back, he pulled out a brown teddy bear. It was a little misshapen from having lived in the back of the narrow drawer for over a year. Shepherd pushed the furry nose around until the face straightened out, and he stared at the only remaining memento from his past. He'd bought the stuffed animal for his unborn child years before and kept it hidden from Maggie. Shepherd had planned to give it to the baby on the day he was born, but that day had come and gone with a storm of violence. Though he'd started over with his life, he could never bring himself to let go of that bear. He used to hold it at night, pretending it was his baby. He told it his darkest secrets, then one day, he locked it up. It was the only tangible reminder of a life that could have been, of a son he'd never know.

And now all that had changed.

Shepherd held the bear by the paw and headed to Kira's room, where the boy was sleeping. When he opened the door, a candle flickered from the draft. Kira's bed was empty, but she'd made him a makeshift bed on the floor beside her.

Shepherd approached the pile of blankets and looked down at the napping boy. He didn't know how long kids slept or at what age they stopped taking naps, but when the boy's eyes became droopy after dinner, Viktor had Kira put him to bed. What did it really matter? None of them were on a set schedule.

He lifted the covers and tucked the bear inside the crook of the boy's arm. Shepherd hadn't been a tender man in a long time, but he felt a glimmer of his old self as he brushed the boy's wispy hair away from his forehead.

Minutes passed. Shepherd couldn't tear his eyes away. Just the sound of the boy's breath and even the whistle in his nose filled Shepherd with heart-tugging emotions like he'd never experienced. He used to think the kid looked a lot like Maggie, but the longer he stared, the more he saw himself. As he traced his finger around the deep scar on his son's face, it reminded him that this kid's first moment in this world had been marked with pain and terror. The moments after that were hollow and joyless.

A boy with no name. A boy whose first years were spent with a man who didn't care about his wants or his happiness. Had that already scarred him more than the mark on his face? The deprivation of love, affection, toys, and even a name?

Shepherd tucked the blanket up to the bear's chin and stroked the boy's cheek. "Good night, Hunter."

Chapter 29

I HAD CONCEALED MY NECKLACE INSIDE my sweater before going back inside. This was a big decision for Shepherd, and I didn't want to draw any attention away from him. When he finally returned to the dining room, he told Viktor he wanted to raise the boy at Keystone. Whether it was temporary or permanent would remain to be seen, but he also made a big announcement that he'd named his son Hunter Moon.

"What if he doesn't like the name?" Wyatt posed the question while adding ginger ale to his glass of wine. "What about a literary name like Sherlock?"

Shepherd swirled his glass of whiskey. "I'll put you in the ground if you start calling him that."

"I'm only suggesting that we could have had a vote."

Shepherd held his glass and pointed a finger at Wyatt. "I'm warning you, Spooky."

Blue dragged her chair to sit between Viktor and me. "I like it. Children should have strong names with meaning. He'll grow into that name."

"Agreed," Viktor said, raising his glass. "A toast for our newest member of Keystone, Hunter Moon."

"To Hunter," we said in unison, raising our glasses.

Viktor swallowed his merlot and set down his glass. "Tonight, Christian and I will question each of you."

Blue wrung her hands. "You're not asking details about our past, are you?"

"Nyet. Not specific questions. As a precaution, I only want to make sure that none of you will bring harm to the boy. I have the utmost faith that I have chosen good men and women, but this will bring Shepherd the thing he needs. What thing?" he asked Gem.

"Assurance," she answered.

Viktor nodded. "Assurance. Niko will be present for each session."

"I'll join him when it's Christian's turn," Shepherd said, inviting no argument.

Christian folded his arms. "Now is that any way to treat a dear old friend? What's the matter? Afraid I'm going to get thirsty in the middle of the night?"

"Friend or not, you put one fang on him, and I'll make a necklace out of it."

I laughed. "Why not make a set of earrings?"

Viktor cleared his throat, his eyes glazed over from the wine. "We should also have rules."

"Like bedtime?" Claude admired his bicep as he stretched his arms. "Children should be on a schedule."

"Nyet. I do not care if he stays up all night and sleeps all day. But he will need his own room, and I think it would be best if it's not across the hall from the medical room. If one of you comes in injured and he sees the blood and hears the screaming, it might give him nightmares."

Wyatt chortled. "You mean like the ones I might have of Bloody Mary sitting across the table from me?"

"I have no problem with him seeing that," Shepherd said. "He already knows the world is full of pain. You can't keep suffering a secret and shelter him from it. Maybe he can watch me patch someone up or watch Niko use his Healer abilities."

"Shepherd makes a valid point," Niko said. "This is an opportunity for him to learn about anatomy. His Relic knowledge has to do with human genetics, but he might grow up to be a gifted healer himself. We shouldn't coddle him. He'll also learn what it means to live among a group of people who are different from him. Blue heals by shifting, and Raven has her own unique abilities."

Shepherd lit up a cigarette. "One rule I wanna lay down is he doesn't leave the house without gloves on. A car ride is fine, but walking out in public isn't."

Blue swept her long hair behind her shoulders. "What about around the house?"

Shepherd looked across the table with hesitation. "Only if you're careful where you leave your emotions. I don't know how strong his talents are—if they're like mine. I'll have to work with him and teach him control, but that'll take years."

Christian smirked. "Translation: if you're feeling randy, don't sit in one of the public chairs and have your wet fantasy."

"Same goes for thinking about killing someone," Shepherd added.

Wyatt shrugged playfully. "I guess that means I won't be able to eat at the table with you anymore."

Shepherd pulled in a drag from his cigarette and then set it in the slim groove on the ashtray. "Most Sensors can only feel emotions on an object when it's been recently touched, but others can feel it days or years later."

"Maybe you should get him in the habit of wearing gloves around the house until we figure it out," I suggested. "That way, he'll get used to wearing them."

Shepherd scratched his jaw. "I gotta go to a Sensor shop and find a decent pair. They sell specialty gloves that are thin and breathable. Maybe I'll do that tomorrow."

Everyone turned their head when a little visitor crept into the room. Hunter reached the edge of the table and rested his arms on it. You couldn't help but notice the scar on his face, but somehow, it made him one of us.

Claude looked down at him and smiled warmly. "Hey there, sleepyhead."

The boy's lip twitched, but he was still waking up. His dark hair was sticking up on one side from how he'd slept on it. He reached for one of the empty glasses and started playing with the narrow stem.

Shepherd got up, rounded the table, and squatted next to him. "Hey, little man. I got some news."

The boy kept fiddling with the glass, probably nervous that we were all watching him closely and he didn't know why.

"Do you know what my name is?" Shepherd asked in his rough voice. "I'm Shepherd Moon. Everyone here has a name. Did you know that?"

The boy shrugged and pulled the glass closer to him.

Shepherd continued. "That tall guy next to you is Claude Valentine. And that's Gem Laroux, Wyatt Blessing, Viktor Kazan, and Blue. See, Blue doesn't tell us her last name, but she's still got a name. That dirty woman over there is Raven Black. I think she's been playing with a lot of red paint."

The boy looked at me and giggled. Great.

"And that scary man you should never go near is Christian Poe."

Christian smiled and gave Shepherd the finger. "Feck off."

"And this guy here with the long hair is Niko. They all wanna know your name, but you don't have one, do you?"

Despite him being a child of five, he comprehended the one thing that set him apart from everyone else. His ruddy cheeks and glistening eyes revealed his embarrassment.

Shepherd gently poked the boy's arm. "But guess what? You've had a name all along, but bad people just kept it a secret from you. Wanna know what it is?"

A tear slipped down the boy's cheek, and he nodded.

"Hunter Moon."

Niko tilted his head to the side and smiled. "That is the very best name I can imagine for a boy."

Shepherd looked as if he were struggling with something. "And I'm Shepherd Moon. We both have the same last name. Do you know what that means?"

The boy shook his head, and I glanced over at Gem, who was crying.

Shepherd's chin quivered, and he pressed his lips into a thin line as he touched the boy's hand. I wasn't sure what kind of emotion transferred between them, but something undeniable was transpiring.

"I'm your real father."

The boy spun to face Shepherd, his arm knocking the glass, which toppled and shattered on the floor.

Hunter retreated several steps, terror etched in his face as he stared at the broken glass. When he wet his pants, I wanted to cry.

Claude's nostrils flared, and he clenched his fists, forcing himself to look away.

We all knew exactly what he was thinking. No kid's normal reaction to an accident was fear, but Hunter had received a punishment that frightened him enough to wet his pants.

"Accidents happen. No big deal. See?" Shepherd shot up to his feet, grabbed a glass, and threw it against the far wall.

We all jumped from his unexpected reaction.

Niko repeated the gesture, and before we all knew it, we were smashing our glassware on the floor, creating a mess for Kira to clean up.

By the time Wyatt had dramatically hurled his against the wall, only to tip a vase, the boy had erupted into laughter, tears still wetting his ruddy cheeks.

Shepherd scooped him up in his arms. "You're gonna stay here from now on, Hunter. This is your new home. You don't get in trouble for breaking things."

Wyatt raised a finger. "Except my computers."

Shepherd stared daggers at him. "Fuck your computers. If he does something wrong, nobody punishes him. I'll sit down and talk to him." Shepherd turned his attention to the kid and jerked his neck back, trying to see his face. "We got lots of games and a big yard outside. I'll even buy you toys. Crayons, trucks, dolls, bubbles—whatever the hell you want. What do you say, little man? You wanna stay with us?"

Hunter didn't answer. I had yet to hear him speak. But he wrapped his arms around Shepherd's neck and whispered something in his ear.

Shepherd squeezed him tight and turned to leave the room. "Let's go find you some pj's. You know what pj's are?"

Gem had her feet up in the chair, knees bent, her face buried in them. "That was the sweetest thing I've ever seen," she said, sniffling and finally lifting her head.

"Patrick hurt that kid," Claude informed us. "I could smell it. Men who hurt children should be torched from the earth."

Wyatt scratched his smooth jaw. "Shep's gonna have to curb that dirty mouth of his around the kid, or the first word we're going to hear is cocksucker."

Christian laughed darkly and stood up. "That'll make trips to the ice cream parlor fun. I'll just be upstairs, picking glass from the bottom of my shoes."

I grimaced and looked at the mess on the floor. But I was glad we'd had that moment. It reminded me of what really mattered.

Gem rubbed her puffy eyes. "Hooper's ashes were scattered today by his family in a private ceremony."

Niko lowered his head. "I'm sorry for your pain."

"I just don't feel like I got closure," she admitted. "But at least I've learned my lesson. I'm not relationship material, especially since I work with a bunch of killers."

Wyatt leaned across Shepherd's chair and squeezed her shoulder. "Want me to pour you a tall glass of apple juice to drown your sorrows in?"

I scooted my chair back. Now that I had my memories restored, I couldn't stand it any longer. I needed to see Christian. "I should probably shower."

"Feel free to take three," Wyatt offered. "You look scarier than some of the spooks that used to live here."

Blue found a spare wineglass and filled it for Viktor. "We have some major celebrating to do. Who wants another drink?"

Viktor smiled warmly. "What would I do without my Blue?"

Christian's room wasn't far from mine. Like me, he was a recluse and enjoyed his privacy. That was the nice thing about our relationship—we understood each other's basic needs. I knocked and heard him murmur something unintelligible before swinging open the door.

I leapt into his arms, ravishing him with a passionate kiss that could have stopped time. The heat between us culminated to a scorching degree as he slammed the door and backed up to the bed. He'd just lit a fire, and the wood crackled and popped in the hearth. When he sat down, I straddled him, my hands cupping his face.

He growled, clawing at my hips and rocking me against him. "Keep doing that, Precious."

I threw my head back and tried to control the energy spiraling through me like a cyclone. Christian lifted my sweater and put his head inside, his hands peeling away my bra as he sucked on my nipple.

When his kisses ceased, I looked down, out of breath. "Don't stop."

"Where did this come from?" he asked, his tone so sharp that it made me shiver.

"The bra?"

Then I felt a tug around my neck. He'd found the necklace tucked beneath my sweater.

Christian's head reappeared, his hair disheveled and lips tinged red. I didn't like the look on his face, so I climbed off him and pulled the necklace into view.

"I didn't want to create a distraction during Shepherd's meeting. The others don't know the importance, but you do."

Christian shot to his feet, his rage barely contained. "He was just here? On *our* property?" Just then, it was as if Christian had switched off his emotions. His face became ashen and his gaze hollow as he stared at the necklace. "You remember."

I clutched the heart. "He gave it back to me. All my memories. Our kisses, the fire, the necklace—everything. Maybe he felt guilty."

Christian clasped his hands behind his back and walked to the fire. "And knowing everything, how do you feel about it? About us?"

"You couldn't tell when I walked in the room?"

"What if you had never gotten it back? Knowing what you know now, would you have seen me as more than just a sex object?"

I snorted. "You have a high opinion of your prowess as a lover."

"I'm serious, Raven. We'd lost all those other moments, and you weren't giving me that same tenderness. Not like before. You felt passion for me, to be sure, but if you couldn't give me your heart a second time, then maybe—"

"We're not meant to be?"

He turned on his heel and gave me a pensive look.

I knew what he meant. There's an idea that lives within each of us that if you're meant to love someone, you could meet that same person in a thousand lifetimes and always fall in love. After losing my memory, I'd felt residual emotions for Christian that had no memory connection. Our sexual chemistry was off the charts, but something kept holding me back.

"I don't know," I admitted. "Maybe it would have taken us longer to get back to that same place. I never thought you'd be more afraid of this thing than me."

"When a man has been burned once before, he learns to guard his heart."

I turned toward his bedside table and approached it, my eyes lost in the warm glow of the lantern. "So this isn't about us. It's about another woman. That's why you've always had a low opinion about love and relationships. It's not easy making this work under Viktor's watchful eye, but you're the only one holding back. You just don't see it that way. When someone's coming, you push me away. I know we have to be careful, but do you ever think how that makes me feel?"

"I said it before, and I'll say it again. I'm not a thing to love. It doesn't mean I'm not capable of having feelings for you, but everything you buy in the store comes with a warning label."

"Do not use while sleeping?"

"I want you, Raven. I just don't know how to have you." His voice moved away as he turned to look at the fire again.

Someone must have really done a number on him. I feared losing everything in my life that I'd worked hard for, but Christian feared trusting me. I had every reason not to trust a Vampire, but I'd given him that much, and my trust wasn't something I gave out freely.

It made me wonder… if Viktor allowed relationships to flourish between partners, would Christian find another reason to push me away? I'd always felt safe with him, and despite my head telling me one thing, my heart trusted him implicitly. We'd made a pact never to lie to each other as partners, but I'd always felt that our agreement carried over to our complicated relationship.

What was he hiding from me besides his heart?

I sat on the edge of his bed. "What changed? You wanted me to remember everything, and now that I do, you're running scared."

"I'm not running."

"You left skid marks on the floor."

He drew in a deep breath and sighed. "You deserve to have your memories back. They're yours. I can't tell you what to do with them, but I never wanted you to have them back just for my own benefit. I could have kept our relationship platonic when you lost them."

"I don't think that will ever be possible."

Maybe he *was* scared. Scared that I'd love him so hard that he couldn't give me the same love in return. And that scared me too. Scared me because the word "love" was suddenly popping in my head a whole lot.

"Was it easier when I was the one pushing back?" I asked. "Maybe your flaw is that you're attracted to people you can't have because it's safe. Now that I'm all in, you're the one who's spooked."

I reached for the candy dish and knocked a small slip of paper onto the floor. When I bent down to pick it up, I noticed papers poking out from beneath his bed. The bold letters caught my attention, because it was a printed receipt for renting out a doublewide trailer.

"If you need time to think, I'll understand," he went on.

I lifted the papers onto my lap and scanned the top. The date was shortly after my abduction, and the signature was Christian's name. "What is this?"

I never heard his footsteps or saw him round the bed since I was flipping through pages and pages of receipts for food and utilities. Then I found a document that made me stand up. The papers scattered to the floor in a messy pile. I gripped the wrinkled paper between my hands and stared at the address. This was the last electric bill for my father's trailer.

Chapter 30

"WHAT IS ALL *THIS*?" I gestured to the papers on the floor, my heart still pounding against my ribs. Christian held the look of a man caught in a web of lies. "You don't like my house in the woods, so I thought I'd upgrade. Every man needs a second home."

"Don't lie to me. This is my father's mail." I flourished the paper in front of his face and then crumpled it in my fist before letting it drop to the ground. "The dates are right after I went missing. Start talking."

"Went missing. That's an interesting way to put it." His eyes flicked down to my necklace. "After your maker sold you to Fletcher, I knew your da was in trouble. So I arranged for him to stay in a secret location."

The truth slipped out with Christian's confession, but I wanted him to say it out loud. "And he went willingly… with a complete stranger?"

"He's an obstinate man and wouldn't go without his fecking chair."

"Did you charm him?"

Christian opened his mouth as if to say something but snapped it closed.

"You lied to me. I want the truth."

"I didn't have to charm your da because… he already knew me."

I shut my eyes. "He knew because you never erased his memory of our meeting, did you?"

"Your da knows about the Breed world, Raven. I had no choice. You think his friends wouldn't have figured it out before long?"

"Then why didn't you tell me?"

"He saw you were happy and didn't want you holding on to the past." Christian folded his arms. "I saved the man's life."

"Do you think that justifies lying to me? You kept a secret from me about the most important person in my life. I could have gone back to visit with him instead of sitting around, terrified that Fletcher might show up and kill him."

"Have you seen his gun collection? The man can take care of himself. Once we found you, he demanded to go back home."

It was one thing to keep trivial secrets, but this was the biggest and baddest betrayal of them all. Christian was denying me the right to continue a relationship with my father. Had I never found the receipt, what then?

"You can't be mad at me for saving your da."

"I'm not. I'm grateful my father's alive, but that doesn't negate the damage you've done. If I hadn't found out, you wouldn't have told me. This wasn't a little white lie, Christian. You had *no* fucking right to keep my family from me. You were stealing away years of time I had to be with him that weren't yours to take. It wasn't your secret to keep. As soon as I walked out of that trailer and he told you the truth, you should have called me back inside. That's a game changer. We could have worked it out. All this time, you've been telling me to let go of the past, forget my father, and move on. But now I find out that he remembers our meeting and knows about our world? Jesus, how does he know about our world?"

Christian shrugged.

I held the ruby heart in my hand. "I'm starting to wonder if Houdini wasn't trying to protect me when he erased my memories of you."

Christian's eyes narrowed. "You're going to forgive him because he gave you something back? Don't forget who gave you that necklace to begin with. That was *my* heart on a chain, not his."

Christian's words cut through me like a knife.

"The truth hurts, doesn't it, Precious?"

I squared off with him. "Don't call me that."

"I've always called you that."

"Not when you're angry. Don't call me a name of affection when you're berating me, or I'll never want to hear that word again."

"What'll you have me do? Apologize? I can't. I did what I had to do."

"Even if it meant betraying me?"

"Jaysus wept. Would you be this vexed if I'd slept with another woman?"

"Is there something else you're not telling me?"

Christian's eyes became evasive, and he shifted his stance.

"That's my point."

My shoe kicked the wadded-up paper as I walked past him to the door.

"Come back when you've had time to think it over," he said.

"Don't count on it."

"You'll see I had no choice about the matter."

After closing the door behind me—though it was more like slamming—I went to my room.

Christian was threatened by Houdini. At first, I thought it had to do with him being my maker, but now I could see the jealousy in Christian's eyes just as clearly as his printed name on those receipts. His good deed was eclipsed by the deception. All those private conversations we'd had, in which I poured out my heart about my father, and Christian never seized the opportunity to confess the truth. He could have saved me so much anguish.

Even if I never went back home, at least I could have called my father on the phone every now and again when I felt down and needed a good kick in the ass. I could have sent him money when he needed it. I could have had more time with him before he grew old and died.

What else had he lied about? When someone betrays you once, what's to stop them from doing it again? Where is the line drawn?

Maybe I would have been better off if Houdini had kept those memories, because now it hurt so much worse to remember them.

Especially knowing that Christian originally bought my necklace for someone else. As much as I wanted to confront him about it now, my heart couldn't take another blow.

I needed to think.

I needed space.

I needed to get out.

How could I ever trust him as my partner? This went infinitely deeper than just a lie. I was more prepared for Christian ruining my heart than my life. If I couldn't trust my partner, how could I do my job effectively?

After a brief stop in my bedroom to do a few things, I took a dazed walk to the first floor, grabbed my leather jacket, and headed out to my truck, still parked out front. No one noticed me leave.

When I started the engine, I felt like throwing up. The more distance I put between us physically and emotionally, the more I knew I'd fallen in love with Christian.

I'd never experienced a conventional relationship, and that had always been okay. But now I selfishly wanted more. Trust was only one piece of the pie. I wanted him to fight for me. Even after finding out I had my memory restored, he'd backed away like a spooked horse. Maybe he was afraid I'd go public or tie him down in a real commitment. As far as I knew, all his relationships had been casual and brief.

Well, except for whoever ruined him.

As I turned out of the driveway, I glanced toward the garage and noticed Christian's Honda parked outside.

"Houdini," I whispered.

He'd spied on our date. Was he jealous of Christian? It would certainly explain why he'd taken my memories, but it didn't explain why he'd returned them.

Or the car.

When I reached the gate, I passed another car turning in. Viktor must have forgotten to call the people picking up Hunter and cancel.

I switched on the radio, and "Sara" by Fleetwood Mac poured through the speakers.

The headlights lit up a thin layer of fog rolling across the fields, and I imagined myself driving through the timeline of my life. As long as it seemed, this was only the beginning. The great unknown lay before me, and centuries would pass by like an open stretch of road beneath my tires. Places, people, tragedies, laughter, and change.

My life had been nothing *but* change, and only now did I realize how much change scared the hell out of me. Most of all, the decisions that couldn't be undone. I'd set myself up to fail by inviting a relationship with Christian. Whether we worked out or not, it would alter my course with the organization.

Deep down, had I wanted to screw up my life all along? To create yet another reason for someone else to give up on me? I'd spent my whole life feeling as though I'd let everyone down, that I was somehow not good enough. Keystone was the last stop, and here I was, screwing it up by seeking out a doomed relationship.

But that wasn't the whole truth.

Deep down, I *wanted* Christian to love me enough to risk everything. Being with him wasn't some subconscious form of self-sabotage. I wanted to tell Viktor that I'd fallen in love with my partner, but each time Christian pushed me away or avoided eye contact, it made me doubt that day would ever come.

Swimming in my thoughts, I checked my speed and slowed down. If a cop pulled me over, he'd lock me up and throw away the key after one look at my bloody clothes. I tilted the rearview mirror and wondered who was staring back at me. I didn't recognize that girl anymore. She was heartbroken and sad, and I'd always been tough. I'd fought my way through every tragedy and survived.

Hours passed.

With my tank running on empty, I made a final turn home. I'd needed that temporary escape to put things into perspective. It was time for me to stop avoiding risks because I was afraid of the consequences. Matters of the heart were more important, and right now, there was only one thing that mattered.

After parking the truck, I walked around outside and stared upward at the dark sky. The clouds had moved in and obscured the lights from a thousand directions. The night had created its own blackout, and there were no favors in the world that could bring back the stars.

My thoughts crystallized with each step I took, leading me to the only conclusion that felt right. I knocked on the door, my heart in my throat.

Had he left, or was he ignoring my knock? I blew out a nervous breath, my palms sweaty and legs restless. The second time I knocked, the door slowly opened.

When he looked at me, I'd never felt more certain of his love.

Tears welled in my eyes.

Fear gripped my spine.

And joy filled my heart.

I looked into his eyes and knew right then and there that everything would be okay. Somehow, he just had a way of making it so.

"Daddy?"

Crush wrapped his arms around me in a bear hug, his love never more felt. "I knew you'd come home, Cookie."

Epilogue

CHRISTIAN TOSSED THE LAST RECEIPT into the flames. The fire devoured the paper, disintegrating it into ash. He should have burned them weeks ago, but no one ever came into his room. Like almost everyone else, he'd leave his laundry outside the door for Kira, so he was the only person who ever crossed that threshold.

Maybe part of him wanted to get caught.

Or maybe he was just getting careless. It was arrogant of him to believe that Raven would forgive his deception. He knew what he'd done was wrong. Crush wasn't a stranger to their world, so there wasn't a need to keep it from Raven.

It had been difficult for him to do this recent assignment while constantly worried about Raven's whereabouts and safety. But what confused him the most was how reckless she was getting about their on-again, off-again relationship. Was she trying to get them kicked out or just hoping to drive him away? They couldn't afford to be careless. Christian had a feeling that Viktor would send them both away, and if that happened, neither of them would remember each other. There was always a chance they could work out a deal with him, but Viktor would have to be convinced that what they had was permanent. Casual got dangerous, but nothing about this felt casual.

He strolled across the room and sat on the edge of his bed. Turning the onyx ring around his finger, he couldn't help but wonder how her restored memories would change things. She'd only had a short time to process everything, and the way she'd tackled him gave him unexpected reservations. Christian wasn't ready to go public, especially without knowing if what they had was true.

And the odds of that weighed heavily on his mind. He had experienced firsthand how easily women trampled on the hearts of men. They were just as conniving as their male counterparts. He felt like two halves of a whole—the cynical side constantly warring with the other side that wanted to believe true love was possible for a lost cause like him.

He clenched his fists when he thought of that shitebag returning her necklace like some kind of hero. Part of the deal was restoring her stolen memories, *not* the gemstone. Houdini *had* to have known the value of that necklace. No man in his right mind would give away a priceless find such as that. So why throw it back in Christian's face?

Because he knew it would put him in a good light.

Houdini worked all angles, and Christian was beginning to dread what might be in store for him. Raven's memories had come at a price, and he pondered over what that price might be.

Footfalls in the outside hall drew him out of his thoughts, and when he cocked his head to the side, they ceased.

A light knock sounded at his chamber door.

He'd known she wouldn't be vexed for long. Raven wasn't the kind of woman who flounced off and held a grudge. She preferred looking a person right in the eye and telling it like it was.

Keeping secrets about her father was reprehensible, but he knew she'd eventually come to her senses and see it had been a necessary evil.

He rounded the bed, straightening his shoulders and masking the grin on his face as he opened the door… and peered into darkness. Christian heard a familiar ticking that he hadn't heard in many years.

Was he dreaming?

It was a rhythm without a tune, and when a ghost from his past stepped into view, Christian drew back.

"Lenore?"

A smile widened her unmerciful red lips. "Christian Poe. So, we meet again."

95999237R00204

Made in the USA
Lexington, KY
15 August 2018